The Vagrants

The Vagrants

A NOVEL

Yiyun Li

RANDOM HOUSE

NEW YORK

This is a work of fiction. All incidents and dialogue, and all characters with the exception of some well-known historical and public figures, are products of the author's imagination and are not to be construed as real. Where real-life historical or public figures appear, the situations, incidents, and dialogues concerning those persons are entirely fictional and are not intended to depict actual events or to change the entirely fictional nature of the work. In all other respects, any resemblance to persons living or dead is entirely coincidental.

Published in the United States by Random House, an imprint of The Random House Publishing Group, a division of Random House, Inc., New York.

RANDOM HOUSE and colophon are registered trademarks of Random House, Inc.

Grateful acknowledgment is made to Random House, Inc., for permission to reprint seven lines from "The Shield of Achilles" from *Collected Poems* by W. H. Auden, copyright © 1932 by W. H. Auden. Reprinted by permission of Random House, Inc.

LIBRARY OF CONGRESS CATALOGING-IN-PUBLICATION DATA
Li, Yiyun.
The vagrants : a novel / Yiyun Li.
p.   cm.
ISBN 978-1-4000-6313-0
1. City and town life—China—Fiction.   2. China—Politics and government—20th century—Fiction.   3. China—Social conditions—20th century—Fiction.   4. China—History—20th century—Fiction.   I. Title.
PL2946.Y59V34 2008
813'.6—dc22   2008023467

Printed in the United States of America on acid-free paper

www.atrandom.com

2 4 6 8 9 7 5 3 1

FIRST EDITION

For my parents

The mass and majesty of this world, all

That carries weight and always weighs the same

Lay in the hands of others; they were small

And could not hope for help and no help came:

What their foes liked to do was done, their shame

Was all the worst could wish; they lost their pride

And died as men before their bodies died.

—W. H. AUDEN, "THE SHIELD OF ACHILLES"

Part I

ONE

The day started before sunrise, on March 21, 1979, when Teacher Gu woke up and found his wife sobbing quietly into her blanket. A day of equality it was, or so it had occurred to Teacher Gu many times when he had pondered the date, the spring equinox, and again the thought came to him: Their daughter's life would end on this day, when neither the sun nor its shadow reigned. A day later the sun would come closer to her and to the others on this side of the world, imperceptible perhaps to dull human eyes at first, but birds and worms and trees and rivers would sense the change in the air, and they would make it their responsibility to manifest the changing of seasons. How many miles of river melting and how many trees of blossoms blooming would it take for the season to be called spring? But such naming must mean little to the rivers and flowers, when they repeat their rhythms with faithfulness and indifference. The date set for his daughter to die was as arbitrary as her crime, determined by the court, of being an unrepentant counterrevolutionary; only the unwise would look for significance in a random date. Teacher Gu willed his body to stay still and hoped his wife would soon realize that he was awake.

She continued to cry. After a moment, he got out of bed and turned on the only light in the bedroom, an aging 10-watt bulb. A red plastic clothesline ran from one end of the bedroom to the other; the laundry his wife had hung up the night before was damp and cold, and the clothesline sagged from the weight. The fire had died in the small stove in a corner of the room. Teacher Gu thought of adding coal to the stove himself, and then decided against it. His wife, on any other day, would be the one to revive the fire. He would leave the stove for her to tend.

From the clothesline he retrieved a handkerchief, white, with printed red Chinese characters—a slogan demanding absolute loyalty to the Communist Party from every citizen—and laid it on her pillow. "Everybody dies," he said.

Mrs. Gu pressed the handkerchief to her eyes. Soon the wet stains expanded, turning the slogan crimson.

"Think of today as the day we pay everything off," Teacher Gu said. "The whole debt."

"What debt? What do we owe?" his wife demanded, and he winced at the unfamiliar shrillness in her voice. "What are we owed?"

He had no intention of arguing with her, nor had he answers to her questions. He quietly dressed and moved to the front room, leaving the bedroom door ajar.

The front room, which served as kitchen and dining room, as well as their daughter Shan's bedroom before her arrest, was half the size of the bedroom and cluttered with decades of accumulations. A few jars, once used annually to make Shan's favorite pickles, sat empty and dusty on top of one another in a corner. Next to the jars was a cardboard box in which Teacher Gu and Mrs. Gu kept their two hens, as much for companionship as for the few eggs they laid. Upon hearing Teacher Gu's steps, the hens stirred, but he ignored them. He put on his old sheepskin coat, and before leaving the house, he tore a sheet bearing the date of the previous day off the calendar, a habit he had maintained for decades. Even in the unlit room, the date, March 21, 1979, and the small characters underneath, *Spring Equinox,* stood out. He tore the second sheet off too and squeezed the two thin squares of paper into a ball. He himself was breaking a ritual now, but there was no point in pretending that this was a day like any other.

Teacher Gu walked to the public outhouse at the end of the alley. On normal days his wife would trail behind him. They were a couple of habit, their morning routine unchanged for the past ten years. The alarm went off at six o'clock and they would get up at once. When they returned from the outhouse, they would take turns washing at the sink, she pumping the water out for both of them, neither speaking.

A few steps away from the house, Teacher Gu spotted a white sheet with a huge red check marked across it, pasted on the wall of the row houses, and he knew that it carried the message of his daughter's death. Apart from the lone streetlamp at the far end of the alley and a few dim morning stars, it was dark. Teacher Gu walked closer, and saw that the characters in the announcement were written in the ancient Li-styled calligraphy, each stroke carrying extra weight, as if the writer had been used to such a task, spelling out someone's imminent death with unhurried elegance. Teacher Gu imagined the name belonging to a stranger, whose sin was not of the mind, but a physical one. He could then, out of the habit of an intellectual, ignore the grimness of the crime—a rape, a murder, a robbery, or any misdeed against innocent souls—and appreciate the calligraphy for its aesthetic merit, but the name was none other than the one he had chosen for his daughter, Gu Shan.

Teacher Gu had long ago ceased to understand the person bearing that name. He and his wife had been timid, law-abiding citizens all their lives. Since the age of fourteen, Shan had been wild with passions he could not grasp, first a fanatic believer in Chairman Mao and his Cultural Revolution, and later an adamant nonbeliever and a harsh critic of her generation's revolutionary zeal. In ancient tales she could have been one of those divine creatures who borrow their mothers' wombs to enter the mortal world and make a name for themselves, as a heroine or a devil, depending on the intention of the heavenly powers. Teacher Gu and his wife could have been her parents for as long as she needed them to nurture her. But even in those old tales, the parents, bereft when their children left them for some destined calling, ended up heartbroken, flesh-and-blood humans as they were, unable to envision a life larger than their own.

Teacher Gu heard the creak of a gate down the alley, and he hurried to leave before he was caught weeping in front of the announcement. His daughter was a counterrevolutionary, and it was a perilous situation for anyone, her parents included, to be seen shedding tears over her looming death.

When Teacher Gu returned home, he found his wife rummaging in an old trunk. A few young girls' outfits, the ones that she had been unwilling to sell to secondhand stores when Shan had outgrown them, were laid out on the unmade bed. Soon more were added to the pile, blouses and trousers, a few pairs of nylon socks, some belonging to Shan before her arrest but most of them her mother's. "We haven't bought her any new clothes for ten years," his wife explained to him in a calm voice, folding a woolen Mao jacket and a pair of matching trousers that Mrs. Gu wore only for holidays and special occasions. "We'll have to make do with mine."

It was the custom of the region that when a child died, the parents burned her clothes and shoes to keep the child warm and comfortable on the trip to the next world. Teacher Gu had felt for the parents he'd seen burning bags at crossroads, calling out the names of their children, but he could not imagine his wife, or himself, doing this. At twenty-eight—twenty-eight, three months, and eleven days old, which she would always be from now on—Shan was no longer a child. Neither of them could go to a crossroad and call out to her counterrevolutionary ghost.

"I should have remembered to buy a new pair of dress shoes for her," his wife said. She placed an old pair of Shan's leather shoes next to her own sandals on top of the pile. "She loves leather shoes."

Teacher Gu watched his wife pack the outfits and shoes into a cloth bag. He had always thought that the worst form of grieving was to treat the afterlife as a continuity of living—that people would carry on the burden of living not only for themselves but also for the dead. Be aware not to fall into the futile and childish tradition of uneducated villagers, he thought of reminding his wife, but when he opened his mouth, he could not find words gentle enough for his message. He left her abruptly for the front room.

The small cooking stove was still unlit. The two hens in the cardboard box clucked with hungry expectation. On a normal day his wife would start the fire and cook the leftover rice into porridge while he fed the hens a small handful of millet. Teacher Gu refilled the food tin. The hens looked as attentive in their eating as did his wife in her packing. He pushed a dustpan underneath the stove and noisily opened the ash grate. Yesterday's ashes fell into the dustpan without a sound.

"Shall we send the clothes to her now?" his wife asked. She was standing by the door, a plump bag in her arms. "I'll start the fire when we come back," she said when he did not reply.

"We can't go out and burn that bag," Teacher Gu whispered.

His wife stared at him with a questioning look.

"It's not the right thing to do," he said. It frustrated him that he had to explain these things to her. "It's superstitious, reactionary—it's all wrong."

"What is the right thing to do? To applaud the murderers of our daughter?" The unfamiliar shrillness had returned to her voice, and her face took on a harsh expression.

"Everybody dies," he said.

"Shan is being murdered. She is innocent."

"It's not up to us to decide such things," he said. For a second he almost blurted out that their daughter was not as innocent as his wife thought. It was not a surprise that a mother was the first one to forgive and forget her own child's wrongdoing.

"I'm not talking about what we could decide," she said, raising her voice. "I'm asking for your conscience. Do you really believe she should die because of what she has written?"

Conscience is not part of what one needs to live, Teacher Gu thought, but before he could say anything, someone knocked on the thin wall that separated their house from their neighbors', a protest at the noise they were making at such an early hour perhaps, or, more probably, a warning. Their next-door neighbors were a young couple who had moved in a year earlier; the wife, a branch leader of the district Communist Youth League, had come to the Gus' house twice and questioned them about their attitudes toward their imprisoned daughter. "The party and the people have put trusting hands on your shoulders, and it's up to you to help her correct her mistake," the woman had said both times, observing their reactions with sharp, birdlike eyes. That was before Shan's retrial; they had hoped then that she would soon be released, after she had served the ten years from the first trial. They had not expected that she would be retried for what she had written in her journals in prison, or that words she had put on paper would be enough evidence to warrant a death sentence.

Teacher Gu turned off the light, but the knocking continued. In the darkness he could see the light in his wife's eyes, more fearful than angry. They were no more than birds that panicked at the first twang of a bow. In a gentle voice Teacher Gu urged, "Let me have the bag."

She hesitated and then passed the bag to him; he hid it behind the hens' box, the small noise of their scratching and pecking growing loud in the empty space. From the dark alley occasional creaks of opening gates could be heard, and a few crows stirred on the roof of a nearby house, their croaking carrying a strange conversational tone. Teacher Gu and his wife waited, and when there were no more knocks on the wall, he told her to take a rest before daybreak.

THE CITY OF MUDDY RIVER was named after the river that ran eastward on the southern border of the town. Downstream, the Muddy River joined other rivers to form the Golden River, the biggest river in the northeastern plain, though the Golden River did not carry gold but was rubbish-filled and heavily polluted by industrial cities on both banks. Equally misnamed, the Muddy River came from the melting snow on White Mountain. In summers, boys swimming in the river could look up from underwater at the wavering sunshine through the transparent bodies of busy minnows, while their sisters, pounding laundry on the boulders along the bank, sometimes sang revolutionary songs in chorus, their voices as clear and playful as the water.

Built on a slice of land between a mountain in the north and the river in the south, the city assumed the shape of a spindle. Expansion was limited by both the mountain and the river, but from its center the town spread to the east and the west until it tapered off to undeveloped wilderness. It took thirty minutes to walk from North Mountain to the riverbank on the south, and two hours to cover the distance between the two tips of the spindle. Yet for a town of its size, Muddy River was heavily populated and largely self-sufficient. The twenty-year-old city, a development planned to industrialize the rural area, relied on its many small factories to provide jobs and commodities for the residents. The housing was equally planned out, and apart from a few buildings of four or five stories around the city square, and a main street with a department store, a cinema, two marketplaces, and many small shops, the rest of the town was partitioned into twenty big blocks that in turn were divided into nine smaller blocks, each of which consisted of four rows of eight connected, one-storied houses. Every house, a square of fifteen feet on its sides, consisted of a bedroom and a front room, with a small front yard circled by a wooden fence or, for better-off families, a brick wall taller than a man's height. The front alleys between the yards were a few feet wide; the back alleys allowed only one person to squeeze through. To avoid having people gaze directly into other people's beds, the only window in the bedroom was a small square high up on the back wall. In warmer months it was not uncommon for a child to call out to his mother, and for another mother, in a different house, to answer; even in the coldest season, people heard their neighbors' coughing, and sometimes snoring, through the closed windows.

It was in these numbered blocks that eighty thousand people

lived, parents sharing, with their children, brick beds that had wood-stoves built underneath them for heating. Sometimes a grandparent slept there too. It was rare to see both grandparents in a house, as the city was a new one and its residents, recent immigrants from villages near and far, would take in their parents only when they were widowed and no longer able to live on their own.

Except for these lonely old people, the end of 1978 and the beginning of 1979 were auspicious for Muddy River as well as for the nation. Two years earlier, Chairman Mao had passed away and within a month, Madame Mao and her gang in the central government had been arrested, and together they had been blamed for the ten years of Cultural Revolution that had derailed the country. News of national policies to develop technology and the economy was delivered by rooftop loudspeakers in cities and the countryside alike, and if a man was to travel from one town to the next, he would find himself, like the blind beggar mapping this part of the province near Muddy River with his old fiddle and his aged legs, awakened at sunrise and then lulled to sleep at sundown by the same news read by different announcers; spring after ten long years of winter, these beautiful voices sang in chorus, forecasting a new Communist era full of love and progress.

In a block on the western side where the residential area gradually gave way to the industrial region, people slept in row houses similar to the Gus', oblivious, in their last dreams before daybreak, of the parents who were going to lose their daughter on this day. It was in one of these houses that Tong woke up, laughing. The moment he opened his eyes he could no longer remember the dream, but the laughter was still there, like the aftertaste of his favorite dish, meat stewed with potatoes. Next to him on the brick bed, his parents were asleep, his mother's hair swirled around his father's finger. Tong tiptoed over his parents' feet and reached for his clothes, which his mother always kept warm above the woodstove. To Tong, a newcomer in his own parents' house, the brick bed remained a novelty, with mysterious and complex tunnels and a stove built underneath.

Tong had grown up in his maternal grandparents' village, in Hebei Province, and had moved back to his parents' home only six months earlier, when it was time for him to enter elementary school. Tong was not the only child, but the only one living under his parents' roof now. His two elder brothers had left home for the provincial capitals after middle school, just as their parents had left their home villages twenty years earlier for Muddy River; both boys worked as apprentices in factories, and their futures—marriages to suitable female workers in the provincial capital, children born with legal residency in that city filled with grand Soviet-style buildings— were mapped out by Tong's parents in their conversations. Tong's sister, homely even by their parents' account, had managed to marry herself into a bigger town fifty miles down the river.

Tong did not know his siblings well, nor did he know that he owed his existence to a torn condom. His father, whose patience had been worn thin by working long hours at the lathe and feeding three teenage children, had not rejoiced when the new baby arrived, a son whom many other households would have celebrated. He had insisted on sending Tong to his wife's parents, and after a day of crying, Tong's mother started a heroic twenty-eight-hour trip with a one-month-old baby on board an overcrowded train. Tong did not remember the grunting pigs and the smoking peasants riding side by side with him, but his piercing cries had hardened his mother's heart. By the time she arrived at her home village, she felt nothing but relief at handing him over to her parents. Tong had seen his parents only twice in the first six years of his life, yet he had not felt deprived until the moment they plucked him out of the village and brought him to an unfamiliar home.

Tong went quietly to the front room now. Without turning on the light, he found his toothbrush with a tiny squeeze of toothpaste on it, and a basin filled with water by the washstand—Tong's mother never forgot to prepare for his morning wash the night before, and it was these small things that made Tong understand her love, even though she was more like a kind stranger to him. He rinsed his mouth with a quick gurgle and smeared the toothpaste on the outside of the cup to reassure his mother; with one finger, he dabbed some water on his forehead and on both cheeks, the amount of washing he would allow himself.

Tong was not used to the way his parents lived. At his grandparents' village, the peasants did not waste their money on strange-tasting toothpaste or fragrant soap. "What's the point of washing one's face and looking pretty?" his grandfather had often said when he told tales of ancient legends. "Live for thirty years in the wind and the dust and the rain and the snow without washing your face and you will grow up into a real man." Tong's parents laughed at such talk. It seemed an urgent matter for Tong's mother that he take up the look and manner of a town boy, but despite her effort to bathe him often and dress him in the best clothes they could afford, even the youngest children in the neighborhood could tell from Tong's village accent that he did not belong. Tong held no grudge against his parents, and he did not tell them about the incidents when he was made a clown at school. Turnip Head, the boys called him, and sometimes Garlic Mouth, or Village Bun.

Tong put on his coat, a hand-me-down from his sister. His mother had taken the trouble to redo all the buckles, but the coat still looked more like a girl's than a boy's. When he opened the door to the small yard, Ear, Tong's dog, sprang from his cardboard box and dashed toward him. Ear was two, and he had accompanied Tong all the way from the village to Muddy River, but to Tong's parents, he was nothing but a mutt, and his yellow shining pelt and dark almond-shaped eyes held little charm for them.

The dog placed his two front paws on Tong's shoulders and made a soft gurgling sound. Tong put a finger on his lips and hushed Ear. His parents did not awake, and Tong was relieved. In his previous life in the village, Ear had not been trained to stay quiet and unobtrusive. Had it not been for Tong's parents and the neighbors' threats to sell Ear to a restaurant, Tong would never have had the heart to slap the dog when they first arrived. A city was an unforgiving place, or so it seemed to Tong, as even the smallest mistake could become a grave offense.

Together they ran toward the gate, the dog leaping ahead. In the street, the last hour of night lingered around the dim yellow street-lamps and the unlit windows of people's bedrooms. Around the corner Tong saw Old Hua, the rubbish collector, bending over and rummaging in a pile with a huge pair of pliers, picking out the tiniest fragments of used paper and sticking them into a burlap sack. Every morning, Old Hua went through the city's refuse before the crew of young men and women from the city's sanitation department came and carted it away.

"Good morning, Grandpa Hua," Tong said.

"Good morning," replied Old Hua. He stood up and wiped his eyes; they were bald of eyelashes, red and teary. Tong had learned not to stare at Old Hua's afflicted eyes. They had looked frightening at first, but when Tong had got to know the old man better, he forgot about them. Old Hua treated Tong as if he was an important person— the old man stopped working with his pliers when he talked to Tong, as if he was afraid to miss the most interesting things the boy would say. For that reason Tong always averted his eyes in respect when he talked to the old man. The town boys, however, ran after Old Hua and called him Red-eyed Camel, and it saddened Tong that the old man never seemed to mind.

Old Hua took a small stack of paper from his pocket—some ripped-off pages from newspapers and some papers with only one side used, all pressed as flat as possible—and passed them to Tong. Every morning, Old Hua kept the clean paper for Tong, who could read and then practice writing in the unused space. Tong thanked Old Hua and put the paper into his coat pocket. He looked around and did not see Old Hua's wife, who would have been waving the big bamboo broom by now, coughing in the dust. Mrs. Hua was a street sweeper, employed by the city government.

"Where is Grandma Hua? Is she sick today?"

"She's putting up some announcements first thing in the morning. Notice of an execution."

"Our school is going to see it today," Tong said. "A gun to the bad man's head. Bang."

Old Hua shook his head and did not reply. It was different at school, where the boys spoke of the field trip as a thrilling event, and none of the teachers opposed their excitement. "Do you know the bad man in the announcement?" Tong asked Old Hua.

"Go and look," Old Hua said and pointed down the street. "Come back and tell me what you think."

At the end of the street Tong saw a newly pasted announcement, the two bottom corners already coming loose in the wind. He found a rickety chair in front of a yard and dragged it over and climbed up, but still he was not tall enough, even on tiptoes, to reach the bottom of the paper. He gave up and let the corners flap on their own.

The light from the streetlamps was weak, but the eastern sky had taken on a hue of bluish white like that of an upturned fish belly. Tong read the announcement aloud, skipping the words he did not know how to pronounce but guessing their meanings without much trouble:

Counterrevolutionary Gu Shan, female, twenty-eight, was sentenced to death, with all political rights deprived. The execution will be carried out on the twenty-first of March, nineteen seventy-nine. For educational purposes, all schools and work units are required to attend the pre-execution denunciation ceremony.

At the bottom of the announcement was a signature, two out of three of whose characters Tong did not recognize. A huge check in red ink covered the entire announcement.

"You understand the announcement all right?" asked the old man, when Tong found him at another bin.

"Yes."

"Does it say it's a woman?"

"Yes."

"She is very young, isn't she?"

Twenty-eight was not an age that Tong could imagine as young. At school he had been taught stories about young heroes. A shepherd boy, seven and a half years old, not much older than Tong, led the Japanese invaders to the minefield when they asked him for directions, and he died along with the enemies. Another boy, at thirteen, protected the property of the people's commune from robbery and was murdered by the thief. Liu Hulan, at fifteen and a half, was executed by the White Army as the youngest Communist Party member of her province, and before she was beheaded, she was reported to have sneered at the executioners and said, "She who works for Communism does not fear death." The oldest heroine he knew of was a Soviet girl named Zoya; at nineteen she was hanged by the German Fascists, but nineteen was long enough for the life of a heroine.

"Twenty-eight is too early for a woman to die," Old Hua said.

"Liu Hulan sacrificed her life for the Communist cause at fifteen," replied Tong.

"Young children should think about living, not about sacrificing," Old Hua said. "It's up to us old people to ponder death."

Tong found that he didn't agree with the old man, but he did not want to say so. He smiled uncertainly, and was glad to see Ear trot back, eager to go on their morning exploration.

EVEN THE TINIEST NOISE could wake up a hungry and cold soul: the faint bark of a dog, a low cough from a neighbor's bedroom, footsteps in the alley that transformed into thunder in Nini's dreams while leaving others undisturbed, her father's snore. With her good hand, Nini wrapped the thin quilt around herself, but hard as she tried, there was always part of her body exposed to the freezing air. With the limited supply of coal the family had, the fire went out every night in the stove under the brick bed, and sleeping farthest from the stove, Nini had felt the coldness seeping into her body through the thin cotton mattress and the layers of old clothes she did not take off at bedtime. Her parents slept at the other end, where the stove, directly underneath them, would keep them warm for the longest time. In the middle were her four younger sisters, aged ten, eight, five, and three, huddled in two pairs to keep each other warm. The only other person awake was the baby, who, like Nini, had no one to cuddle with for the night and who now was fumbling for their mother's breast.

Nini got out of bed and slipped into an oversize cotton coat, in which she could easily hide her deformed hand. The baby followed Nini's movement with bright, expressionless eyes, and then, frustrated by her futile effort, bit with her newly formed teeth. Their mother screamed, and slapped the baby without opening her eyes. "You debt collector. Eat. Eat. Eat. All you know is eating. Were you starved to death in your last life?"

The baby howled. Nini frowned. For hungry people like the baby and Nini herself, morning always came too early. Sometimes she huddled with the baby when they were both awake, and the baby would mistake her for their mother and bump her heavy head into Nini's chest; those moments made Nini feel special, and for this reason she felt close to the baby and responsible for all that the baby could not get from their mother.

Nini limped over to the baby. She picked her up and hushed her, sticking a finger into the baby's mouth and feeling her new, beadlike teeth. Except for Nini's first and second sisters, who went to elementary school now, the rest of the girls, like Nini herself, did not have official names. Her parents had not even bothered to give the younger girls nicknames, as they did to Nini; they were simply called "Little Fourth," "Little Fifth," and, the baby, "Little Sixth."

The baby sucked Nini's finger hard, but after a while, unsatisfied, she let go of the finger and started to cry. Their mother opened her eyes. "Can't you both be dead for a moment?"

Nini shuffled Little Sixth back to bed and fled before her father woke up. In the front room Nini grabbed the bamboo basket for collecting coal and stumbled on a pair of boots. A few steps into the alley, she could still hear the baby's crying. Someone banged on the window and protested. Nini tried to quicken her steps, her crippled left leg making bigger circles than usual, and the basket, hung by the rope to her shoulder, slapped on her hip with a disturbed rhythm.

At the end of the alley Nini saw an announcement on the wall. She walked closer and looked at the huge red check. She did not recognize a single character on the announcement—her parents had long ago made it clear that for an invalid like her, education was a waste of money—but she knew by the smell that the paste used to glue the announcement to the wall was made of flour. Her stomach grumbled. She looked around for a step stool or some bricks; finding none, she set the basket on the ground with its bottom up and stepped onto it. The bottom sagged but did not give way under her weight. She reached a corner of the announcement with her good hand and peeled it off the wall. The flour paste had not dried or frozen yet, and Nini scraped the paste off the announcement and stuffed all five fingers into her mouth. The paste was cold but sweet. She scraped more of it off the announcement. She was sucking her fingers when a feral cat pounced off a wall and stopped a few feet away, examining her with silent menace. She hurried down from the basket, almost falling onto her bad foot, and sending the cat scurrying away.

At the next street corner Nini caught up with Mrs. Hua, who was brushing paste on the four corners of an announcement when the girl walked up.

"Good morning," the old woman said.

Nini looked at the small basin of paste without replying. Sometimes she greeted Mrs. Hua nicely, but when she was in a bad mood, which happened often, she sucked the inside of her mouth hard so that no one could make her talk. Today was one of those days—

Little Sixth had caused trouble again. Of all the people in the world, Nini loved Little Sixth best, yet this love, a heavy knot in her stomach, as Nini sometimes felt it, could not alleviate her hunger.

"Did you have a good sleep?"

Nini did not reply. How did Mrs. Hua expect her to sleep well when she was always starving? The few mouthfuls of paste had already vanished, and the slight sweet taste in her mouth made her hungrier.

The old woman took a leftover bun from her pocket, something she made sure to bring along every morning in case she saw Nini, though the girl would never know this. Nini reminded Mrs. Hua of the daughters she had once had, all of those girls discarded by their parents. In another life she would have adopted Nini and kept her warm and well fed, Mrs. Hua thought. It seemed that not too long ago life had been a solid dam for her and her husband—with each baby girl they had picked up in their vagrancy, they had discovered once and again that, even for beggars, life was not tightfisted with moments of exhilaration—but the dam had been cracked and taken over by flood, their happiness wiped out like hopeless lowland. Mrs. Hua watched Nini take a big bite of the bun, then another. A few bites later, the girl started to hiccup.

"You are eating too fast," Mrs. Hua said. "Remember to chew."

When half of the bun was gone, Nini slowed down. Mrs. Hua went back to the announcement. Years of sweeping the street and, before that, wandering from town to town and rummaging through the refuse had given the old woman's back a permanent stoop, but still she was unusually tall, towering over most men and other women. Perhaps that was why the old woman got the job, Nini thought, to put the announcements out of people's reach so nobody could steal the paste.

Mrs. Hua patted the corners of the announcement onto the wall. "I'm off to the next street," she said.

Nini did not move, looking sharply at the basin of paste in Mrs. Hua's hand. The old woman followed Nini's eyes and shook her head. Seeing nobody in the street, she took a sheet from the pile of announcements and folded it into a cone. "Take it," she said and placed the cone in Nini's good hand.

Nini watched Mrs. Hua scoop some paste into the paper cone. When there was no sign of any more, Nini licked her hand clean of the dribbles. Mrs. Hua watched her with unspeakable sadness. She was about to say something, but Nini began to walk away. "Nini, throw the paper cup away after you finish it," the old woman said in a low voice behind her. "Don't let people see you are using the announcement."

Nini nodded without looking back. Between hiccups she was still biting the inside of her mouth hard, making sure she did not say a word more than necessary. She did not understand Mrs. Hua's kindness toward her. She accepted the benevolence of the world, as much as she did its cruelty, just as she was resigned to her body being born deformed. Knowledge of human beings came to Nini from eavesdropping on tales—her parents, in their best mood, walked around her as if she were a piece of furniture, and other people seemed to be able to ignore her existence. This meant Nini could learn things that other children were not allowed to hear. At the marketplace, housewives talked about "bedroom business" with loud giggles; they made mean jokes about the teenage peddlers from the mountain villages, who, new in their business, tried hard not to notice the women's words yet often betrayed themselves by blushing. The neighbors, after a day's work and before dinner, gathered in twos and threes in the alley and exchanged gossip, Nini's existence nearby never making them change topics hurriedly, as another child walking past would do. She heard stories of all kinds—a daughter-in-law mixing shredded grass into the dumpling filling for her mother-in-law, a nanny slapping and permanently deafening a baby, a couple making too much noise when they made "bedroom business," so that the neighbor, a mechanic working at the quarry, installed a mini–time bomb to shock the husband's penis into cotton candy—such tales bought Nini pleasures that other children obtained from toys or games with companions, and even though she knew enough to maintain a nonchalant expression, the momentary freedom and glee offered by eavesdropping were her closest experiences of a childhood that was unavailable to her, a loss of which she was not aware.

The six-thirty freight train whistled. Every morning, Nini went to collect coal at the train station. The Cross-river Bridge, the only one connecting the town to the other bank of the Muddy River, had four lanes, but at this early hour, trucks and bicycles were scarce. The only other pedestrians were women and teenage peasants coming down the mountains, with newly laid eggs kept warm in their handkerchiefs, small tins of fresh milk from goats and cows, and homemade noodles and pancakes. Walking against the flow of the peasants, Nini eyed them with suspicion as they looked back at her, not bothering to hide their revulsion at the sight of her deformed face.

The railway station near the Cross-river Bridge was a stop for freight only. Coal, timber, and aluminum ore from the mountains were loaded here and carried on to big cities. The passenger trains stopped at a different station on the west end of the town, and sometimes, standing on the bridge, Nini saw them rumble past, people's faces visible in the many squares of windows. Nini always wondered what it felt like to go from one place to another in the blink of an eye. She loved speed—the long trains whose clinking wheels sparked on the rail; the jeeps with government plate numbers, racing even in the most crowded streets, stirring up dust in the dry season, splattering mud when it was raining; the ice drifts flowing down the Muddy River in the spring; the daredevil teenage boys on their bicycles, pedaling hard while keeping both hands off the handlebars.

Nini quickened her steps. If she did not get to the railway station fast enough, the workers would have transferred the coal from trucks to the freight cars. Every morning, the workers, out of intentional carelessness, would drop some coal to the ground, and later would divide it among themselves. Nini's morning chore was to stand nearby, staring and waiting until one of the workers finally acknowledged her presence and gave her a small share of the coal.

Everyone worked for her food, Nini's mother had said many times, and all Nini wanted was to reach the station in time, so she would not be denied her breakfast.

WALKING ACROSS THE BRIDGE in the opposite direction from Nini, among the clusters of peasants, Bashi was deep in thought and did not see the girl, nor did he hear two peasant women commenting on Nini's misshapen face. He was preoccupied in his imagination with what a girl was like *down there* between her legs. Bashi was nineteen, had never seen a girl's private parts, and was unable to picture what they would be like. This, for Bashi, son of a Communist hero—the reddest of the red seeds—was an upsetting deficiency.

Bashi's father had served in the Korean War as one of the first pilots of the nation, and had been awarded many titles as a war hero. The American bombs had not killed him but a small human error had—he died from a tonsillectomy the year Bashi was two. The doctor who injected the wrong anesthesia was later sentenced to death for subverting the Communist nation and murdering one of its best pilots, but what happened to the doctor, whether it had been a life or a death sentence, meant little to Bashi. His mother had left him to his paternal grandmother and remarried herself into another province, and ever since then his life had been subsidized by the government. The compensation, a generous sum compared to other people's earnings, made it possible for his grandmother and him to live in modest comfort. She had hoped he would be a good student and earn a decent living by his wits, but that did not happen, as Bashi had little use for his education. She worried and nagged at him, but he forgave her because she was the only person who loved him and whom he loved back. Someday she would die—her health had been deteriorating over the past two years, and her brain was muddled now with facts and fantasies that she could not tell apart. Bashi did not look forward to the day she would leave him for the other side of the world, but in the meantime, he was aware that the house, although owned by the government, would be his to occupy as long as he lived, and the money in their savings account would be enough to pay for his meals and clothes and coal without his having to lift a finger. What else could he ask of life? A wife for sure, but how much more food could she consume? As far as Bashi was concerned, he could have a comfortable life with a woman, and neither of them would have to make the slightest effort to work.

The problem, then, was how to find a woman. Apart from his grandmother, Bashi had little luck with other women. Older ones, those his grandmother's or his mother's age, used him as a warning for their offspring. They would be too ashamed to meet their ancestors after their deaths if it turned out that they would have to endure a son, or a grandson, like Bashi—these comments, often loud enough for Bashi to hear, were directed at those children who needed a cautionary tale. Younger women of a suitable age for marriage avoided Bashi as a swan princess in the folktales would avoid a toad. It was Bashi's belief that he needed to gain more knowledge of a woman's body before he could gain access to her heart, but who among the young women looking at him despisingly would open up her secrets to him?

Bashi's hope now lay with much younger girls. He had already made several attempts, offering little girls from different neighborhoods candies, but none of them had agreed to go with him into the high grasses by the riverbank. Even worse, one of the girls told her parents, and they gave him a good beating and spread the news around so that wherever he went now, he felt that people with daughters were keeping a watchful eye on him. The little girls made up a song about him, calling him a wolf and skunk and girl-chasing eel. He was not offended; rather, he liked to walk into the girls' circle in the middle of their games, and he would smile when they chanted the song to his face. He imagined taking them one by one to a secret bush and studying what he needed to study with them, and he smiled more delightedly since none of the girls would ever have guessed what could have been happening to them at that very moment, these young girls singing for him in their fine, lovely voices.

Bashi had other plans too. For instance, hiding in the public out-house after midnight, or in the early morning, when females would arrive in a hurried, half-dreaming state, too sleepy to recognize him as he squatted in a place where the light from the single bulb did not reach. But the idea of squatting for a long stretch of time, cold, tired, and stinking, prevented Bashi from carrying out this plan. He might as well dress up in his grandma's clothes and wrap his head in a shawl to go to a public bathhouse. He could talk in a high-pitched voice and ask for a ticket to the women's section, go into the locker room and feast his eyes on the women undressing. He could stay for a while and then pretend he had to go home to take care of some important things, a chicken stewing on the stove maybe, or some forgotten laundry on the clothesline.

Then there were other possibilities that offered more permanent hope, like finding a baby girl on the riverbank, which was what Bashi was trying to do now. He had searched the bank along the railway track, and now he walked slowly on the town side of the river and looked behind every boulder and tree stump. It was unlikely that someone would leave a baby girl out here in this cold season, but it never hurt to check. Bashi had found a baby girl, one February morning two years earlier, underneath the Cross-river Bridge. The baby had been frozen stiff, if not by the cold night, then by death it-self. He had studied its gray face; the thought of opening the blanket and looking underneath the rags, for some reason, chilled him, so he left it where it had been deserted. He went back to the spot an hour later, and a group of people had gathered. A baby girl it must be, people said, a good solid baby but what a pity it wasn't born a boy. It takes only a few layers of wet straw paper, and no more than five min-utes, people said, as if they had all suffocated a baby girl at least once in their lives, talking about the details in that vivid way. Bashi tried to suggest that the baby might have frozen to death, but nobody seemed to hear him. They talked among themselves until Old Hua and his wife came and put the small bundle of rags into a burlap sack. Bashi was the only one to accompany the Huas to where they buried deserted babies. Up the river at the western end of town it was, where white nameless flowers bloomed all summer long, known to the children in town as dead-baby flowers. On that day the ground was too frozen to dig even the smallest hole; the couple found a small alcove behind a rock, and covered the baby up with dry leaves and dead grass, and then marked the place. They would come back later to bury her, they told Bashi, and he replied that he had no doubt they would send her off properly, good-hearted people as they were, never letting down a soul.

Bashi believed that if he waited long enough, someday he would find a live baby on the riverbank. He did not understand why people did not care for baby girls. He certainly wouldn't mind taking one home, feeding her, bathing her, and bringing her up, but such a plan he had to keep secret from his townsfolk, who treated him as an idiot. And idiocy seemed to be one of the rare crimes for which one could never get enough punishment. A robber or a thief got a sentence of a year or more for a crime, but the tag of idiot, just as counter-revolutionary, was a charge against someone's very being, and for that reason Bashi did not like his fellow townsfolk. Even a counter-revolutionary sometimes got depurged, as he often heard these days. There were plenty of stories on the radio about so-and-so who had been wronged in the Cultural Revolution and was reabsorbed into the big Communist family, but for Bashi, such redemption seemed beyond reach. People rarely paid attention to him when he joined a conversation at an intersection or a roadside chess party on summer evenings, and when they did, they all held disbelieving and bemused smiles on their faces, as if he made them realize how much more intelligent they themselves were. Bashi had often made up his mind never to talk to these people, but the next time he saw these gatherings, he became hopeful again. Despite being badly treated, he loved people, and loved talking to them. He dreamed of the day when the townspeople would understand his importance; perhaps they would even grab his hands and shoulders and apologize for their mistake.

A dog trotted across to the riverbank, its golden fur shimmering in the morning light. In its mouth was a paper cone. Bashi whistled to the dog. "Ear, here, what treasure did you find?"

The dog looked at Bashi and stepped back. The dog belonged to a newcomer in town, and Bashi had studied both the dog and the boy. He thought Ear a strange name for a dog, and believed the boy who had named it must have something wrong with him. They were two of a kind, village-grown and not too bright. Bashi put a hand into his pocket, and said in a gentle voice, "A bone here, Ear."

The dog hesitated and did not come to Bashi. He held the dog's eyes with his own and inched closer, calling out again in his gentle voice, then without warning he picked up a rock and hurled it at the dog, which gave out a short yelp and ran away, dropping the paper cone on the ground. Bashi continued to hurl rocks in the direction where the dog had disappeared. Once before, he had been able to lure Ear closer so he could give it a good kick in its belly.

Bashi picked up the paper cone and spread it on the ground. The ink was smeared, but the message was clear. "A counterrevolutionary is not a game," Bashi said aloud. The name on the announcement sounded unfamiliar, and Bashi wondered if the woman was from town. Whose daughter was she? The thought of someone's daughter being executed was upsetting; no crime committed by a young woman should lead to such a horrible ending, but was she still a maiden? Bashi read the announcement again; little information was given about this Gu Shan. Perhaps she was married—a twenty-eight-year-old was not expected to remain a girl, except . . . "A spinster?" Bashi spoke aloud to finish his thought. He wondered what the woman had done to earn herself the title of counterrevolutionary. The only other person he knew who had committed a similar crime was the doctor who had killed his father. Bashi read the announcement again. Her name sounded nice, so perhaps she was just someone like him, someone whom nobody understood and no one bothered to understand. What a pity she would have to die on the day he discovered her.

■ ■ ■

TONG CALLED OUT Ear's name several times before the dog reappeared. "Did you bother the black dog again?" Tong asked Ear, who was running toward Tong in panic. The black dog belonged to Old Kwen, a janitor for the electric plant who, unlike most people living in the blocks, occupied a small, run-down shack at the border between the residential and industrial areas. Old Kwen and his dog were among the few things Tong's father had told him about the town when Tong had first arrived. Leashed all its life in front of the shack and allowed to move only in a radius of less than five feet, the dog was said to be the meanest and the best guard dog in town, ready to knock down and bite through the throat of anyone who dared to set foot near his master's shack; stay away from a man who keeps a dog like this, Tong's father had warned him, but when Tong asked why, his father did not give an explanation.

Too curious and too friendly, Ear had approached the black dog several times, and each time the black dog had growled and jumped up, pulling at the end of his chain with fierce force; it would then take Tong a long time to calm Ear down. "You have to learn to leave other dogs alone," Tong said now, but Ear only whined. Maybe he was chastising Ear for the wrong reason, Tong thought, and then he realized that he hadn't heard the black dog bark. "Well, maybe it's not the black dog, but someone else. You have to learn to leave others alone. Not all of them love you as you think they do," Tong said.

They walked on the riverbank. The clouds were heavy in the sky. The wind brought a stale smell of old, unmelted snow. Tong stripped a layer of pale, starchy bark off a birch tree, and sat down with his stump of pencil. He wrote onto the bark the words he remembered from the announcement: *Female. Counterrevolutionary. School.*

Tong was one of the most hardworking students in his class. The teacher sometimes told the class that Tong was a good example of someone who was not bright but who made up for his shortcoming by thorough work. The comment had left Tong more sad than proud at first, but after a while he learned to cheer himself up: After all, praise from the teacher was praise, and an accumulation of these favorable comments could eventually make him an important pupil in the teacher's eyes. Tong longed to be one of the first to join the Communist Young Pioneers after first grade so that he would earn more respect from the townspeople, and to realize that dream he needed something to impress his teachers and his peers. He had thought of memorizing every character from the elementary dictionary and presenting the result to the teacher at the end of the semester, but his parents, both workers, were not wealthy enough to give him an endless supply of exercise books. The idea of using the birch bark had occurred to Tong after he had read in a textbook that Comrade Lenin, while imprisoned, had used his black bread as an ink pot and his milk as ink, and had written out secret messages to his comrades; on the margins of newspapers, the messages would show up only when the newspaper was put close to fire; whenever a guard approached Lenin would devour his ink pot with the ink in it. "If you have a right heart, you'll find the right way," the teacher said of the story's moral. Since then Tong had tried to keep the right heart and had gathered a handful of pencil stumps that other children had discarded. He had also discovered the birch bark, perfect for writing, a more steady supply than the paper Old Hua saved for him.

Ear sat down on his hind legs and watched Tong work for a while. Then the dog leapt out to the frozen river, leaving small flowerlike paw prints on the old snow. Tong wrote until his fingers were too cold to move. He blew big white breaths on them, and read the words to himself before putting away his pencil stump.

Tong looked back at the town. Red flags waved on top of the city hall and the courthouse. At the center of the city square, a stone statue of Chairman Mao dwarfed the nearby five-storied hospital. According to the schoolteachers, it was the tallest statue of Chairman Mao in the province, the pride of Muddy River, and had attracted pilgrims from other towns and villages. It was the main reason that Muddy River had been promoted from a regional town to a city that now had governing rights over several surrounding towns and villages. A few months earlier, not long after Tong's arrival, a worker assigned to the semiannual cleaning of the statue had an accident and plummeted to his death from the shoulder of Chairman Mao. Many townspeople gathered. Tong was one of the children who had squeezed through the legs of adults to have a close look at the body—the man, in the blue uniform of a cleaning worker, lay face up with a small puddle of blood by his mouth; his eyes were wide open and glassy-looking, and his limbs stuck out at odd and impossible angles. When the orderlies from the city hospital came to gather the body, it slipped and shook as if it were boneless, reminding Tong of a kind of slug in his grandparents' village—their bodies were fleshy and moist, and if you put a pinch of salt on their bodies, they would slowly become a small pool of white and sticky liquid. The child standing next to him was sick and was whisked away by his parents, and Tong willed himself not to act weakly. Even some grown-ups turned their eyes away when the orderlies had to peel the man's head off the ground, but Tong forced himself to watch everything without missing a single detail. He believed if he was brave enough, the town's boys, and perhaps the grown-ups too, would approve of him and accept him as one of the best among them. It was not the first time that Tong had seen a dead body, but never before had he seen a man die in such a strange manner. Back in his grandparents' village, people died in unsurprising ways, from sickness and old age. Only once a woman, working in the field with a tank of pesticide on her back, was killed instantly when the tank exploded. Tong and other children had gathered at the edge of the field and watched the woman's husband and two teenage sons hose down the body from afar until the fire was put out and the deadly gas dispersed; they seemed in neither shock nor grief, their silence suggesting something beyond Tong's understanding.

Some people's deaths are heavier than Mount Tai, and others' are as light as a feather. Tong thought about the lesson his teacher had taught a few weeks before. The woman killed in the explosion had become a tale that the villagers enjoyed telling to passersby, and often the listeners would exclaim in awe, but would that give her death more weight than an old woman dying in her sleep in the lane next to Tong's grandparents'? The counterrevolutionary's death must be lighter than a feather, but the banners and the ceremony of the day all seemed to say differently.

The city came to life in the boy's baffled gaze, some people more prepared than others for this important day. A fourth grader found to her horror that her silk Young Pioneer's kerchief had been ripped by her little brother, who had bound it around his cat's paw and played tug-of-war with the cat. Her mother tried to comfort her—didn't she have a spare cotton one, her mother asked, and even if she wore the silk kerchief, nobody would notice the small tear—but nothing could stop the girl's howling. How could they expect her, a captain of the Communist Young Pioneers in her class, to wear a plain cotton kerchief or a ripped one? The girl cried until it became clear that her tears would only make her look worse for the day; for the first time in her life, she felt its immense worthlessness, when a cat's small paw could destroy the grandest dream.

A few blocks away, a truck driver grabbed his young wife just as she rose from bed. One more time, he begged; she resisted, but when she failed to free her arms from his tight grip, she lay open for him. After all, they could both take an extra nap at the denunciation ceremony, and she did not need to worry about his driving today. In the city hospital, a nurse arrived late for the morning shift because her son had overslept, and in a hurry to finish her work before going to the denunciation ceremony, she gave the wrong dose of antibiotics to an infant recovering from pneumonia; only years later would the doctors discover the child's deafness, caused by the mistake, but it would remain uninvestigated, and the parents would have only fate to blame for their misfortune. Across the street in the communication building, the girl working the switchboard yelled at a peasant when he tried to call his uncle in a neighboring province; didn't he know that today was an important day and she had to be fully pre-pared for the political event instead of wasting her time with him, she said, her harsh words half-lost in a bad connection; while she was berating him, the army hospital from the provincial capital called in, and this time the girl was shouted at because she was not prompt enough in picking up the call.

*T*he girl was dressed in a dark-colored man's suit, a size too big for her, her hair coiled up and hidden underneath a fedora hat of matching color. Her hands, clad in black gloves, held tightly on to the handle of a short, unsheathed sword. The blade pointed upward, the only object of light color in the black-and-white picture. The girl's unsmiling face was half shadowed by the hat, her eyes looking straight into the camera. Think of how Autumn Jade was prepared to give up her life, Kai remembered her teacher explaining when she was chosen to play the famous heroine in a new opera. Kai was twelve then, a rising star in the theater school at the provincial capital, and it was not a surprise that she was given every major role, from Autumn Jade, who had been beheaded after a failed assassination of a provincial representative in the last emperor's court, to Chen Tiejun, the young Communist who had been shot alongside her lover shortly after they had announced each other husband and wife in front of the firing squad. Kai had always been praised for her mature performances, but looking at her picture now, she could see little understanding in the girl's eyes of the martyrs she had impersonated. Kai had once taken pride in entering adulthood ahead of her peers, but that adulthood, she could see now, was as false and untrustworthy as her youthful interpretation of death and martyrdom.

She returned the framed picture to the wall where it had hung for the past five years along with other pictures, relics of her life onstage between the ages of twelve and twenty-two. The studio, a small, windowless room on the top floor of the administration building, with padded walls and flickering fluorescent lights, had struck Kai at first as a place not much different from a prison cell. Han was the one who decorated the room, hanging up her pictures on the walls and a heart-shaped mirror behind the door, placing vases of plastic flowers on the shelves so they could bloom all year round without the need for sunshine or other care—to make the studio her very own, as Han insisted—when he helped her get the news announcer's position. One more reason to consider his marriage proposal, Kai's mother urged, thinking of other less privileged jobs that Kai could have been assigned to after her departure from the provincial theater troupe: teaching in an elementary school and struggling to make the children sing less cacophonously, or serving as one of those clerks who had little function other than filling the offices with pleasant feminine presence in the Cultural and Entertainment Department. Han, the only son of one of the most powerful couples in the city government, had been courting Kai for six months then, a perfect choice for her, according to her parents, who, both as middle-ranked clerks, had little status to help Kai, when younger faces had replaced Kai onstage. The most important success for a woman is not in her profession but in her marriage, Kai's father said when she thought of leaving Muddy River and seeking an acting career in Beijing or Shanghai; it is more of a challenge to retain the lifelong attention of one audience than to win the hearts of many who would forget her overnight. In her mother's absence, Kai's father explained all this, and it was not only his insight into the ephemeral nature of fame but also his unmistakable indication that Kai's mother—the more dominating and abusive one in their marriage—had failed, that made Kai reconsider her decision. A child who catches for the first time a glimpse of the darker side of her parents' marriage is forced to enter the grown-up world, often against her nature and will, just as she was once pushed through a birth canal to claim her existence.

For Kai, who had left home for the theater school at eight, this second birth came at a time when most of her school friends had ventured into marriage and early motherhood, and she made up her mind to marry into Han's family. That Kai's father had passed away shortly thereafter with liver cancer, discovered at a stage too late, had made the decision seem a worthy one, at least for the first year of the marriage.

Kai placed a record on the phonograph. The needle circled on the red disc, and dutifully the theme song for the morning news, "Love of the Homeland," flooded out of loudspeakers onto every street corner. Kai imagined the world outside the broadcast studio: the dark coal smoke rising from rooftops into the lead-colored morning sky; sparrows jumping from one roof to the next, their wings dusty and their chirping drowned out by the patriotic music; the people underneath those roofs, used to the morning ritual of music and then the news broadcast. They would probably not hear a single word of the program.

The chorus ended, and Kai lifted the needle and turned on the microphone. "Good morning, workers, peasants, and all revolutionary comrades of Muddy River," she began in her standard greeting, her well-trained voice at once warm and impersonal. She reported both international and national news, taken from *People's Daily* and *Reference Journal* by a night-shift clerk in the propaganda department, followed by provincial news and local affairs. Afterward she picked up an editorial, denouncing the Vietnamese government for its betrayal of the true Communist faith, and hailing the ideological importance of Pol Pot and his Khmer Rouge despite the temporary setback brought about by the Vietnamese intrusion. While she was reading, Kai was aware of the note taped to the microphone, instructing her to announce to the townspeople Gu Shan's denunciation ceremony, and her execution to follow.

Gu Shan was twenty-eight, the same age as Kai, and four years younger than Autumn Jade when she had been beheaded after a hasty trial. Autumn Jade had left two children who were too young to mourn her death, and a husband who had disowned her in defense of the last dynasty she had been fighting against. Kai had a husband and a son; Gu Shan had neither. The freedom to sacrifice for one's belief was a luxury that few could afford, Kai thought. She imagined sneaking the words *pioneer* and *martyr* into the announcement of the execution. Would Shan, who was probably being offered her last breakfast and perhaps a change of clean clothes, hear the voice of a friend she had perhaps long ago ceased hoping for in her long years of imprisonment? Kai's hands shook when she read the announcement. She and Shan were allies now, even though Shan would never know it.

Kai clicked off the microphone, and someone promptly knocked on the door, two short taps followed by a scratch. Kai checked her face in the mirror before opening the door.

"The best tonic for the best voice," said Han, as he lifted the thermos and presented it with a theatrical gesture. Every morning, before Han went to his office in the same building, he stopped by the studio with a thermos of tea, brewed from an herb named Big Fat Sea and said to be good for one's voice. It had begun as a habit of love after their honeymoon, and Kai had thought that it would cool down and eventually die as all unreasonable passions between a man and woman did. But five years and a child later, Han had not given up the practice. He must be the only husband in this town who would deliver tea to his wife, Han sometimes said, full of marvel and admiration, as if he himself was happily baffled by what he did; other people must think of him as a fool now, he said, out of self-mockery, yet it was the pride he did not conceal in the statement that filled Kai with panic. Getting married and becoming a mother had once seemed the most natural course for her life, but Kai could not help but wish, at times, that everything she had mistakenly decided could be wiped away.

"I've told you many times I don't need it," said Kai of the tea, and her reply, which often sounded like a loving reprimand, sounded more impatient to her ears today. Han seemed not to notice. He pecked her on the cheek, walked past her into the studio, and poured a mug of tea for her. "It's an important day. I don't want the world to hear that my wife's voice is anything less than perfect."

Kai smiled weakly, and when Han urged her to drink the tea, she took a sip. He gazed at her. How was his preparation for the day going, she asked, before he had a chance to compliment her beauty, as he often did.

"All set but for the helicopter," Han replied.

The helicopter? Kai asked. Something that was not his responsibility, he said, and he left it at that. Kai asked, as if out of innocent curiosity, what he needed a helicopter for, and Han replied that he was sure someone would set things straight, she should not bother herself with his boring business. "Worrying makes one grow old," he said, as a joke, and Kai said that perhaps it would soon be time for him to look for a younger woman. He laughed, taking Kai's reply as a flirtation.

It amazed her that her husband never doubted her in any way. His faith and confidence in her—and more so in himself—made him a blind worshipper of their marriage. How easy it was to deceive a trusting soul, but the thought unsettled Kai. She looked at the clock, and said it was about time for her to go. She was expected to be at her position at the East Wind Stadium, one of the major sites for the denunciation ceremony, by eight. He would walk her there, Han said. Kai wished she had an excuse to reject his offer, but she said nothing.

She put a few pages of the news away and adjusted her hair before leaving the studio with him. Her husband placed a hand on her elbow, as if she needed his guidance and assistance to walk down the five flights of stairs, but when they exited the building, he let go of her, so that they would not be seen having any improper physical contact in public.

"So I'll see you at Three Joy?" Han asked, as they turned at the street corner.

What for? Kai asked, and Han answered that it was the celebration banquet. Nobody had told her about it, Kai said, and Han replied that he thought she would have known by now that it was the regular thing after such an event. "The last couple of dinners, the mayor asked why you were not there," Han said, and added that he had found excuses for her both times.

Kai could envision it: her place at the table with the mayor and his wife, Han and his parents and a few other families, a close-knit circle of status. It had been part of the allure of the marriage, that once she was a member of this family she would enter a social group that clerks like her parents had dreamed of reaching all their lives. Kai was unwilling to admit it now, but she knew that vanity was one of her costly errors. She was a presentable wife and daughter-in-law: good-looking, having had no other boyfriend before she met Han, and capable of giving birth to a son for the first baby. Her in-laws treated her well, but they would never hesitate to let her know that she was the one to have married up in the family.

She had told the nanny that she would be home around lunch-time, Kai said. The new nanny, having just started the week before, was fifteen and a half, too young to take care of a baby, in Kai's opinion, but when the previous nanny had quit to go back to work on the land with her husband and sons—after many years of the people's commune, the central government had finally allowed peasants to own the planting rights to their own land—a girl from the mountain village was the only one they could find as a replacement.

He would send his parents' orderly to check on the nanny, Han said. What could an eighteen-year-old boy know about an eleven-month-old baby, Kai responded, and Han, detecting a trace of impatience in her words, studied her and asked if she was feeling all right. He squeezed her hand quickly before letting it go.

Kai shook her head and said she only worried about Ming-Ming. Han replied that he understood, but his parents would not be happy if she missed important social events. She nodded and said she would go if that was what he wanted. The baby had been an easy excuse for her distraction at the breakfast table, the dinners she missed at Han's parents' flat, fewer visits to her own mother, her tired apologies when Han asked for sex at night.

"My parents want you to be there," said Han. "So do I."

Kai nodded, and they resumed their walk in silence. A few blocks away they saw smoke rising at an intersection. A group of people had gathered, and there was a strong odor of burned leather in the air. A piece of silk, palm-sized and in a soft faded color, was carried across the street by the wind. An orange cat, stretching on a low wall, followed the floating fabric with its eyes.

Han asked the crowd to make way. A few people stood aside, and Kai followed her husband into the circle. A man sporting the red armband of the Workers' Union security patrol was staring down at an old woman, who sat in front of a burning pile of clothes. She did not look up when Han asked her why she was blocking traffic on the important day of a political event.

"The old witch is playing deaf and mute," the security patrol said, and added that his companion had gone to fetch the police.

Kai looked at the top of the old woman's head, barely covered by thin gray hair. She bent down toward the old woman, and told her that she was violating a traffic regulation, that she'd better leave now. There was a slight ripple in the crowd as Kai spoke; in this town, people recognized Kai's voice. When she stood up, she could feel the woman standing next to her inching away, so as to study her face at a better angle.

"You may still have a chance, if you walk away by yourself now," Han said, and in a lower voice, he told Kai to go on to the ceremony, as he would wait for the police.

The old woman looked up. "You'll all see her off in your way. Why can't I see her off in mine?"

The security patrol explained to Han and Kai that this woman was the mother of the soon-to-be-executed counterrevolutionary. Only then did Kai recognize the defiance in Mrs. Gu's eyes. She had seen the same expression in Shan's eyes twelve years ago, when they had been in rival factions of the Red Guards.

"Our way to send your daughter off is not only the most correct way but also the only way permitted by law," Han said, as he ordered the security patrol to fetch water. Mrs. Gu poked the fire with a tree branch, as if she had not heard him. When the patrol returned with a heavy bucket, Han stepped back and motioned the man to put out the fire. Mrs. Gu did not shield her face from the splashing water. The pile hissed and smoldered, but she poked it again as if she were willing the flame to catch again.

Two policemen, summoned by the other patrol, were now pushing through the crowd and shouting, telling people to move on. Some people left, but many only retreated and formed a bigger circle. "Let's not make a big fuss out of this," Kai said to Han, as he strode up to meet the policemen.

"Those who seek punishment will get what they ask for," Han said.

The patrol greeted the police, and pointed out Han and Kai, but Mrs. Gu paid little attention to the men surrounding her, mumbling something before she wiped tears from the corners of her eyes.

"Why don't you just let her go?" Kai said to Han, and she quoted an old saying, *Favors one does will be returned to him, and pains one causes will be inflicted on him.*

Han glanced at Kai, saying that he did not know that she could be superstitious.

"If you don't want to believe in it for yourself, at least believe in it for your son," Kai said. The urgency in her voice stopped Han, who looked at her with half-smiling eyes. He said he had never known she would take up the beliefs of the old generation.

"A mother needs all the help possible to ensure a good life for her child," Kai said. "What if people direct curses at Ming-Ming because of what we do?"

Han shook his head, as if amused by his wife's logic. He greeted the policemen and told them to escort the old woman home and find someone to clean up the street. "Let's not make a big fuss this time," he said, echoing Kai's words and adding that there was no need to put additional stress on this day. The other men complimented Han for his generosity: More power to him who lets someone off without pursuing an error, the older policeman said, and Han nodded in agreement.

THREE

*M*rs. Hua did not see the police-
men remove Mrs. Gu from the site of her crime; nor would Mrs. Hua
have realized, had she witnessed the scene, that the woman who was
half dragged and half carried to the police jeep was Mrs. Gu.

Like Mrs. Hua herself, Mrs. Gu would never become a grandmother. Mrs. Hua was sixty-six, an age when a grandchild or two
would provide a better reason to live on than the streets her husband
scavenged and she swept, but the streets provided a living, while the
dreams about grandchildren did not, and she was aware of the good
fortune to be alive, for which she and her husband often reminded
themselves to be grateful. Still, the urge to hold a baby sometimes
became so strong that she had to pause what she was doing and feel,
with held breath, the imagined weight of a small body, warm and
soft, in her arms. This gave her the look of a distracted old woman.
Once in a while her boss, Shaokang, a man in his fifties who had
never married, would threaten to fire her, as if he was angry with her
slow response to his requests, but she knew that he only said it for
the sake of the other workers in the sanitation department, as he was
one of those men who concealed his kindness behind harsh words.
He had first offered her a job in his department thirteen years ago,
when he had seen Mrs. Hua and her husband in the street, she running a high fever and he begging for a bowl of water from a shop. It
was shortly after they had been forced to let the four younger girls be

taken away to orphanages in four different counties, a practice believed to be good for the girls to start anew. Mrs. Hua and her husband had walked for three months through four provinces, hoping the road would heal their fresh wound. They had not expected to settle down in Muddy River, but Shaokang told them sternly that the coming winter would certainly kill both of them if they did not accept his offer, and in the end, the will to live on ended their journey.

"The crossroad at Liberation and Yellow River," said Shaokang, when Mrs. Hua came into the department, a room the size of a warehouse, with a desk in the corner to serve as an office area. She went to the washstand and rinsed the basin. There was little paste left; he had given her much more flour than needed, but she knew he would not question the whereabouts of the leftover flour.

Mrs. Hua went to the closet but most brooms had not yet been returned by the road crew. When all present, the brooms, big ones made out of bamboo branches and small ones made out of straw, would stand up in a line, like a platoon of soldiers, each bearing a number in Shaokang's neat handwriting and assigned to a specific sweeper. Sometimes Mrs. Hua wondered if in one of Shaokang's thick notebooks he had a record of all the brooms that had passed through the sanitation department: how much time they had spent in the street and how much they had idled in the closet; how long each broom lasted before its full head went bald. The younger sweepers in the department joked behind Shaokang's back that he loved the brooms as his own children, but Mrs. Hua saw nothing wrong in that and knew that the joke would come only from young people who understood little of parenthood.

Mrs. Hua picked up the brooms that belonged to her and told Shaokang that the night before she had dreamed of painting red eggs for a grandchild's birthday. Mrs. Hua spoke to Shaokang only when there was no one around. Sometimes it would be days or weeks before they had a chance to talk, but neither found anything odd in that, their conversations no more than a few words.

"A dream is as real as a blossom in the mirror or a full moon in the river,"

said Shaokang. He did not look up from the notebook he was study-ing. Mrs. Hua sighed in agreement and headed to the door. Earlier that morning she had told the same dream to her husband, and he had replied that it was a good dream, if nothing else.

"Do you want some time off today?" Shaokang asked.

Why would she, replied Mrs. Hua. He worried that the denuncia-tion ceremony might bore Mrs. Hua, Shaokang said, and added that enough workers would be representing the sanitation department. As if boredom was something that people like her should be con-cerned about, Mrs. Hua thought, but she could use a day off to help her husband sort out the bottles that had been accumulating in their shed. Indeed, she was trying to fight off a cold, Mrs. Hua said, lying for the sake of the office desk and the brooms and the four empty walls. Shaokang nodded and said that after she cleaned up the crossroad she need not report to the denunciation ceremony.

The pile at the intersection was scattered by the indifferent tramping shoes of adults as well as the kicking feet of children for whom the half-burned fabric and scorched shoes all provided end-less amusement. Mrs. Hua shooed a few persistent children away and cleaned the street while thinking about her dream from the night before.

"Morning, Mrs. Hua," a voice whispered to her, too close to her ears.

Mrs. Hua, startled, saw Bashi, that good-for-nothing idler, smile at her. She mumbled that she wished he had better things to do than frighten old folks in the street.

"Frighten? I didn't mean to. I was only going to remind you that Old Hua might be waiting for you at home."

"Home? Rubbish collectors do not boast about home," said Mrs. Hua. "It's a temporary nest."

"But my home is your home, Mrs. Hua. I've told my grandma many times that you and Old Hua could move in with us any day you like. You know she's a bit lonely and wouldn't mind some old friends around," Bashi said, looking sincerely into Mrs. Hua's eyes.

Mrs. Hua shook her head and said, "Nobody believes your sweet talk except your grandma."

"I mean it, Mrs. Hua. Ask anyone in town. Everyone knows I am generous about my wealth, and ready to help anyone in need."

"Your wealth? That's the money your father earned with his life."

Bashi shrugged and did not bother to refute the old woman.

"Son, don't you worry about your future?"

"What do I have to worry about?" Bashi said.

"What can you do, son?" she said. "I worry about you."

"I can go rubbish collecting with Old Hua," Bashi said. "I can sweep the streets with you too. I'm a hard worker. See my muscles. Here and here. I'll tell you, Mrs. Hua, it's not a joke to lift dumbbells every morning." There were neither dumbbells nor muscles worth bragging about, but such stories came readily and convincingly to Bashi.

"Street sweeping is a hard job to get now," Mrs. Hua said. In the past two years, the end of the Cultural Revolution had brought many young people back from the countryside, where they had been sent over the past decade. Even a street sweeper's position was something people fought over now. She would not be surprised one of these days to find herself replaced.

"There's no permit required to go rubbish collecting," Bashi said. "That's an easy thing to do."

"It's a hard life."

"I don't mind. Honestly, Mrs. Hua, I would love to go rubbish collecting, and baby collecting too, with you."

Mrs. Hua gathered the wet ashes on the ground without replying. It had been years since she and her husband had given up the seven girls they had found in their wandering lives as rubbish collectors, and she did not know what continued to capture the young man's interest, when the story had long ago lived out its due in people's gossip and curiosity. He asked them often, and she never offered much to satisfy him.

"Would Old Hua and you bring up a baby girl again if you found a live one now?"

Mrs. Hua looked at the sky and thought about the question. Hard as she tried—often at night when she was unable to sleep—she could not summon up clear images of the seven faces. How could she forget their looks when she had raised them from rag-covered little creatures left by the roadside? But old age played tricks, dulling her memory as well as her eyes.

"Would you, say, keep an eye out for a baby girl?" Bashi persisted.

Mrs. Hua shook her head. "Too hard a life. A hard life for everybody."

"But I could bring up the girl along with you, Mrs. Hua. I have the money. I can work too. I'm young."

Mrs. Hua studied Bashi with her cataract-bleared eyes. Bashi stood straighter and arranged his hat. The young man in front of her had not had the first taste of hardship in life, Mrs. Hua thought, and said so to Bashi.

"I lost my parents when I was young," Bashi said. "I'm as much an orphan as your girls were before you picked them up."

Caught off guard, Mrs. Hua could not think of what to say. She had not known that Bashi would remember his parents. After a moment, she said, "Better to have left them to die in the first place."

"Where are your daughters now?" Bashi asked. "How old are they?"

"Wherever their fates have brought them to. Where else can they be?"

"Where is that?" Bashi persisted.

"Three of them we left with people who were willing to take them in as child brides. The four younger ones were confiscated by the government and sent to orphanages because we were not the legal parents. What do you think of that, son?" Mrs. Hua said, unaware of her raised voice. "We fed them spoonful by spoonful and brought them up and then we were told it was illegal to keep them in the first place. Better just to let them die from the start."

Bashi sighed. "It makes no sense, this life, does it?"

Mrs. Hua did not reply. Bashi repeated the line to himself and let it stay in the air between them for a beat longer.

NINI SLOWED DOWN when she approached the alley where Teacher Gu and Mrs. Gu lived. She had managed to get to the railway station in time, and the workers had given her coal and then shooed her away. None of them seemed to like her, and she often wondered if someday they would find her unbearably ugly and change their minds. That had not happened, but she often worried about it.

She worried too about Mrs. Gu's hospitality. For the past two years, Mrs. Gu had never failed to show up where her alley joined the street. Standing by a half-dead plum tree, she would put a hand on the trunk and swing her legs, one and then another, as if she were doing some halfhearted exercises, and when people walked past her she did not greet them. At the sight of Nini, Mrs. Gu would nod imperceptibly and turn toward her alley, and Nini would know that she was welcome in the house for another day.

This morning ritual had started not long after Nini's parents had made her responsible for providing coal. Since the Gus' house was out of Nini's way, Mrs. Gu had been the one to seek Nini out one morning, asking politely if she would like a few bites of breakfast before going home. Nini thought the invitation odd and suspicious, but a hungry child all her life, she found it hard to turn away.

Nini did not know why Mrs. Gu and Teacher Gu invited her to breakfast. They seldom talked between themselves, at least when she was around. They asked her about her family once in a while, and when Nini offered the briefest answers to their questions, they did not press for more information, so Nini knew they had no more interest in the topic than she did. Teacher Gu ate fast, and while waiting for Nini to finish her breakfast, he folded a frog out of the piece of paper he had ripped off the calendar and had kept neat and flat on the table. For your sisters, Teacher Gu said when he placed the paper frog in her hand, though she never passed it on to them. She had thought of keeping all the paper frogs but there was no corner in her house to save anything. In the end, she left them in the rubbish can, picked up later by Old Hua, unfolded, and sold to the recycling station.

Nini always worried that one day Teacher Gu and Mrs. Gu would stop caring about her, and her bowl would be missing from the table. When she saw now that no one was standing next to the half-dead plum tree she wondered, for a second, if Mrs. Gu and Teacher Gu had overslept; they could have gotten ill also, she thought, old people as they were, their bodies no longer reliable. Still, her instincts told her that they must have stopped wanting her around, and she decided to go to the Gus' house, if only to make sure that was true.

Several steps into the alley a police jeep drove toward Nini with short impatient honks, and she hurried to make way for the vehicle, almost twisting her bad foot. When the jeep turned out of the alley Nini said a curse she had picked up at the marketplace—even though she understood little of its meaning, it fitted her mood and she used it often. She lingered in front of the Gus' gate for a few minutes and made small coughing sounds, but neither Mrs. Gu nor Teacher Gu rushed out of the gate to apologize for their lateness. Nini pushed the gate ajar and let herself into the yard. The front room was unlit, and the window that faced the yard was covered with thick layers of old newspaper for insulation. Nini looked in, but could see nothing through the opaque newsprint. "Mrs. Gu," she said quietly, then raised her voice a little. "Teacher Gu." When no one answered, she tried the door, and it opened without a sound. The front room, dark and cold, was lit only by a long stripe of orange light on the floor that came from the half-closed door of the bedroom. "Mrs. Gu," said Nini. "Are you feeling all right today?"

The bedroom door opened and Mrs. Gu stood in the frame, a dark silhouette. "Go home now, Nini," she said in a flat voice. "We don't owe you any more. Never come to my door again."

Nini had been waiting for moments like this all her life. She was not surprised, but relieved. She had not made a mistake: People changed their minds all the time, often without a reason. She sucked the inside of her mouth hard and did not move. She could not see Mrs. Gu's face in the dark shadow, but any moment now the old woman would come closer, grab her arms, and push her out of the door, and Nini's small body tensed up at the expectation. She wondered whether Mrs. Gu's hands would feel differently on her face than her own mother's slapping. "Nini," Teacher Gu said, appearing behind Mrs. Gu, his voice gentler. He walked past Mrs. Gu and took the rope off Nini's shoulder. She let the basket go and followed him to an old desk that served as both the kitchen counter and a dinner table. There was no porridge and no pickled cabbage waiting. Teacher Gu looked around, and before he spoke, there came a muffled cry from Mrs. Gu in their bedroom. He rubbed his hands. "Mrs. Gu is not feeling well today," he said. "I'll be back, and you wait here."

Nini nodded. When Teacher Gu closed the bedroom door behind him, she tried the two drawers at the side of the desk. From the dim light coming through the newsprint that covered the window, Nini could see that the first drawer was filled with chopsticks, cutting knives, matchbooks, candles, used batteries, and other knickknacks. She shut it without making a sound and opened the other one: a few pencils, a black velvet box, some scratch paper, a thick notebook in which many receipts were pasted, a plastic barrette. Nini opened the box and found a fountain pen inside; she stroked the smooth and dark blue body before putting it back into the box. She then picked up the barrette and slipped it into her own pocket; Mrs. Gu deserved this. The two hens, quiet and forgotten by Nini, scratched and cooed; startled, she almost gave out a cry. When no one came, she paged through the notebook. There was a loose receipt, and she pocketed it too, just in time before Teacher Gu came out of the bedroom. He turned on the lamp and Nini blinked in the sudden harshness of the light. He walked to the cabinet and took out a tin of biscuits. "Nini, take the biscuits with you," said Teacher Gu. "For you and your sisters."

Nini looked up at Teacher Gu, and his eyes, tired and sad, seemed not to register her presence. She thought about the receipt in her pocket, something he would be looking for later; if he said a few kind words to apologize for Mrs. Gu, Nini thought, she would find a way to sneak the receipt back into the drawer, or just drop it by the door.

Teacher Gu did not notice her hesitation. He picked up her basket. "Mrs. Gu is not feeling well these days, and she does not wish to see you for some time," Teacher Gu said, pushing Nini gently out of the door. "Don't come back to see us until Mrs. Gu feels better."

In the street Nini opened the tin and put a biscuit in her mouth. The biscuit tasted sweet and stale. Teacher Gu had changed his mind too, dismissing her with a tin of biscuits that must have been sitting on the shelf for ages. Nini took the receipt out and looked at the red official stamp on it. She could not read, but a red stamp must mean something important, which made her happy. She squeezed the receipt into a small ball and threw it into a nearby dumpster. She took out another biscuit, nibbling and walking slowly home when someone tapped her on the shoulder.

Nini turned and saw a familiar face that belonged to a young man who spent most of his days wandering in and out of the marketplace. She stepped back and looked at him.

"Nini's your name, isn't it?" he said, baring his yellow and crooked teeth.

She nodded.

"You must be wondering how I know your name," said the man. "Do you want to know how I know your name?"

Nini shook her head.

"And you have five sisters. Do you want to know what else I know about you?"

Nini stared at the young man without replying. On another day, in a different mood, she might ask the young man who he thought he was to bother with other people's business. She had heard grown-ups talk this way and she believed she had learned the right tone, impatient, and with authority. At least, when she talked to her sisters in that tone, they all seemed intimidated. She could make the young man speechless and embarrassed, but she was not in the mood for that today. The only thing she wanted to do was to bite the inside of her mouth until she could taste blood.

"If your mother gives birth to another daughter, they will become the Heavenly Emperor and Empress, do you know why?"

Nini shook her head.

"Only the Heavenly Emperor and Empress gave birth to seven daughters, the Seven Fairy Sisters," said the man. "Ha."

The man waited for her to laugh. He seemed disappointed when she did not. "My name is Bashi, *Eighty*."

What an odd thing to have a number as his name, Nini thought. She wondered if the man had any brothers and sisters, and if they had names like Seventy, Sixty, and Fifty. As if he had guessed her question, the man said, "You know why Bashi is my name? Because I ate eighty dumplings the day I was born."

Nini knew it was a joke too, but it was not funny, and she decided not to smile.

"Are you a mute?" Bashi said.

"Of course not. What a stupid question."

"Good, you can speak. How old are you?"

"It's none of your business," Nini said.

"I'm nineteen—well, nineteen and a quarter. I was born in July. July 7, an important day, because I was born on that day. Have you seen a history textbook? It lists all the birthdays of all important people, and someday it will include mine."

Nini shifted the coal basket to another shoulder. She knew enough not to believe his words, but nobody had wanted to talk to her at this length before.

"How old are you? If you don't tell me, I'll have to guess."

"Twelve," Nini said. She did not know why the man was so persistent.

"Twelve? Wonderful."

"What's wonderful?"

Bashi looked baffled by Nini's question. "Do you want to come and chat with me?" he said.

"Why?"

Bashi scratched his scalp hard and Nini watched big flakes of dandruff fall. "You can come to talk to me so you don't have to walk all the way to the railway station for coal. What you're doing is really stealing, I'm sure you know that. Nobody saying anything about it now doesn't mean someone won't pursue you in the future. Wait and see. Any day now they may come and charge you with stealing from state property. 'What a pity,' people will say. 'What a nice little girl but look at the trouble she's got herself into.' Do you want to be caught like a thief? And paraded around town in a cage for people to throw stones at?" Bashi asked. "We have plenty of coal in our house. My grandmother and I live together, and she likes to talk to little girls like you. We can buy extra coal for you to bring home, and you don't even have to tell your parents. Think about it, all right?"

Nobody had ever used *nice* to describe her, and for a moment Nini wondered if the man was blind. But he was right that what she did was not legal. It had not occurred to her before, but she wondered now whether it was the reason she was sent to do it. She imagined the policemen coming to arrest her. Her parents would be relieved, and her sisters would celebrate because a competing mouth was eliminated from the dinner table. Mrs. Gu and Teacher Gu might not even wonder what had happened to her. The neighbors and strangers would all say it was their good fortune that the ugly girl had finally been plucked out of their life. No one would miss her.

Bashi told her again to think about what he could offer. Nini did not understand why people decided to be nice or, more often, mean to her. She imagined a house with good, solid lumps of coal. A few men and women walked past them in the street, all wearing their best Mao jackets and carrying colorful banners in their gloved hands. Some of them looked at Nini's companion with disdain, but most ignored him. Bashi seemed not to notice. He grinned and waved back at them. "Morning, Uncles and Aunties. Are you having a parade today? For the execution?" he said. "Who's this woman, anyway? Does anyone know her story?"

When none of the adults replied, Bashi turned back to Nini. "They are executing someone today. A woman. Think about it. One can't commit a crime and think one can run away without punishment." Then, in a lower voice, he added, "Say, do you want to come and chat with me?"

"Where?"

"Come with me. I can show you my house now."

Nini shook her head. It was getting late, and her mother would be cursing her and her bad leg for being slow. "I need to go home," she said.

"Will you be free after breakfast? I'll wait for you upriver, by the old willow tree. You know that place?"

The willow was an old, gnarled tree with a full head of branches, like a madwoman. It was quite a walk from Nini's home, past half the town, past the birch woods on the riverbank, until one could see not the low row houses but the high chimneys of the generation plant. Nini had been there before Little Sixth's birth; she had not been charged with most of the chores then, and in the spring, sometimes she had been sent to dig new dandelions and shepherd's purses. Through the spring and early summer, her family ate the edible grass, boiled in water and salted heavily; they ate it long past the season, until their mouths were filled with bitter, hard fibers. The memory made Nini's mouth full of the grassy taste.

"How about it?" Bashi said. He looked at her as if her face were any other girl's face, her mouth not skewed to the left, her eyes not drooping in the same direction. Her left hand and left foot were bad too, but he seemed not to have noticed them either. "Are you coming?"

Nini nodded.

"Great," Bashi said. He took a biscuit out of the tin in Nini's hand and popped it into his mouth before he walked away.

TEACHER GU STARTED the fire and poured water on the leftover rice. He watched the yellow flame lick the bottom of the pot, the murmuring of the water inside soothingly hypnotic. A grain of sand is as complete as a world, he said to the fire, his voice audible only to his own ears. The thought that someone sitting above the clouds could gaze into this small cocoon in which he and his wife were trapped in pain comforted him; their suffering to the eyes above could be as tiny and irrelevant as the piece of coal in his own eyes, a burning ember that would soon cool into a gray ball of ash.

The water boiled, and the lid of the pot let out sighs of white steam. Teacher Gu stirred the rice and sat down at the table. There was no sound from the bedroom, and he wondered if his wife had been falling into sleep; she had been escorted back by two policemen earlier, and they had made some harsh threats before taking off her handcuffs. He had worried that she would become hysterical, but she had kept herself still until the moment Nini arrived, the last person in the world who should be receiving his wife's anger.

Teacher Gu's hands probed around on the table as if they belonged to a blind man. Over the years he had developed a habit of busying his hands with anything they could reach, a sign of some disturbing psychological problem perhaps, but Teacher Gu tried not to dwell on it. Apart from a bowl of leftover soup, the table was empty. Another broken ritual, Teacher Gu thought, gone with Nini and the folding of a paper frog out of the calendar. It had started when Shan was fourteen, a young Red Guard ready to rip the world apart. He had folded paper compulsively, his busy fingers saving him from the sorrow of watching his daughter transform before his own eyes into a coldhearted stranger. At breakfast on an early summer day, when Shan had given a speech on how he should bow to the revolutionary youths instead of resisting with his silence, he made the paper frog jump and it landed in his wife's unfinished porridge. Neither Mrs. Gu nor Teacher Gu removed the frog, and he knew then that they would never laugh together as a family again. On the same morning, when Shan's young revolutionary friends came over, she suggested that they go out and "kick the bottoms of some counterrevolutionaries." So easily she had let these vulgar words slip out, this daughter whom he had taught to recite poetry from the Tang dynasty since she was very young. Later, someone came to his school with the news that besides booting some people's bottoms, Shan had also kicked the belly of a woman eight months pregnant. Teacher Gu hid himself in his office and wrote a long essay, a meditation on the failing of poetry as education in an unpoetic age. Upon finishing and rereading the essay, he tossed it into the fire and braced himself to face his wife, with whom he shared the responsibility of having brought a near murderer into this world.

How Shan had escaped the consequences of her action was beyond Teacher Gu's understanding. His wife began to break down and weep often, first thing in the morning or sometimes in the middle of a savorless meal. What wrong had she done to deserve Shan? his wife asked him. Was heaven punishing them because they had both been married before and thus brought impurity to their marriage? This notion was superstitious nonsense, Teacher Gu wanted to remind his wife, but she was lost too, led astray by the belief that she herself was responsible for the crimes committed by their daughter. In his quiet disapproval she grew into an ordinary, witless woman, trying to find a reason for every calamity and failure, as if the world were explainable and life would have to make sense for one to continue living.

Teacher Gu shook his head. He was no better than she, he told himself. He was a man who had foolishly let himself be deceived by his own wishes. When he had first met his wife, she had just stopped belonging to her previous husband, as one of his five wives. She was the only one to leave the family of her own will when the newly established Communist government banned polygamy; the other wives had to be dragged away from the family by government officials. She was the first one to enroll in Teacher Gu's class for illiterate women—she was eighteen that year, her hair black and smooth as silk, her cheeks peach-colored, and her eyes two deep wells of sad water. She was born with an *ill-favored* face, people in town warned Teacher Gu when he decided to marry her. Look at her cheekbones, which are too high, her lips, which are not full enough, people said. He shrugged off their comments. Ill-fortuned she was, losing her parents at twelve, sold to a husband by her uncle at fourteen, serving a man forty years her senior as half wife and half handmaiden, but Teacher Gu did not want to listen to any of the talk. Husband and wife were birds of the same fate—so said the ancient poems. Wasn't it why they had become husband and wife in the first place? The day they got married, his first wife sent a telegram to him; *keep each other alive with your own water,* said the message. He hid the telegram, even though his new wife was not yet able to read all the characters in it. He never told her about the blessing, nor the fable behind those few words—two fish, husband and wife, were stranded in a puddle; they competed to swallow as much water as they could before the puddle vanished in the scorching sun so that they could keep each other alive in their long suffering before death by giving water to their loved one.

It was not a surprise that Teacher Gu and his first wife, being in love, had wished to be the two fish in the story, nor was it a wonder that this wish, along with other dreams and plans, was left unspoken at the end of their marriage. Nothing went wrong except, as she put it in her application for divorce, their marriage could not live up to the demands of the new society, she as a model Communist Party member, he a counterrevolutionary intellectual once serving in the Nationalist government as an education expert. She stayed in the university after the divorce, the first female mathematics professor in the tri-province area, later promoted to be president of a prestigious college in Beijing; he, the founder of the first Western-style high school in the province, was demoted to the local elementary school. If husband and wife were indeed birds of the same fate, he was not a good match for his first wife. He wished her better fortune in finding a husband appropriate for her position, someone approved by the party, or, even better, someone assigned by the party. But she remained single, childless. He never gathered enough courage to ask why. They exchanged a letter or two each year, saying little, because he felt that he had nothing, or too much, to say. Her letters were plain greetings for him and his family, and he dared not imagine her anguish beneath the calm politeness.

Teacher Gu's first marriage had lasted three years, and what he remembered, afterward, was many of their intellectual talks. Even on their honeymoon they had spent more time reading and discussing Kant than enjoying the beach resort. Early in his second marriage, he would sometimes watch his young wife asleep at night and hope that she would eventually offer more than her physical beauty, that he would be able to share his intellectual life with her—he was then thirty-two, still too young to understand how limitless men's desires were, or the absurdity of such greed.

When he had finally come to terms with what he could expect from his young wife, he did not love her less. He felt more responsible for her, not only as a husband and a man, but also as a parent and educator. He had always thought of her as his first child, before Shan and the other children they could not save—their firstborn, a baby boy, had lived for three days, and when Shan was two they had made one more effort that ended with a miscarriage. They gave up after that, counting it their blessing that they had Shan, a healthy, strong, and beautiful girl.

A son might have been different, Teacher Gu thought now, a son who would have grown up into an intelligent young man, someone with whom he could have had a true conversation. A son would take care of his parents on this day of loss, and for all the days that were coming. But these were foolish thoughts, wishing for something in vain. He'd better put a stop to such irrational wanderings of his mind. Teacher Gu opened the drawer. He had not done his book-keeping since the previous day.

He paged through the notebook carefully, but there was no trace of the receipt. He went over the day before in his mind, the two offi-cials, not impolite, and the pink, yellow, and white copies of the re-ceipt they had produced. It had never occurred to Teacher Gu that he and his wife were to pay for the bullet that would take their daughter's life, but why question such absurdity when it was not his position to ask? He signed, and counted out the price of the bullet, twenty-four cents, for the two men. The price of two pencils, or a few ears of corn—what he had often bought for his poorer students. He remembered folding the receipt once in the middle and putting it into the notebook when his wife came back from the market, a cab-bage and a radish in her string bag. In the alley, she did not question the two men leaving; perhaps she had not seen them, or perhaps she had already guessed who they were. He and his wife had not talked about Shan's case since the appeal had been turned down.

Teacher Gu went over the notebook again. His wife never touched it, trusting him with all monetary matters. He himself had not opened the notebook since last night. "It must be taking a walk with a ghost," a familiar voice said to Teacher Gu, and for a moment he was startled but then he recognized his nanny's voice from decades ago. She had been a servant for his grandparents, and she called him Young Master, but she was more like his mother—his own mother had been the headmistress of a boarding school for girls and had spent most of her time fund-raising for students from poor families to receive secondary education. Your mother is more capable than a man, he remembered his nanny saying with admiration. She herself, like the generation of women from her background, did not have any education, but she had theories and explanations for the small-est incidents in life. A misplaced hairpin must be taking a walk with a ghost, so too a lost coin or a missing tin soldier; sometimes the ghosts returned the runaway items but to different locations, because ghosts were forgetful, which also explained the permanent disappearance of things. She had a husky voice, which she said was a result of having cried too much over her husband and children, all of them caught in an epidemic of cholera. Gone to pay off their debts, she would talk about her family as if their deaths had just been another ordinary circumstance that required some straightforward explanation.

Teacher Gu closed his eyes; in his drowsiness he felt as if he had been returned to his childhood, nodding off on the stories told in an unhurried manner by the nanny.

The bedroom door opened, and before Teacher Gu could put away the notebook, his wife rushed to the stove and moved the pot away from the fire. The porridge had long ago stopped gurgling, and the front room was filled with a heavy, smoky smell. Teacher Gu looked at his wife apologetically, but she averted her eyes and scooped the meal out for them both, the less burned portion for him and the black bottom for herself.

They ate without talking and without tasting either. When they had both finished, she got up and washed the bowls. He waited until she finished. "Nini's done nothing wrong. You should not treat her like that."

The words, once out of his mouth, sounded more accusing than he had intended. His wife stared at him. He tried to soften his voice. "What I mean is, after all, we've done more harm to her and her family. They've done nothing to us."

"They're part of the world that will celebrate your daughter's murder," his wife said. "Why do we have to feel that we owe other people, when we're owed more than anybody?"

"*What I own is my fortune; what I'm owed is my fate,*" Teacher Gu answered. The words sounded soothing and he repeated them one more time to himself, in a low, chanting voice. His wife did not reply and shut herself in the bedroom.

NINI FINISHED all the biscuits and threw the tin away before she pushed open the gate. Unlike most families in Muddy River, hers did not have a rudimentary storage shed in their small yard. She poured the coal into a wooden crate covered by an old tarpaulin. The white hen, one of the two that her family owned, flapped its wings and leapt onto the crate. With a smack Nini sent the bird fluttering to the ground. The nosiest creature in the world, the white hen came to check on the coal every morning as if she had been assigned by Nini's mother to supervise her; in a low admonishing voice, Nini told it to mind its own business. The white hen strolled away, unruffled.

In the front room that served as a kitchen, Nini's mother was cooking over hot oil, and Nini wrinkled her nose at the unusual aroma. The other hen of the family, a brown one that was not as diligent as the white hen in laying eggs, flapped her wings when she saw Nini come in, though her legs, bound together and tied to a stool, forbade her to move far. Without turning to look at Nini, her mother raised her voice over the sizzling pan and asked what had made Nini late. Nini, expecting her mother's anger, and a punishment with no breakfast, spoke haltingly of the long wait in the railway station, but her mother seemed not to hear her.

Inside the bedroom, Nini's father and her sisters sat around the table on their brick bed. The small wooden bed table was the only good furniture they owned; the rest of the house was filled with cardboard boxes that served as closets, trunks, and cabinets. The brick bed was where every family function took place, and the bed table served as their dinner table, her sisters' desk for homework, as well as their workbench. Nini's father worked in the heavy-metal factory and her mother packed ginseng and mushrooms in the wholesale section of the agricultural department; they earned barely enough to feed Nini and her five sisters, and clothes were passed down in order, from the parents to Nini and then to the rest of the girls. Every evening, the family sat together around the bed table and folded matchboxes to earn extra money. Even the three-year-old was given a small batch to finish. Besides the baby, Nini was the only one who did not fold matchboxes. Her bad hand made her useless for the job, and it was made clear to her many times that she was living not only on her parents' blood and sweat but also on that of her younger sisters.

The fire had been built up in the belly of the brick bed. Nini's father was sipping cheap yam liquor from a cup, but he did not look as gloomy as he did when he drank in the evenings. Her mother came in with a plate of fried bread. Nini was shocked to find such an extravagant breakfast.

Nini's father beckoned to her and said, "Come on. If you don't hurry, we'll finish yours for you."

Her sisters all giggled, a little nervously at first, more boldly when their mother did not shout and tell them to stay quiet. Even Little Sixth was making loud and happy noises. Nini's father dipped the end of his chopsticks into the liquor, and then let the liquid drip into the baby's mouth. Nini's mother raised her voice to stop him but only in a laughing and approving way. The three-year-old and the five-year-old clamored and asked for a taste of the liquor, and their father gave them each drops of liquor too. The two older girls, already in school, knew better and did not ask, but they both sat close to their father. Lately they had begun to compete for his attention, the second daughter running to get his slippers and tea when he came home. But hard as she tried, replacing their mother in many ways to care for their father, Nini could see that she was no rival for the third daughter. The eight-year-old was a barometer of their father's mood—when he was in a good humor, she acted as if she had been his only love, demanding more attention with soft whining and intimate gestures; when he was in a bad mood, she kept to herself and tiptoed around the house.

Nini climbed up on the bed. She huddled at the corner of the table farthest from her mother and asked the ten-year-old, "What happened to the brown hen?"

"We'll make a chicken stew tonight for celebration," her mother answered. "Feast on. *Every wronged soul has a day to be compensated.* I'm happy to see the day finally come."

Every spring, peasants from the mountain came down to Muddy River with bamboo baskets full of new chicks, yellow, fluffy, all chirping and pecking. Young children timidly asked for one or two as their pets and were surprised when their parents paid for ten or fifteen. The chicks died fast, breaking many children's hearts, but by the time summer came, with luck a few chickens would still be alive, among them a hen or two that would soon begin to lay eggs. Nini's parents did not have the money to buy in large numbers, so they farmed out Nini's sisters to watch the chicks in the spring so that they would not be devoured by hungry stray cats. In the evenings, when Nini cooked for the family, her sisters helped the neighbors round up the chickens for the night. Sometimes a family had an extra chicken left by the end of the summer, and they would give it to Nini's family. The transaction was based on trust and understanding, but the neighbors were often left with none after a whole season, and no one could be blamed for that.

Nini thought about the brown hen, which liked to peck around Nini when she washed the family laundry in the yard, in the warmer season. It did not surprise Nini that her mother would choose to kill the brown hen over the white one. Nini had never tasted chicken before, and she wished the brown hen was not the first she would be eating.

Nini's father downed another cup of liquor. Despite his heavy drinking, he was gentle with Nini's mother and never beat her as other drinkers in the neighborhood did their wives. Except for the eight-year-old, most of the time he ignored the rest of his daughters. He sighed often, and sometimes wept while drinking alone at night, when he believed that the girls had fallen asleep. Nini stole glances at him on those nights from her corner of the bed. Her mother, leaving him alone as if his tears did not exist, folded matchboxes quietly.

"Let me tell all of you," Nini's mother said. "Always be kind to others. Heaven has an eye for mean people. They never escape their punishments."

Nini's sisters nodded eagerly. Their mother lovingly slapped the biggest piece of fried bread onto their father's plate. "That whore of Gu's is your example," she said. "Learn the lesson."

"Who's the whore?" asked the eight-year-old.

Nini's mother poured another cup of liquor for her husband, and a cup for herself. Nini had never seen her mother touch alcohol, but she now sipped the liquor with relish. "Nini, don't think your parents are unfair to you and make you work like a slave. Everybody has to be useful in some way. Your sisters will marry when they are old enough, and their husbands will take care of them for the rest of their lives."

The eight-year-old grinned at Nini in a haughty way that made Nini wish she could slap the girl.

"You, however, won't find someone willing to marry you," Nini's mother continued. "You have to make yourself useful to your father and me, do you understand?"

Nini nodded and squeezed her bad hand beneath her leg. She liked to sit on her bad hand until it fell asleep. In those moments the hand was like someone else's, and she had to touch each finger to know it was there.

"Someone has put a curse on us through you, Nini, and that's why we never get to have a boy in our family. But today, the one who has done this to us gets to see her final day. The spell is over now, and your father and I will have a son soon," their mother said, and their father held out a hand to stroke her belly. She smiled at him before turning to the girls. "You've all heard of the denunciation ceremony today, haven't you?" she said.

The ten-year-old and the eight-year-old replied that they were going with their school, and Nini's mother seemed satisfied with the answer. "You too, Nini, take Little Fourth, Little Fifth, and Little Sixth to the East Wind Stadium."

Nini thought about the young man Bashi in the street, and the willow tree past the birch woods by the river. "Why, Mama?" asked the eight-year-old.

"Why? Because I want all my daughters to see what happens to that whore," her mother said, and divided her own bread into four pieces, and handed them to all of Nini's sisters but not to Nini or the baby.

Nini's father put down his cup. His face was flushed, and his eyes seemed unable to focus. "Let me tell you this story, and all of you will have to remember it from now on. Your mother and I, we grew up together in a village in Hebei Province, where your uncles and aunts still live. Your mother and I—we fell in love when we were in the fifth grade."

The ten-year-old looked at the eight-year-old, and both giggled, the younger one bolder than the other. Nini's mother blushed. "What are you telling them these old stories for?" she said, and for a moment, Nini thought her mother looked like a different person, bashful as a young girl.

"Because I want all my children to know what you and I have gone through together," Nini's father said. He lifted the cup and sniffed the liquor before turning to the girls. "In our village, if you go back there now, people will still tell you our love story. When we were fourteen your mother went to Inner Mongolia to visit her aunt. For the summer, your mother and I wrote to each other, and together we used more stamps than all the village would ever use in a year. The postman said he had never seen such a thing in his career."

"Honestly, where did you find the money for the stamps?" Nini's mother said. "I took money from my aunt's drawer and never dared to ask her if she noticed the missing bills."

"I stole copper wiring from the electric plant, remember, the one next to the Walnut Village. And I sold them."

It must have been the first time Nini's mother had heard the story, for her eyes turned as soft and dreamlike as Nini's father's. "I'm surprised they didn't catch you," she said. "And you didn't get yourself electrocuted."

"Had I been electrocuted, who would give you the sparks now?" Nini's father replied with a chuckle.

Nini's mother blushed. "Don't tell these jokes in front of your children."

He laughed and put a piece of pickled tofu into her mouth. The liquor made both of them daring, with happy oblivion. Nini watched them and then turned her eyes away, half-fascinated and half-disgusted.

"Your mother's father—your grandfather—was a tofu maker, and my father was the best farmer in the area, and earned enough with his own labor to buy land."

"And remember," Nini's mother said. "My father was an honest tofu maker, and never cheated a single soul in his life."

"But this young girl, this Gu Shan, said your grandfathers were capitalists and landlords. She was a leader of the Red Guards, and she led a group of young girls to come and beat up your mother. Your mother was pregnant with Nini, and this young girl kicked your mother in the stomach. That's why Nini was born this way."

The ten-year-old and the eight-year-old stole quiet glances at Nini; Little Sixth babbled and grabbed Nini's hand to chew on. Nini picked up Little Sixth and fed her a small bite of fried bread. "Is it why they have this denunciation ceremony for her today?" the eight-year-old asked after a long moment of silence.

"No," Nini's mother said. "Who would care about what she did to us? Nobody remembers our misfortune, because we are unimportant people. But that's all right. Justice serves one way or another. One day you are the leader of the Red Guards, the next day you are a counterrevolutionary, waiting for a bullet. Whatever she is sentenced for, I'm just happy to see that she is paying off her debt today."

Nini hugged the baby closer, and Little Sixth ran her hand along Nini's cheek until the small fingers got ahold of Nini's ear; she pulled at Nini's ear, a gesture comforting to both of them.

"I've been thinking," Nini's mother said after a while, her voice calmer now. "I want to have a perm done tomorrow. Many of my colleagues have had it."

"Will it be safe for the baby?" Nini's father asked.

"I've checked, and they say it's safe," Nini's mother said. "It's time for me to look more like a woman than a ghost."

"You've always been the most beautiful woman to me."

"Who believes your drunken nonsense?" Nini's mother smiled, and raised her cup to meet the cup of her husband.

BASHI WHISTLED and walked home in long and bouncy strides. Every ten or fifteen steps he saw people gather in front of an announcement, and more were walking along the road to join their work units, holding banners and slogans. His mind occupied with Nini, Bashi did not have time to stop and distract himself by talking with these people. He wondered why the idea had never occurred to him before. For several years, he had seen Nini in the street, hauling baskets of coal from the railway station in the early morning; during the day she went to the marketplace and gathered half-withered vegetable leaves the housewives peeled off before they paid. A despicable creature, he had thought of her then. She was still an ugly thing, but she definitely looked more like a girl now. Twelve years old, Bashi said to himself, savoring the pleasure of saying the sweet number out loud. With all the girls growing up healthily and beautifully in the world, who, besides him, would have thought of Nini as a desirable girl? He whistled, loudly and off-key, a love song from a romantic film in the fifties. Two girls in front of the gate of the middle school pointed at him and snickered, and he smiled back nicely, blowing a kiss to them as he had seen an actor do in a movie that, imported from some eastern European country, was the first foreign film ever shown in Muddy River. Bashi had been impressed with the man's ease and had practiced the gesture many times in front of his grandmother's dressing table. The girls walked faster, their faces flushed with indignity, and he laughed and blew another kiss, one of hundreds of kisses he'd blown, and would be blowing, that landed nowhere.

Bashi thought about Mrs. Hua, and then let his thoughts wander to the seven girls the old woman no longer had as daughters. They, although deserted by their parents, must have better faces and bodies than Nini. He wondered why it had never occurred to Nini's parents to leave her on the riverbank to die when she had been born with that horrible face, or why her parents had kept Nini's sisters as well, when obviously a son was what they were trying to get, baby after baby. He thought about the daughters that Mrs. Hua had left with other people as child brides. Perhaps that was what he needed, a young girl purchased from someone like the Huas as a future wife. But a thing like that would take some time. Meanwhile, he had Nini to think about, the ugly yet real girl Nini, who would be expecting him soon.

When Bashi got home he found a bamboo steamer on the table, kept warm by a small square of cotton blanket. Underneath, six white buns nestled together, fresh and inviting. He pinched one and was amused to see his fingers leave dents on the smooth crust. He called out to his grandmother that breakfast was ready; hearing no answer, he walked into the bedroom that he shared with her. Both beds had been made, and the curtain between the beds had been pulled back and tied with a ribbon. The curtain had been installed by Bashi two years earlier, when he had learned the exciting things he could do with himself in bed. Not that his grandmother would ever wake up to spy on him, her senses already dull as a rusty knife unearthed from an ancient tomb, but Bashi insisted on the necessity of a curtain, which added pleasure to his secret games.

Bashi took a bite of the bun and walked closer to his grandmother, who was dozing in a cushioned armchair on her side of the bedroom. He put a finger under her nostrils and felt her breath. She was alive. "Get up, get up, lazy piglet. The sun is shining and the house is on fire," Bashi said, squeezing his voice into that of a woman—his grandmother's voice when he had been a young boy—and singing, but she did not open her eyes. "Breakfast is ready, and the ants are waiting for your crumbs," Bashi chanted again. She opened her eyes, nodded briefly, and went back to dozing. He gave up. She was eighty-one and she had the right to indulge herself in anything she liked: short naps in the mornings, a bite now and then, long moments spent sitting and snoozing on a chamber pot. It was no longer safe for her to go to the public outhouse, where people hopped in and out, through the stinky swamp, on boulders and rocks. Someday, Bashi knew, someday he would have to start to take care of her, cooking for her, making her bed, cleaning the chamber pot, cleaning her. He did not fear it. His grandmother had taken care of him all his life, and he would look after her when she needed him. If he was ever to have a baby girl, he would do the same thing for her. If he could find a baby girl now, Bashi thought, he would name the baby Bashiyi, *Eighty-one,* after his grandmother, the eighty-one-year-old baby. Bashi himself had been named the same way, as he had been born the year his great-grandfather had turned eighty. "Bashiyi," Bashi said aloud to the room, and thought that only a genius could have come up with the name—it would make the baby girl his sister, as even a fool could see, but the girl would also belong to him. Eighty-one existed only because eighty did, and where would you find Bashiyi without Bashi? He felt the urge to share this thought with someone, but his grandmother was becoming more forgetful by the day; conversation between them was often interrupted by irrelevant comments about events that had happened years or even decades before. Perhaps he could tell Nini. Would she understand him? She looked like a stupid little thing, but people in town had agreed that he himself was dumb. "You never know," Bashi said, and nodded in a knowing way, as if someone were standing right next to him. "She may be much smarter than you expected."

Bashi squeezed the rest of the bun into his mouth, and left the house when the clock was striking eight. The main street was in a festive mood. Two men with red armbands were locking up the marketplace. Students from a nearby elementary school were marching and singing a Soviet song, the tune familiar to Bashi's ears though he had never learned the lyrics, and he could not make out the words while listening to the children, shouting more than singing, their mouths a string of Os. In a side street, two day care teachers were hurrying twelve small children to join the parade, their hands holding a rope with its two ends in the teachers' hands. The workers from the candy factory, men and women in blue overalls, chatting and laughing, were waiting for the students to pass and two men whistled at a few older girls from the elementary school who probably had been kept back many times and were old enough to be ogling back.

"Where's the denunciation ceremony?" Bashi asked a policeman at a crossroad.

The policeman pulled Bashi back by his arm and said, "Don't block the traffic."

"What harm do I do standing here, comrade?" Bashi said. "Do you see that slogan on the wall? It says SERVE THE PEOPLE. Do you know who wrote that? Chairman Mao. Is that what you do to serve the people, huh, shout at them and almost break their wrists?"

The policeman turned to look at Bashi. "Who are you?"

"I'm a member of the people whom you serve."

The policeman retrieved a small notebook from his pocket. "What's your name? What's your work unit?"

Bashi tried to make something up, but before he spoke, the policeman turned away to shout at someone who was trying to push through the children's parade. Bashi shrugged and said under his breath, while he slipped away, "My name is Your Uncle and my work unit is your mother's bed."

A few steps later, Bashi asked someone else, and found out that people in this district were all marching toward a high school, one of six sites for the denunciation ceremony before the execution.

"Do you know who the woman is?" Bashi asked.

"A counterrevolutionary," the man replied.

"I know, but who is she?"

The man shrugged. "What's that got to do with you?"

"Where do you get the ticket?" Bashi asked.

"Ticket? Go with your school."

"I'm out of school now."

"Go with your work unit."

Bashi thought of explaining that he was a free man, but he stopped midsentence when the man seemed not to be listening to him. Bashi stood and watched men and women, students, and retired workers march by. They all looked happy, singing songs, shouting slogans, and waving colorful banners to the sky. Bashi had never considered the importance of being a member of a unit. He thought of tagging along behind the high school students, but without a banner in his hand, he would look suspicious. After a while, he said to himself, "What's so special about the denunciation ceremony? I'm going to the island to see the execution itself."

Once the words were said, Bashi's mind was made up. Why should he be one of the marching crowds when he had all the freedom in the world to do what he wanted? "Bye-bye," he said, smiling, and waved at these people who pushed along in the street like a herd of sheep.

FOUR

The East Wind Stadium, built at
the peak of the Cultural Revolution, in 1968, and modeled on the
Workers' Stadium in Beijing, though with much less seating capacity, was not an unfamiliar stage for Kai. Several times a year she
served as the master of ceremonies, celebrating May Day, the birthday of the Chinese Communist Party, National Day, and achieve-
ments of various kinds that the city government decided to honor in
mass gatherings. From where she stood, she could not see most of
her audience, and she had learned to gauge the attention of fifteen
thousand people through her own amplified voice, which, it seemed,
could be affected by even the smallest change in the air. Sometimes
the echo of her voice came back with a life of its own, vibrant with
energy, and Kai knew that she was being watched with admiration
and perhaps benign desires, replacing a lover, a wife, or a child in a
stranger's heart, no matter how fleetingly. But these moments had
occurred less and less in the past year; more often now she felt like a
beggar, her voice lost in an intricate maze and bouncing off cold and
uninterested walls.

"Are you nervous?" Han said when they stopped at the side gate.
He looked around before touching her face with the back of his
hand. Things would be all right, he said. She shook her head without replying. The previous fall, after she had returned to work from
her maternity leave, she had lost control of herself onstage at the cel-

ebration for National Day. Her choked voice and uncontrollable tears had passed within a minute, and the audience, if baffled by her behavior, had not reacted in any way detrimental to the event. Still, the tears must have been noticed and talked about by the officials sitting closest to the stage as distinguished guests. It must be the hormones, the mayor's wife commented to Kai at the banquet afterward, and Han's mother, in a less generous and forgiving mood, warned Kai in front of the other guests not to let a woman's petty sentiments get in the way of her political duties.

"People will always pay attention to a woman about to be executed," Han said. Kai looked up at him, taken aback by the simple and cruel truth she had not known he was capable of speaking. Days after the crisis on National Day, Han had asked her what had happened; she had been worrying about the inattentiveness of the audience, Kai lied, knowing that she could never explain to Han or to anyone else the immense desolation that had engulfed her onstage.

Han assured her again that she would not lose her audience today, and Kai nodded and said she had to go into the stadium. He would see her at the banquet, he said, and she looked at the rehearsed curving of his mouth—like a teenager who was very aware of his handsome looks, Han practiced his facial expressions in front of the mirror, smiling, grinning, frowning, and staring—and felt a moment of tenderness. Had Han been born to parents of less status, perhaps the boyish innocence would have made him, in addition to being a good husband and a good father, a good person, but then that innocence might have long ago been crushed by the harshness of life. For the first time that morning, she looked into his eyes and wished him good luck for the day.

"Luck's always on my side," Han replied.

Kai left him for the side gate of the stadium. He would be watching her until she disappeared from his sight, and she had to restrain herself from turning to see him and asking his forgiveness. She had, earlier that morning, kissed Ming-Ming with a burst of passion that had surprised the nanny. The girl had retreated to a less noticeable corner of the nursery and waited, with lowered eyes and a stoic face, to take over the position of mothering the baby. Ming-Ming probed Kai's face with his plump and soft fingers, unconscious of his mother's love or of her resolution to depart from the world fenced in by that love.

Backstage, people were busy with last-minute preparations. A colleague went over the procedure with Kai, and then invited her to rest in a small room where a mug of fragrant tea was waiting for her. A moment later a secretary of the propaganda department came in and said someone was looking for her at the side gate. Was it Han, Kai asked, and the other woman said that it was not Kai's husband but a stranger. A secret admirer, the secretary said with a grin, and Kai dismissed the joke, saying that she had no need for an admirer in her life now. The secretary said she would go and tell the man that Kai was already a happy wife and mother if that's what Kai preferred. Kai thanked her and said no, she would go tell him herself. The secretary was called then to some small task, her laughter trailing her in the hallway. The world could be as trusting and oblivious as an unsuspicious husband.

Across the street from the stadium, Jialin stood under a tree, his gray jacket blending in with the wall behind him. An old Soviet-style cotton cap sat low on his eyebrows, the earflaps let down and tied under his chin; a white cotton mask, the kind worn by men and women alike in Muddy River in the long season of winter, covered most of his face. If not for his glasses, the frames broken and then fixed by layers of surgical tape, Jialin could be as inconspicuous as a worker coming home from a night shift or a shop owner on his way to his cagelike store. Still, it was unlike him to ask to see her in public on this day.

"Is there anything I can do for you?" Kai said. In the world outside the library where they occasionally met, he and she could only act as strangers.

He had come to make sure everything would be all right, he said, and then, caught in a bout of coughing, he turned his face away. She did not know what he meant, Kai replied when his coughing passed, and she wondered if he could catch the falseness in her voice.

"I was wrong to worry, then?" Jialin said. "I wanted to make sure you didn't have some secret plan to carry out all by yourself."

"Why?"

"Any premature action equals suicide."

"I meant why did you think I'd do something without telling you."

Jialin studied Kai and she did not shy away from his gaze. Behind her she heard a whistle, the security guards shouting at some passerby. Soon she would have to finish this conversation with him; soon she would be expected onstage, and he, already deemed more than half-deceased by the world, would not be in the audience.

"You said something the last time I saw you," Jialin said, and then shook his head. "I hope I was wrong."

A revolution required some impulse, was what she had said two weeks ago, when she had been informed of the date set for Gu Shan's execution. She had come to his shack, an unplanned visit. It's time for them to act, she said, her hope to save Gu Shan's life transforming her into a more passionate speaker than she had been after leaving the theater troupe. The masses had to be motivated, public attention had to be drawn to the case; with the right action they should be able at least to impede the execution, if not reverse the sentence. The whole time she was talking, Jialin listened with a frown. It was an impulsive and unwise proposal, Jialin said afterward, and for the first time they argued.

"I want to act as much as you do," Jialin said now.

Kai looked at his eyes behind the glasses. They seemed perplexed, as if he could not find the right words. Outraged by his reasoning, which she had not been able to argue against, she had called him a coward that afternoon two weeks ago. He was closer to his grave than most people he had known in this world, Jialin replied then, and it was not his life or his death he was concerned about but choosing the right time. The statement was delivered with a cold anger that she had not known existed behind his calm gentleness, and Kai had to leave his shack without an apology. He had informed her of his condition when they had first met, six months earlier, but afterward the tuberculosis had never been brought up. Jialin was four years older than Kai, but his ailment made him ageless, a fact that Kai was aware of when she decided to befriend him; it must have occurred to him too, she imagined—that as a dying man he was exempted from many social rules—when he first wrote her a letter that, with its talk about democracy and dictatorship, could have led him to prison. She was baffled by his faith in a stranger, a woman whose voice represented, more than anything, the government in Muddy River, though she never asked him why he had chosen to entrust not only his idealism but also his life to her in the first place. Despite their fast friendship they had few opportunities to talk in person. In their letters to each other, they focused only on political topics and social changes, sharing little about their lives.

"Why did you think I would act on my own?" Kai asked again.

He hoped he was wrong, Jialin said, but it was a feeling that he might regret later had he not come to talk to her this morning. His intuition was not wrong, Kai thought of telling him: She had decided, since they had parted the last time, to carry out her own plan; reserved as he was, she had hoped that once she initiated a public outcry at the denunciation ceremony, he and his friends would have to choose action. Like a child forced to banish his mother from his world before she turned her back on him, Kai thought that she had prepared herself for a day, a battle, a life without Jialin. That he would sense her decision and come to stop her both moved and frightened her.

Jialin studied her. "Have you already started something I don't know?"

"No."

"And are you thinking about starting a protest without telling me?" he said. "Am I right to worry?"

A few people walked past them in the street, and both Jialin and

Kai remained silent for a moment. A bicycle bell clanked impatiently, followed by a crashing noise. Neither looked away to search for the accident.

She had seen his face only once, when she searched for his address on his letter one early afternoon. The letter, delivered to the mailbox that bore her name outside the propaganda department, had caught her eye among the fan letters expressing admiration for her performance at various events or commentaries, which the letter writers hoped would be chosen and read aloud by her in the program: The handwriting on the envelope reminded her of an older man of her father's generation who had devoted himself to the life-long practice of calligraphy, and out of curiosity she singled it out before passing the others to a secretary in the propaganda department.

He answered her knock on the gate with a familiar greeting that afternoon six months earlier, and later she would guess rightly that she was not his only visitor. She pushed the gate open and let herself into a small yard, and after a while, he came out of a low shack and was surprised that she was not whom he was expecting. He was a tall man, much younger than she had pictured, his face pale and thin. As he spoke he broke from time to time into a bout of coughing, and his face would take on an unhealthy red color. He did not invite her into his shack that first time. Please come with masks and gloves next time, he said to her; when they knew each other better he suggested that they meet in the reading room of the only public library in town.

"I know I can't keep you here for long," said Jialin now, when no one was within earshot. "But can you at least promise me not to do anything before we talk again?"

The pleading tone was unfamiliar to Kai; between the two of them he had always been the confident one. Sometimes Kai had to rewrite a letter many times for fear that she would let him down.

"Sooner or later we have to give up what we have for what we believe, no?" Kai asked.

"We don't sacrifice ourselves for any irrational dream."

"So we'll let Gu Shan sacrifice for us?" Kai said. She wondered if Jialin would find her passion unwise and childish, as he had indicated two weeks earlier. But it was not a disagreement with his principle but more of a sense of failing that made her question him. They had done nothing to save Gu Shan's life, she said now; would they also just let her die without waking the public up to the injustice? He was not wrong that she was planning to act on her own, she said; she had her microphone and she had her voice.

Someone called her name, and Kai turned around and saw the secretary waving at her and then pointing out Kai and Jialin to the security guards. She had to go, Kai said. Could she at least think over his words before doing anything, Jialin asked, but Kai, having little time to answer, left him without the promise he was hoping for. The guards looked at her with concern when she crossed the street. One of those people who was determined to discuss political issues with her, Kai said when the secretary asked her, and no, they might as well leave him alone, she said to the guards.

SOMEDAY, SHE WOULD LOSE her oldest son, Jialin's mother thought when she left his breakfast on the tree stump that served as a table. Apart from the tree stump, a chair, and a narrow cot, there was no other furniture in the shack. A heater made out of a gas can, which Jialin's mother filled three times a day with hot water, kept the shack slightly warmer than outside, and dampness clung to the sheet and quilt all year round. On one side of the shack there were piles of books placed on flattened cardboard boxes, a plastic sheet underneath. A shoe box of wires, tubes, and knobs—his radio, as Jialin had called the crudely assembled thing—sat on his cot, and a pair of headphones, a skeleton of wires and metal rings, sat alongside.

Jialin was not in the shack, and she wondered where he could be on this morning. He did not leave home often, and she was almost happy that she had a moment alone in his shack. When he was around he was polite; he thanked her for the food and hot water and clean laundry she brought over but he did not invite her to sit down. That Jialin was someone she would never understand was a fact she had long ago accepted, but like all mothers whose children are growing up and drifting away from them, she felt an urge to stay in his shack as long as she could, to cling to anything that she could use, when he vanished from her life, to reconstruct a son from memory. She picked up a book and flipped to a random page; someone had underlined the paragraph with thick red and blue marks—Jialin perhaps, or the previous owner of the book, but she would prefer to think that the book had no history but belonged entirely to her son. She looked at the words that she could not read—she was illiterate, and it was for that reason, Jialin believed, that she had been assigned as an undertaker of banned books in the factory that produced paper products. He had begged her to save some of the books for him; he had by then been ill with tuberculosis for a year, and a son isolated from the world was enough to turn a mother into a petty thief. Every day she took a book or two from the piles to be pulped and hid them under her clothes. The books came home with her body temperature. His face brightened when he saw the books, and for that rare happiness she, an honest woman who had not cheated a soul in the world, never regretted her crime.

Someone called out from the house to complain about the late breakfast, and she hurried back to the kitchen to get the meal ready for the rest of the family: her three younger sons, aged nineteen, sixteen, and fourteen, who would do no more than pick up the chopsticks laid out for them next to their hands, and her husband, who praised the boys for behaving like men.

Jialin was a son from a previous marriage that had ended with a drowning accident; her first husband, a strong man who had grown up near the sea, had dived into the Muddy River and broken his neck, three months before Jialin's birth. A son who came to claim his own father's life, people said when they came to her with marriage offers and advice to give up the baby for adoption. She did not want to hear this nonsense, and waited for ten years before remarrying,

but sometimes she wondered if she had made a mistake. Had Jialin
been taken in by another couple, perhaps he would have had a different life, free of illness and unhappiness, neither of which she understood. Jialin was thirty-two, old for a marriage, too young for death.
She would never see him get married to a woman but she would live
to see him die. She took a deep breath but tears no longer came to
her eyes. She did not know where he had contracted tuberculosis,
just as she did not know where his bookishness came from; his own
father, like her present husband, was a man without much education. Her three other sons were all robust, rude, boisterous—each a
younger version of their father, who worked as a laborer at the loading station. Jialin was different, as if he had come from a different
breed, not the son of her first husband but of a kind, graceful man
of knowledge. Such a thought sometimes occurred to her, too
strange to articulate even to herself.

Jialin's mother had once dreamed about another man, when she
had been a new wife and attended a class for illiterate women set up
by Teacher Gu. She had been married less than a year. Already her
husband had caused her all the pain a man could inflict on a wife.
Teacher Gu was the gentlest man she had ever met, his eyes sad behind black-rimmed glasses, his shirt and trousers impeccably clean.
She noticed his fingernails, kept neatly short, when he showed her
the right way to grip the pencil, and the image made her blush afterward when she lay awake next to her snoring husband. She was disappointed when she heard that Teacher Gu was going to marry one
of her classmates, a landlord's concubine, a used woman with a
small heart-shaped face, and it was the indignity she felt, as much as
her pregnancy, that stopped her from attending the classes. Over the
years she caught sight of Teacher Gu in town, quiet and melancholy,
as she remembered him. He did not recognize her, but the fact that
she could see him from afar was strangely comforting. She imagined
how the old man would feel, losing a daughter at gunpoint; even
Teacher Gu's wife, once the object of her secret envy, was forgiven
now because, after all, a son was what Teacher Gu needed but she

had given him just a counterrevolutionary daughter. If only he had a son like Jialin, who, with his pale complexion and the unhealthy blush on his cheeks, was as sad a man as she remembered Teacher Gu to be. They would understand each other, she thought for a long moment, and shook her head. She carried the food to the dining table and sat down next to her husband. Jialin would die a young man; what kind of solace would he be as a son to Teacher Gu? They had kept him in the sanitarium for some time but he had shown little hope of recovering. There was no point in wasting money on him, when the three younger boys seemed to be outgrowing their clothes overnight; she didn't need her husband to remind her of this, before she agreed to take Jialin home. Her husband had built a shack in the yard for Jialin, and it was expected, though not said, that Jialin would spend the rest of his days there.

TEACHER GU LEFT HOME after breakfast, avoiding the eyes of the neighbors who were walking or riding bicycles to their work units. A few students from his school shouted out greetings to him. He nodded, unable to tell if there was a difference in their attitudes toward him. Would their parents tell them about his daughter? He wondered what the children would think of him when he returned to his lectern the next day, teaching the same lessons from which his own daughter had gone astray.

It was a half-hour walk from his house to the west end of town. When he turned into the main street, Teacher Gu was aware that his hands, thrust into his coat pockets, held no banners, and his tired legs could not keep up with the others. He decided to take smaller side streets and alleys, where, after the departure of people for the denunciation ceremony, came the chickens, cats, and dogs, as well as old widows and widowers, to claim the space between the rows of houses. An elderly man, sitting on a low stool, looked up at Teacher Gu and mumbled something through his toothless mouth; Teacher Gu nodded, not grasping what he had been told, and a woman, younger than the man but old nonetheless, stooped close and wiped the drool off the old man's chin with a handkerchief pinned on his coat, before she walked across to where she had been sitting, balancing on a chair with a broken leg and knitting something with used, rust-colored yarn.

When Teacher Gu walked past the passenger station, the train running to the provincial capital was making its brief stop. The guardian, who had been sitting in the booth during the day and sleeping in an adjacent cabin as long as Teacher Gu could remember, was yawning by the track. A girl of seven or eight was selling hard-boiled eggs through the windows to the passengers, her fingers frost-bitten and as swollen as baby carrots. Teacher Gu slowed down and looked at her. Out of habit, he thought of finding out where she lived, and if she ever went to school, but he dismissed the idea. For thirty years, he had helped children from poor families, mostly girls, to go to school, paying their tuition and fees when their parents could not spare the money. He saw the joy of being able to read, in his wife's eyes, as well as in the eyes of each new generation of girls; he hoped that he had done his share, even if it was only a little, to make this place a better one. But now he saw that the messages from those books, coming from men and women full of the desire to deceive and to seduce, would only lead these girls astray. Even his two best students—his wife and his daughter—had failed him. Shan would never have become a frantic Red Guard if she hadn't been able to read the enticements of the Cultural Revolution in newspapers; nor would she have become a prisoner, by spelling out her doubts, had he never taught her to think for herself, rather than to follow the reasoning of the invisible masses. His wife would have simply endured the loss of Shan in painful silence, as all illiterate women endured the loss of their children, surrendering them to an indisputable fate and putting their only hope in the next life.

The old guardian rang a bell. Teacher Gu stopped and watched the white steam in the cold morning air, and the passengers who were being taken away from him, a man stuffing an egg into his mouth, a woman nibbling on a homemade sausage. Soon the train sped up, and he could no longer identify faces. This was where he and his wife were in their life, where one day could be indistinguishable from the next, and they shouldn't be worrying about a moment or a day being too long or too miserable. At least that's what he had told his wife when she returned from burning the clothes; they were to look forward and understand that the pains would not be as acute a year or two from now. "Everybody dies," he had said. "We're not the first parents, and won't be the last, to lose a daughter." It was not the first time they had lost a child either; he had not said it but hoped his wife would remember that.

The train passed, and a conductor standing at the rear of the train waved at Teacher Gu. After a few seconds, Teacher Gu gathered some energy to wave back, but the man was a small dot already, too far away to see his gesture.

Teacher Gu walked across the track. Where the street became an unpaved dirt road that pointed to the rural areas in the mountains, Teacher Gu found the Huas' cabin. Old Hua was squatting in front of the cabin and sorting glass bottles. Mrs. Hua was stirring a pot of porridge on the open fire of a small gas stove. Teacher Gu watched them, and only when Mrs. Hua looked up did he greet them.

The Huas stood up and greeted Teacher Gu. "Have you had your breakfast? Please join us if you haven't eaten," Mrs. Hua said.

"I've eaten already," said Teacher Gu. "Sorry to disturb your breakfast."

"Don't apologize," Mrs. Hua said, and she placed an extra bowl of porridge on the wooden table inside the cabin door. "Do join us. We don't have a lot to offer."

Teacher Gu rubbed his hands and said, "You are so very kind, Mrs. Hua."

Mrs. Hua shook her head. She placed a misshapen pan on the fire and dripped some cooking oil from a small bottle that had once been used to keep honey. "A fried egg, Teacher Gu?"

He tried to stop her, but a few minutes later, she put a fried egg onto a small plate for him. Old Hua stopped his sorting and again invited Teacher Gu to sit down for an extra bite. Finding no way to start the conversation without accepting their hospitality, Teacher Gu took Old Hua's chair, while Old Hua stacked two baskets for a makeshift seating for himself.

"Spring is late this year," Old Hua said. "Quite unusual, wouldn't you say?"

"Indeed," Teacher Gu said.

"You are doing well?" Old Hua asked.

"Yes, yes."

"And Mrs. Gu, is she all right?" Mrs. Hua asked.

"She is a little unwell from the season, but nothing too much."

"I hope she gets well soon," Mrs. Hua said, and nudged the plate toward Teacher Gu. "Please help yourself."

"This is too much," Teacher Gu said, and passed the plate to Old Hua. "I'm rather full."

After a minute of pushing to and fro, Old Hua, accepting that Teacher Gu would not touch the egg, divided it with his chopsticks and passed one half to his wife. Teacher Gu waited in silence until the couple finished their breakfast. "I've come to ask a favor from you," Teacher Gu said. The couple sat quietly, both looking down at their empty bowls.

Teacher Gu brought out a package and pushed it toward Old Hua. "A big favor, in fact, and I hope this is enough compensation for your trouble."

Old Hua exchanged a look with his wife. "Are you trying to find someone to take care of your daughter today?"

"Yes," Teacher Gu said. "It's our shame not to have educated her well enough to be a useful human being . . ."

Mrs. Hua interrupted, almost with vehemence, saying that her husband and she had little use for such official talk in their place. Teacher Gu apologized and, for a moment, was unable to speak.

"We're sorry," Mrs. Hua said in a softened voice. "For you and Mrs. Gu."

Old Hua nodded in agreement.

"You are very kind," said Teacher Gu.

"But you have to forgive us," Mrs. Hua said, and pushed the package of cash across the table. "We can't help you."

Teacher Gu felt a sharp pain in his chest and could not find the words to reply. Old Hua coughed with embarrassment and looked away. "We're sorry," he said, echoing his wife.

Teacher Gu nodded and stood up. "No, I'm the one to apologize for having come and bothered you with this inappropriate request. Now if you will forgive my visit, I will leave."

Mrs. Hua picked up the package and passed it to Old Hua. Old Hua put it into Teacher Gu's hands and said, "We thought you might come so I asked around to see if anyone would be willing to help. Do you know Old Kwen?"

Teacher Gu replied that he did not know Kwen, nor did he want to bother Old Hua further. It was irresponsible of him to think that the Huas would step in as undertakers for every unwanted child, Teacher Gu thought of adding, but he stopped himself.

"Not a trouble," said Old Hua. "He's a bit unfriendly but an old bachelor can come to that. He does a good job with whatever he puts his hands on. If you don't mind, I'll walk with you to his place."

"Too much trouble for you," Teacher Gu repeated. He felt a weakening in his legs and had to support himself with both hands on the table.

"Are you feeling all right?" Mrs. Hua said.

Teacher Gu nodded, wishing, for a moment, that the couple would change their minds. He imagined walking to another house and waiting for a stranger to despise him or, even worse, to take pity on him. Fatigue overtook him.

"Old Kwen lives not far from here," Old Hua said, and put on his sheepskin coat. "A five-minute walk."

Mrs. Hua put an old woolen hat on her husband's head and flicked off some dust. "We wish we could help you, but we have our own difficulties," she said.

"Yes, I understand."

"We do wish to help," Mrs. Hua repeated, as if she were afraid that Teacher Gu would not believe her. "Don't think we are holding a grudge against Shan."

Teacher Gu nodded. He had nothing to say to defend his daughter—Old Hua and his wife had been among the ones Shan had whipped and kicked in a public gathering in 1966. All the condemned ones on that day had been old people, widows of ex-property owners, frail grandparents whose grandchildren screamed with fear in the audience and then were silenced by their parents. Teacher Gu and Mrs. Gu themselves were among the accused on the platform that day, but at least their daughter had the mercy to leave her parents to her companions for punishment. Teacher Gu did not know why the Huas were there—they were both from poor back-grounds, after all, but crazy as the young revolutionaries were, it seemed that being human was a sufficient reason for humiliation. On that day Teacher Gu lost any remaining hope for his daughter. She was not the only wild one there; one of her comrades, a girl a year younger than Shan, with baby fat still on her cheeks, beat an old woman's head with a nail-studded stick. The woman stumbled and fell down onto the stage with a thud. Teacher Gu remembered watching her thin silver hair become slowly stained red by the dark sticky blood; afterward Shan forced the audience to hail her com-rade's feat.

"We know how you have felt all these years," Mrs. Hua said.

Teacher Gu nodded. The Huas were among the few to accept Teacher Gu and his wife when, at the end of the Cultural Revolution, the Gus visited the people once beaten by Shan with presents and apologies on their daughter's behalf; many of the people, including Nini's parents, turned them away at the door.

"It wasn't your fault. She was still a child then."

"A student's wrongdoing lies with the teacher's incapability," quoted Teacher Gu from ancient teaching. *"A child's fault is the father's fault."*

"Don't put this burden on yourself," said Old Hua.

They were getting old, Mrs. Hua said, and they hoped to stay in

Muddy River for the rest of their lives. They did not have legal residencies so they could not risk being called sympathizers, Mrs. Hua explained. "If we were younger, we would not hesitate to help you. We were always on the road then."

"Yes."

"And we were less afraid then."

"Yes."

"We will help you with anything else."

"Yes, I understand."

"Do come back for a cup of tea whenever you feel like it," Mrs. Hua said. Old Hua waited for his wife to finish the conversation, then pulled gently on Teacher Gu's arm. "Teacher Gu, this way, please."

Teacher Gu nodded, trying to cover his disappointment. "Thank you, Mrs. Hua."

"Bring Mrs. Gu over for a cup of tea when she feels like it," Mrs. Hua said. She hesitated and added, "We've lost daughters too."

FIVE

*T*he stadium was half-full when the Red Star Elementary arrived. "Communism Is Good," a song Tong remembered by heart, was broadcast through the loudspeakers, and he hummed along. The students were assigned seats in the front rows, and once they settled down, some children in Tong's class started to open the snacks their parents had packed into their school bags; others drank from their canteens. Tong, feeling solemn and important, did not make these childish mistakes.

The denunciation ceremony started at nine. A woman, in a brand-new blue woolen Mao jacket and wearing a red ribbon on her chest, came onto the stage and asked the audience to stand and join the Workers Choir to sing "Without the Communist Party We Don't Have a Life." Tong sprang to his feet and looked up at the woman with admiration. When Tong had first arrived at Muddy River, before he had learned the streets of the city by heart, he used to sit in the yard with Ear in the morning and late afternoon and listen to the news announcer's voice from the loudspeakers. He had little understanding of the news she reported, but her voice, warm and comforting, reminded him of the loving hands of his grandmother from when she had put him to sleep.

It took several minutes for the grown-ups to get onto their feet, and even when the choir began singing, half the people were still talking and laughing. The woman signaled the audience to raise their voices, and Tong flushed and sang at the top of his lungs. The different sections of the stadium proceeded at different speeds, and when the choir and the accompanying music ended, it took another minute for the audience to reach the end of the song, each session taking its time to finish. There was some good-humored laughter here and there.

The first speaker was introduced, a party representative from the city government, and it took a few seconds for the grown-ups to quiet down. More speakers, from different work units and schools, went onto the stage and denounced the counterrevolutionary, their speeches all ending with slogans shouted into the microphone and repeated by the audience. The speech Tong admired most was presented by a fifth grader from his school, the captain of the school's Young Pioneers and the leading singer of the Muddy River Young Pioneers Choir. She recited harsh, condemning words in a melodious voice, and Tong knew that he would never sound as perfect as she did, nor would he have the right accent to gain him the honor of speaking in a solemn ceremony like this.

After a while, there was still no sign of the most exhilarating moment of the gathering—the denouncing of the counterrevolutionary in person, before she was escorted to the execution site. The criminal had to be transported from site to site, the woman explained, and then she called for more patriotic music.

The grown-ups started to wander around, talking and joking. Some women brought out knitting needles and balls of yarn. A teacher told the children to eat their snacks. A boy reported in a loud voice that his mother wanted him to pee at least once at the stadium, which led to several boys and girls raising their hands and making the same request. The teacher counted, and when she had gathered enough children, she led them single file to the back of the stadium.

Tong sat straight in his seat, the crackers his mother had packed for him untouched in his bag. He wished the woman announcer would come onstage and chastise the children and grown-ups who had turned the ceremony into a street fair, but he had learned, since his arrival in Muddy River, that the opinions of a child like him held no meaning in the world. Back in his grandparents' village the peasants respected him because he had once been chosen by a famous fortune-teller as an apprentice. Tong had been two and a half then, before he could remember the story, and all he knew were the tales repeated by his grandparents and their neighbors: The old blind man, weakened by years of traveling from village to village and telling other people's fortunes, had foreseen his own death coming, and decided to choose a boy who would inherit his secret wisdom and knowledge of the world. He had walked across three mountains and combed through eighteen villages before finding Tong. Legend had it that when the old man came to the village, he studied the shape of the skulls of all the boys under age ten, disappointed each time until he reached Tong, the youngest in the line; the old man touched Tong's head and instantly shed tears of relief. In the next six months, the old man settled down in the village and came to Tong's bed every morning before sunrise, teaching Tong to chant, and to memorize rhymes and formulas that Tong would need for his fortune-telling career.

Tong no longer remembered his master. The old man had died shortly after Tong turned three, surprising the villagers, as the master fortune-teller failed to foretell his own death with accuracy. It was a pity that the blind man's wisdom was lost to the world; still, the short stint as the fortune-teller's apprentice marked Tong as a boy with a special status, revered by the villagers. But these stories meant little to Tong's parents and the townspeople. They did not look into Tong's eyes, which old people back in the village had always said were profoundly humane. An extraordinary boy, they had said of him, and Tong knew he was meant for a grand cause. But how could he convince Muddy River of his importance, when his existence was not much more noticeable than the existence of dogs and cats in the street?

A squad of policemen marched into the stadium and guarded both ends of every aisle. The announcer called for the audience to return to their seats. Her voice was muffled, as if she had caught a cold, and from the front row where Tong sat, he could see her knitted eyebrows. He wondered if she felt hurt as much as he did by people's lack of enthusiasm, but she did not see his upturned and concerned face when she announced the arrival of the counterrevolutionary.

Hushed talk rippled through the stadium when the counterrevolutionary was dragged onto the stage by two policemen dressed in well-ironed snow-white uniforms. Her arms were bound behind her back, and her weight was supported by the two men's hands, her feet barely touching the ground. For the first time since the beginning of the ceremony, the audience heaved a collective sigh. The woman's head drooped as if she were asleep. One of the two policemen pulled her head up by her hair, and Tong could see that her neck was wrapped in thick surgical tape, stained dark by blood. Her eyes, half-open, seemed to be looking at the children in the front rows without registering anything, and when the policeman let go of her hair, her head drooped again as if she were falling back into sleep.

The audience was called to its feet, and the shouting of slogans began. Tong shouted along with his classmates, but he felt cheated. The woman was not what he had expected: Her head was not shaved bald, as his parents had guessed it would be, nor did she look like the devil described to him by a classmate. From where he stood, he could see the top of her head, a bald patch in the middle, and her body, small in the prisoner's uniform that draped over her like a gray flour sack, did not make her look like a dangerous criminal.

After a few minutes the woman was escorted off the stage and disappeared with the two policemen to the back of the stadium. The slogan shouting trailed off until there was nothing for the audience to do but go home. Some grown-ups started to move toward the exits, but the security guards refused to let them pass. A fight or two broke out, attracting more security guards, and soon the woman announcer hurried back to the stage and signaled the audience to join the choir for a few more revolutionary songs. Already losing interest, most grown-ups just crowded toward the exits, the banners they had brought with them abandoned on the seats.

On the way back to school, Tong listened to the boys behind him talk about the event. One boy swore that the woman had threatened to come off the stage and attack him, if it were not for the two policemen holding her; another boy told a story that he had heard from his grandfather: Sometimes a woman is a snake in disguise—if she succeeds in locking your eyes with hers, at night she can slither into your dreams and eat your brain.

What nonsense, Tong thought, but his spirit was low and he did not want to contradict the childish notions of his peers.

NEITHER LITTLE FOURTH nor Little Fifth was willing to take Nini's bad hand, so she had to let Little Fourth run free. Little Fifth tried to wiggle her hand out of Nini's grip too, and Nini said in a fierce tone that if she did not obey, a car would run over her, or someone would steal her and sell her to strangers and she would never see their parents again. Frightened, the girl started to cry, and Little Sixth, who had been happily babbling in a cotton sling on Nini's back a moment ago, watched her crying sister for a moment and then joined the howling.

For a moment, Nini thought of bringing all three sisters back home and locking them inside the house, as she often did when she went to the marketplace. She would go to the riverbank by herself. The young man Bashi, odd as his talk was, was an interesting person, and Nini was curious to find out if he had lied about the coal he would give her for free. But the girls would tell on her, and certainly her mother would send her to a corner to kneel through lunch. She should have hidden the tin of biscuits, Nini thought, and then remembered the barrette in her pocket. She hushed her sisters and displayed the blue plastic butterfly in the palm of her good hand. It took Nini five minutes of coaxing and threatening to persuade the older girls to agree to wait for their turns. Nini sat Little Sixth on the sidewalk and plaited her soft brown hair into a tiny braid on top of her head, and then clipped the barrette at the end. The braid wobbled, and Little Fourth and Little Fifth clapped with laughter. Nini smiled. At moments such as this, she liked her sisters.

When they reached the East Wind Stadium, all the entrances were closed; the only people walking around were the security guards in red armbands. "What are you doing here?" a guard shouted at Nini as they walked closer to the entrance. Little Fourth was no longer running, her hand nervously gripping Nini's sleeve.

Nini held Little Fourth closer and replied that they were coming for the denunciation ceremony.

"Which unit do you belong to?"

"Unit?" Nini said.

"Yes, which unit?" the man said with half a smile.

An older guard came closer and told his colleague not to tease the young girls, and the first man replied that he was not teasing but teaching them the most important lesson of life, which was to belong to a unit. The second guard ignored the young man and said to Nini, "Go home now. This is not a place for you to play around."

Nini thought of explaining to the old man why she had to go to the denunciation ceremony with her sisters, but he was already waving his arms and shooing them away. Nini walked her sisters to the alley closest to the stadium, and told them to sit down at the corner. "Let's wait here."

"Why?" Little Fourth asked.

"We're supposed to take a look at this daughter of the Gu family before she's executed," Nini said. "If we don't see her, there'll be no dinner for us tonight."

The two girls sat down immediately. A few minutes later, they started to play games with pebbles and twigs, chanting in whispers. Nini walked around in a circle, and soon Little Sixth fell asleep, her head heavy and warm on Nini's neck. Slogans, songs, and angry voices came from the loudspeakers in the stadium, but Nini could not tell what they were saying. She thought about Mrs. Gu, laying out pickled string beans and scrambled eggs and telling her to eat as much as she wanted, and Teacher Gu, handing her the paper frogs, his hands gentle yet not quite touching hers. They must have wished all along that Nini had never existed, since Nini's deformity was proof of their daughter's crime.

An ambulance and a police car drove down the main street and turned into the alley. The drivers turned off the sirens, but left the blue and red lights blinking. Little Fourth and Little Fifth stopped their game and asked, "What is it?"

Before Nini could reply, a policeman came out of the patrol car and yelled to the girls, "Where is your home? Go home now. Don't stay in the alley."

Little Sixth was startled from her dozing and started to cry. Nini grabbed Little Fifth's hand and told Little Fourth to come with her. A few steps into the alley Nini saw one of the row houses without a fence. She pulled her sisters in and hid behind the fence of an adjoining house, and told them to keep quiet. Little Sixth was squirming on Nini's back. She put a finger into the baby's mouth and calmed her. The two younger girls wandered around the yard, checking the pile of firewood at a corner, crushing a few pieces of soft coal into powder.

Nini peeked out from behind the fence. A few people jumped out of an ambulance, all of them wearing white lab coats, white head covers and masks. One of them pulled a gurney out of the ambulance, and the two shorter ones—two women, Nini realized, as their hair crept out from underneath the head covers and reached their necks—pulled from the ambulance white and blue packages, tubes, and a strangely shaped lamp that connected to the inside of the ambulance with long metal arms. One of the women switched the lamp on and off for a test, and the four policemen, uncurious, patrolled nearby with black batons.

All of a sudden, someone started to shout. A dog darted across the alley, yelping, chased by a policeman waving his baton. "Quick, they're coming," a voice shouted. The man who had been chasing the dog ran back, and Nini looked out again. Someone was dragged into the alley. For a brief moment, Nini thought she saw the black hair of a woman, but before she could take another look, several men lifted the person onto the gurney, which was at once covered by a piece of white cloth. The body struggled under the sheet, but a few more hands pinned it down. "What is it?" Little Fourth asked. Nini did not answer, her heartbeat quickening when she saw a red spot on the white sheet covering the body, at first about the size of a plate, then spreading into an irregular shape.

A few minutes later, the body was lifted off the gurney, its legs kicking; yet strangely, no noise came from the struggling body. Nini felt an odd heaviness in her chest, as if she was caught in one of those nightmares where, no matter how hard you tried, you could not make a sound. The policemen shuffled the body inside the police car. The men and women in the white lab coats climbed back into the ambulance, and a moment later, both vehicles turned onto the main street and, with long and urgent siren wails, disappeared.

"What is it?" Little Fourth asked again.

Nini shook her head and said she did not know.

"What is it? What is it?" Little Fifth said. Nini told her to stop being a parrot. She led them to the entrance of the alley where the ambulance had parked a few minutes ago. Before the younger girls could notice the drops of blood on the ground, Nini dragged her bad foot across them and smeared them into the dust. Little Fourth pointed to a black cotton shoe on the ground, and Little Fifth picked it up. There was a hole in the rubber sole; she pushed a finger through it and wiggled the finger. Nini told Little Fifth to get rid of the shoe, and when she refused, Nini grabbed it and threw it as hard as she could across the alley. Little Fifth started to cry and then stopped when a huge rumble came from the sky. Nini and her sisters looked up. An army helicopter flew over them like a huge green dragonfly. "Helicopter," Little Fourth said, and Little Fifth echoed her, both of them pointing their fingers at the sky.

Soon the gates to the stadium opened, and people swarmed out, all chattering. Nini grabbed her sisters by their hands and walked closer to the crowd.

"The woman did not say a word throughout the meeting," a man said. "I wonder if they drugged her."

Another man swore that he had seen the woman open her mouth during the meeting. "She didn't look drugged at all to me," he said.

"How could she speak? They must have cut her trachea," another man said. "Didn't you see her neck was covered by a bandage?"

"Trachea? You fool. How could she live if her trachea was cut? It was her vocal cords that they cut."

The first man shrugged. "She couldn't speak, for sure."

"Pardon me," Nini said, and raised her voice when she was not heard. "Pardon me, Uncles. Is the counterrevolutionary still in the stadium?"

"What's that to do with you?" one of the men said.

Nini stuttered and said they wanted to see the woman counter-revolutionary, but before she finished her sentence, she was cut off by the men. "What's there to see? They took her away first thing after the meeting was over. By now she's probably been shot."

Disappointed, Nini told her sisters to stand farther away from the entrance so the crowd would not step on them. They waited until the crowd thinned and the last group of elementary students marched away. There was nothing for them to do now but go home.

THE ARMY PILOT did not look down at the city of Muddy River and its many upturned heads when he flew the helicopter over the giant statue of Chairman Mao. The flight to the provincial capital was no more than thirty minutes, and after that was the lunch he looked forward to. The meal, after a special operation, with roast chickens, beef ribs, and steamed fish, was fought over even among the best-maintained pilots. He thought about the first year he had joined the army, sixteen and a half and a full head shorter than the training of-ficer who, at formations, liked to spit in his face and kick his legs. For the first three months they had not had a taste of meat. The pilot wished his training officer could see him now, one stripe and three stars on his shoulders. His father had often said that he who could suffer the insufferable would one day become a man above all men. A man above you all, the pilot thought, imagining the boys running in the crowded alleys, pointing out the helicopter to one another.

Among the upturned heads was Bashi's. He was standing across the river from Hunchback Island. The island, located at the eastern end of town where the Muddy River widened and turned down south, was a long and narrow piece of land in the shape of a whale's back. In the summer it was overrun by wild geese and ducks when their migration brought them north; in those months, children liked to swim out to the island and steal the eggs, which, unless cooked with the strongest spice, had a strong, unpleasant taste; the egg hunting was more for the fun of it than for practical reasons. Apart from the wild birds and children, once in a while other visitors included the police, who would clean up the island, as it was the site where executions for Muddy River and several of the surrounding counties took place. The last time someone had been shot dead on the island was the summer two years before, when a man from a neighboring county had been found guilty of raping a young woman and nearly strangling her to death. The policemen had cleared the island ahead of time, but a few daredevil young men swam there and hid underwater just offshore. Later they claimed to have seen the man's head pop like a watermelon at the single shot. Bashi was not one of the young men, but after a while he believed that he had been; he told people about how the man's member had pointed to the sky, inside his pants, even after he dropped dead like a heavy sack. "A man like him, you know, with problems down there," Bashi said to men and women alike, with a knowing smile.

Bashi watched the red flags and the yellow tape that circled the island. With the unthawed river, there was no place to hide underwater, and Bashi was plagued by the yearning to outwit the authorities so he could get onto the island. If only he could will himself to become invisible! He would slip onto the island easily, walk around the policemen, and blow cool and tickling exhalations onto their cheeks. He could even talk to them in the charming and breathy voice of a young woman, calling them intimate nicknames, thanking them for finishing her painful life for her, inviting them to join her for some real fun on the other side. Bashi imagined the policemen, especially the one who had threatened him earlier in the street, scared out of their wits and wetting their white uniform pants. He guffawed until he had to lean on a tree to catch his breath. No one would dare to set foot on the haunted island again; he could build a hut on the island and live with the woman, who would certainly devote her life to him because he was her savior.

Twenty-eight the woman was, Bashi remembered from the announcement. Twenty-eight was not too old. Bashi lived with his grandmother, a much older woman, without a problem, and he was sure the woman would love him as his grandmother did. If she became too lonely on the island when he had to go home and spend time with his grandmother—certainly the woman would understand such an arrangement—he could ask Nini to be her companion, a handmaiden even, a trustworthy one because no one would be interested in what Nini knew. He then realized that Nini was probably waiting by the willow tree now, her small crooked face looking serious. Oh well, he could always find her later and spin some tall tales about the execution so she would be entertained. It was hard to make her smile, her little rag face with the scowl, but Bashi would not mind trying again.

Someone tapped Bashi's shoulder and said, "What are you doing here, smiling like an idiot?"

Bashi looked up and saw Kwen studying his face. Kwen had never married, and Bashi had always wanted to ask him what it was like being an old bachelor, having no woman to warm the bed or wash his feet for him; Bashi wondered whether Kwen dreamed about women the way he himself did, but such questions might be offensive. There were only a handful of people in the world that Bashi would not bother with his chattiness, and Kwen was one of them. People said Kwen was not an easy character. All the dogs in town behaved like kittens in front of him. Rumors were that the mountain wolves were scared of him; snakes too, and even the black bears. Bashi had never doubted these claims. He had once seen Kwen whip his black dog, a cigarette dangling from the corner of his mouth; his face had been almost gentle, with a patient smile, but the dog, the beast that had been mean to nearly every creature in the world, had been docile as a lamb, its head low to the ground, as if begging for mercy.

"Did you hear me?" Kwen said again. Close-up, Kwen looked like any old man, a face with its usual wrinkles, squinting eyes, two front teeth missing and the rest stained yellowish black from cigarette smoking. Bashi smiled and raised both hands as if in surrender. "What a surprise. What are you doing here?"

"I'm here for what you're here for."

"What am I here for?" Bashi asked with great interest.

"The execution, no?"

"Wrong. I'm here for a meeting," Bashi said. "With a beautiful woman."

Kwen shook his head. "If you said you were here for a date with death, I'd be more inclined to believe you."

Bashi spat three times onto his palm. "Bad omen. Don't say that."

"Where did you get that womanish habit?"

Bashi pretended not to hear Kwen. "So what are you doing here?" Bashi said.

"I'm having a date with death."

"Come on," Bashi said. He searched both coat pockets and finally found in his pants pocket the pack of cigarettes he had bought two weeks earlier—he had tried smoking four or five times, but he had found, once again, that he did not like the charred taste. Bashi tapped the bottom of the pack until one cigarette dropped out into his palm. "Here," he said, and pinched the cigarette into a perfect round shape before handing it to Kwen.

Kwen looked at the cigarette dubiously. Bashi sighed and handed over the pack. Kwen lit the cigarette and put the rest of the pack away. A police car drove to the riverbank, followed by a covered truck. A squad of policemen jumped out of the truck, and a moment later, the counterrevolutionary was carried out of the police car by her arms. Kwen and Bashi watched the group cross the frozen river silently. From where they stood they could barely see the woman's face.

"Is she what you're here for?" Bashi said.

Yes, Kwen replied; he was coming to collect her body.

"Why is it you who collects the body and not me?" Bashi said.

"Because I'm paid to."

"By whom?"

"Her parents."

"Where is the money?" Bashi said.

Kwen patted the breast pocket of his jacket. "Here."

"Can I see?" Bashi asked. He did not trust Kwen's words. A woman was a woman, and Bashi knew that Kwen was here because he wanted to take a look at her, in whatever condition they would find her.

Kwen brought out a small package from his pocket. It looked like a thick pad, but who could guarantee that Kwen had not wrapped up some toilet paper in it? Bashi was going to inspect the package more closely, when Kwen slid it back into his pocket and said, "Keep your paws off my money."

"How much did they pay you?" Bashi asked.

"Why should I tell you?"

"Because I can pay the same amount to you for not collecting her body."

"Who will, then? You can't leave a body to rot by itself on the island."

"I will," Bashi said.

Kwen grinned. "You are more fun than I thought," he said.

"Why?"

"Because I've never seen an idiot as interesting as you."

Bashi thought of acting offended, but on second thought, he laughed with Kwen. Perhaps they could become friends if he could keep entertaining him. People would regard him in a different light if they saw that he alone could befriend Kwen. A fox feared by all animals because he befriended a tiger, the old story occurred to Bashi, but what was wrong with being a smart fox? "Can I help you collect the body? It must be heavy for one person," Bashi said.

"I don't have money to pay for your help," Kwen said.

"I can pay you if you let me help," Bashi said. "At least let me take a look at her."

Kwen looked at Bashi for a long moment and laughed aloud. A few sparrows pecking on an open field between the trees flew away. Bashi smiled nervously. Then they heard a single shot, crisp, with an echo of metal. Kwen stopped laughing, and they both looked at the flocks of birds flying away from the island. Nothing happened for a few minutes, and then the squad of policemen marched across the river, their heavy boots treading on the old snow. "Crack," Bashi whispered to himself, and imagined a big hole in the broken ice devouring all those people he despised.

"It's my job now," Kwen said when the police car and the truck drove away.

"How about me?" Bashi said.

"How much can you pay?"

Bashi stuck two fingers out; Kwen shook his head and Bashi added one finger, and then another. Kwen looked at him with raised eyebrows.

"Okay, a hundred, is that okay?" Bashi said, almost begging. "A hundred is probably more than the family is paying you, no?"

Kwen smiled. "That is my business," he said, and signaled Bashi to follow him onto the ice.

SIX

*M*rs. Gu did not reply when Teacher Gu told her that lunch was ready. He had found her sitting still in a chair when he returned from his visit to Old Kwen, and ever since then she had been a statue. He tried to make small noises with every little chore that he could invent for himself. When he ran out of things to do, he sat down and forced himself to take a short nap. He was awakened by people returning from the denunciation ceremony, men talking and locking their bicycles, women calling their children for lunch. He got up and started noisily cutting, boiling, frying things to prepare lunch. He tried not to think about what had happened outside his home—the only way to live on, he had known for most of his adulthood, was to focus on the small patch of life in front of one's eyes.

Teacher Gu sat down at the table with a full bowl of rice and reminded his wife again to eat at least a little. She replied that she had no appetite.

"One has to be responsible for one's body," Teacher Gu said. He had always insisted on the importance of eating regular and nutritious meals for a healthy body and mind. If there was one thing he prided himself on, it was that he never gave in to difficulties to the point where he ignored his duty to his body. Life was unpredictable, he had taught his wife and daughter, and eating and sleeping were among the few things one could rely on to outwit life and its capriciousness. Teacher Gu chewed and swallowed carefully. He might not have added enough water, and the grains of rice were dry and hard to eat. The fibers from the cabbage hurt his already loosened teeth, but he chewed on, trying to set a good example for his wife, as he had always done.

When he finished the meal, he walked over to her. She did not move and after a moment of hesitation, he put a hand on her shoulder. She flinched and he withdrew his hand. It could have been worse, he said; they should look at the positive side.

"Worse than what?" she said.

He did not answer. After a while, he said, "The Huas cannot do it. I've asked a janitor from the electric plant to help."

"Where will she be?" Mrs. Gu asked.

"He'll find a spot. I asked him not to mark it."

Mrs. Gu stood up. "I need to go and find her," she said.

"I thought we had agreed," Teacher Gu said. Together they had made the decision, he suggesting and she consenting, that they would not bury her themselves. They were too old for the task, their hearts easily breakable.

She had changed her mind, Mrs. Gu said, and she looked for her coat; she could not let a stranger send off her daughter.

"It's too late," Teacher Gu said. "It's over now."

"I want to see her one last time."

Teacher Gu did not speak. For the past ten years, he had visited Shan only twice, at the beginning of her sentence and right before the retrial. The first time he had gone with his wife, and they had both been hopeful despite the fact that Shan had been given a ten-year sentence. Shan was eighteen then, still a child. Ten years were not hard to go through, he said to his wife and daughter, just a small fraction of one's long life. Things could be worse, he told them.

Shan was sneering the entire time that he spoke. Afterward she said, "Baba, doesn't it make you tired to talk about things yourself don't even believe in?"

"I believe in good patience," replied Teacher Gu. It did not surprise him that his daughter behaved this way toward him. The arrest had come as a shock for Teacher Gu and his wife; they had thought of their daughter as a revolutionary youth. Only later did they learn that Shan had written a letter to her boyfriend and expressed doubts about Chairman Mao and his Cultural Revolution. Teacher Gu and his wife had not known she had a boyfriend. He would have warned Shan had he been told about the man; he would have said—once and again, even if she did not listen—that betrayals often came from the most intimate and beloved people in one's life. He would have demanded that she bring the boyfriend to meet them. But would they have been able to make a difference? The boyfriend turned the letter in to the city Revolution Committee. Shan got a ten-year sentence and her boyfriend was awarded the privilege of joining the army, even though his background—a family of capitalists and counterrevolutionaries—had not been good enough for him to enlist.

People were the most dangerous animals in the world, Teacher Gu thought of telling his daughter during that visit ten years ago; stay small and unimportant, like a grain of dust, he thought of advising her, but before he had the chance, his daughter refused to stay in the room and signaled for the guards to take her away.

Teacher Gu had not visited his daughter after that. His wife had gone but only once or twice a year. She had worried that too many visits would harm Shan's record and add more time to her term. They rarely talked about their daughter, each in secret hoping that ten years would somehow pass without any incidents. What came at the end of the term, however, was a notice saying that Shan would receive a retrial—she had been unrepentant in prison and had written, year after year, letters of appeal for herself, and personal journals that contained the most evil slanders of Communism.

At the weekly meeting at his school, the party secretary asked Teacher Gu to share his thoughts on his daughter's upcoming retrial. He had nothing to say, Teacher Gu answered, and all the party members shook their heads at him in disappointment. "Let me tell you what I think, since you have nothing to say," said the party secretary. "Last time your daughter was sentenced for her slander of our Communist cause. She was young and educable then, and was given this chance to correct her wrong notion. But what happened? She didn't take the opportunity. She not only refused to reclaim her love and trust for our party and our Communist cause, she also argued against us from the most counterrevolutionary point of view. That," the secretary said, his index and middle fingers pointing at Teacher Gu, "will never be tolerated."

Teacher Gu did not tell his wife about the meeting. Such a meeting must have taken place in her work unit too, and a similar message conveyed. He heard her weeping sometimes at night. When he tried to comfort her, she acted cheerful and said that they should not worry too much. Shan was still a young woman, she said, and she had already spent ten years in prison; the judge would be lenient and the retrial would be only a form of warning.

Teacher Gu did not say anything to encourage his wife's blind confidence. A few days later he went to the prison for a visit. The guards were rude to him, but he had become used to people's abuse over the years and thought nothing in particular about their behavior. What shocked him was Shan's condition—she was not the defiant, lively girl he had known ten years earlier. Her prison uniform, gray and torn, smelled of filth; her short hair, filthy too, had thinned and there was a big bald patch in the middle of her scalp; her skin was so pale it was almost transparent, and her eyes were wide and dreamy. She recognized him immediately, but it seemed that what had happened ten years earlier was all gone from her memory. She started talking when she sat down. She told him that she had written letters to Chairman Mao and he had replied, apologizing for the wrong decision and promising a release. It had been two years since Chairman Mao had passed away, but Teacher Gu, sitting in a cold sweat, did not point that out to Shan. She talked fast, about all the things she planned to do after her release. In her mind, she had a fiancé waiting for her outside the prison walls, and the first thing they would do was go to city hall to apply for a marriage license. Teacher Gu did not protest when, at the end of the visiting period, two guards grabbed Shan's arms roughly and forced her out of the room. She was still talking, but he did not hear her. He stared at her uniform pants, stained with dark menstrual blood. Death was far from the worst that could happen to a human being. Something bigger than fear crept over him; he wished he could finish his daughter's life for her.

Teacher Gu did not know how long his daughter had been mad, nor did he know if his wife was aware of this fact. Perhaps she had been keeping it from him for years. In turn he lied about a note from the prison informing them that Shan's visiting rights had been stripped away because of disobedience. His wife sighed but did not question further, which made him wonder if she accepted the order willingly for his sake. The death sentence came to him as a relief; perhaps it was for his wife too, but he had no way of knowing. With the failure of the appeal, Mrs. Gu started to talk about seeing Shan one last time, but her request for a visit was turned down, no reason given.

Mrs. Gu put on her coat. Women were like children, Teacher Gu thought, the way they tenaciously held on to things that had little meaning. When he begged her to stay, she raised her voice and asked why he did not let her see their daughter.

"*Seeing is not as good as staying blind,*" Teacher Gu said, quoting an ancient poem.

"We've been blind all our lives," said Mrs. Gu. "Why don't you want to open your eyes and see the facts?"

In her eyes he recognized the same defiance that he had once seen in Shan's eyes. "The dead have gone. Let's forget about all of it," he said.

"How can you forget so easily?"

"It's a necessity," he said. "A necessity is never easy but we must accept it."

"You've always wanted us to accept everything without questioning," his wife said. "Why do we have to live without backbones?"

Teacher Gu averted his eyes. He had no answer for his wife, and he wished she would let it go without prolonging this suffering for both of them. Before he could say something, he felt a sudden deadness in the left side of his body and he had to kneel down. He looked up at his wife for help but his eyes could no longer see. She rushed to support him but he was too heavy for her; she let him lie down slowly and he felt the coldness of the cement floor seeping through his clothes and numbing his whole body. "Don't go," he begged, longing for a fire, for her warm and soft body. For a moment he was confused and thought he saw his first wife's face, still as young and beautiful as thirty years ago. "Don't leave me," he said. "Don't make me lose you again."

THE WOMAN'S BODY was lying facedown on the crystallized snow, her arms wrenched and bound behind her back in an intricate way. Her head, unlike what Bashi had imagined, was in one complete piece. He stopped a few steps away and looked at the bloodstains on her prisoner's uniform. "Is she dead?" he asked.

"Why, are you afraid now?" Kwen said, and bent down to study the body. "I didn't pay you to tag along."

"Afraid? No, no. Just making sure she has no chance."

"No chance at all," Kwen said, kicking one leg of the body and then the other. He squatted down next to the body and pointed to the woman's back. "Look here. They bound her arms this way so her left middle finger was pointing right at where her heart was."

"Why the heart?"

"So that the executioner knew where to aim his gun."

On the walk across the frozen river to the island, Bashi had conjured a vivid story about a blown-away head, a bloody brain blooming on the snow like spilled paint. He had imagined telling the tale to the townspeople who stood around him in awe. He went closer now and squatted beside Kwen. The bloodstain on her back was about the size of a bowl, and it amazed Bashi that such a little wound could finish a life. The woman's face was half-hidden in the snow, impossible for one to make out her features. Bashi touched her scalp; it was cold, but the hair, soft and thin, felt strangely alive.

"Let's get down to work," Kwen said. He cut the bonds with a knife, but the woman's arms stayed where they were behind her back. Kwen shrugged. He took out a used towel from his coat pocket, wrapped it around the woman's head twice, and tied it with a knot on the back of her head.

"What's that for?" Bashi asked.

"So we don't have to see her eyes."

"Why?"

"That's where her ghost looks out, to see anybody responsible for her death. Once the ghost sees you, she'll never let you go," Kwen said. "Especially a young female ghost. It'll come and suck you dry."

"Superstition," Bashi said. "I would rather have someone to suck me dry."

Kwen snorted a half laugh. "I've eaten more grains of salt than you've eaten rice. It's up to you whether you believe me, but don't cry for help when you need me."

"What are you afraid of? We're only helping her," Bashi said. He pointed to the middle part of the body. "What's that? Did she get another shot there?"

The two men came closer to examine the body's lower back, where the uniform had been soaked in blood that already was dry and dark brown. Unable to lift the clothes by layers, Kwen tore hard at the fabric and tried to separate the clothes from the body.

"Be careful," Bashi said.

"Of what? She won't feel a thing now."

Bashi did not reply. When Kwen ripped the clothes off the body, they both looked at the exposed middle part of the woman, the bloody and gaping flesh opening like a mouth with an eerie smile. Bashi felt warm liquid rise in his throat and threw up by a bush. He grabbed a handful of snow and wiped his face, its coldness refreshing, reassuring.

"Not pretty, huh?" Kwen muttered. He had already put the body

into two burlap sacks, and was working to bind the two sacks together with ropes.

"What did they do to her?" Bashi said.

"They probably took something from her before they shot her."

"Something?"

"Organs. Kidneys maybe. Or other parts maybe. Old stories."

"What are they for?"

"Haven't you heard of transplants?" Kwen said.

"No."

"I thought you had some education," Kwen said. "Who knows
who has her body parts now? Sometimes it's not even for a transplant, but the doctors need to practice so that their skills remain
sharp."

"How do you know?"

"If you live to my age, there's nothing you don't know," Kwen
said.

"How old are you?"

"Fifty-six."

"But I bet there's one thing you don't know," Bashi said. With the
body secured in the sacks, he felt safe and in good humor again.

"That is?"

Bashi walked closer and whispered to Kwen: "Women."

"How do you know I don't know women?" Kwen said, looking at
Bashi with half a grin.

"You're an old bachelor, aren't you?"

"There are so many ways to know women," Kwen said. "Marrying
one is the worst among them."

"Why?"

"Because you only get to know one woman."

"Do you know a lot of women?"

"In a way, yes."

"What way?"

Kwen smiled. "I heard people in town talking about you as a fool.
You are too curious to be a fool."

"What do you mean?"

"You are a man with a brain, and you have to use it."

Bashi was confused. Other than his grandmother, he had never been close to a female. "Can you show me the way?" he asked.

"I can show you where the door is, but you have to get in and find the way by yourself," Kwen said, and lit a cigarette. "Let me tell you a story. I heard it from older people when I was your age. Once upon a time, there was a woman whose husband liked to sleep with other women. The wife, of course, was not happy. 'What makes you leave me and seek other women's bodies?' she asked. Her husband said, 'Look at your face—you're not a pretty one.' The wife looked at her face in the mirror and then came up with a plan. Every evening, she cooked vegetable dishes and made them as fancy-looking as possible: radishes carved into peonies, peas linked into necklaces and bracelets as if they were made of pearls, bamboo shoots cut into the shape of curvy women."

Bashi swallowed loudly without realizing it.

"At the beginning, the husband was impressed. 'You've become a wonderful cook,' he said to his wife, but after dinner he still went out to sleep with other women. After days of eating the vegetable dishes, the husband asked, 'Where are the pork chops and beef stew you cook so well? Why are you not cooking them for me now?' The wife smiled and said, 'But, my master, they don't look pretty at all.' The husband laughed and said, 'Now I understand you.' And from then on he never went out with another woman again."

Bashi stared at Kwen when he stopped talking.

"The story is over," Kwen said.

"What happened?"

"I just told you a story, and the story is over."

"What happened to the man? Why did he stop going to the other women?"

"Because his wife taught him a lesson."

"What lesson?"

"Use your head. Think about it."

"I'm bad at riddles. You have to tell me the whole story," Bashi said.

"Why do I have to?" Kwen said with a smile.

"Oh please," Bashi said. "Do you want another pack of cigarettes? A bottle of rice liquor?"

"If you promise me one thing, I will tell you."

"I promise."

"Don't you want to know what the promise is?"

"As long as you don't want me to kill a person."

"Why would I want you to kill a person?" Kwen asked. "If I want to, I can handle it much better than you."

Bashi shivered, as Kwen looked at him and laughed. "Don't worry," Kwen said. "Why would I want to kill someone? So this is what's going on: Her parents gave me the money for a coffin and for the burial. But what I think is a coffin won't make a difference to anyone, her or her parents or you or me, so I'm going to spare the trouble."

"It's understandable."

"But you have to promise me not to tell anyone. I don't want people to know this."

"Of course not."

Kwen looked at Bashi. "If I hear anything, I'll wring your neck, do you understand?"

"Hey, don't frighten me. I don't do well with bad jokes."

Kwen picked up a branch thick as a man's arm and broke it in half with his hands. "I'm not joking with you," he said, looking at Bashi severely.

"I swear—if I tell Kwen's secret to anyone, I will not have a good death," Bashi said. "Now can you tell me the lesson?"

Kwen looked at Bashi for a long moment and said, "The lesson is this: A pretty face is nothing; for a real man, what matters is the meat part, and in that part all women are the same."

"Which part is that?"

Kwen shook his head. "I thought you were a smart boy."

"Then tell me," Bashi said, slightly agitated.

"I've told you enough. The rest you have to figure out for yourself," Kwen said, and went back to work on the sacks. When he had secured them together, he grabbed one end of the body and tested the weight.

"If you don't explain, I won't help you with the body anymore," Bashi said.

"That suits me fine."

"I'll die if you don't tell me."

"Nobody dies from curiosity," Kwen said with a smile.

"I'll stop being your friend then."

"I had no idea we were friends," Kwen said. "Now, why don't you go your way? I'll go mine."

Bashi sighed, not ready to leave Kwen. "I was only kidding," Bashi said, and when Kwen grabbed one end of the body, Bashi took the other end, and together they heaved the body onto their shoulders. It was heavier than Bashi thought, and a few steps later, he was panting and had to put the body down. Kwen let go of his end and the body hit the ground with a heavy thump. "What a straw boy," Kwen said. "What would you do with a woman even if you had one?"

Bashi breathed hard and bent down to hurl the body onto his shoulder. Before Kwen caught up with him, he started to walk fast, and then stumbled across a tree stump and fell down with the body pressing on top of him.

Kwen roared with laughter. Bashi pushed the body hard to get free. "I thought she looked very tiny," he said, and he massaged his chest, hit hard by the corpse. "But she must have weighed tons."

"Don't you know that once dead, the body weighs a hundred times more?"

"How come?" Bashi asked.

Kwen shrugged. "Death's trick, I suppose."

THE BANQUET ROOM on the second floor of Three Joy was known to some as the place where the fates of many in Muddy River were determined, but for most people in town it was a room with double doors that were kept closed all the time; what was behind the heavy doors was beyond their meager salaries and imaginations. The ground floor, with ten wooden tables painted dark red and benches in matching color, was no more than a dingy diner. Food was ordered and paid for at a window where a moody female cashier would accept the cash and throw out the change along with a bamboo stick, which, oily to the touch, had an almost illegible number engraved on one side. Later the number would be called from an equally narrow window, where the platters were to be picked up by the customers right away, before they were chided for their tardiness. The dishes were greasy, heavily spiced, and overpriced, as was expected for restaurant food. Apart from salespeople on business trips whose meals would be reimbursed, around town only those who needed to put on an extravagant show—a wedding to impress the townspeople or a meal to dazzle some village relatives—would dine at Three Joy.

Kai arrived at the restaurant a little past twelve. The ground floor was empty but for two men with traveling cases set next to them on the floor. The men looked up at her from their cloud of cigarette smoke when she came in, one of them nodding as if he had recognized Kai. She stared at them, and only when the men exchanged a look between themselves did Kai realize that she had fixed her eyes on them for a moment too long. She turned toward the stairs and walked up to the banquet room. Would those men, when they arrived home, entertain their wives with the tale of an execution, Kai wondered; or, buried by other pointless memories accumulated on their trips, would the incident surface only when a cautionary tale was needed for a disobedient child? A death that happened to a stranger could be used for all sorts of purposes. Time and space would add and subtract until the death was turned into something else. A martyr's blood, Kai had once sung onstage, would nurture the azaleas blooming in the spring, their petals red as the color of the revolution; the lyrics and the music had filled her heart with a vast passion that made the earthly world she occupied seem small and temporary, but what could a fourteen-year-old have seen in death but an illusory exterior of grand beauty? Kai had envisioned a different scene at the ceremony, her last encounter with Shan: A speech from Kai would only be a prelude to what Shan would have to say; together their words would awaken the audience and change the course of the day. But what was left of Shan after the murder of her spirit and before the execution of her body—soiled prison uniform and severed vocal cords, half-opened mouth and empty eyes, and a weightless body in a policeman's grip—had filled Kai with a sickness. The drafted speech, with its empty words, had been killed easily by the slogans that had overtaken the stadium.

A young man wearing the armband of a security guard pushed the double doors open for Kai when she approached the banquet room. The air, warm with the smells of fried food, hard liquor, and cigarette smoke, rushed at Kai's face. The mayor's wife and another official's wife greeted Kai and congratulated her on her excellent performance at the denunciation ceremony, and Kai had to demur, as modesty was expected under these circumstances, speaking of her inability to complete her task as well as she had hoped for. The conversation soon drifted to different topics. The mayor's wife, whose daughter-in-law was going into labor any day now, asked Kai about the injection she had gotten after the labor to stop her milk from coming. Han's parents, like all people of their social status, believed that breast-feeding was a backward way to raise a baby; Kai, unaware of the arrangement, had received the injection that later made her weep into Ming-Ming's bundle. No, Kai replied now, she found nothing uncomfortable in the treatment.

"Young women in your generation are so privileged," said a middle-aged woman, joining the conversation. "We had never heard of dried-milk powder in our time."

"Nor fresh cow milk," Han's mother said. "I tell you—that suckling pig Han was enough to make me decide not to have another child after him."

The women laughed, and one of them congratulated Kai on her good fortune of marrying the only son of Han's parents before another woman would have a chance. Kai listened with a trained smile, nodding and replying when it was expected. At the other end of the room, Han smiled at her before turning to crane his neck in a reverent manner at the mayor, who was speaking and gesturing to a small group of men next to him. The mayor's wife continued the discussion on childbirth, and Han's mother prompted Kai to visit the mayor's daughter-in-law. "Not that Kai has any better knowledge about childbirth than you and I, but she is of Susu's age, so they may have more to say to each other," Han's mother said. She looked at Kai for a moment and then turned to the mayor's wife. "Besides, these young women are probably eager to be spared our old women's wisdom for a moment."

Gu Shan could have easily been a daughter-in-law of these women, Kai thought, and tried her best to stay with the conversation. Perhaps some strangers' painless decision had contributed as much to Kai's misplacement in life as had her own decision to marry into Han's family. If the judges had chosen Gu Shan instead of Kai as the winner in the singing and dancing contest in second grade, Shan might have been the one sent to the theater school in the provincial capital. It would have been different then, Shan growing into the leading actress's role while Kai herself remained an ordinary girl in Muddy River. Would she have met Jialin earlier then, before his illness even? The thought made Kai dizzy, and she tried to maintain a calm voice as she told the mayor's wife about the dish, three-cup chicken, that Han's mother had taught her to make. It was Han's favorite, his mother said to the mayor's wife, and Kai added that when she made it herself, it was far less successful, her comment winning approving smiles from the older women in the circle.

Before that day, Kai had not seen Gu Shan for years. They had been classmates in the first grade, but Kai could not recall how Shan looked at that age; rather, she remembered Shan's parents from around the time—Teacher Gu, who had been their teacher that year, and Mrs. Gu, whom Kai had seen only once at a school festival, when Mrs. Gu stood out among the many mothers. Kai remembered, even as a first grader, that she felt jealous of Shan not only because her father was their teacher but also because her mother was beautiful— she had worn a silk blouse on the day of the school festival, under her plain gray Mao jacket, the pomegranate red fabric escaping at the cuffs and the neckline. A plastic barrette, in a matching color, adorned her smooth black hair, grown a few centimeters longer than the allowed style for a married woman. It was Mrs. Gu's posture that Kai had tried to mimic when, at fourteen, she had played a young mother who had given up her newborn baby to save the child of a top Communist Party official; straight-backed, she had clutched the plastic doll to her breast while another doll, wrapped up in a blue print cloth, was thrown into the river onstage. The ballad that followed the drowning was Kai's favorite song from her acting career, a mother's lullaby to a child who would never wake up to all the sunrises of the world.

The last time Kai and Shan had seen each other was in the autumn of 1966. Shan was the leader of a local faction of Red Guards, and when Kai returned from the provincial capital to Muddy River with her touring Red Guard troupe, the two groups faced each other in a singing and dancing duel in the city square. The competition to become the most loyal followers of Chairman Mao, and the animosity stemming from that rivalry, seemed pointless now; but Kai remembered that autumn as the beginning of her adult life, and sometimes she imagined that Shan would share with her the same recollections, of the September sun shining into their eyes on the makeshift stage, the workers from a road crew hitting the ground with their shovels to accompany the beats of their singing, the old people and small children gathering to watch them with great interest, and a lanky boy, who looked not much older than Kai or Shan, standing apart from the crowd with half a smile, as if he alone remained unimpressed by the performances of both groups.

The boy, with a grandfather and two uncles serving in the Nationalist army and fighting against Communism in the civil war, was an outcast from all the Red Guards' factions in town. Two years after that, news came from Muddy River that Shan was imprisoned as an anti–Cultural Revolution criminal. The lanky young man, Shan's boyfriend then, had turned her letters in to the government in exchange for the opportunity to enlist. Had she remained in Muddy River, Kai thought now, would she have fallen for that deceitful smile?

The mayor called for the guests to sit down now at the two tables, where bowls of soup and platters of food were waiting, steaming hot. A show of humbleness and reverence began, as people gently pushed each other around the table, declining the most privileged seats close to the mayor and his wife; only once the act was fully played out did the mayor announce that he would take the liberty of assigning seats for the sake of everyone's grumbling stomach. The guests sat down and began to enjoy the midday banquet.

NINI DID NOT GO HOME after visiting the marketplace in the afternoon. Instead, she limped across the town, her basket, half-filled with withered vegetable leaves, on her shoulder, until she reached the riverbank. The sun had left the heaviest clouds behind and was now midway in the western sky, a pale and cold disk. She had not spotted Bashi on the way back from the stadium, nor in the marketplace, where she remembered sometimes seeing him. She wondered if he was still waiting for her by the willow tree—Bashi seemed to be the kind of person who would stand there and wait—and she decided to go and look for him. Her sisters would certainly wake up from their naps by the time she made it back home, but she had padlocked the door from the outside. The only window was double-sealed. They could cry as much as they wanted; she did not mind as long as she didn't hear them.

Walking upstream along the river, Nini thought about her future. Her mother referred to all her daughters as debt collectors. She couldn't wait to marry every one of them off, she often said. They'd better learn to behave so that when they went off to their husbands' houses, their mothers-in-law wouldn't whip the rascal souls out of their bodies. Her mother made it clear that if the girls offended their in-laws, they'd better brace themselves for their punishment and never expect their parents to help them. But these warnings were never meant for Nini. It was accepted that Nini, the meanest debt collector of the six girls, would remain a burden for her parents; no one would ever come to Nini with a marriage offer. If only they could have a son, and a daughter-in-law to see them off to the next world, Nini's mother said, and Nini understood that her mother was more interested in having one daughter-in-law than six daughters. Without a son, Nini, the unmarriageable daughter, would have to tend to her parents for as long as they lived.

Until that very morning, Nini had wished to become the Gus' daughter. She had loved Teacher Gu and Mrs. Gu, their voices gentle when they said her name, their quiet household abundant with hot meals. The wish had become a dream that sometimes lasted for hours or days, in which Nini pictured herself living with the Gus. Misunderstandings would occur between her and her new parents— a smashed china bowl that had slipped from her bad hand, a misplaced wallet Teacher Gu could not find, or an overcooked dinner that Nini had forgotten to tend to. But they would never speak a harsh word or cast a look of suspicion at her; they knew she was innocent, they knew she always tried her best, but the mere thought of disappointing Teacher Gu and Mrs. Gu drove Nini to tears. She would pinch herself or bite herself on the useless part of her body when they were not looking at her, but sooner or later they would discover the marks and bruises on her body, and this would hurt their hearts more than it had hurt her body. Mrs. Gu would beg Nini not to do it again. Teacher Gu would sigh and rub his hands in helplessness. Nini would push them away and pinch and bite herself harder because she was not worthy of their love. Didn't they know that she was so ugly she would rather die, she would scream at them;

then she would hurt herself more, because she deserved such punishment for screaming at the two dearest people in her life.

The moment would come when, in gentle yet firm words, Mrs. Gu and Teacher Gu would forbid her to hurt herself again. She was not ugly at all, they would tell her, embracing her when she did not resist. They loved her, they would say, and in their eyes she was as precious as a jewel. She would not believe their words, but they would tell her again and again, until she softened and cried. Nini had learned to make her stories longer each time until she could not stand the wait for the final moment when her loneliness and hunger were soothed by the two people who cherished her as dearly as their own lives. When the moment came—it could arrive anytime, on the way to the marketplace or the train station, or when she was patting the baby to sleep or cooking supper—Nini held her breath until she was on the edge of suffocation. Her heart would pump hard afterward, and her limbs would remain weak with a pleasant numbness.

Then, inevitably, a guard in a red armband shouting into her face, a slap on her shoulder from her mother, or a curse from one of her sisters awoke Nini from her dream. It was then that Nini would dream other dreams, conjuring other worlds that would make her the Gus' daughter. Sometimes her parents had died, and she was on the verge of being sent to an orphanage with her sisters, when Mrs. Gu and Teacher Gu ran to her rescue. Other times Nini's parents kicked her out of the house, and the Gus, hearing a knock at their door, would come and pull her from the dark and cold street into their warm house; they had been waiting for the moment as long as she had, they told her, saying that all would be well. In one dream Nini's mother beat her to unconsciousness and she woke up to find herself in Mrs. Gu's arms, the woman's eyes full of thankful tears because Nini had not died.

What would she live for, now that she knew Mrs. Gu and Teacher Gu had never been the gentle parents she dreamed about? In her dreams they would never turn their backs on her.

"Now, now. Why are you so sad? Are you missing me already?"

Nini looked up and saw Bashi, spinning a sheepskin hat in his hand like a magician, his forehead shining with sweat. She took a deep breath and looked around. She was halfway to the birch woods; the snow was dirty on the frozen river. She licked the inside of her mouth and tasted blood from having bitten herself so hard. "Why are you here?" she asked, sniffling.

"I've been waiting for you, remember? Since this morning." Bashi made an exaggerated gesture of pointing twice to his wrist, though he did not wear a watch. "But you didn't come."

"My mother sent me to the denunciation ceremony."

"Did you see the woman?"

"No."

"Of course not, because you don't belong to any work unit," Bashi said. He walked closer and put his hat on Nini's head. It was too big for her. He adjusted the hat but it still sat low on her eyebrows. "You look like a girl soldier in a movie," said Bashi.

"Which movie?"

"I don't know. Every movie has a girl soldier. *The Guerillas, The Tale of a Red Heart, The Pioneers.* Have you seen them?"

Nini shook her head.

Bashi clicked his tongue and made a sound of being surprised. "One of these days I'll take you to a movie."

Nini had never been to a movie theater. Once in a while, her parents would go to see a film with their work units; her two sisters went with their school too. In the summer, a white screen would be set up in an open field by the Muddy River, and every other week a film would be shown, but Nini was always the one left with the baby at home. They would stay in the yard as long as they could, listening to the faint music coming from the river, until swarms of mosquitoes came and buzzed around them.

Bashi watched Nini closely. "Why, you don't want to see a movie with me?"

"But you'll still give me the coal even if you take me to a movie?" Nini asked.

"Coal? Yes, anytime," Bashi said, and circled an arm around Nini's shoulder. Taken aback, she struggled slightly, and Bashi let her go with a chortle. "Why don't we find a log and sit down," Bashi said, directing Nini upstream. She tried to catch up with his long stride; when Bashi realized this, he slowed down.

"Do you know who I saw today?" he asked.

"No."

"Do you want to know?"

Nini hesitated and said yes.

"I saw the counterrevolutionary."

Nini stopped. "Where is she?"

"Dead now."

"Did you see her alive?"

"I wish I had. No, she was dead already," Bashi said, and twisted Nini's left arm gently behind her back. "They bound her arms this way, so her middle finger was pointing at her heart. And bang," he said, pushing his index finger into Nini's back.

Nini shuddered. She withdrew her arm, and hid her bad hand in her sleeve. "Where is she now?" she asked.

"Why?"

"I want to see her."

"Everybody wants to see her. But believe me, there's nothing to see. She is as dead as a log. Heavier than a log, in fact. Do you know how I got to know this?"

"No."

"Because I just helped this man move her body off the island. Oh, she's heavy, believe me."

"Is she with the man?"

"He's digging a grave for her."

"Where are they?"

"On the other side of the woods. It's quite a task to dig a hole now. They shouldn't really execute someone in this cold season. Summer would be much easier for everyone. I told the man not to waste his time. Old Hua and his wife would never dig a hole in the

winter. But the man said he would take care of it and told me to go
home first. Of course I didn't want to stay with the poor man and
watch him work. Maybe we could go there tomorrow morning and
see if he's got a hole the size of a bowl by then."

"Can we go there now?"

"Why?"

"I want to see her."

"But there's nothing to see. She's in a couple of sacks now."

Nini looked upstream. The fire in their stove would be dead by
the time she returned home. It would take her another fifteen minutes to start the fire, and dinner would be late. Her mother would
knock her on the head with her hard knuckles. Bashi might change
his mind and never give her the coal again. Still, she pushed away
Bashi's hand and started to walk toward the woods.

"Hey, where are you going?"

"I want to see the body."

"Don't leave me here. I'm going with you," Bashi said, putting his
hand back on Nini's shoulder. "The man who's burying her, you
know, he is not easy to talk to, but he's a friend of mine. Ask him
anything and he'll do it for you."

"Why?" Nini asked.

"Silly, because you're my friend, no?"

THE WIND PICKED UP after sunset, and Bashi realized that he had left
his hat on Nini's head. He chuckled when he thought about her serious little face. She rarely smiled, but her eyes, even the bad one with
a droop, would become larger with attention when he was talking to
her. He didn't know how much she understood of the rules between
boys and girls, or how much she had heard about his reputation, but
she had not said anything when he put a hand on her shoulder.

Before they parted, Bashi had asked Nini to come out again the
next day, and she had neither agreed nor refused. The old bastard
Kwen must have frightened her out of her poor soul, Bashi thought.
He picked up a rock from the ground. It was suppertime now, the

street deserted except for the leftover announcements, swept up and swirling about in the wind. Bashi looked around, and when he saw nobody in sight, he aimed the rock at the nearest streetlamp. It took him three tries to break the bulb.

Kwen had not behaved like a friend at all when Bashi and Nini had found him. It had taken them a while, and only when he saw a trail left by the body on the dead leaves did Bashi realize that Kwen had moved it farther, into another patch of woods. Kwen was half rolling, half carrying a big boulder toward the body, which was already partly covered by stones of different sizes. It was unrealistic of the parents to expect him to bury her underground in this weather, Kwen said when they approached him.

"As if I hadn't told you," Bashi observed.

"Could you shut up just for once?" Kwen said.

That was not a way to speak to a friend, especially in front of his new companion, but Bashi tried not to protest. "If you're worried about wild dogs, you could cover the body with some heavy branches. Old Hua does that," Bashi said. "You don't need to move all those stones."

"I thought you were a smart man, and knew not to interfere with other people's business."

"Just a friendly suggestion," said Bashi.

Kwen looked at Bashi sharply. "I'd appreciate it if you'd leave me alone."

"Don't worry. Your secret sits well with me," said Bashi, running his finger along his mouth and making a zipping sound. He walked closer to Kwen. "But my friend there, she wants to have a look at the body."

"Why?"

"Who doesn't want to see?"

Kwen shook his head and said it was not possible.

"Come on," Bashi said, patting Kwen on the shoulder as he had seen men do to each other. "The girl only wants a quick look. It won't hurt anyone. I'll move the stones and I'll put them back. You can stand here and supervise us. It won't take more than a minute."

Kwen brushed Bashi's hand away. Bashi made a face at Nini, hoping she would understand that brusqueness was normal between men. Wouldn't he want to help a friend to impress his girl? Bashi said in a low voice; she's just a girl to whom nobody paid any attention, and why not make her happy for a day, Bashi whispered. Kwen shook his head, and when Bashi pressed again and insisted that he himself would open the sack for the girl, Kwen looked at Bashi with cold eyes. "You'd better leave before my patience runs out."

"What's the matter with you?" Bashi said. "It's only a counter-revolutionary's body, not your mother's."

With a curse Kwen told Bashi to shut up. Bashi was shocked. He had thought that Kwen was fond of him; only an hour earlier Kwen had been the storyteller. Nini stared at them, and it hurt Bashi to see her unblinking eyes stay on his own face, hot and probably red as a beet now. "Fuck *you*," Bashi said to Kwen. "Fuck your sisters and your mother and your aunts and grandmas and all your dead female ancestors in their tombs."

Before Bashi had time to react, Kwen held a long knife to his throat, the sharp blade pressed into his skin. In a cold voice Kwen told Bashi to get down on his knees.

For the next five minutes, Bashi did everything Kwen ordered him to do. He called himself all sorts of names, slapping his own face and begging for forgiveness. Kwen looked down at him with a smile. "You're a useless man, Bashi, do you know that?"

"Yes, of course," Bashi said. It was then that Bashi noticed the suspicious stain on Kwen's crotch, near his fly, light gray on the dark corduroy overalls. Bashi moved closer, as if he wanted to let his head touch Kwen's feet, and stole another glance. Kwen could have given Bashi a thousand other explanations for the stain, but Bashi would never believe him.

It was dark when Bashi and Nini got back to town. She looked nervous, and did not reply when he suggested a meeting the next day. She was late, she said, and quickened her pace with a desperate effort; her parents might not be happy, he thought, but he decided not to ask her about the punishment she was to receive. He had enough to worry about, and would prefer not to take on her misery.

A block away, Bashi broke another bulb. He kicked the half bulb into the ditch. "You corpse rapist!" Heaven knows what else such a man could do, Bashi thought; the townspeople needed someone to watch out for them. He decided to go back and find out why Kwen had been so stubbornly guarding the body from them, but before that, he had to know Kwen's whereabouts. Think as a good detective, Bashi urged himself. He moved quietly toward Kwen's shack, and approached it facing the wind so the dog would not catch his scent. About sixty feet away, he hurled a rock in the direction of the shack. The black dog started to bark and jump at the invisible enemy. Bashi turned into a side alley quickly and heard Kwen shouting from inside the shack. After a few minutes, Kwen came out of the shack and headed to the electric plant for his night shift. All safe for him to explore, Bashi thought. Who would have imagined that he, Bashi, the man whom everybody called an idiot, would be the one to work for the town's safety on this dark night? He rubbed his ears roughly with his hands; he wished he had not forgotten to retrieve his hat from Nini.

Stumbling in the darkness, Bashi had a hard time finding the spot. He made a mental note to buy some appropriate tools the next day, a good knife, a long and slim flashlight that he had seen a safety guard carry, a compact notebook and a pen of matching color, a pair of gloves, a magnifying glass, and some other things he imagined a detective needed. It was too late to make the purchase now, but at least the moonlight on the snow and a few weak stars made the search less difficult. Bashi fumbled in his pocket and found half a matchbook. He lit a match to make sure he was in the right place, and then started to work in the near darkness. The boulders were heavy, and he had to take a break from time to time.

At least he had to give that bastard Kwen credit for being a strong man despite his age.

Bashi cleaned off all the boulders and then tried to untie the strings holding the sacks, but his fingers, too tired, could not finish the task. He bent down and broke the strings between his teeth. When he peeled the burlap sack away, his hand touched something hard and cold, not the ripped prisoner's uniform he had seen earlier but the woman's frozen body. Bashi gave a little startled cry, and then laughed at himself. "You'd better get used to this from now on," he said in a hushed voice to himself.

The body, entirely uncovered now, looked eerie in the dim light. Kwen's old towel was still around the woman's head, and Bashi thought he'd better leave it there. "Sorry, miss, I don't mean to disturb you twice," he said. "I'm just doing my job. For your good too."

He lit another match and bent down to check the body, and it took him a long moment to register what he saw. His hand shook hard and the match dropped onto the snow, hissing for a moment before going out. Bashi sat down and panted, his legs too weak to support the weight of his knowledge. After a while, he lit another match and checked again. He was not mistaken: The woman's breasts were cut off, and her upper body, with the initial wound from the transplant operation and the massive cuts Kwen had made, was a mess of exposed flesh, dark red and gray and white. The same mess extended down to between her legs.

The match burned Bashi's finger and he flipped it away. He half squatted beside the body for a moment and started to gag. It had been a long day and he had nothing left to throw up. Still, he coughed and retched until his face was smeared with tears and bile dribbled down his chin. After a while, he calmed down and grabbed some snow to clean up his face. He wrapped the body up in the burlap sacks and tried to put back the boulders, but his arms and legs were shaking too hard. He spread dead tree branches and dry grass on top of the body, and when he felt sure the body was concealed well enough, he sat down and panted again, then cried.

The walk back home was exhausting. A few blocks away from his house, Bashi saw the dog, Ear, run by. He shouted at it and tried to muster his last energy to kick it. The dog yelped and ran away, dropping something by the roadside.

Bashi picked it up. It was a woman's shoe, the sole worn through with a hole. Bashi aimed it at a garbage can, but missed. "The world is becoming a hell of a place," he said to no one in particular.

THE WIND HOWLED all evening, shaking windows, seizing loose tiles from roofs and hurling them across the empty yards and alleys. Kwen's black dog, tied to his post, whined and shivered, but his suffering meant little to the world, let alone to his master, who dozed off in the small cubelike janitor's shack, an empty flask on the floor next to his feet.

Elsewhere Mrs. Hua sipped from a chipped cup the rice liquor that her husband had poured for her earlier to numb the throbbing pain in her palm, and listened to the whistling of the wind through the woods. Old Hua and Mrs. Hua had sorted bottles and paper all afternoon and evening, and it was at the very end, when she was lost in her reverie, that she punched her palm with half of a broken bottle. There was not much bleeding, her aged body having little to offer now. Her husband washed it with saltwater and then poured a cup of rice liquor for her. They did not touch alcohol often, but a bottle had always been around, kept with the iodine and the rags they cleaned and boiled; it was the best medicine they could get, and once when Old Hua had had to remove gangrene from his leg by himself, he had downed half a bottle and later poured the other half onto the cut.

How was her hand? Old Hua asked, sitting down in his chair. Unless it was necessary they did not light the kerosene lamp, and she replied in the darkness that there was little to worry about. He nodded and did not talk for a while, and she felt the hard liquor slowly warming her body. Morning Glory, Mrs. Hua said, the name of their first daughter; did he want to talk about Morning Glory? The baby had been found on a summer dawn when morning glories, pink and blue and white and purple, had taken over the wilderness outside the mountain village where the Huas had passed through as beggars. The dew had soaked the rags that were bundling the little creature, her bluish gray face cold to the touch. For a moment Mrs. Hua thought it was another baby who had died before having ever enjoyed a day of her life, but her husband was the one to notice the small lips sucking.

Old Hua lit the tobacco pipe now and inhaled. The amber-colored tip flickered, the only light in the room. What's there to talk about? he asked, more out of resignation than rebuttal. Earlier that afternoon she had told Old Hua, while they were sorting, that it was time they began to tell themselves the stories of the seven daughters, before old age wiped out their memories. Neither Old Hua nor Mrs. Hua could read or write, and already Mrs. Hua had been frustrated when one girl's face was overlapped by another's in her dreams.

They could start with Morning Glory, Mrs. Hua said now, but she was momentarily confused. Where would they begin? When they had picked the bundle up from the grass, or when she had been sneaked out of the village before daybreak by her helpless mother? Mrs. Hua and her husband had looked for anything left by the parents—a name, a birthday, or a message they could later find people to read for them—but the rags that swaddled the baby, ripped from old sheets and worn-out undershirts, had said enough about the reason she had been discarded.

She was the prettiest, Old Hua said. He was as biased as a father could be, Mrs. Hua thought, but did not point it out to him. Morning Glory had been seventeen when Mr. and Mrs. Hua were forced to give up the girls. Seventeen was old enough for a girl to become a wife; still, when they found a family who was willing to take Morning Glory in as a child bride for one of their grown-up sons, they made the family swear to wait until Morning Glory turned eighteen before they would let the husband touch her. Mrs. Hua wondered aloud how well the other parents had kept their promises; they had

had daughters themselves, she said, and as parents of girls they must have understood.

Old Hua nodded. He could have said that it made no difference now, and she was glad that he only smoked silently and listened.

"She liked to drink vinegar," Mrs. Hua said.

Old Hua shook his head as if he did not trust her memory, but she knew she was not wrong about that. Once, when a younger girl had tipped over the vinegar bottle, Morning Glory had cried; she was seven or eight then, old enough not to shed tears over this, and Mrs. Hua remembered later catching the girl munching on clover stems for the tart juice and thinking that it must be one of those things that only her birth parents would have understood. Mrs. Hua wondered if Morning Glory would crave something odd in her pregnancies. Mrs. Hua had never been able to bear a baby herself, and she was always curious about the stories she heard of a pregnant woman's wants.

"How old is Morning Glory?" Mrs. Hua asked suddenly.

Old Hua thought for a moment and replied that she must be forty-one or forty-two now.

Mrs. Hua counted the years, but the liquor made it hard to keep the numbers straight. Middle-aged, she thought, with a litter of children of her own by now. Mrs. Hua wondered what Morning Glory would be like as a mother. She had been gentle with stray cats and wounded birds, and Mrs. Hua remembered her husband had once said that of the seven girls Morning Glory was the one to have the most of a Buddha's heart; a hard thing for a girl to live with, Mrs. Hua remembered herself replying then, but perhaps a full house of children to feed and many in-laws to please had long ago hardened that heart into a rock.

Night fell, and Mrs. Hua poured a cup of liquor for her husband and another cup for herself. The liquor was the best medicine, if only they could afford it, Old Hua said. But it did little to heal the wound left when their daughters were taken away, Mrs. Hua thought, and before she knew it, she felt her face wet with tears. Was she all right?

Old Hua asked when he heard her sniffling, and she replied that it was the trick of the liquor and the wind howling outside.

Disturbed too were other souls. A female prison guard, off duty for the next two days, claiming she had a minor cold, woke up from a fitful dream and gasped for air; her husband, half-asleep, asked her if she felt unwell. A ridiculous nightmare, she answered, knowing enough not to tell him that she had fainted at work earlier that morning, when the warden had ordered that Gu Shan's vocal cords be severed so that she could not shout counterrevolutionary slogans at the last minute. The woman had been among the four guards assigned to pin the prisoner down for the procedure, but it had not gone as smoothly as promised by the warden and the doctor; the prisoner had struggled with a vehemence that one would not have imagined could come from her skinny body, and the female guard, whose nerve was usually up to her work, had fallen backward and bumped her head hard on the floor before the doctor finally finished the operation.

Unable to sleep, in another house, was an old orderly for the police station. I tell you, he said to his wife, who answered that she did not want to be reminded for another time about the bucket of blood he had washed off the police jeep that had transferred the prisoner. But it was unusual, he said; I tell you, it was a horrible thing, to clean up so much blood. What did they do to her? Why couldn't they wait until they got her onto the island to finish her off? He threw one question after another at his wife, who was no longer listening. He was getting old, after waiting for answers that his wife would not give him, the man thought sadly; he had fought in the war against the Japanese when he was a boy and he had seen plenty of bodies, but now he could not sleep because of a bucket of blood from a woman who was no longer alive. The story would make his old platoon friends laugh at the next reunion, the old man thought, and then he realized that he was the last one remaining who had not reported to the other side.

She had to die anyway, one of the two surgeons who had operated on Gu Shan told himself one more time—so it didn't matter, in the end, that they had changed the protocol because the patient did not believe in receiving something from a corpse and insisted that the prisoner be kept alive when the kidneys were removed. This was not the most challenging operation for him, but it would be the one to make him the chair of the surgery department, and put his wife into the position of head nurse in internal medicine, though she was still unaware of her promotion and would be overjoyed when she found out about it. It would also help their twin daughters, fourteen and a half and blossoming into a pair of young beauties, to get a recommendation from the city government so that they could go to an elite high school in the provincial capital. The man thought about his wife and his daughters—they were fast asleep in their innocent dreams, unplagued by death and blood; the burden was on his shoulders, the man of the household, and he found it hard not to ponder the day when he could no longer shelter them, the two daughters especially, from the ugliness of a world that they were in love with now, rosebudlike girls that they were. What then? he wondered, painfully aware of his limitations as a man trapped between practicality and conscience. In the end, he had to make himself believe that he had chosen the best for his family. The long-needed sleep rolled over him like a tide and washed him offshore.

In an army hospital a hundred miles away, medicine dripped into an old man's vein. He was surrounded by people congratulating themselves on the success of the transplant operation. And in Muddy River, in a hospital populated by many more patients and fewer doctors and nurses, sat Mrs. Gu, who was dozing off at the drip-drip of the saline solution into her husband's arm. Now and then she woke up and watched her husband's face, shrunken and suddenly too old for her to recognize.

Part II

*T*he nanny stood by the doorway of the nursery, watching Kai and Ming-Ming with detached patience. The morning leave-taking was never easy, but before the girl's gaze Kai felt more incapable than ever. The nanny was young, fifteen and a half, but there was a look of resignation on her face that made the girl look old, as if an aged woman had taken over and lived out all that was to come in her life before her time.

"Now, now," said the nanny finally, when Kai failed to pry Ming-Ming's small fingers off her hand. He screamed in protest when he was pulled out of Kai's arms, and the nanny caught the small wrist and shook it gently. "Ming-Ming will be a good boy. Wave to Mama and let Mama go to work. Without work Mama doesn't make money. Without money there is no food. Without food Ming-Ming's tummy will rumble. And when Ming-Ming's tummy rumbles Mama will be too sad to go to work."

The girl had a way of talking in circles, her tone flat and unhurried, as if she was telling an old folktale that no longer held any suspense, and Ming-Ming always calmed down. In those moments Kai felt that the girl was innocent and mysterious at once, a child and an old woman sharing the space within her skinny body, neither aware of the other's existence.

Han came out of the bathroom, buttoning the last button on his Mao jacket. "Let Mama go to work, yes," he said, and tickled Ming-

Ming under his chin. "But your baba will make more than enough money even if Mama doesn't work. Aren't you a lucky boy?"

Ming-Ming turned away and hugged the nanny's neck, having already banished his parents from his world before he was abandoned for the day. The child's attachment and indifference, both absolute, were a mystery to Kai. She did not recall ever being close to her mother, an unhappy woman who had been easily disappointed by everything in her life: her husband's lack of social status, the three children close to their father but stingy with their affection for her, promotions given to her colleagues, the tedious life, year after year, in a provincial city. Han's mother, a shrewd woman who had been credited with both her husband's political career and her own—she had been a nurse in the civil war, and had tended several high-ranking officials—was attentive to Han's needs, a better mother than Kai's own perhaps, but Kai had never thought of apprenticing herself to her mother-in-law. Until Ming-Ming's birth Kai always had someone to rely on for advice, teachers for instruction at the theater school, an older actress as a mentor in the theater troupe, her father. In her new motherhood, she felt not much different from a young child in a fishermen's village—her father had once told her and her siblings about the practice in his hometown near the East Sea, where a boy, upon turning three, would be thrown into the sea without warning; the child was expected to use his instinct to stay afloat, and those who could not save themselves were banished from the fishing boats, to live out their humility onshore, mending fishing nets and harvesting air-dried fish and seaweeds from clotheslines among women. Life is a war, and one rests only when death comes to fetch him, Kai remembered her father saying. She looked at Ming-Ming's small limbs; in another life he would soon be expected to fight in his first battle.

Kai repeated to the nanny a few details about feeding and napping. The girl looked patient, and Kai wondered if the girl was eager for them to go to work so that she could mother Ming-Ming more capably than Kai could herself. When the girl had been hired, her parents had told Kai that, as the eldest daughter of the family, she had helped to bring up six siblings, the youngest not much older than Ming-Ming. She had become a mother before she had grown into adulthood, Kai thought now, and Ming-Ming's plump arms, circling the nanny's neck with trust and familiarity, reminded Kai how easy it could be to replace a mother with another loving person in a small child's life.

Han insisted on walking Kai to the studio. The well-orchestrated denunciation event of the day before and, more so, the successful transplant—by now Han felt little need to keep it a secret from Kai that a top official had received Gu Shan's kidneys, and that Han himself was to be praised for that—had made Han more talkative.

"Is that why her trial was expedited?" asked Kai.

Han smiled and said they need not be concerned about irrelevant details; they had more important things to look forward to now, he said, and when she asked him what he meant, more pointedly than she had intended, he brought up the possibility of a second baby.

But Ming-Ming was no more than an infant himself, Kai said. Han studied her face and told her not to be nervous. By the time his little sister was born Ming-Ming would be old enough to be a big brother, he said. Even before Ming-Ming Han had hoped for a daughter, though he knew a boy as the firstborn would please his parents more.

They might get another boy, Kai reminded Han.

"Then we'll have another baby. I won't stop until I get a daughter as beautiful as her mother."

Kai was silent for a moment and then said that she was not a sow. Han laughed. He could easily find a joke in everything she said, and she thought he would have failed as an actor, unable to recognize or deliver the subtlety in his lines.

It was time to think about a second baby, and soon a third, Han said, more seriously now. Ming-Ming was for his parents, Han explained, as the first grandchild was born for the sake of satisfying and entertaining the grandparents. For her mother too, he hastily added when he found Kai gazing at him, though she was not upset—rather, she was thinking that he had stumbled into the truth: Kai's mother doted on Ming-Ming in a timid way, as if she had less right to claim him as a grandchild than Han's parents did.

The second baby would be for Ming-Ming, as he needed a companion more than they needed another baby to deprive their sleep, Han said. Only the third child could they have as their own. "I'm not a selfish person but I want us to have something for ourselves," Han said.

Kai walked on without replying. She had always convinced herself that the decision to marry was not much different from serving a meal to a tableful of guests, with different people to consider: her parents' elation at being taken more seriously by those who had previously treated them with little respect, the futures of her two younger siblings—a brother whom Han had arranged to send to Teachers College in the provincial capital, and a sister who had been delighted to be courted as the relative of an important figure in the government. The heroines Kai had once played onstage had all given up their lives for higher callings, but it was not for a grand dream that she had decided to marry Han, but for a life with comfort and convenience.

When they arrived at the studio, Han assured Kai that there was no pressure. He handed her the mug of herb tea he had carried for her. "Sometimes a man can talk like an idiot when he is dreaming."

Kai smiled and said she was only tired. She had no right to stop a husband from dreaming up a future to share with his wife. She wondered if the foundation of every marriage was made up of deceptions, and whether to keep the marriage from collapsing the deceived party had to maintain a blind confidence or a willingness to look away from the unwelcome truth. In his last year of life Kai's father had admitted, in one of his few private conversations with Kai, that marrying Kai's mother had been the most unfortunate decision he had ever made, and that he had stayed in the marriage only for the sake of the three children; this confession was not to be shared with her mother, as both father and daughter understood without having to make any promises to each other.

"I know I may not be the perfect husband for you," Han said. "But I also know that you may not find someone who wants to do as much for you as I do, or someone who can do as much as I do for you."

"Why are we talking like a new couple who needs to prove our love to each other?" Kai said, trying to make her voice light. "Isn't Ming-Ming enough for what we are to each other?"

Han gazed at Kai with a strange smile. "How many children do you think would make you settle down?"

She had never been unsettled, Kai said.

She had not been the only girl, Han said. Kai had never asked him about other suitable matches, and he had questioned little about her own past, though she knew he had the connections to investigate if he had wanted to. There was little mystery about what the other girls wanted, Han said, and there was little doubt that he could easily give them what they were after. "But you were different. I knew it the moment I saw you. You were more ambitious than all the other girls, and I thought maybe even I couldn't get for you what you wanted."

Kai had never seen Han speak with such candor, nor had she expected his insight, and this alarmed her. She had thought that there was little in him beyond the spoiled boy, and she had found it suffocating to tend the boy both as a mother and a playmate. Now she wished that was all he was. She looked at her watch. She needed to get ready now, she said, and Han nodded. In a lighter voice he told her to forget their conversation. Spring fever, he said of himself, and promised to recover from the illness by the time he saw her for lunch.

IT TOOK BASHI A FEW SECONDS to realize that the night had long been over. The patch of sky in the high bedroom window was blue and cloudless, and through the half-open door of the bedroom he could see the living room filled with bright sunlight. He had missed the best time to see Nini. He wondered if the girl had looked for him. It had been a restless night for Bashi. He had been going over the different ways he could reveal Kwen's crime to the town, but none of them seemed right. In the meantime, he had a feeling that the woman's ghost was perched at the foot of his bed, and when he shut his eyes and refused to acknowledge her presence, she took over the space inside his eyelids. After an hour of tossing and turning, he masturbated. The woman's ghost retreated, taking with her his usual joy in the activity. In the end, he exhausted himself, in pain more than enjoyment, and fell into a series of dreams. In one, a double wedding was taking place, Nini and himself the first couple, the executed counterrevolutionary and Kwen the other. What a horrifying dream, Bashi thought now, but perhaps it was a sign that justice would send Kwen to his dead bride.

His grandmother did not answer when Bashi asked her for the time. He raised the curtain between them and found her in her bed. What dreams had kept her in bed? he asked. Had his grandfather come for a visit? Bashi thought of joking, but before the words came out, he noticed that there was something odd about his grandmother, her cheeks ashen-colored.

After five minutes Bashi was convinced that she was dead, even though her skin still felt lukewarm to the touch. He sat down next to her on the bed, unsure what to do next. She had been less of a nuisance than any other woman her age when she was alive, but she had chosen the most inconvenient time to die. It was the beginning of a new life for Bashi, with Nini to befriend and Kwen to battle with, and he needed his grandmother to live a while longer to take care of him. Bashi checked a few more times over the next half hour, but she was colder with each inspection.

His grandmother had been preparing for her own ending for some time. A few years ago she had hired two carpenters and a painter to make a casket, and she had supervised the whole process to ensure that no effort was spared and that the casket turned out as she desired. She also accumulated stacks of embroidered outfits for

the burial—black silk robes with blooming golden and pink chrysanthemums, ivory-colored shoes and sleeping caps, made of fine satin,
with dozens of the embroidered symbol *shou*—long life—arranged in
intricate patterns. A box of cheap replicas of her jewels would go to
the next world with her; the authentic ones—gold and silver and jade
and emerald—had been sold for cash when Bashi failed to secure a
job after graduating from high school. "I've arranged everything for
you," she said to him when she went over her inventory for the next
world, once or twice a month. "I won't be a burden to you."

How could she call herself a burden, when she was the dearest
person he had in life? Bashi often told her, but instead of making her
happy, the words would bring her to tears. "What a bitter life you
were born into. Not knowing one's own parents! Thank heaven that
I was given a long life to watch you grow up," Bashi's grandmother
said, and would repeat stories from different eras of her life.

This talk had always made Bashi laugh. What did he need an old
woman for, when he could take care of himself perfectly well? But
now he wished she were here to help him. She had said she was ready
to go, but what were the things he needed to do to make her really
go, out of the house and into the ground? Bashi sat by her bedside
for some time and decided to seek help. The neighbors wouldn't
do—even though they were friendly with his grandmother, they all
despised him; putting her into their hands would only make him
more of a talking point at their dinner tables. Nini wouldn't know
anything other than her baskets of coal and rotten vegetables. Kwen
seemed to be a man of the world, as he had been sought by the other
family to bury their daughter, but with Kwen's dark secret fresh in
his own mind, Bashi would never want him near his grandmother.
The only people left were Old Hua and his wife. They took care of babies thrown out like rags; surely they would help to bury an old, re-
spectable woman.

The street was the same one as the day before, but people on the
way to their work units would not look at Bashi and understand his
loss. He walked south to the riverbank and, from there, along the

river to the west. When he was out of sight of the townspeople, he sat down on a boulder and wept.

"What are you crying here for, first thing in the morning?" asked someone, kicking his foot lightly.

Bashi wiped his face with the back of his hand. It was Kwen, a heavy cotton coat on his shoulders and a bag of breakfast in his hand. He must be coming back from the night shift. "Leave me alone," Bashi said.

"That's not the right way to answer a friendly greeting. Would you care for a piece of pig-head meat?"

Bashi shook his head. "My grandma died," he said, despite his determination to keep Kwen an enemy.

"When?"

"Last night. This morning. I don't know. She just died."

"Sorry to hear that," Kwen said. "But how old was she?"

"Eighty-one."

"Enough to call it a joyful departure," Kwen said. "There's no need for the tears. Be happy for her."

Bashi's eyes reddened. These were the first words of condolence he'd heard, and he almost felt he had to forgive Kwen. "I'm wondering what kind of funeral would honor her life. She's been father and mother and grandmother to me," Bashi said. The thought of being an orphan made him feel small again, as he had felt on the day his mother deposited him, years earlier, with his grandmother. He tried to cough into his palm but it came out as sobbing.

"Hey, we know you're sad, but if you want to do her a favor, don't waste your time on tears now."

"What can I do? I've never taken care of a dead person," he said.

Kwen looked up at the sky. The wind from the night before had died out, and the weather forecast predicted a warm front. The sun, halfway beyond the mountain, promised a good early spring day. "It will thaw in two weeks," Kwen said. "I would find a place to keep her before thawing. Go to the city hospital and rent her some space."

"Why didn't the family yesterday rent from the hospital?" Bashi asked, but once the question came out, he regretted it.

"The morgue only accepts bodies from natural deaths."

"What's a natural death?"

"Like the one with your grandmother."

The image of the woman's body came back to Bashi. He breathed hard, trying to control a bout of nausea. "Thanks for reminding me," he said. "I'm going there now."

"But you're walking in the wrong direction," Kwen said.

Bashi looked at the road, leading west into the mountain where the woman's body lay butchered under a bush. He wondered if Kwen had seen through him. He wanted to report the news to Old Hua and his wife first, Bashi said, as they were old friends of his grandmother's.

Kwen studied Bashi, and he felt his scalp tighten under the man's gaze. "So I'm going," Bashi said, raising a hand hesitantly.

Kwen lit a cigarette. "You know I don't like anyone to be naughty around me?"

"Why would I want to? I have my own grandmother to take care of."

Kwen nodded. "Just a reminder."

Bashi promised that he would behave and left in haste. He should have returned the boulders to their place the night before. A good detective did not leave any traces of his investigation around. He wondered if it was too late for him to correct his mistake.

The Huas' cabin was padlocked. Bashi picked up a small piece of coal and wrote big scrawling characters on the door: *My grandma is dead—Bashi.* He looked at the characters and then wiped out the word *dead* and wrote *gone.* There was no need to disturb two old people with the harshness of reality, Bashi thought, and then it occurred to him that the Huas might not be able to read.

The visit to the morgue was disappointing, one more sign that this world was becoming as bad as it could get. The woman at the front desk threw a pad across the table, before Bashi could explain things to her. When he opened his mouth, she pointed to the papers. "Fill them out before you open your mouth."

It took Bashi some time to work out how to answer the questions. He had forgotten to bring the household register card; the woman wouldn't be too happy about it, but she would certainly understand negligence from a bereft grandson. Perhaps people would regard him differently now that his grandmother was dead; perhaps they would forgive him and love him because he was an orphan. He dipped the pen into the ink bottle and said to the woman as he wrote, "You know, she is the only one I have and I'm her only one too."

The woman raised an eyebrow and glanced at Bashi without replying. Perhaps she did not know who he was. "My grandma, she left me today," he explained. "I don't have parents. I never did, as long as I can remember."

"Did I say not to open your mouth before finishing the forms?"

"Yes, but I'm just being friendly," Bashi said. "You don't have many people to talk with you here, do you?"

The woman sighed and put a magazine up in front of her eyes. He looked at the magazine cover; *Popular Movies,* the title said, and a young couple leaned onto a tree and looked out at Bashi with blissful anticipation. Bashi made a face at the couple before going back to work on the forms. The last paper was a permission sheet for cremation. Bashi read through it twice before he could understand it. "Comrade," he said in a hoarse, low voice, intending to earn the sympathy that he fully deserved.

"Done?"

"I have a question. My grandmother—she was eighty-one and she raised me from very young—she already had a casket made. She didn't like the idea of being burned," Bashi said. "I don't know about you but I myself would rather not be burned, alive or dead."

The woman stared at Bashi for a long moment and grabbed the registration from his hand. "Why are you wasting my time then?"

she said. She ripped the sheets off, squeezed them into a ball, and targeted the wastebasket by the entrance. She missed, and Bashi walked over to pick the ball up. "I don't get it, comrade," he said, trying to sound humble. "You asked me to fill out the forms and open my mouth afterward, and I did as you told me." Most women were ill-tempered at work, according to Bashi's observation; at home they served their grumpy husbands, so women had to show, at work, that they were fully in control. Bashi was willing to humor this one despite her looks—she was no longer young, and the dark bags underneath her eyes made her look like a panda.

The woman pointed to a poster on the wall. "Read it," she said and went back to the magazine.

"Of course, comrade, anything you say," said Bashi. He read the poster: The city government, in accordance with the new provincial policy to transform the old, outdated custom of underground burying, which took up too much land that could otherwise be used to grow food for the ever-growing population, had decided to make cremation the only legal form of undertaking; the effective date was two and a half months away.

"It seems we still have some time till the policy becomes effective," Bashi said to the woman. "Enough time to bury a little old woman, isn't it?"

"That's your business," the woman said behind the magazine. "Not ours."

"But can I rent some space in your freezer, until the ground starts to thaw?"

"We only take in bodies for cremation."

"But the regulation says—"

"Forget the regulation. We don't have enough space here for everyone, and our policy now is to take bodies that are for cremation only," said the woman. She left the front desk and entered an inner office.

Bashi left the morgue with a less heavy heart. His grandmother, a wise woman, had chosen the right time to die. Two more months of living would have sent her into an oven; just like she had always said—heaven assigned punishment to any form of greed. The death of his grandmother, instead of being a tragedy, had become something worth celebrating. One must always look on the good side of things, Bashi reminded himself. His usual energy was restored. The sunshine was warm on his face, a cheerful spring morning.

"Bashi," said a small voice, coming from a side alley. Bashi turned and saw Nini, bareheaded, with his hat in her good hand, standing in the shadow of the alley wall. She did not look as ugly as he remembered.

"Nini!" Bashi said, happy to see a friendly face. "What are you doing here?"

"I've been looking for you. I didn't see you this morning," Nini said. "You said yesterday you would give me coal if I talked to you."

Bashi knocked on his head harder than he'd meant to and winced. "Of course, it's my mistake," he said, and walked over. "But it was only because I was running an important errand this morning. Do you want to hear about it?"

Nini opened her eyes wide, and for the first time Bashi noticed her lovely, dense eyelashes and dark brown irises. He blew at her eyelashes and she winked. He laughed and then rubbed his eyes hard to look sad. "My grandma died last night," he said.

Nini gasped.

"Yes, my grandma who brought me up alone and loved no one but me," said Bashi.

"How did it happen?"

"I don't know. She died in her sleep."

"Then why are you sad?" Nini said. "You should be happy. I've heard people say if a woman dies in her sleep, it means she's been rewarded for her good deeds."

"Happy I am!" Bashi said. "But the thing is, nobody is willing to help me with her burial."

"Where is she now?" Nini asked. "Did you clean and change her? You don't want her to leave unwashed and in old clothes."

"How do I know these things?" Bashi said. "Nobody has died before. You know a lot. Do you want to come and help me?"

Nini hesitated. "I need to go to the marketplace."

"We have enough vegetables to feed you and all your fairy sisters. Coal too. You can get as much as you want. Just come and help a good old woman," Bashi said. "Come on, don't make a friend wait."

A FEW STEPS BEHIND BASHI, Nini counted the lampposts. It was his idea not to walk side by side, so that people would not suspect anything. From the marketplace they turned north and followed the road halfway up the northern mountain. Here the blocks were built in the same fashion as in the valley, but Bashi's house was unusually large. He looked around the alley, which was empty, before unlocking the gate and motioning to Nini to enter. She looked at the mansion in front of her, impressed. The yard was twice the usual size, with a wooden storage cabin as big as the front room of her family's home and with a high brick wall to separate it from the neighbors' yards. His father had been a war hero, Bashi explained, so they were granted more space for their house; however, he added, the construction team hadn't bothered to make it presentable, building a two-room house like every other house on the street, only twice as big.

"You must need a lot of coal to keep this house warm," Nini said when she entered the front room. It was divided by a high shelf into a kitchen—with a sink and a water tap, a stove for cooking, and several cabinets with painted flowers—and a living room, which had its own stove for heating. The wall of the living room was covered with posters showing scenes of heroes and heroines from revolutionary movies and operas. Nini touched the table in the middle of the living room, heavy-looking with old-fashioned carvings on its four sides. Two armchairs, dark red, with intricate patterns carved on their backs, showcased soft, inviting cushions. "Where is your mother?" Nini said.

"Heaven knows. She remarried and left me here."

Stupid woman, Nini thought. No one would ever make her give

up this luxury. Before she voiced her opinion, she heard some familiar rustling. "Mice," she said, and squatted down to look for the source of the noise. Her own house was infested with mice, their nibbling keeping her awake at night. They ripped old clothes and, sometimes, new sheets of cardboard that her family used to fold into matchboxes. Except for the baby, every one of the girls in her family was trained to hunt down the mice and put them to death with a single twist of the neck.

"Don't worry, I've got my cure," Bashi said. He went into the kitchen and, a minute later, came back with a box wrapped in fine red satin. Inside were a few dry roots, wrinkled and earth-colored. "Ginseng roots," Bashi said, and handed the box to Nini.

She touched the red satin with her finger. She did not know how much money the ginseng roots cost; the box itself was expensive-looking and finer than anything her family owned.

"My grandpa was a ginseng picker, and my grandma loved ginseng roots. The best medicine in the world," Bashi said. "But of course they don't make you live forever."

"Where is she now?"

Bashi gestured at the bedroom. "We'll get to it in a minute, but let's take care of the mice first." He broke a small branch from one of the roots and put it by Nini's mouth. "Do you want to taste? Sweet as honey."

Nini opened her mouth but Bashi took the ginseng root away before she had a bite. "Ha, I'm kidding you, silly girl. Only people older than seventy can eat ginseng. Too much fire in it. It'll make your nose bleed and your skin and flesh burn and rot."

Nini shut her mouth tight, a little angry. She did not know why she had agreed to help Bashi. She thought of leaving him with his grandmother and returning to her own life, finding a few deserted cabbage leaves and then going home, watching her little sisters play with the baby, telling them horrible stories if they made Little Sixth cry, threatening to feed them ginseng roots if they dared to complain. But Nini found it hard to move her legs. Bashi had promised many things, coal to take home, vegetables too. Friendship, and something else that Nini could not put into words.

Bashi found a jar of honey and dipped the ginseng root into it. When he got the root out, it looked dewy and delicious. Nini had eaten honey only once, in Teacher Gu's house. Her stomach grumbled.

"Here," Bashi said, pushing a spoon and the jar into Nini's hands. "Eat the whole jar if you like. I don't care for honey myself." He wiped the ginseng root clean of the dripping honey. Nini stuffed her mouth with a spoonful of honey. He was a good person, after all, generous and kind, even though his jokes left her confused at times. "What are you doing?" she mumbled through the sweet stickiness between her lips.

"This is my invention of mouse poison," Bashi said. "Mice love honey, like you, don't they? So they'll eat the ginseng root without thinking and then they'll get such a fire in their stomachs they will wring themselves to death regretting they took that sweet bite of stolen food."

Nini shuddered. She looked at the jar in her hands. "Did you put poison in the honey?"

"Why would I?" Bashi said. "You thought I would poison you? What a funny thought. You're not a mouse. You're my friend."

Nini looked at Bashi's grinning face and felt slightly uneasy. "Do you have many friends?" she asked.

"Of course," Bashi said. "Half the people in Muddy River are my friends."

"You have other girls as friends too?"

"Yes. Men and women. Young and old. Dogs, cats, chickens, ducks."

Nini could not tell if Bashi was joking again. But, if he did have other girls as friends, did they ever come here? The way he had behaved on the way here, making sure people did not see them together, made her suspicious. "Do you bring girls to your house often?" she asked.

Bashi shook his hand at her, his face taking on a serious look.

"Are you all right?" asked Nini.

Bashi wiggled a finger at Nini. "Don't make a sound," he whispered. "Let me think."

Nini looked at Bashi. With his pouting lips and knotted eyebrows, he looked like a small child pretending to be an adult. He was a funny person. She could never tell what he would do next. She had heard neighbors warn their daughters not to talk to strangers; her parents had told her sisters too, but the warning had never been issued to her, as nobody seemed to think she would ever be in danger. Nini studied Bashi again. If he ever did anything very bad, she had a voice to warn his neighbors. But perhaps her worry was unnecessary. He was not a stranger. He was a new friend, and Nini decided that she liked him, in a different way than she liked Teacher Gu and Mrs. Gu. They made her want to be better, prettier, more lovable, but what difference would it make now? They hated her and wouldn't allow her back into their house. Bashi made her forget she was a monster. Perhaps she was not.

"Yes," Bashi said, clapping his hands after a moment and smiling. "I've got the whole plan worked out."

"What plan?"

Bashi beckoned Nini to follow him into the bedroom. The curtain between the two beds was not pulled up. He sat her down on his unmade bed. "Can you keep a secret for me?" Bashi asked her.

Nini nodded.

"You can't tell anyone," he said. "Can you do that?"

"I don't have other friends besides you," Nini said.

Bashi smiled. He drew the curtain and Nini saw the old woman, eyes closed as if in sleep, the blanket pulled up all the way and tucked tight under her chin. Her thin gray hair was coiled in the style of an old woman's bun, with a few strands escaping the hairnet. She looked like an old woman Nini might have liked, but maybe death made people look kind, as none of the old women she met in the marketplace was nice to her.

Bashi put a finger underneath his grandmother's nose for a moment and said, "Yes, she's as dead as a dead person can be. Now you take a vow in front of her."

"Why?"

"Nobody fools around with dead people," Bashi said. "Say this: I swear that I'll never tell Bashi's secret to other people. If I do, his grandmother's ghost will not let me have a good death."

Nini thought it over. She did not see much harm in it, as her parents reminded her often that, with all the pains and troubles she had brought to the family, there would be nothing beautiful in her death. For all Nini cared, there was nothing good in her life either, so why should she be fearful of an ugly death? She repeated the words and Bashi seemed satisfied. He sat down next to Nini and said, "I'm going to kill Kwen's dog."

"Because Kwen beat you yesterday?" Nini asked. She was disappointed. A dead dog didn't seem to fit with a solemn vow in front of a grandmother's body.

"More than that. He's a devil, and I'm going to make the whole town see it. There's a lot I'll tell you later. For now, you just have to know that I'm going to kill that black dog of his before I can go on with the rest of my plan."

Nini nodded. She did not know if she wanted to hear more of Bashi's plan. The old woman, no more than five feet away, distracted her.

"So here's how it will work. Dogs are not old women and they don't take a liking to ginseng roots, right? What is to a dog as a ginseng root is to an old granny?"

Nini looked at Bashi, perplexed.

"Think, girl. A sausage, or a ham, no? Dogs like meat, so do you and I, but we are smarter than dogs," said Bashi. "This is what I'm going to do: I will give the dog a sausage a day until he wags his tail at me whenever he sees me, and then, bang, a sausage cured with pesticide. The poor dog will never imagine that his only friend in this world has killed him. How does that sound?"

Nini fidgeted. It seemed that Bashi could sit here talking to her, or to himself, all morning. If she did not return in time to cook before her parents came home for lunch, as she hadn't the night before for dinner, her mother would let that bamboo broomstick rain down on her back again.

Bashi looked at her. "Don't you like my plan?"

"It's not good to think of other things before taking care of your grandmother," she said. "I don't have all day to sit here talking to you."

"The business of the living comes before that of the dead," Bashi said. "But you're right. I need your help to get her into the casket before you leave."

"You don't want to hire some professionals?"

"I'd have to burn her for them to be hired," Bashi said. "It's all right. We can do it ourselves." He pulled a trunk from the corner of the bedroom. "I think she got everything ready here. Find what you need and dress her up well. I'll get the casket."

Bashi left for the storage cabin before Nini replied. She opened the trunk. Silk and satin clothes lined the inside in orderly layers: coats, jackets, blouses and pants, shoes, and caps. She touched the one on the top with her good hand and her chapped palm caught a thread. What a waste, to bury such fine clothes with a dead woman, Nini thought. She rubbed her hands on the outside of her pants hard before she touched the clothes again. Piece by piece she took them out of the trunk and piled them neatly next to the old woman on the bed. When she reached the bottom of the trunk, she saw several envelopes, each bearing a number. She opened the first one and saw a stack of bills, mostly of ten or five yuan. Nini had never seen so much money. She bit her lips and looked around. When she was sure Bashi was not in sight, she put the money back into the envelope, folded the envelope once in the middle, and slipped it into her pocket.

"The casket is too heavy for me," Bashi said when he came in a moment later. "I wonder if the carpenters put some lead in it. Let's not worry about that part now."

Nini's voice quavered when she pointed out the envelopes to Bashi. He checked their contents and whistled. "I thought she saved everything in our bank account," he said. He pulled out two ten-yuan bills and handed them to Nini.

She shook her head and said she did not want the money.

"Why not? Friends stick together, so why don't we share the good fortune?"

Nini accepted the money. She wondered if the ghost of the old woman was around supervising her afterlife business like old people said, and if so, whether she would be outraged by the envelope in Nini's pocket. But why did she need to worry about a ghost? Nothing could make her life worse than it was now, with Mrs. Gu and Teacher Gu turning their backs on her. Nini pulled back the blanket and peeled off the old woman's pajamas. There was a strange smell, not pungent but oily sweet, and Nini felt nauseated. When her hand touched the old woman's skin, it was leathery and cold. So this was what it would be like when her parents died. The thought made Nini less scared. After all, it would be her job to care for her parents when they got old, and eventually clean them up for burial. She wondered who would see off Teacher Gu and Mrs. Gu. She had more trouble imagining them dead and naked in bed than her own parents. She wished things could be different for the Gus—perhaps the wind would carry them away like smoke before someone's hand touched their skin—but why would she let them off so easily, when they had thrown her out without hesitation?

Bashi loitered on the other side of the curtain without helping Nini. She thought it strange until she realized that perhaps it was not good for a boy to see the naked body of his grandmother. He was a good and honorable person, after all, despite his oddness.

When it came to cleaning the body, Bashi suggested that they use the cold water from the tap in order to spare unnecessary trouble.

Nini disagreed. The folded envelope threatened to jump out of her pocket and reveal itself to Bashi and to the world—she wished she had thought of a better way to hide it, in her shoe so she could step on it firmly—and out of guilt, she insisted on starting a fire so she could bathe the old woman with warm water one more time. Bashi followed her to the kitchen, leaned against a cabinet, and watched her stoke the fire. "What a nice granddaughter-in-law you would make!" he said with admiration.

Nini blushed and pretended that she had not heard. Bashi placed a chair by the stove and sat astride it, both arms hugging the back of the chair. "Have your parents arranged someone for you to marry?" he asked.

What a strange question, Nini thought, shaking her head.

"Have you heard of the saying that the bird with the weakest wings needs to take off earlier?"

"No."

"You should think about it. You don't want to wait too long be- fore looking for a husband."

Nini said nothing and wondered if Bashi was right. Her parents had no wish to marry her off; they would have no one else to wash them before their burials. Had she been the daughter of Mrs. Gu and Teacher Gu, would they have started to worry about her marriage by now, so that when they exited the world, she would not be left alone?

"I'll keep my eyes open for possible candidates, if you like," said Bashi.

Nini watched the fire without replying. The water hummed. When he pressed again, she said, "Let's not let your grandma wait too long."

Bashi laughed. "She won't know now," he said. He helped Nini carry the kettle to the bedroom and then sat down on his own bed on the other side of the curtain. Nini wiped the old woman gently, trying not to study the dry and creased skin, the eerily long and sag- ging breasts, the knotted joints. If not for the stolen envelope in her pocket she would have finished the job in a minute or two. When she finally did, she tried to slip the silk clothes onto the body, but the old woman, completely still and stiff, would not cooperate. Nini yanked one of the old woman's arms out of her sleeve when she felt a small crack. She must have broken the old woman's arm, Nini thought, but she did not care anymore. It took her a long time, with her one good hand, to fasten the coiled buttons of the robes. When she finished with the sleeping cap and silk shoes, she said to Bashi, "Now you can come and see her."

The two of them stood side by side. The old woman looked serene and satisfied in the finest outfit for the next world. After a while, Bashi circled an arm around Nini's shoulder and pulled her closer to him. "What a nice girl you are," he said.

"I need to go home now," she said.

"Let's get whatever you need from the storage cabin."

"Not too much," Nini said when Bashi put several cabbages in her basket. "Otherwise, my parents would question."

"I'll walk you home."

Nini said she would rather he did not walk with her.

"Of course," Bashi said. "Whatever you prefer. But when do I get to see you again? Can you come this afternoon?"

Nini hesitated. She would love to come to this house again, with food and coal and a friend, but it was impossible. In the end, Bashi found the solution—Nini could spend an hour or so every morning in his house and she could get the coal from his storage bin; later in the day, she could come to see him at least once, with the excuse of going to the marketplace.

Nini was sad when they said goodbye. On the way home, she turned into a side alley and took the envelope out of her pocket. Her parents would certainly discover this by the end of the day. She wondered if they would send her to the police because she was a thief, or just happily confiscate the money. She disliked either possibility, so she changed direction and walked toward the Gus' house. When she reached their gate, she could not help but hope that they would throw the door open and welcome her into their arms.

A man walked past Nini and then turned to her. "Are you looking for Teacher Gu and Mrs. Gu?"

Nini nodded, a small hope rising—perhaps they had known she would come, and had asked a neighbor to watch out for her.

"Teacher Gu is ill, and Mrs. Gu is taking care of him in the hospital. They won't be back for some time."

Nini thought of asking for more details, but the man went on before she could say anything. She waited until he was out of sight and slipped the envelope beneath the gate. They would never guess that the money had come from her, but perhaps they would change their minds, when they realized that they were well treated by the world while they themselves had mistreated her; perhaps they would come and look for her when Teacher Gu was released from the hospital.

TONG LEFT HOME after lunch. His parents were taking their midday nap, and Ear was running around somewhere in town. Tong's father was not fond of Ear, and thought it a waste of Tong's life to play with the dog. Tong was happy that Ear found places to wander about until sunset, when the darkness made him less of a nuisance to Tong's father, who would by then have begun his nightly drinking.

It was early for the afternoon class, and Tong took a longer route to school. In the past six months he had explored the many streets and alleys of Muddy River, and he never tired of watching people busy with their lives. The marketplace, where many mouths seemed to be talking at the same time without giving anyone the time to reply, was an exciting place, while the back alleys, with men and women gossiping in different groups, were full of overheard tales about other people's lives. Only an old man pondering over nothing or a loitering cat mesmerized by the sunlight at a street corner would make Tong feel lost, as if they belonged to a secret world to which he had no access.

Life seemed the same after the previous day's event. All these people must have attended the denunciation ceremony, but none of the faces betrayed any memories. The announcements, some torn down and others now only fragments glued to the walls, were no longer noticed by the passersby. In the marketplace, housewives bargained in loud, accusing voices, as if the vendors were all shameless liars. At a state-run vegetable stand, a male sales assistant, bored and idle, formed a pistol with his hand, aiming it at a female colleague's bosom. The woman, in her twenties with a round, full moon face, waved her hand as if chasing away an annoying fly, though every time the man made a banging noise, she laughed. Tong smiled, but when she caught sight of him, she called him a little rascal. "What are you looking at? Be careful or I'll scoop out both your eyeballs."

Tong blushed and turned away. Behind him the male assistant asked the woman why he himself hadn't the right to such a luxury. She replied that she would oblige him on the spot by removing his eyeballs if he really wanted to be blind; the man urged her to do so, saying that he had no use for his eyes now that he had seen her heavenly beauty. Tong walked on. There was a secret code to the adults' world, Tong realized once again, and without knowing the rules, he would always be found offensive for reasons he did not understand.

Around the corner a few chickens sauntered in an alley. Tong fixed his eyes on a bantam hen, willing her to stop pecking, but she searched attentively for food, oblivious. A feral cat quietly approached the chickens from behind a three-legged chair, but before the cat could move closer, an older woman, sitting on a wooden stool in front of a yard, hit the ground with her stick and shrieked. The chickens scattered, flapping their wings and cooing frantically. Caught off guard, Tong took a few breaths to calm down before asking the old woman if everything was all right.

"Things could've gone wrong if not for my vigilance," replied the old woman.

Tong turned to look at the feral cat, studying them at a safe distance. "That cat probably just wanted to play," he said.

"I'm not talking about the cat," the old woman said. Tong looked up at the woman, baffled. "I'm talking about you, boy. You thought you could snatch the hen when nobody was around, huh?"

Tong stammered and said he had never thought of stealing any-one's chicken.

"Don't think I didn't hear that little abacus clicking in your belly when you looked at my chickens," the old woman said. "A village boy like you!"

Tong retreated from the alley. There was little he could say to defend himself.

AFTER LUNCH KAI WENT to the one-room clinic on the first floor of the administration building and told the doctor that she didn't feel well. The doctor, around sixty-five years old, was entitled to give out only cold medicines and slips for a sick leave—with any problem bigger than a cough or a runny nose, the officials and clerks would go to the city hospital across the street.

Three days? the doctor asked while writing Kai's name neatly on top of the slip.

An afternoon would be fine, Kai replied. The doctor put down a cold that required a half day's rest, and then studied his old-fashioned penmanship for a moment with satisfaction before signing his name. Could he run it over to the propaganda department? Kai asked; she did not want her colleagues to make a fuss about a small cold, she explained, and the doctor nodded understandingly, saying he would personally deliver the slip.

Kai went up to the studio through the back stairs and unlocked the bottom drawer of her desk. Inside was an old cotton jacket of brownish gray color, with mismatched buttons, and patches sewn on both elbows. A scarf was tucked into one pocket, and in the other pocket was a white cotton mask. The jacket and scarf had belonged to their previous nanny, and Kai had traded with the woman for a jacket and a scarf of her own. For possible out-of-town assignments, Kai had told the nanny, and even though she had tried to keep the explanation vague, the nanny had replied that of course Kai would not want to wear her woolen jacket or silk scarf to some of the filthy places the lower creatures dwelled in.

Kai changed into the outfit. Underneath where the outfit was kept were a stack of letters, in unmarked envelopes, all from Jialin. Before she locked the drawer again she took one envelope randomly from the stack. Inside she found a long letter about the nature of a totalitarian system, and Kai, having reread it many times and memorized the content by heart, scanned the page; it was written more as a meditation than a letter, and she always wondered if the same letter had been sent to and read by many of Jialin's friends. On a separate page in the same envelope there was a note, a brief paragraph about a new program from Britain, broadcast in Mandarin, which Jialin said he had picked up recently on his shortwave transistor radio. Once again Kai wondered if it was pure imagination when she had sensed his eagerness to share the news with her; it was these shorter notes, addressed to her and about the small details of his life that were largely unknown to her, that made her unwilling to burn his letters as he had instructed her to do.

Jialin and Kai did not see each other often, and sometimes a week or two would pass before she could find an excuse to walk to the town library. They did not talk much, but quietly exchanged letters tucked inside magazines. Sometimes there would be several letters in the envelope he passed to her, and she tried not to wonder whether he might be waiting for her in the reading room day after day, or about his disappointment when she did not show up. The librarian was his friend, Jialin had once said; she allowed him to sit in the reading room as long as he had his mask and gloves on. Kai made herself believe that the librarian, a quiet woman in her late forties, offered enough friendship to Jialin so that his trips to the library were not futile.

Jialin and Kai never planned their encounters, and in their letters they dwelled little on the world where they would have to find excuses to see each other for just five or ten minutes; rather, they wrote about topics they could not discuss in person. She saved every letter from him. She wished she could bring herself to burn them, as she knew he must have dutifully done with every letter she had written to him, but one day she would have nothing left of him but his words, written on sheets of paper from a student's notebook, his handwriting slender and slanted to the right. Sometimes the ink from the fountain pen would run out and the dark blue words turned pale in the middle of a long passage; only when the words became as light as the paper, seemingly engraved onto the page rather than written, would he remember to refill the fountain pen.

Kai put the sheets back into the envelope and locked it with the others. A few minutes later, she left the building, her head wrapped up in the old scarf, her face covered by the mask. Few would recognize her now as the star announcer, and she felt momentarily free.

The library, the only one in town that was open to the public, was in a house that had once served as the headquarters for a local faction of Red Guards. Before that the house had belonged to an old man, but soon after the beginning of the Cultural Revolution the man had killed himself with rat poison. His action baffled the townspeople. The man, said to have been an orphan adopted by a doctor and his wife, had grown up as half son, half apprentice to the doctor, who was the only medical expert in town when Muddy River was no more than a trading post; when the old couple passed away, the man inherited their money and the old-style house, built as a quadrangle around a small and well-groomed garden, near the town center. The man practiced acupuncture occasionally but only for older patients troubled by back pain and arthritis; he was sage-looking, polite, and friendly, and it seemed that there was little reason for him to fear the upcoming revolutionary storms. But as any death had to be accounted for—suicide in particular, since any suicide could be a sinful escape from Communist justice—rumors started that the man was a Manchurian prince who had been biding his time to resurrect the last dynasty; as a famous general had said, a lie repeated a thousand times would become truth, and after a while the old man was deemed a political enemy who had slipped through the net of justice with an easy death. The local Red Guards soon occupied the property, printing out propaganda leaflets and storing ammunition; for months the back rooms also served as a makeshift interrogation room and prison cell.

The library, established now for a mere year and a half, occupied the two front rooms of the house. A few desks and chairs lined one side of the reading room, and on the other side was a butcher's workbench, where a dozen magazines were on display. The librarian sat at a desk at the entrance to the reading room, and if one asked for a book from the collection, she would unlock the door to the other room, where there were no more than ten shelves of books. There were no cards or catalogs; rather, when one was looking for a specific subject, the librarian would go into the collection and then come out with a book or two she had deemed fit for the subject at hand.

Few people in town used the library, and it had not surprised Kai that Jialin chose this place to wait for her. The librarian nodded at Kai distantly when she arrived, and went back to her reading. Kai wondered if the woman recognized her as the news announcer, but probably she just remembered Kai as the woman who stopped by once in a while to check out the few magazine subscriptions in the reading room. Kai did not talk, so that the librarian would not recognize her voice. The woman was a widow, and her late husband, a clerk in the city government, had jumped into the Muddy River when two young boys called for help; the man himself could barely swim and had saved neither his life nor the two boys', in the end. The city government granted the man the title of hero, and when his wife, once a schoolteacher, requested a less challenging job, the government gave her the newly established position as the town's librarian, a position with an abundance of time for her to mourn in quiet.

Jialin was the only person in the reading room. Sitting in a corner and facing the door, he looked at Kai from above his cotton mask before resuming his writing in a thick notebook. She always looked for a change of expression on his face, but there never was one, and she wondered if her own eyes above her mask looked as blank as his. She walked to the magazine display and picked one up, the front cover showing an enlarged picture of the new national leader.

Kai read a few words on one page and then turned to another. The librarian, behind her desk, seemed to pay little attention to the two people in the reading room. Kai took out a piece of paper and scribbled a few words on it before walking past Jialin for another magazine. *We need to talk,* said the note that she dropped next to him. She wondered if he could sense the urgency in it. She had never requested anything before; a letter, drafted and revised, was what she usually passed to him.

Jialin put his notebook away in a bag and got ready to leave. Meet him at his place, instructed the note left inconspicuously next to the magazine that Kai was feigning interest in.

After waiting for a while she left too, walking away from the city center and into a more crowded world where cats, dogs, and chickens shared the alleys and the afternoon sunshine with dozing old men. It was a world Kai had once been familiar with—before she had moved away to the provincial capital she had lived in one of these alleys with her parents and siblings. The shabby house had been one of the reasons for her mother's unhappiness, as she believed that Kai's father had not climbed up the ladder fast enough to move them into one of the modern buildings. Only after Kai's marriage to Han did her parents get the flat that her mother had been dreaming of all her life. Their farewell to the alley was celebrated by Kai and her family at the time, but now she wished she had never left this world.

Kai found Jialin's house and pushed the slate gate ajar. The yard, the standard size of fifteen feet by twenty, was filled with all sorts of junk: unused pickle jars placed haphazardly on top of one another; inner tubes twisted and hung from the handlebars of a rusty bicycle, its two wheels missing; cardboard boxes crushed flat and piled high; three metal chain locks displayed prominently, forming a triangle inside which were three bayonets. They belonged to his three younger brothers, Jialin had told Kai the first time she visited him; he was walking her out to the gate then, and the passing comment about his brothers, along with the clutter, were mere facts about some strangers' lives. But six months later, seeing them again, Kai knew she would one day remember these details as part of the world Jialin had inhabited; one day they would be used to construct him in her memory.

The door to the house opened. "Do you need help?" asked an older woman wrapped in a long cotton coat.

Kai pointed to the shack and said in a muffled voice that she was looking for Jialin. The older woman, who was no doubt Jialin's mother, with traces of him recognizable in her face, nodded and waved before closing the door.

His mother had learned not to ask about his life, Jialin explained when he caught her glancing back at the closed door of the house. He let Kai into the shack and pointed to the only chair.

"Your mother—she's not working today?" Kai asked.

"She has a cold."

"And your brothers—are they at school?"

Jialin looked surprised by the small talk that never occurred between them. He hoped they were at school, he said, but rumors were that they had become part of a street gang and skipped school for their own business.

"Do your parents know?"

"The parents are always the last to learn of any bad news."

"Don't you want to talk to your brothers, or at least let your parents know?"

They expected him not to interfere with their lives, Jialin said; in return they left him to his own world. Besides, they were only his half brothers, and there was little reason for him to step in front of their birth father and claim any responsibility. Did he share these stories about his life with his other friends? Kai wondered, thinking of all the questions she could not ask him.

Jialin waited for a moment, and when Kai did not speak, he asked if there was anything she needed to speak to him about. Yes, Kai replied, the same request she had put to him all along: a protest on Shan's behalf, not for her life now but for her rights to be recognized as wrongfully executed. Kai spoke of the suspiciously expedited trial and of Shan's kidneys, transplanted into another man's body; she spoke of Mrs. Gu's insubordinate action at the crossroad, remembering Mrs. Gu's straight back when she had been dragged away from the smoldering fire. It was time to wake up the townspeople of Muddy River to the atrocity and injustice done to a daughter and a mother.

Neither spoke for a moment after Kai had finished her speech. Then Jialin beckoned her to a corner of the shack and removed some plastic sheeting. Underneath were a mimeograph set and a pile of newly printed leaflets. Kai picked one up; she recognized Jialin's handwriting. It was a letter addressed to the townspeople of Muddy River, dated on the day of the execution. Kai looked up, perplexed. "Did you have them ready yesterday?"

"Yes."

"I didn't know you had done everything by yourself."

Jialin shook his head and said it had been done with the help of several other friends.

"But why did we wait if you had the leaflets ready?" Kai asked.

"Situations change every day," Jialin said. Then he asked her if she had heard any news about the democratic wall in Beijing. Kai shook her head, and Jialin seemed surprised. He thought she would have heard the news even though she would not be allowed to broadcast it, Jialin said. She replied that she was no more than a voice for the government, and she relied on him more than anyone else for real news about the world.

A wall had been set up in the national capital, Jialin said, where people could express their opinions freely; in the past few weeks many had posted comments, requesting a more open and democratic government. As he spoke Kai felt a strange sense of loss. She did not know how long Jialin had been following the news, but he had never told her this in his letters. She imagined young people gathered in groups in the nation's capital, sharing their dreams. Even in Jialin's shack his other friends must stay up late at night sometimes, hoping for any positive news on the shortwave radio.

Where was she on those nights, but playing out her role as a dutiful wife and a good mother?

Could she meet Jialin's friends? Kai asked.

Jialin took off his glasses. He massaged his eyes, wiped the lenses with his sleeve, and put the glasses back on. "You do understand you're not as free as most of us are, don't you?" he asked gently. "My hope is not for you to be part of this. At least not yet."

"Why? Can't you trust me?"

Jialin shook his head. Once the leaflets were delivered to the world, he said, waving a hand at the pile, there was no turning back for anyone, and he would have not only his own life but also the lives of his friends to be responsible for.

"Am I different from your other friends?" Kai asked.

"I'd be lying if I said no," Jialin said, and explained that there had been some disagreement among his friends; he was vague in his explanation but Kai realized right away that it was not Jialin but his friends, whoever they were, who did not trust her. She wondered if he had spoken up for her in front of his friends, and if they had questioned him about how he had known her, to defend her. Her letters, read and then burned by him, would not be of any assistance, but even if he had kept them, she could not imagine his showing her letters to his friends. "They may not know you as well as I do," Jialin said, apology in his eyes.

"And you won't help them get to know me better?"

He had to protect everyone, Jialin said, and it was his averted eyes, more than his words, that made Kai understand there was more than the simple unfriendliness of his cohorts that he was concealing.

"So if I went to the police to report on you, your friends would be spared, as I would not know who they are?" Kai asked.

"I'm protecting you too," Jialin said. "Each one of us could be the one to sell out our friends."

"Was it a decision agreed to by all your friends, for you to write to me?" Kai asked. "Or was there disagreement in the first place?"

It mattered little, Jialin said, now that he had let her down. But she wanted to know, Kai insisted. They had thought of finding someone in the government, Jialin said, but then the plan was determined to be immature.

"So you wrote to me on your own?"

Jialin looked away without replying.

"Why?" Kai asked.

Years ago he had seen her act as Autumn Jade, Jialin said finally, and he had always wondered since then what kind of person she was, whether she could put on a performance like that without having the purity and nobleness of a martyr in her heart. "You could've been a different person and I'd have been sitting out my sentence now. You could say I took a bet with myself, writing to you, because I wanted to know, but how I did not lose the bet I do not know. By pure chance, perhaps. I'd not have been surprised if it had turned out the other way," Jialin said, trying to suppress the cough that threatened to overtake him at any moment.

So that was the history they had been avoiding all along, Kai thought, imagining Jialin as an audience, before his illness had taken over perhaps, before her marriage. That one's existence could extend beyond one's knowledge was not a new discovery; many times in the theater troupe Kai had received letters from her fans, some written under real or made-up names, others left unsigned. But the crossing of paths at a wrong time—too early or too late, and Kai could no longer tell which was the case in her encounter with Jialin— could not be understood. It was to be endured, as anything beyond one's control. Had she met Jialin not as a new mother but as an older woman, Kai thought, imagining the time when Ming-Ming would be a young man, she would perhaps be grateful for this encounter; she would even be free to choose again. But illness would soon be replaced by death on Jialin's part, before she was liberated by time; soon their paths would part.

"You must know I am not turning you away as a friend," Jialin said gently.

He had enough to work on now, and she would respect his friends' wishes and leave them alone, she said; there was no need for him to worry about how she felt. She knew where to find him, as he knew where to find her. For a moment her voice wavered, and she left abruptly before they might weaken and let out all that was better left unsaid.

THE OTHER PATIENTS in the ward must have heard about his daughter. They glanced at Teacher Gu when they thought he was not paying attention. When he looked back, they turned their eyes away and lowered their heads. Teacher Gu saw their efforts to refrain from talking about the case. A pitiful man, they must be thinking, unable to stand up straight, easily defeated. Teacher Gu did not talk to his ward mates. When visiting time came, and their wives and children swarmed into the ward, he hid under the striped blanket and pretended to be asleep. His wife did not talk to the other patients and their families either. She came with a thermos of chicken soup and sat on a chair by his bedside; half past the visiting hour, when he still refused to acknowledge her, she rocked him gently and told him that he'd better drink the soup before she had to leave. He let her prop him up on the pillow; she moved from the chair to the bedside, spoon in her hand. He obeyed and drank the soup without making a fuss and waited for three days before asking why she had killed their two hens for a useless man; the hens were their only children, he thought of saying, but did not let the cruel remark slip out. She had not touched their hens, she said, offering no explanation as to how she had managed to afford the chickens. She bought other food too, from the expensive store next to the hospital—canned fruit of all kinds, dried-milk powder, dates cured with honey, condensed orange juice that Teacher Gu believed to be made of nothing but saccharine and orange dye. After another day, he could not help but ask about the money for these unnecessary luxuries. She hesitated and said that someone kindhearted and sympathetic had slipped money into their yard. He imagined that she had withdrawn money from their meager savings account and then agonized over how to cover the expense, making up philanthropic strangers he no longer believed existed. He didn't cross-examine her lies. The world was cold enough; if she wanted to light a small fire of hope, he would let her, but he refused to be drawn into her fantasy.

The stroke, not a fatal one, had left Teacher Gu's left side paralyzed, though it was not a serious case compared to a few other old men in the ward, and he was expected to recover some ability to move. Dr. Fan, a woman in her forties, harshly ordered about all the patients in the ward when she oversaw their physical therapy; and the other patients and their relatives, despite the deference they showed to her face, had nicknamed her the Tigress.

On the fifth day of Teacher Gu's stay in the hospital, Dr. Fan was late for her morning rounds, and when she did come she wasn't wearing her doctor's white cap. Teacher Gu noticed that her short hair had been transformed into many small and busy curls. She must have wanted not to destroy her new perm—indeed it was the first perm she'd had in her life, as her generation had grown up at a time when a permanent wave was an illegal bourgeois legacy. After being ordered to lift his arm and leg, which he could not possibly do, Teacher Gu complimented Dr. Fan on her new hairstyle.

Taken aback, Dr. Fan blushed without saying anything. She moved quickly to the next bed and soon regained control of herself by chiding the man lying there. Her flustered gesture saddened Teacher Gu. He took pity on Dr. Fan, and a generation of women like her, who had spent their best years in dull-colored and baggy clothes and short straight hair that had stripped them of their feminine beauty, and who were now trying to catch the last of their no longer youthful days, hoping to look beautiful. But then what right did he have to think of these women in such a way, when he himself, old and invalid, was the object of people's pity?

There were eighteen beds in the recovery ward, fifteen of them occupied, mostly by old people suffering from strokes and cerebral hemorrhages. One man, however, had a unique condition that fascinated everybody. Teacher Gu too paid attention to the discussions among the patients, families, and nurses, even though he never let it show. From what he had overheard, Dafu, who was in his late forties and had lost his wife a year earlier, had been a healthy man before he committed himself for a special operation to take out his gallbladder—he had gallstones but did not suffer much, and it seemed that there was little surgical necessity for it. However, news came that the army hospital in the provincial capital needed a model patient to demonstrate a new, drugless anesthetic method. Dafu, through some connection, got himself chosen for this political assignment on the condition that his two daughters would be granted positions in factories. The daughters, both educated youths who had been sent down to the countryside for years and had just returned to the city, had not been able to find jobs. The father underwent surgery without anesthesia, except for five acupuncture needles in his hand. Told to stay still while he was filmed, Dafu suffered so much pain during the procedure that afterward both his legs were paralyzed for no clear medical reason, and his ability to urinate was permanently impaired. After a few days of observation, the perplexed army doctors decided that the problems were psychological and sent Dafu back to Muddy River.

It amazed Teacher Gu that a man could exercise such stoicism for his daughters. Dafu, however, did not think himself a hero, as his ward mates did. A low-ranking clerk, he was easily embarrassed when his selflessness was commented upon. He apologized when he failed to urinate. "Relax," Nurse Shi, the older one who had gentler hands than the others, urged him. The doctors had told Dafu that because he had used such great control to endure the pain of the operation, his muscles were in a constant seizure, which explained his symptoms. "Relax," Nurse Shi repeated. "Use your imagination. Think of when you were young and could not hold your pee. Did you wet your bed when you were a boy?"

"Yes," Dafu said.

"Close your eyes and think of the time you wet your bed. You want to hold it but you can't because oh, oh, it's coming out. It's coming out." Nurse Shi's voice became breathy and urgent, and at such moments, the patients, even the four old men on the far end of the ward who enjoyed drawing attention by moaning and complaining about nonexistent problems, dared not make a noise. To further stimulate his imagination, Nurse Shi would order a young nurse to turn on the tap at the washstand and have the water drip into an empty basin. Dafu sat awkwardly at his bedside, supported by Nurse Shi and another nurse, his pants rolled down to his ankles and a white enamel bedpan waiting between his legs. The water would drip, Nurse Shi would murmur encouragements, and everyone else in the room would hold his breath until, eventually, one of the four old men at the far end of the room would break the silence and yell that he could not hold his pee anymore, and could someone please pass him a bedpan. A young training nurse would try to conceal her joy as she obliged the old man; Nurse Shi would comfort Dafu, saying he was doing better and she believed that the next time he would succeed. His face the color of a beet, Dafu would apologize for all the trouble he had brought to the nurses and everyone else in the room. He apologized constantly, even to his two daughters, who came to the ward to show him the white lab coats they wore for their positions at the pharmaceutical factory, white rather than the regular blue, which would, in the eyes of people unfamiliar with their jobs, promote them to the same level as a nurse or perhaps even a doctor. The daughters did not talk about the possibility of attracting suitable men with the coats, but the father saw such hope in their eyes; they were twenty-six and twenty-seven, no longer young for marriage. At night he practiced secretly in the darkness, willing his legs to move so he would not become a burden to his daughters; the prospect of marrying a woman with a bedridden father might frighten away potential suitors, and Dafu imagined his dead wife looking down at him with disapproval from the heavens. On the morning of the day when she had been run over by a truck, they had had an argument over some small household chores; she had married the worst man in the world, who was of little use to his wife and daughters, she complained then, the last words she said to him. He had wondered ever since if she believed it, but she was known to be unable to choose the right words when she was overtaken by her temper, and perhaps the comment was not meant to harm him. There was no way he could know now, Dafu thought; all he could do was prove to himself otherwise.

At the moment Dafu wept into his pillow, parental worries plagued many more hearts outside the hospital. A mother who had just helped her panicking daughter with her first period could not close her eyes next to her snoring husband. She remembered her own mother, constantly checking the panties of all her daughters for fear they would be raped or seduced by strangers. The daughter who had escaped the sad fate envisioned by her mother had become a mother herself, and was now horrified that the ghost of her mother's fear had decided to make its home in her own heart.

In another bed in the same block, a man reminded his wife to warn their two teenage daughters not to dress up in bright colors. But it was no longer forbidden to look beautiful, his wife pointed out, defending their daughters and thinking about her own youthful years that had withered before she had ever blossomed. People would notice and talk, the father said, unwilling himself to broach the awkward topic with his daughters, who had, with their swelling breasts and fuller lips, made him avert his eyes and feast instead on other girls' young bodies along the street.

Nini's parents did not sleep. Her father's hand on her mother's belly, which was starting to show, they talked with hope about a son, not wanting to share their dread about yet another girl. On the other end of the brick bed, Nini eavesdropped, praying to unknown gods and goddesses that they would be given a baby girl.

Jialin's mother worried too, about the remaining time in Jialin's life, but more about his three younger brothers, who had stolen her money to buy three pairs of sunglasses. Earlier that day they had come home with the shining black things on their faces, and when she looked at them she saw in their lenses six duplicates of herself, face tired and hair gray. She wondered if they were on their way to becoming the newest gang members in the city, but when she talked to her husband about this worry, he replied that it was natural for the boys to grow into men.

In the Huas' shack, Mrs. Hua dreamed about her seven daughters. Sometimes they would come to talk with her about a newborn baby girl who did not please the husband's family, or a long-awaited son whose arrival had finally stopped another husband's beating; the younger ones talked about their orphanages, where they were too cold or too hungry or had too much labor. On this specific night the youngest daughter, born with a cleft palate and nicknamed Bunny by her older sisters, came and told Mrs. Hua that she had decided to go home; she was coming to say goodbye to her parents because the years she had lived with them were the happiest of her life. For a moment, Mrs. Hua felt the girl's breath on her cheeks, and then the girl vanished, leaving Mrs. Hua in a cold sweat. She bit her finger; the pain was real, so she was not dreaming. She lay in the darkness for a moment and started to cry. Bunny's ghost had come to say her final farewell, Mrs. Hua told her husband when he was woken up; something had happened and the poor girl was now on her way to the otherworld. Old Hua held Mrs. Hua's hand; after a while Mrs. Hua calmed down. They would never know what or who had killed their little girl, she said, and he replied that perhaps heaven had known it would be harder for the girl to live on.

$\mathcal{A}$ middle-aged carpenter and his apprentice, both in their undershirts and covered with sawdust and sweat, moved their sawhorse to let Kai enter her flat. The hallway shared by the four families on the floor had been turned into a temporary workshop, and out of curiosity Kai asked which family they were working for. The harmless question, however, seemed to throw both men into instant confusion; they glanced at each other, and when the older man lowered his head, the young apprentice replied that they had been assigned a political task by the city government.

Kai frowned. Before she had a chance to question the men further, the door to her flat opened and Han smiled at her mysteriously. He had a surprise for her, he said, and told her to close her eyes. The young carpenter glanced at Kai and Han with timid curiosity, and Han told the boy to keep working, before he pulled Kai into the flat. What was it? she asked, but Han insisted that she keep her eyes closed. Kai sighed and let him hold her hand and guide her into the living room. When she was told to open her eyes, she saw in the middle of the room a huge cardboard box with a blue television set printed on it.

"When did you get out of town?" Kai asked. The only place to buy a television set was in the provincial capital, with a special permit, and even though Han had been talking about buying a TV for days, Kai thought it would take weeks before permission could be granted.

"I didn't take one step out of my office today," Han said. "And I didn't have to spend a penny."

Kai nodded absentmindedly. Han seemed to be disappointed by her lukewarm reaction. "It's a present," he said. "And only three families in Muddy River got them. Guess who?"

"Your parents and the mayor, and us?"

"Nothing escapes your eyes," said Han. "Who else deserves such a prize?"

"For the kidney transplant?"

Han smiled and said that the mayor and his wife had recommended the carpenters, as they had finished a top-quality TV stand for them just two days earlier, and he had asked that the carpenters finish by the next day. Shouldn't the neighbors be consulted before they let the carpenters use a public space? Kai asked, but Han dismissed the question and said that he believed the neighbors would feel just fine about it—the men in the three other families occupied positions not much lower than Han's, yet they were the ones who had reached their limits, as Han put it; he himself was the only one on their floor with a future.

Kai nodded, and then asked if there was other news.

"I need to talk to you about something," Han said as the door to the nursery opened. Ming-Ming walked out on tiptoes, his hands pulled up by the nanny's hands. He looked at his parents and led the nanny toward the sofa. Han had rearranged the furniture in the living room to make room for the TV stand, and when Ming-Ming climbed onto the sofa, now close to the light switch, he reached out to turn on the light, and then off, and then on and off. Kai and Han, both preoccupied with their own thoughts, watched the baby in the blinking light.

Finally, Han made a gesture toward the nanny. Kai picked Ming-Ming up and kissed him, but he wiggled out of her arms to go to the sofa. Kai asked the nanny about the baby's lunch and then told her to dress the baby warmly and take him for a stroll around the city square. A walk before the nap? the nanny asked in surprise, and Kai answered that it was a warm day and he might as well get some fresh air.

Han stood next to the window and watched the street. "I'm sure you've heard of the situation out there," he said, once the nanny had shut the door to the flat.

Fifteen hundred copies of the first leaflet had been distributed three nights earlier, but by noon the next day they had been torn down by the sanitation squad, and no one had mentioned it since. A couple of nights later a second leaflet showed up, this time talking not only about Gu Shan's execution but also about a democratic wall movement in Beijing. By now Kai thought it would be suspicious to pretend to be unaware of it. "The leaflets," she said, feeling her words filled with a bitterness that only she herself could detect. She wished she had been part of what was happening in Muddy River.

"This nonsense about the democratic wall, and the talk of the dead woman, neither would be much of a headache if treated separately."

"Why?"

Han waved a hand to dismiss the topic. Lunch was ready, he said, and they might as well enjoy a good homemade meal.

Rarely did Kai ask Han about the affairs he managed, though he had a habit of recounting his daily activities when they lay in bed at night. Kai decided to wait before asking any more questions. They sat down and ate their lunch, neither talking for a moment, and then Han cheered himself up by turning the conversation back to the new television set. It was a fourteen-inch black-and-white, imported from Japan, bigger and of better quality than the one he had originally set his heart on; the three sets had come as a surprise that morning, a gesture of gratitude, no doubt, from their powerful friend in the provincial capital.

It seemed a perfect invitation for Kai to ask questions. "Who is this mysterious friend you keep talking about?"

Han thought about this and then shook his head. "I'll let you know as soon as we find out where these leaflets are coming from."

"Is there anything wrong?"

"Not from what I can see," Han said, and reached across the plates of food to pat Kai's hand. "These are things you shouldn't bother yourself about. Politics is not for women. The last thing I want is for you to become my mother," Han said with a grin. Before Kai could reply, he straightened his face and imitated his mother's speech at the May Day gathering the previous year; Kai's mother-in-law was nicknamed the "Iron Woman" behind her back by her inferiors.

Kai didn't expect Han to be aware of such talk, as he and his father were known to be admirers of the woman they shared. "You should be thankful for your mother," Kai said. "You wouldn't have been so lucky, if not for her."

"Oh, I love her dearly. Still, you wouldn't want our son to have a mother like her, would you?" said Han with a wink. There was a knock at the door. Kai, expecting the nanny with the baby asleep in her arms, went to the door but found Han's parents, both waiting, unsmiling, to be let in. She greeted them, and they nodded and entered the flat without a word. In a low, stern voice they told Han, who had already gone to the kitchen and poured two cups of tea for them, to come up to their flat right away.

Kai stood by the door and said farewell to her parents-in-law. Neither explained anything to her, and Han only squeezed her shoulder and told her to relax, before he ran to catch up with them. The carpenter's apprentice stopped his work and watched Kai. When the older man coughed and told him to mind his own business, he smiled shyly at Kai and went back to sanding the wood.

Han did not wait for the carpenters to finish their work before setting out for the provincial capital that afternoon. A special liaison for the mayor, Han explained when he returned from his parents' flat; the mayor and Han's parents wanted him to be at the capital to gather firsthand information about how Beijing was reacting to the democratic wall before they could make a decision themselves about the leaflets. He did not know how long he would have to be there, Han said, his spirit unusually low. Kai imagined that he had been warned not to reveal anything to her, but when she pressed him for details, he admitted that the situation was difficult for everyone in the administration, as the central government in Beijing did not have a clear attitude toward the democratic wall. Would it mean that some change would be introduced in national policies? Kai asked. That would be the end of his career, Han answered. He looked despondent. A boy put into a man's position by his parents. Kai looked at him almost with sympathy. She touched his cheek with her palm, but even before she could find some empty words to comfort him, Han grabbed her hand, and asked her if she would still love him if he lost the game.

What was there for him to lose? she wondered, but when she put the question to him, Han only sighed and said that she was right, that it was too early to give up, and he would remain hopeful.

Kai asked for another sick leave slip from the doctor and took the afternoon off. She did not know Teacher Gu's address, but when she searched the area, the first housewife she asked about the Gus led Kai to the alley. Number 11, the woman told her, and as a passing comment she said how miserable Mrs. Gu's life was now, with no children to share the burden of an invalid husband.

Kai knocked, and it took Mrs. Gu a while to come to the gate, a hen clucking under her arm. She must have the wrong address, Mrs. Gu said before Kai could open her mouth.

"I heard Teacher Gu was not feeling well," Kai said. "I've come to see you both."

"We don't know you," Mrs. Gu said. She studied Kai for a moment and her stern face softened. "Were you the one to leave the money here?"

Money? Kai said, her confusion disappointing Mrs. Gu. Who could it be then? she mumbled to herself.

Kai looked around at the alley, empty but for an old man dozing in the sun. Could she come into the yard and talk to Mrs. Gu for a few minutes? Kai asked, and Mrs. Gu, looking skeptical, nonetheless let her through the gate. The hen cooed and Mrs. Gu released it, telling it in a conversational tone to stay in the sun so as not to get a cold. The hen sauntered away, pecking at its own shadow.

Kai brought out the copies of the two leaflets she had saved. "I came to talk to you and Teacher Gu about these," she said.

Mrs. Gu looked at the unfolded sheets without reading them. "My husband is in the hospital," she said. "He can't talk to you."

They were leaflets posted on Gu Shan's behalf, Kai said, and explained that not all the people in Muddy River supported the court's decision. Mrs. Gu looked at Kai for a moment and asked sharply if she was the news announcer.

"Yes," Kai said.

"Did you know my daughter?"

Kai told her that she had moved to Muddy River after graduating from a theater school in the provincial capital. She had always been an admirer of Shan, Kai said, but what difference would her words make?

"My daughter, she wouldn't have done your job any less well than you. She was a good singer. She was always the best," said Mrs. Gu. She glanced at the leaflets. "Did you write those?" she asked.

She wished she had, Kai said, but no, she had done little to help.

"But you know who did it? Are they your friends?"

Kai hesitated and said yes, some of them were her friends.

"Tell your friends they are very kind," Mrs. Gu said. "But no, we don't need them to do anything like this." Mrs. Gu added that she was only happy her husband was in the hospital. It would have upset him had he seen the leaflets.

"But we—they—are only trying to help," Kai said. "The mistake has to be corrected. Shan was a pioneer among us. And she would be comforted to know that friends and comrades are fighting for what she fought for."

Mrs. Gu gazed at Kai for a long moment and sighed. She was

grateful, Mrs. Gu said, to hear that Kai and her friends had not forgotten Shan. Nor had she herself, Mrs. Gu said. But she had a sick husband to tend to and there was little she could do for them, nor they for her. They were not asking for anything, Kai assured her; she said that the only reason she had come to visit the couple was to let them know that they were not alone in this world, where her daughter's memory lived on as an inspiration.

"You're very good at giving speeches," Mrs. Gu said. Kai blushed at the comment, but Mrs. Gu seemed to mean little ill. "Shan was like that too. She was the most eloquent child," Mrs. Gu said gently. "How old are you?"

"Twenty-eight."

"And you're married? Do you have children?"

Kai replied that she and her husband had a young boy.

"And your parents, are they well?"

Her father had passed away, Kai replied. Mrs. Gu nodded without adding words of sympathy. "It's kind of you to come and see us, and to let us know how you care about Shan. I don't know your friends and what their stories are, but you are a mother and a daughter. Have you thought how your mother would feel about your doing this? Have you ever thought of her?"

Kai did not know how to answer the question. She hadn't visited her mother for a few weeks now, even though they lived within a five-minute walk of each other.

"You haven't thought of her at all, have you?" Mrs. Gu said. "Daughters are all alike. Their parents weigh little in their decisions, and I don't blame you for it. Have you thought about your son?"

Yes, Kai said; she was doing this so that her son could live in a better world. But all parents would think that way, Mrs. Gu said; they wanted to make everything better for their children, but the truth was that what they ended up doing was making their children's lives worse.

"I don't understand that, Mrs. Gu."

"Think of Shan," Mrs. Gu said, more vehemently now, her face flushed. "We thought we could give her the best education possible because my husband was one of the most knowledgeable people in town. But what did we do but turn her into a stranger? Your parents must have worked hard to get you a good job, but what are you doing except putting yourself in danger without thinking of them? You think you're doing something for your son, but the last thing he needs is for you to go out and talk about secret leaflets with people."

Her family was not her sole responsibility, Kai replied. Mrs. Gu stared at Kai; she felt for Kai's mother, she said, her narrowing eyes filled with gentle sadness for a brief moment, before it was taken over by a coldness. It was time for Kai to leave now, Mrs. Gu said, as her husband was waiting for her in the hospital.

FOR TONG, spring this year had started on March 21, the day of the equinox, when he had seen the first swallow coming back from the south and had noted it in his nature journal. Swallows were the messengers of spring, Old Hua said; they were the most nostalgic and loyal birds, coming back year after year to their old nests. But that meant they would never get a family of swallows to live under their roof, Tong worried aloud, because there was no nest there. In that case, Old Hua said, they had to wait for a young couple who would not return to their parents but would make a new home of their own.

The next day, Tong saw a flock of geese flying across the sunny afternoon sky, the head goose pointing north. Like swallows, geese never mistook where they were flying to, Old Hua said, but when Tong asked him why they never got lost, the only answer Old Hua had was that they were born that way.

Every afternoon after school, Tong went to the city square, where the day's newspapers were displayed in glass cases. There were more than a dozen to choose from, newspapers printed both in Beijing and in the provincial capital, but for Tong, the most important one was *Muddy River Daily,* from which he copied the temperatures of the local weather forecast into his journal. Tong had read, in an outdated copy of *Children's Quarterly,* that Old Hua had found a few weeks earlier, about a boy who had for years recorded temperatures three times a day in a nature journal. The year the boy turned thirteen, he noticed a change in the temperature pattern and successfully predicted an earthquake, earning him the title of "Science Hero" for saving people's lives. The story did not say what kind of change the boy had noticed, leaving Tong to construct his own theory about that, but the article showed him a new way to become a hero. His parents, of course, would say they did not have money idling in their pocket for a thermometer, so Tong did not ask. Instead, he decided to use the local newspaper. When Old Hua heard about the nature journal, he wondered why anyone needed to rely on the numbers at all, when one's own skin was the best way to detect minute changes in the air temperature. Tong did not tell the old man of his plan, holding on to the secret and hoping that one day Muddy River would thank him for his vigilance.

According to the weather forecast, the temperature had climbed above the freezing point on March 22, the day after the denunciation ceremony, and the wind in the midafternoon no longer felt like a razor on one's face. Children left school bareheaded, some throwing their hats high into the sky and then catching them as they fell. Ear came home in the evening with a girl's pink mitten, a hole in the tip of the thumb; Tong tried it on, the right size for his hand, and he wiggled his thumb out of the hole, pretending it was a puppet. He told Ear that they would put the mitten by Chairman Mao's statue the following morning, in case the girl, like himself, liked the city square.

The next morning, Tong went out into the alley and saw leaflets posted on the wall, within his reach if he stood on a stack of bricks. Tong peeled one off the wall and read it. The leaflet talked about things that Tong did not understand, and two days later, another leaflet found its way to their alley. The secretive way they came to his door alarmed Tong. They reminded him of the stories he had learned in school, about underground Communist Party members risking their lives to spread the truth to the people, but in the new China, where everybody lived as happily as if in a jar of honey, like it said in the new song they had just learned at school, what use did they have for the leaflets?

Tong wondered whom he could talk to. His parents would not be interested in listening to him, and his schoolteacher taught as if nothing had happened. He patted Ear and said they should team up and solve the mystery together. "Show me anything suspicious," Tong said. "Nothing is too small."

Ear circled Tong agitatedly. Tong did not know that Ear had heard, the previous nights, muffled steps in the alley, stopping and then continuing. Ear had jumped as high as he could and then stood with his front paws on the fence, sniffing, but his latest training prevented him from sounding the alarm. Both nights it was the same person, whose scent, of earth and horse manure and winter haystacks and harvested wheat, reminded Ear of his home village. Like Tong and Ear himself, the night stranger had come from the countryside, where Ear had once chased a squealing piglet until he bumped into the mountainlike body of a sow unperturbed by her baby's dilemma, and where he had barked many times at the passing horse wagon, on which sat a hitchhiking peddler, his rattle drum flipped briskly in his skillful hand, the plimp-plump, plimp-plump never overpowered by the barking of Ear and his companions. In the past six months, Ear had gotten used to the villagers from the mountains who brought with them the smell of stale snow and ancient pine trees, of freshly skinned hares and newly gathered mushrooms, but they were different from the smell of his home on the plain. The stranger at night made Ear fretful.

Fretful too were the members of the city council, the Muddy River Communist Party branch, and other officials. The first leaflet, a letter questioning Gu Shan's retrial, had not induced much alarm; it was more of a nuisance, some people dissatisfied with their lives, for whatever reason, using the dead woman's body as an excuse to make a fuss. Better to wait, the mayor had decided, and he had requested increased surveillance at night. But the extra security guards, cold and hungry in their late-night patrolling, were not able to catch the people who posted the second leaflet. A democratic wall movement in Beijing had begun a new page in the nation's history, the leaflets informed the citizens of Muddy River; why did they never get a chance to hear the news, to know what was going on in the national capital; why could they not speak their minds without being put to death like Gu Shan?

The news of the protest had been accessible to only a few high-ranking officials, and the connection made between Gu Shan's execution and the situation in Beijing seemed a sinister conspiracy, more so when uncertainties raged over how to react to the democratic wall movement not only in the provincial capital but also in Beijing. Daily these veterans of local politics read and reread the news, fresh off the classified wire service, about developments in Beijing. There were clearly two camps, both with significant representation in the central government and among party leaders. Were the leaflets in Muddy River the spawn of the democratic wall seven hundred miles away? And what should they do, which side should they take?—the questions puzzled these people who had never worried over the lack of a meal, a bed, or a job. Offices became minefields where one had to watch out for oneself, constantly defining and redefining friends, enemies, and chameleons who could morph from friends to enemies and then back again. With their fates and their families' futures in their hands, these people sleepwalked by day and shuddered by night. What would they do about these leaflets that only spelled trouble?

In the period of indecision and uncertainty, old winter-weary snow began to melt. The ground became less solid, the black dirt oozing with moisture in the sunshine. The willow trees lining both sides of the main street took on a yellow hue, which lasted a day or two before the buds turned green. It was the best green of the year—clean, fresh, shining. Boys from middle schools cut off the tender tips of the willow branches, took out the soft pith, and turned the sheaths into willow flutes. The few musical ones among them played simple melodies on the flutes and made girls their age smile.

The ice in the river rumbled at night, resisting the spring, but when the daytime came, its resolve was melted in the sunshine. The middle school boys, despite repeated warnings from their schools and parents, let the ice drifts carry them downstream, their feet planted on the ice as firmly as possible; when the drifts came closer, they tried to push one another off into the water. Sometimes one of them lost his balance and plunged into the river, and all the other boys would stamp their feet and shriek, making animal-like noises. The soaked boy dodged the ice drifts, scrambled onto the bank, and ran home, laughing too because this kind of failure did not bother him. The same thing could happen to anyone; the next day, he would be one of the winning boys, laughing at another boy falling in. It was a game, and it guaranteed neither a permanent victory nor a loss that would last beyond overnight.

Down from the mountains and over the Cross-river Bridge, villagers came with newly hatched chicks and ducklings in bamboo baskets, the first batch of edible ferns picked by the small hands of children with smaller children on their backs, deer that had not escaped the hunters' buckshot and now came in disjointed forms: antlers, hides, jerky, bucks' members labeled as deer whips and said to improve a man's performance in his *bedroom business.*

April, too, came, and with it the approaching Ching Ming, the long-awaited first holiday of the season, the day for people to bring their ancestors and their recent dead freshly steamed rolls painted with spring grass, newly brewed rice wine, and other offerings. As immigrants in a recently built city, the people of Muddy River did not have family burial grounds and ancestral compounds close by to visit, so Ching Ming became a holiday as much for the dead as for the living. Drugstores and peddlers prepared bunches of candles and incense for sale; edible green dye too, as Muddy River would not see its first real grass till after the holiday. Women shopped for the best meat to make cold cuts to feast on at the holiday picnic; men oiled and cleaned their bicycles for the annual spring outing. Even though the city government had announced a new policy eliminating Ching Ming as a public holiday—communicating with the dead in any form was an act of superstition, unfit for the new era when the country was rebuilding itself after the Cultural Revolution—the holiday this year fell on a Sunday, so the impact of the new policy on the townspeople was minimal.

NINI'S PARENTS DECIDED that this year's Ching Ming was to be celebrated as a special occasion. More than ever they needed the blessings of their ancestors. These dead people whom they had rarely thought of in the past years had no doubt been properly honored by more pious relatives in their home province; still, nobody would refuse an additional offering. At night Nini's parents calculated and discussed the menu of their offerings to these ancestors, who, if pleased, would surely send their blessings for male progeny.

Nini couldn't remember similar preparations for the births of any of her sisters. Ever since the execution of the Gus' daughter, her parents had taken on a more cheerful view of life. Nini's mother moved around with extra caution, her two hands cupped around her belly. Nini's father touched her mother's belly often, in a way that made Nini shiver with disgust, but she couldn't take her eyes off his big-knuckled hand on her mother's body. She kept on looking until one of her parents, usually her mother, caught her staring and gave her a chore to do. Nini's father forbade her mother to do any housework, including the matchbox making that was nothing even for a small child—Nini was told to take all the duties off her mother's shoulders, and now, as well as getting coal, picking up leftover vegetables, and doing grocery shopping, she was going to cook three meals a day and do the laundry for the entire family. Nini pointed out that if they waited for her to cook breakfast after coming back with the coal from the train station, they might be late for work and school; her parents were shocked that she dared to challenge their decision, but what Nini said was true, so they had to reassign the duty to their second daughter, which made her hate Nini more than ever.

Except for the baby, all the girls sensed the importance of this pregnancy. Twice a day, in the morning and in the evening, Nini's mother gagged and threw up into a chamber pot, which it was Nini's duty to clean. Her first and second sisters moved quickly to prepare warm water and a clean towel for their mother. Nini looked on, appalled by how thoroughly the sour, bitter odor of her mother's pregnancy permeated their lives—even though it was warm enough to open the windows now, it seemed that the smell clung to everything in the room, the blankets and the pillows on the brick bed, meals Nini cooked, the laundry that hung from one end of the room to the other, even Nini's own skin. The two younger girls, however, did not wrinkle their noses when they tended their mother, and for that Nini's father praised them; after all, he said, education had made them into sensible and usable human beings. Nini might be the oldest, her mother would say, but she remained a worthless idiot. Nini listened stone-faced; she bit the inside of her mouth and fixed her eyes on a crack on the floor. This made her mother impatient, but when she looked for something to hit Nini with, a broomstick or a ruler, Nini's father would stop her. It was not worth her effort to beat some sense into Nini, he said. What she needed now was to care for the baby; she might hurt him with too much anger.

Nini's mother consented, telling Nini to hide her ugly face so that she would be spared the pain of looking at it. Instead of acting dumb, as she used to, Nini made an obvious effort to look around the small, crowded room for a hiding place before picking up Little Sixth and half burying her face into the baby's soft tummy.

One night Nini overheard her parents, on the other end of the brick bed, discuss whether they should send Nini away for a few months, the general belief being that a pregnant mother would unknowingly pass on physical traits to the baby from the people around her. Nini's mother did not want the baby to inherit anything by accident from Nini; was there a place to send her for a few months? she asked.

There was no place to send her, her father replied. After a while, her mother said, "If only we had finished her when she was born."

Nini's father sighed. "Easy to say so but hard to do," he said. "A life is a life, and we're not murderers."

Nini's eyes turned warm and wet. For this she would, when the time came to bury her parents, give his body a warm bath instead of a cold one. He had never said more than three sentences to her in a day, but he was a quiet person, and she forgave him. The moment of softness, however, lasted only until her father's next sentence. "Besides," he said, "Nini's like a maid we don't have to pay."

Quietly Nini put out the fire and filled the basin with icy cold water.

Little Fourth and Little Fifth, who had recently formed an alliance between themselves and did not participate in much of the life outside their secret world, held hands and watched whenever their mother put on a show of morning and evening sickness. They were less annoying to Nini because they never courted their parents' attention—they were not old enough, or perhaps they had everything they wanted from each other. A few times Nini thought of befriending them, but they showed no interest, their inquiring eyes on Nini's face reminding her that she would never be as beautiful as they—by now there was no mistaking that the two girls would grow up to be the prettiest ones in the family.

But all these things—her parents' impatience with her, her two oldest sisters' scheming to get her punished, and the indifference of Little Fourth and Little Fifth—bothered Nini less now that she had Bashi. She explored her power with a secret joy. She put a pinch more salt into the stew than necessary or half a cup more water into the rice; she soaked her parents' underwear in suds and then wrung them dry without rinsing; she spat on her sisters' red Young Pioneers' scarves and rubbed the baby's peed cloth diapers against her mother's blouses. Nobody had yet noticed these sabotaging activities, but at her most daring moments Nini hoped to be discovered. If her parents kicked her out of their house, she would just move across town to Bashi's place, less than a thirty-minute walk and a world away, freed from her prisoner's life.

Her newly added housework, however, made it inconvenient for her to spend more time with Bashi during the day. Apart from providing coal and vegetables, Bashi did not have the magic to make meals cook themselves, or laundry do itself, or the stove and her sisters take care of themselves. He suggested coming to Nini's house and being her companion when her parents were at work. She thought about the idea, alluring and exciting, and then rejected the offer. Her parents would hear about Bashi's presence in no time, if not from the neighbors, then from her younger sisters; they would throw her out for sure. Was Bashi a reliable backup, despite all her wishful thinking? Nini decided to give him some more time.

The short hour in the early morning became the happiest time of her day. When she arrived at six o'clock, Bashi always had a feast ready—sausages, fried tofu, roasted peanuts, pig's blood in gelatin, all bought at the marketplace the day before, more than they could consume. Nini started the fire—Bashi seemed unable to finish this simple task by himself, but he was a man, after all, the deficiency forgivable—and when she cooked porridge on the stove to go with the morning feast, Bashi would peel frozen pears by her side. The flesh of the pears was an unsavory dark brown color, but when Bashi cut it into thin slices and slipped them into Nini's mouth, she was surprised to find the pear crisp and sweet; the iciness inside her mouth and the heat from the burning stove made her shudder with some strange joy. Sometimes his finger stayed on her lips even after the slice of pear disappeared. She opened her mouth wide and pretended to bite; he laughed and snatched his hand away.

The morning before Ching Ming, between slices of frozen pear, Bashi said, "Old Hua says it's time to bury my grandma now."

"When?" Nini asked.

"Tomorrow. They think it makes sense to bury her on the holiday."

It seemed everyone had something important planned for Ching Ming, Nini thought. Her father had booked a pedicab for the holiday, a luxury they could barely afford. Little Fourth, Little Fifth, and a huge basket of offerings would ride with her mother, while the two older girls and her father would walk. Nini and the baby were to stay home because neither could keep up with the others. Nini found it hard not to feel disappointed; it was the only picnic her family had planned for as long as she could remember, and she longed to go into the mountain where she had never set foot, even though it meant that she would have to endure her family for the entire day.

"Where are you going to bury her?" she asked Bashi.

"Next to my grandpa and my baba. Old Hua said he would go there today to make sure everything is ready."

"I didn't know Muddy River was your hometown."

"Close to here. My grandpa was a ginseng picker. He said the best ones were those that grew into the shape of a woman's body."

"What nonsense."

"Shhh. Don't say that about a dead man," said Bashi. "The ghosts can hear you."

Nini shivered.

"And it's true. Some ginsengs grow into women," Bashi said. He stuffed the last slice of pear into Nini's mouth and told her to wait. He soon came back from the bedroom with a red silk-wrapped box, which he opened for Nini. Inside was a ginseng root, displayed on ivory-colored silk. "See here, the head, the arms and legs. The long hair," Bashi said, and let his finger run across the ginseng, which, to Nini's astonishment, did look like an unclothed woman's body. "Beautiful, no?" said Bashi. "This was the best one my grandpa picked. If he'd sold this, he could've bought seven concubines easily, but he didn't want to part with it. He thought it was a ginseng goddess. When the army came, he and my grandma prayed to this goddess not to take my father with them, but of course she let them down."

"Didn't you say he was a war hero?"

"War hero is rubbish. You know how he was recruited? They came to my father's village and said they would invite all the young men to a house for dinner. Well, if someone invited you to dinner with a gun at your head, you would go. So my father went along with some other young people. And they were treated to a very good dinner and then invited to sit on a big brick bed. A boy soldier kept the fire burning under the bed, adding wood so that in a short time the brick bed became very hot. Like a barbecue plate, you see? And the officer said, 'Young men, we are the People's Liberation Army and we fight for the people. Think about it. If you are interested in our cause, come down and you'll become a glorious member among us.' Nobody moved. Of course all their parents had warned them not to join the army; they said the Communist army would not enlist someone at gunpoint like the Nationalist army. And yes, it was true that the officer was very polite. He kept telling the boy soldier to make the brick bed warmer for the guests, and an orderly kept bringing them hot tea and more tobacco leaves for their pipes. Now, tell me, what would you do? Move, or stay on the bed to have your ass burned? So after a long time my father couldn't stand the heat and came off the bed. He was the first one so he got a higher rank than his companions, and later they sent him to learn how to fly fighter planes. The rest of them became foot soldiers and orderlies."

"They all came off, then?"

"All except one. My father's best buddy. His bottom was so badly burned he was called 'Hot Butt' for the rest of his life."

Nini smiled. Bashi often told stories, and she could never tell which part was true and which was from his imagination.

"Why? You don't believe me? Ask anyone in my father's village! They said my father was clever because he came off the bed early and got the biggest promotion, but where did that get him? On the other hand, Hot Butt didn't end up in a better place. He was executed for sabotage in '59. He and my father died within a month of each other.

They said my father was called by his friend's ghost. What does that tell you?"

Nini shook her head.

"There is only one place for everyone to go."

Nini tried to picture Bashi's grandmother, her body withered like a ginseng root and her ghost floating in the air, eavesdropping on them. She scooped the porridge into a bowl. "Here, you must eat more and talk less," she said to Bashi. It couldn't hurt for the old woman's ghost to see that her grandson was well taken care of.

They sat down and ate. After a moment of quietness, Nini said, "My family will go to the mountain tomorrow."

"Why? Your family didn't have ancestors buried here," said Bashi. "They don't have a wire service in the mountain for them to send the offerings."

"They just want an excuse to waste all the money and go to the mountain for fun."

"Like every other family. Are you going?"

"Me? The sun has to rise from the west for them to take me."

Bashi nodded and then stopped his chopsticks, looking at Nini with a meaningful smile. "So you'll be home, and . . . alone."

"With the baby."

"She can sleep anywhere, no?" Bashi said.

Nini's heart skipped a beat. "But you need to bury your grandma."

"Do you think she'll mind if I don't go?"

"Yes," said Nini. "Don't let her down."

"But I may get sick and unfit for the burial trip."

Nini smiled. She was pleased that the old woman's ghost could not compete with her. Out of modesty and caution, she suggested that Bashi buy a lot of paper money for the old woman's ghost in case she felt offended, and he agreed that it was a good idea. The more they planned, the more it seemed the perfect opportunity, Nini thought, for her to put a chain on his heart so it would not go astray to another girl. "How are you doing with Old Kwen's dog?" Nini asked. She did not believe anything he said about the dog, but it made him happy when she talked about it as if it were serious business.

It was going well, Bashi replied. He had been feeding the dog hams and steaks cured in hard liquor and now it had become his friend; what would a dog with a master like Kwen fancy other than that, Bashi said, and added with a smile that he was ready to launch a test of his poison very soon. Nini listened halfheartedly and ate with concentration.

"Of course, hard work gets rewarded," Bashi said. "While I've been working on Kwen's dog, I've found something else interesting. That woman whose body you didn't see? Some people in town are trying to organize a protest on her behalf."

A slice of pig-blood gelatin dropped from Nini's chopsticks into her porridge. "Why?" she said. "Isn't she already dead?"

"If you ask me, people go crazy for no reason," Bashi said. "Have you seen the leaflets all over town?"

Nini said she had not noticed, and then remembered hearing whispered conversations between her parents in bed. One time her father had said that using a dead person as a weapon was a common trick and would get the troublemakers nowhere; another time he said that they themselves had their victory and justice. Both times her mother cursed with her usual venom.

"Who are these people?" Nini asked.

"They belong to a secret group, coming at night with white skulls as necklaces."

Nini shuddered, even though she knew that Bashi was probably being his exaggerating self. "What do they care about the woman?"

Bashi shrugged. "Maybe the ghost of the dead woman came back and cast a spell so people are under her power now, and work for her."

"That's nonsense," Nini said with a trembling voice.

"Why else are these people willing to act like idiots?"

Nini thought about Mrs. Gu, her former gentleness and her sudden change of attitude. Nini had stopped at the Gus' door several times in the past week, but neither Mrs. Gu nor Teacher Gu had come out to meet her. Perhaps Mrs. Gu herself was under the spell of her daughter's ghost and had become an unreasonable woman. "That old woman," Nini said sullenly. "She hates me."

"Who?"

"The mother of the executed woman."

"Why do you have anything to do with her?"

"How do I know?" Nini said. "People all hate me."

"Not me," Bashi said. "I like you."

"That's what you say now," Nini said. "Who knows when you'll change your mind?"

Bashi swore this would never happen, but Nini was no longer in a mood to listen. She said abruptly that it was time for her to leave, and before Bashi could object, she went straight to the kitchen to get the coal for herself. Bashi scratched his head and begged her to let him know how he had offended her. She thought his eagerness to keep her pleased was ridiculous. If he wanted a smile from her she would give him one, but the way he worried like an ant on a hot pot made her happy. She said she would come back the next day after her parents and sisters left the house. "You can prove yourself to me then," she said, and left without giving Bashi a chance to defend himself.

TEACHER GU SPENT TWO WEEKS in the city hospital, and was released the day before Ching Ming, along with other patients who had requested to go home for the holiday. Teacher Gu's left hand had recovered well, and with a barely usable left leg and a cane, he was able to move slowly. Mrs. Gu hired a pedicab, and on the short ride home from the hospital, Teacher Gu saw several people stop and watch them pass, some nodding at them and one even raising a hand to wave before scratching his head, as if he was embarrassed by his own gesture. Mrs. Gu nodded back, surreptitiously too, which did not escape Teacher Gu's eyes. He pulled up the blanket that was slipping away from his legs, and his wife, startled as if from a secret dream of her own, bent to rearrange it. "You must be cold without the boots," she said. She took off her mittens, stuck her hands into the blanket, and held his feet. Through the cotton socks he could feel the warmth of her palms. "The doctor said to avoid the boots so the circulation wouldn't be blocked," she said, as if she were placating a child. "We'll be home soon."

Teacher Gu looked down at his feet, tucked away in the old woolen blanket, which bore a pair of phoenixes, the red and golden colors already fading. It had been a present from his first wife the day he had left for Muddy River, at the time a small, undeveloped town, perfect for his exile. The blanket, with its gaudy colors and patterns, was an insult to his aesthetics, and he remembered throwing it back to the woman who had decided to stop being his wife. She had picked it up and repacked it in his suitcase. It was time for them to believe in something less intellectual, she had said; it was an error for them to remain blind in their intellectualism.

Go to court your illiterate proletariat master, was his reply, hurled at her out of rage and self-pity. But later, when he calmed down, he puzzled over his first wife's words. She was always the wise one, choosing the winning side even before the civil war had tipped one way or the other. He, however, was a thorough dreamer, living in his ivory tower until an eviction order was slapped in his face.

It was time to leave their intellectualism behind. When Teacher Gu settled down in Muddy River he recalled her words and decided to teach night classes to illiterate women. In their progress he saw his merit, not as an intellectual but as a worker ant, moving the smallest grains of sand away from a mountain that lay between his people and an enlightened, civilized society. On the night of his wedding to his second wife, he brought out the blanket; a present from an old friend, he told his young bride. An expensive present it was, as a woolen blanket was still a rarity in provincial towns. His wife fell in love with it, and for the first few years, she treasured it and used it only on special occasions, holidays and anniversaries, and the first month of each new year. But like everything else cherished in a new marriage, over the years the blanket lost its original importance and was used now for practical reasons—it was a blanket of top quality, good for the severe six-month-long winter of Muddy River.

When they reached the alley, the pedicab stopped, too wide to pass through to the Gus' door. Teacher Gu limped slowly toward home while his wife counted out the bills for the driver. A few chickens jumped aside and watched Teacher Gu, and he recognized his two hens among the group. He pushed the gate open and saw a pile of wood, cut and stacked neatly. A young woman heard his steps and came out of the house. They were back just in time for lunch, she said.

Teacher Gu studied the woman. She was in her late twenties, her medium-length straight hair covering the nape of her neck, parted to one side with a barrette; she wore a gray Mao jacket and a pair of pants in a darker gray. At first glance, she had the standard appearance of a young married woman, neutral-looking, as a wife was expected to no longer reveal any of her femininity and beauty to strangers. Yet a corner of her gauzy, peach-colored scarf spilled over the collar of the Mao jacket, perhaps with deliberate intent. Teacher Gu squinted at the scarf; on their wedding night his first wife had worn a silk robe of the same hue, peach being her favorite color.

The woman smiled, her teeth very white and even. "How are you feeling, Teacher Gu?"

He did not reply. He realized that the woman was prettier than she intended to appear. "Who are you?" he asked, his tone unfriendly.

"This is Kai," said Mrs. Gu, coming through the gate. "She reads the news."

"Ah, of course it's you," Teacher Gu said. It was impossible to forget her voice, which could easily be compared to a sunny autumn sky, a clear creek in the springtime, or any other empty similes that could be used to describe other female announcers, from the central radio stations to the provincial stations, all well chosen because of the lack of individual features in their voices. What a sad thing it was, to be someone who could so easily be replaced by another perfect, almost identical voice, Teacher Gu thought. What a tedious job it must be, to speak day in and day out words that were not one's own. But then what right did he have to despise her? For all he knew she might enjoy the fame this job brought her. "You have a nice voice," Teacher Gu said. "Great for being the *throat and tongue* for the party."

There was a small pause before Kai nodded hesitantly. Mrs. Gu studied both of them nervously and put a hand on Teacher Gu's arm. "You must be tired now. Why don't you have some lunch and take a nap?" She half supported and half pulled him into the house. He wiggled his arm, with more force than he had intended, to free himself.

Kai carried a pot of chicken stew to the table and asked Teacher Gu how the trip home had been for him. He did not answer. There was no space in his heart for small talk, neither with his wife nor with a stranger. While he had been lying in the hospital for two weeks, he had conducted many conversations with his first wife, sometimes arguing, other times agreeing with her; he wanted no one to interrupt them.

Mrs. Gu apologized to Kai in a low voice, saying the trip might have worn him out. Kai said it was not a problem at all, and in any case, she should be leaving to take care of a few things. Teacher Gu tried to return to his preoccupation, yet the young woman distracted him. He looked up and studied her face. "You were my student, weren't you?" he said all of a sudden, taking both Kai and Mrs. Gu by surprise.

"Kai did not grow up in Muddy River," Mrs. Gu said, and explained that Kai had become an announcer after she left the theater troupe in the provincial capital.

Teacher Gu stared at Kai. She would make the bed in case he wanted a rest before lunch, Mrs. Gu said.

He had taught hundreds of students in the past thirty years; only lately had he begun to mix up their names and faces, yet, like any older person, the more forgetful he was in his recent life, the sharper his earlier memories became. "You were my student," Teacher Gu said again.

Kai looked uneasy. "I was in your first-grade class for two months before I moved away," Kai said.

"When was that?"

"Nineteen sixty."

Teacher Gu squinted and calculated. "No, it was in 1959. You were in the same class as Shan."

Mrs. Gu turned to Kai, who looked stricken, and for a moment no one spoke. Teacher Gu tried hard to recollect more about Kai, but all he saw was Shan, in his first-grade class in 1959, a skinny girl with two thin pigtails, the ends yellowed like scorched weeds, a malnourished child among the starved children in the famine that would last three years before losing its grip on the nation.

Mrs. Gu was the first to recover. She ladled stew into a bowl. "Kai brought the chicken and the chestnuts," she said.

"Why did you change schools?" Teacher Gu asked.

"I was chosen and sent to the Children's Theater School," Kai said.

Teacher Gu snorted. "I imagine you were well fed as a selected star, then," he said. Something about this young woman annoyed him, her voice, her being the same age as Shan but with a secure job and an easy life, her intrusion into his home, her lying to his wife about not having met Shan. His own daughter, seven years old back then, had looked up at him with pleading eyes when he divided the meager food he had saved from his own ration for the children who came from bigger families and were hungrier than his daughter. Those children grew up to be the most dangerous youths, their minds as empty and eagerly receptive as their mouths, and they devoured anything fed to them, good and bad and evil. "Have you ever known hunger?" Teacher Gu said to Kai now, not covering his animosity.

"He who is in your house is a guest," Mrs. Gu said, and he recognized the tone of disapproval. "You're not behaving like a good host today."

"Teacher Gu must be tired now," Kai said. "I'll come back later to talk to him."

He did not answer either woman. He stumbled out of the chair and into the bedroom. The stove was burning well, and all of a sudden he was exhausted by the warmth. He listened to his wife apologizing to Kai, and Kai replying that of course she understood, and no, she did not mind it at all. Soon their conversation became inaudible. Teacher Gu looked at the clock on the wall. He wondered how long it would take his wife to remember her sick husband, made too hot and uncomfortable by the burning stove in the middle of a spring day.

Seven minutes Teacher Gu had counted on the clock when Mrs. Gu came in with the untouched bowl of stew. "You really should eat a little," she said.

"Where's that woman?" he said.

"Her name is Kai," Mrs. Gu said.

Teacher Gu struggled to drag himself into a sitting position. He was surprised that his wife did not hurry to help him.

"You were very unfriendly to her, as if she owed you something," Mrs. Gu said.

"She lied to us. Why was she here?" Teacher Gu demanded. "She's a political tool for the government. What does she want from us?"

His wife stared at him with a quizzical look that reminded him of his rebellious daughter ten years earlier. "Didn't you teach your students to use their brains and not to jump to quick conclusions?"

So this was what he had come home for, Teacher Gu thought, an unpleasant wife who questioned his every word. "How long do you plan to remain this person that I don't think I've had the privilege of knowing before I went to the hospital? Do I deserve an explanation?" he said, raising his voice.

"The doctors said to remain calm," she said.

"Never is there a calmer person than a dead one."

His wife put the bowl on a stool next to the bed. He thought she would sit on the stool and feed him. When she did not, he made an effort to reach for the spoon even though he had no appetite.

"There's something you should know—we didn't tell you before because we thought your recovery was more important then," Mrs. Gu said.

"Who are 'we'?"

"Kai and I, and her friends. We're mobilizing the townspeople for a petition for Shan."

The change in his wife—her eyes that were no longer directed downward when she spoke, her clear pronunciation of words beyond her vocabulary—alarmed Teacher Gu. In almost thirty years of being second-class citizens, and especially in the ten years since Shan's imprisonment, they, as a couple, had retreated to a cocoon they had woven together, a flimsy and claustrophobic shell that provided their only warmth; sometimes it was hard to tell where one self ended and the other began; they were the two fish that chose to live the rest of their lives in the same drying puddle—had all this been an illusion? Who was this woman in front of him, trusting young strangers with some crazy and meaningless idea about a protest that could never change his daughter's fate? The feeling of falling down, unable to grab onto something—the same feeling he had experienced when he was first ill—made his breathing difficult.

"I thought I shouldn't hide this from you now," said Mrs. Gu. "It's become the biggest news."

"A new star you've become."

She ignored him. "You can't believe how many people are sympathetic. People are afraid but that doesn't mean they are callous. We just need to find them."

Teacher Gu watched his wife. Her cheeks were flushed, and her eyes, two deep wells of water that had gone dry over the years, looked somewhere beyond his head, with an unusual glimmer. A coldness crept into his body despite the burning stove. It was a disease—this passion for politics, for *mobilizing* the masses as if they were grains of sand that could easily be gathered under a magic spell and turned into a tower—it was a deadly disease. It had claimed his daughter's life, and now it was fastening its grip on the most unlikely person in the world, his wife, an obedient and humble old woman. "What do you want?" he asked finally. "Shan is already gone."

"We want the government to acknowledge the mistake. Shan was innocent. Nobody should be punished because of what she thinks. It's wrong and it's time to correct that mistake."

These words had been fed to his wife, probably by Kai, that young woman whose job it was to read aloud all the grand and empty words created to cast a mirage for suffering souls. "Shan is dead," Teacher Gu said. "Whatever you do, you won't bring back her life."

"It's not her life we're fighting for. It's the justice she deserves," Mrs. Gu said.

Stupid, stupid woman, talking like a parrot and offering their daughter's body as a public sacrifice in return for an empty promise. These women, with their flimsy logic and hungry minds, these women who let themselves be dazzled by magnificent words, their brains washed and refilled by other people. Was it his fate to face such an enemy all his life, first a wife who was so devoted to Communism that a marriage had to be dissolved, then a daughter, and now the only woman left in his life, who had been immune to this disease for the longest part of her life? He stared at his wife. "How long did it take for them to make a heroine out of you?" he asked coldly. "Five seconds, I imagine."

Like him, she had had doubts too, Mrs. Gu said in a calm voice, but they had to keep hoping for a change. They could not let their daughter's life be sacrificed for nothing.

Their daughter had died out of stupidity, because of trusting the wrong people all her life, Teacher Gu wanted to remind his wife, but in the end he only told her to stop what she was doing. "I won't allow this," he said. "I forbid you, or anyone, to use Shan's name as an excuse to gain anything."

Mrs. Gu looked up in shock. After a long moment, she smiled at him. "Teacher Gu, weren't you the one to teach me many years ago that women weren't men's slaves and followers anymore? And what men could not give us, we needed to fight for with our own hands?"

Teacher Gu looked at his wife, his body shaking. The lies he had been forced to teach many years ago had come back to bear down on him, making him into a clown. He thought of throwing the chicken stew against the wall or onto the hard cement floor; he would let the soup splatter everywhere, hot and oily, and he would watch the china bowl smash into pieces. But what would that do except put him down on the level of an uneducated, illogical man? His anger, overwhelming a moment ago, was replaced by disappointment and exhaustion. He looked at his wife with a half smile. "Of course we're living in the Communist era now," he said. "Forgive an old man's confusion, comrade."

WHO WOULD HAVE THOUGHT that Nini could throw a girlish tantrum, requesting a demonstration of loyalty from him? A rose with a thorny stem was worth the risk and pain, but what if it was a wildflower by the roadside that considered itself a rose and grew unpleasant thorns? Bashi chuckled to himself. Perhaps he needed to keep an eye on Nini's temperament and make sure she did not grow into one of those grumpy old hens in the marketplace. He watched a young nurse fresh off the night shift stand in front of a shop window, unsatisfied with the way her hair parted and trying hard to fix the problem with her fingers. He walked up to her and brought out a bag of candies that he always carried with him in case there was a young girl to strike up a conversation with. "Your hair looks great," he said. "Do you want a treat?"

The young woman studied Bashi with a cold look. "Go home and look at yourself in the mirror," she said.

"Why? I don't need a mirror to know what I look like," said Bashi. "It's you who are pruning your feathers in the street."

"What rotten fortune to meet a toad in the morning," the woman said to a cat strolling by, and she hurried away, her hand still combing her hair.

Who does she think she is, a swan in disguise? Bashi looked at his reflection in the shop window, a presentable lad in a new jacket. Three teenage boys, heads shaved bald and all sporting sunglasses, stopped next to him. "Hey, Bashi, what do you need a jacket like that for?"

Bashi looked for their eyes but only saw six figures of himself in the dark lenses. He did not know the boys, and from a few unfortunate encounters with the newly sprouted gangs of Muddy River, he had learned not to attract their attention. "Nice sunglasses," he said, patting his pocket and finding the package of cigarettes he kept for these moments. The boys caught the cigarettes Bashi threw to them. "Can we borrow your jacket for a day?" the youngest one said with a grin.

"Yes," said Bashi. "There's nothing that I don't share with my brothers." He took off the jacket and shivered in the morning breeze. The boys nodded and walked on, the youngest trying on the jacket for the older brothers to assess.

What a dangerous bunch this city is breeding, thought Bashi. He patted a wad of cash in a pocket of his pants—he was wise not to have left any money in the jacket. He went into a nearby store and asked for a small bag of sunflower seeds, and when he came out, he put a few of the seeds in his mouth and chewed them into an inedible mess, imagining all of them to be unfriendly people crushed between his teeth. Only with Nini did he have the respect he deserved. But what did he give Nini, except for a few basketfuls of coal and vegetables? She was right that he needed to prove himself. "Name the people who make you unhappy," he imagined himself saying to Nini first thing the next morning. "Name them all and they are Lu Bashi's enemies too. I won't let them live happily." He would start with that mother of the executed woman, who hated Nini.

At the entrance to an alley, Bashi saw the dog Ear. "Hello, my friend," Bashi said, putting a hand into his pocket. Ear wagged his tail. "Come on," Bashi said sweetly. "How are you? Are you looking for me? I was just thinking about you."

The dog came closer and rubbed his neck on Bashi's leg. What a stupid dog, Bashi thought; he withdrew his hand from his pocket and clapped. "Sorry, I haven't got meat for you today. You see, I'm running some other errands."

The dog circled him for a minute and ran away. Bashi felt satisfied. The new friendship with Ear was a by-product of his plan for Kwen's dog—it had not taken a long time or much ham to win Ear's heart, and what dog could refuse a piece of meat? Dogs were dogs, after all, unable to compete with man's intellect.

Bashi entered a store with a black wooden plaque bearing the golden characters *Long Life*. An old woman stood by the counter, laying out many wrinkled bills for the shop owner. "Granny, what are you buying?" Bashi asked.

Hadn't he heard about the medicine woman from Eastern Village who had discovered new ways to communicate with the dead? asked the old woman. She had just paid a visit to the medicine woman, who had given her the message that her husband did not have enough money for liquor in the next world.

"Ha, you believed him?" Bashi said. He looked at the money on the counter; the husband certainly would not get drunk from that poor amount. "Maybe he uses your money to buy a woman out there?"

The old woman mumbled and said her husband had never been into women; it was drinking that he had lived for and then died from. Bashi thought of this fool dying before knowing the real joy of life and shook his head in disbelief. "What a pity," he said. "What's so good about drinking?"

"You say that because you don't know the real taste," said the shop owner, a middle-aged woman with a new perm. "People always put liquor and a woman's beauty together, you understand why, little brother? Drinking and women are the two best things for men."

Bashi snorted. What did a shop owner know about men? He picked up stacks of paper money, a miniature mansion, carriages pulled by four horses, a chest, and some other knickknacks, all made of white rice paper and ready to be burned into ashes to accompany his grandmother to the otherworld. He asked for some rat poison too, and the shop owner was taken aback. "My store serves those who have stepped into the immortal garden," she said. Like all people in Muddy River, the woman resorted to any euphemism possible to avoid mentioning death, and Bashi smiled. He paid for the paper products and said he had asked for the poison because he did not want any rats to bother his grandmother's body. Frightened, the paled woman bowed to a Buddha that sat in a corner of the store with burning incense in front of him. Please forgive the boy's ignorance, the woman said, and Bashi laughed and decided not to bring any more nightmares to the merchant. A few doors down the street, he bought a packet of rat poison in a drugstore.

When he arrived home, Bashi left the paper offerings next to his grandmother's casket. "Nana, tomorrow Old Hua and his wife are sending you off to my grandpa and my baba," he said, talking to the old woman as he worked; he had developed a habit of talking to her when he was alone. He hacked off a thick slab of ham, punched a few holes in it, and soaked it in liquor. "When you get there, say a few words for me to my grandpa and my baba. Tell them I am doing well and won't bring disgrace to their name. See, I can't go with you tomorrow, because I have something more important to take care of." He unpacked the rat poison and poured some pellets into the mortar his grandmother had used to grind dried chili peppers. The pellets were a nasty, dark grayish brown color. What rat would ever want to touch such a disgusting thing, Bashi wondered aloud as he ground the pellets into powder. He did not know how strong the poison was but the layer of powder seemed unconvincing, so he added a handful more of the pellets to the mortar. "I tell you, Nana, not many people use their brains nowadays. It's hard to find someone as smart as my baba now, no?" Bashi said, thinking that ghosts, like the living, must readily devour compliments. Old women were easily pleased if you praised their sons and their grandsons; perhaps his grandma would forgive him for not going with her to the burial tomorrow. He talked on and praised his father more. When he finished grinding, he brought the mortar close and sniffed—apart from a stale, pasty smell, he did not sense anything dangerous. He took out the ham and dredged it in the powder until it was covered on both sides; with a tiny spoon he tried to insert more powder into the holes. "You must be wondering about this," he said. "But you watch out for me and pray for this to work, and after I finish this big deed, I'll come and burn a lot of paper money for all of you."

The last time his grandmother had taken him to visit his grandfather's and his father's graves, Bashi was twelve. The next time, he thought, he would bring Nini so they would know that they didn't have to worry about their descendants. He looked at the ham for a moment, and carefully brushed some honey onto both sides, making sure none of the poisonous powder escaped. "There," he said. "Beautiful, isn't it?"

Bashi walked across half the city before he found Ear. With a smaller piece of meat he was able to entice the dog to follow him. They walked over the Cross-river Bridge and climbed up South Mountain. It was a beautiful day, the sun warm on his face, the buzz of spring unmistakable in the air. Bashi stopped by a bush of early-blooming wild plums. "I have something really good for you," Bashi said, and laid the ham next to the bush.

Ear sniffed the ham with great curiosity but showed no immediate interest in taking it. Bashi urged the dog on, but it only pawed the ham and sniffed. Bashi became impatient. He grabbed the ham from the dog and pretended that he himself was going to eat it. This seemed to work; when Bashi threw the ham back at the dog, it caught the meat in midair and trotted away.

Bashi loitered, thinking he would give the dog a few minutes before locating it and observing the effect of the poison. If the rat poison did not work on this small dog, it would certainly not work on

Kwen's black dog. Bashi wondered if he would need to go back to the drugstore and make a fuss. He would demand something stronger, saying that the rats in his house were as strong as hogs. His thoughts wandered until he heard the dog's painful yelping. "There," he said, and then he heard a long, painful howl.

Bashi found the dog on the ground, panting, its limbs jerking helplessly. A small ax stuck in its skull, between the eyes, and sticky red blood oozed out. It was obvious that the dog was dying fast. Next to the dog stood a teenage boy in a gray cotton coat as worn-out as a heap of rags; his left hand was bleeding with a dog bite, and his right hand tightly gripped the slab of ham. Bashi looked from the dog to the boy and then to the dog. "Did you kill the dog for that?"

The boy looked at the young man in front of him. He thought of explaining that he had not meant to kill the dog, but who would believe him, when the dog's blood had already stained his ax. The boy, a small teenager who looked not much older than ten, had come to town to sell nothing but his poor, underdeveloped muscles. Sometimes a housewife hired him to chop firewood, kill a live chicken, or unload coal, small chores that she could just as well finish by herself or ask her sons or husband to do, but by hiring the boy, she would feel good about her own heart. Women were all alike, the boy had concluded after a few weeks of working; they talked about their hearts but also watched their wallets carefully. They paid him with food but not money, and the boy, half beggar and half sop for the women's consciences, knew enough not to ask for more than he was allowed.

"Did you kill the dog?" Bashi asked again.

The boy stepped back and said, "He bit me first."

"Of course he did. You stole his meat. I would bite you too." Bashi grabbed the boy's sleeve and dragged him to the dog, whose breathing was shallow and fast and whose paws were trying to dig into the newly thawed ground. "Look what you did. What kind of a man are you to fight with a small dog for food?"

The boy assessed the situation. If he ran, the man could easily catch him. He could fight, but there was not much good in that for him either. He might as well brace himself for a good beating, but besides a beating, there was nothing else the man could do to him. The boy relaxed.

"Look at your eyes," said Bashi. "What trick are you thinking of playing on me?"

The boy knelt down and started to cry. "Uncle," he said. "Uncle, it's all my fault. I thought it was a waste for a small dog to eat that much meat. I thought I could get the meat for my mother. My mother and my sister haven't had a taste of meat for three months."

"So you have a sister?" Bashi said. "How old is she?"

"Nine," the boy said. "My father died six years ago, and my mother is ill." To prove his story, the boy untied a small cloth bag and showed the man its contents—a few buns and half buns he had got, already hard as rocks. His sister had invented a way of re-cooking the leftover buns into a paste, he explained.

Bashi nodded. The boy must have told the story a thousand times to earn the sympathy of those old hens in town. He brought out a few bills. "You're certainly a boy who knows how to take care of your family. If not for this," Bashi said, and bared his teeth, "if not for your mother and your sister, I would send for the police. Now take the money and buy some good clothes for your sister."

The boy looked at the money and swallowed hard. "I killed your dog by accident, Uncle," he said. "How dare I accept your money?"

Bashi laughed. The boy could certainly tell that Bashi was not much older than he, but he knew how to talk properly, and it pleased Bashi. "It's not my dog," he said. "If you killed my dog I would wring your skinny neck like this."

"Are you sure you don't want to send me to the police?"

Bashi knocked on the boy's head with his knuckle. "Don't be silly. The police wouldn't care if you hacked ten dogs to pieces."

The boy accepted the money and thanked Bashi profusely. Bashi stopped the boy with an upturned hand. They both walked toward the dog; it had stopped panting and moving and now lay on the ground, its paws half-covered with mud. It was hard to imagine that a thin boy could kill a dog with such a precise cut.

The boy knelt down and retrieved the ax and wiped it clean on his coat. Bashi told him to throw away the ham. The boy hesitated and said, "But won't it be a waste?"

"Why do you ask so many silly questions?"

The boy watched Bashi hurl the ham with all his might. It made a beautiful arc in the afternoon sky and fell out of sight. "Now hurry back home before my patience runs out," Bashi said.

The boy said yes but did not move, eyeing the dead dog. When Bashi urged him again, he said, "Uncle, what do you think will happen to the dog here?"

"How do I know?" Bashi said. "I told you it's not my dog."

"Do you want a dog-skin hat or mufflers?" the boy asked.

Bashi smiled. "Ha, you cunning little thing. If I need anything I have money to buy it. Take the dog and make something for your sister, if that's what you're thinking."

The boy smiled too. "Uncle, if not for our shabby place, I would treat you to a good meal with dog-meat soup for the holiday."

"Don't sweet-talk me," Bashi said. "Now I need to run on to my own business. Send my greeting to your sister."

The boy watched Bashi disappear before he sat down to work. He dumped the old buns by the roadside and tore the cloth bag into strips. He took off his coat and wrapped it around the dog, and then strapped the body on his back. It was heavier than he'd thought, warm still, which reminded him of the day his sister rode piggyback on him as they followed their father's coffin to the cemetery. His father had held the boy's hands the moment before his death, and told him that he would have to be the man of the house and take care of his mother and sister.

The boy thought about his father's grave, untended in the past six years. He looked up at the sky, still brightly blue; if he hurried up, he would be able to get home before dark and clean up the grave for

Ching Ming. His mother, bedridden for five years now, would not be able to make the trip, but he would take his sister there. He was now a man, responsible for the living as well as the dead. The boy walked fast; then after a moment, he turned back. It took him some thrashing around to locate the meat, which was a little dirty with sand, but with a good scrubbing it would make a fine holiday meal.

KAI TOLD HER COLLEAGUES in the propaganda department that she was going to give her studio a spring-cleaning. An editor raised his eyebrows but said nothing, and Kai realized that cleaning on the day before Ching Ming might be interpreted as a way to celebrate the superstitious holiday, but she decided not to dwell on the matter. Ever since the appearance of the leaflets, her colleagues in the propaganda department had been courteous to one another, yet no one dared mention anything about the situation; they were all seasoned barometers, fine-tuned to detect any minute change in the political atmosphere.

A secretary offered to help, and Kai politely refused, saying that the studio was too small for two people to move around in. It was two o'clock in the afternoon, the slowest time of the day, and when Kai left the office for the studio, she saw that many offices in the administration building were closed. People had started to take the afternoon off for the holiday the next day, even though as government employees, they were not allowed to celebrate Ching Ming publicly. Earlier that morning, when Kai had stopped by her mother's flat, her mother had told her that she had hired a trustworthy helper to send paper money and other offerings to Kai's father; Kai did not know if her in-laws had similar plans, as Han was not back yet from the provincial capital. It was about two weeks since he had left, and apart from a few phone calls he had made to her office—despite their status, they did not have a telephone in their flat, though Han had promised that would change very soon—they had not talked much. The office was not a good place for any exchange of information, nor, she imagined, did the provincial capital allow Han much freedom. All they talked about was Ming-Ming, who had missed Han for the first two days and then settled down as if nothing was out of the ordinary.

Kai locked herself in the studio. She had expected some hostility from Teacher Gu, as she had also encountered resistance when she had first met Mrs. Gu—distrust of a stranger, more so in her case, as her voice represented the government. It had taken Kai a few visits for Mrs. Gu not to turn down the fruit and dried milk Kai brought for Teacher Gu, and after a while they had begun to talk, neither about Gu Shan nor about the protest, but, in the most harmless way, about the changing of the seasons. Slowly Mrs. Gu warmed up. One day she asked Kai about her parents, and Kai replied that her father had passed away several years ago. Mrs. Gu pondered this for a moment and said that it was a daughter's good fortune to see off her parents. Mrs. Gu quoted an old saying about the three utmost misfortunes in life—losing parents in childhood, losing a spouse in midlife, and losing a child in old age. Of the three misfortunes she had already experienced two, said Mrs. Gu, and Kai had to avert her eyes, as she could not find words of comfort. It was time for an old woman like her to make herself useful in some way, Mrs. Gu said, looking into Kai's eyes with neither self-pity nor sadness.

Kai had never expected Teacher Gu to recognize her as a former student. His hostility reminded her how she was bound, against her wishes, to her past, her family, and her status. She could, if she wanted to, go back to her old life; apart from introducing Mrs. Gu to Jialin, she did not have much involvement in the upcoming protest, nor did she have much contact with Jialin's friends, who, along with Jialin, had put out the leaflets and planned the event for Ching Ming. The fact that everything could be reversed was disconcerting. She did not need another option, and she wanted Teacher Gu, of all people, to understand and acknowledge her.

Someone banged on the door. Kai's heart pounded. When she opened the door Han squeezed in and locked it behind him.

"You frightened me," Kai said. Her cheeks felt warm, caught, as she was, in a secretive moment, but Han seemed not to notice her unease. He looked equally flustered. "What's wrong?" Kai asked. "Is Ming-Ming all right?"

"I haven't been back home," Han said. "I need to leave in ten minutes."

"Why?"

Han gazed at Kai and did not reply. Could it be possible that he had heard about the protest planned for tomorrow? She wondered who could have leaked the information, but she did not know Jialin's friends. Things were under control, in trustworthy hands, Jialin had informed Kai, the stage set for Kai and Mrs. Gu on the day of Ching Ming. But perhaps his trust was misplaced. She wished she had met his friends.

"If I ever became a nobody," Han said, and sat down on the only chair in the studio, "or worse than a nobody—if I became a criminal and was never able to give you anything again, would you still love me?"

Kai looked at Han, his eyes filled with an agony that she wished she could share. The heroines she had performed onstage never faced a husband proclaiming his love: They were maidens giving up their lives for a higher calling, mothers leaving embroidered kerchiefs in the swaddling clothes of their babies before taking the journeys that would not return them to their children, and wives of fellow revolutionaries; in the case of Autumn Jade, her husband was the villain, who had not loved Autumn Jade or had the right to love anyone.

Han walked toward Kai and embraced her. She made herself remain still; after a moment, when he broke down weeping into her hair, she touched the top of his head. He had heard speculation in the provincial capital that the faction standing behind the democratic wall would win in Beijing, Han said, after he had calmed down; the man they had supported with the kidneys would lose the power struggle, if the rumor was true.

"Do your parents know?"

"I came to meet them and the mayor an hour ago," Han said. "My parents are worried that the mayor might give me up to protect himself."

Kai looked at Han; his smooth, almost babylike face had a day-old stubble now, and the whites of his eyes were bloodshot. "How could you be made responsible?" she said.

"The kidneys," Han said, and explained that their enemy in the provincial capital, who seemed to be winning so far, was now investigating the transplant and Gu Shan's execution, which he claimed had violated legal procedures.

"Is that true?"

"If not for this, he'd find another excuse to attack us," Han said. "It's the same old truth—*the one who robs and succeeds will become the king, and the one who tries to rob and fails will be called a criminal.*"

Kai grabbed the edge of the table where she was leaning, and tried to steady herself. When Han finally looked up, the tears in his eyes had been replaced by a rare look of resolution. "Can you promise me one thing?" Han said. "Can you write up a divorce application and sign it, with today's date, just in case? I don't want anything horrible to happen to you."

She was not the type to abandon a family because of some rumors, Kai said weakly.

"This is no time for emotion," said Han. "I know you love me, but I can't destroy your future. Write an application. Say you no longer love me and you want to raise our child by yourself. Pretend you know nothing and let's hope they won't demote you. Draw the line now, and don't let me ruin your future and Ming-Ming's."

Kai shook her head slowly.

"Do you want me to write a draft for you? You need only to sign."

Kai had long ago stopped loving the man in front of her; perhaps she had never loved him. But she felt an urge to hug him as a mother would, to comfort a child who had tried hard to act like a brave man. Han broke down again in her arms, and she let him bury his face in her hair, feeling the dampness on her collar. Nobody would love her as much as he did, she remembered his saying on their wedding night; she had looked up at a poster of Chairman Mao on the wall of the hotel room when he whispered the secret into her dark hair, uncut and long as a maiden's.

APRIL 4, 1979, Tong wrote in his nature journal, and then read the weather forecast on the right-hand corner of *Muddy River Daily*. *Sunny. Light wind. High 12° C, low –1° C.* He recorded the numbers and then went out to look for Ear. Saturday was a half day at school, and he was surprised that Ear had forgotten; he had told Ear that morning to come home around midday, and Ear had never failed to do so on Saturdays. Tong wondered what the dog was up to. He was no longer a puppy and had secrets of his own. Some evenings Ear looked indifferently at the food Tong brought out to the cardboard box. Tong wondered if Ear had been up to something naughty, stealing food from other dogs or from the marketplace.

He called Ear's name as he walked from alley to alley. He spotted several dogs, but they turned out not to be Ear, all busy with their own lives on this spring afternoon. Perhaps he shouldn't blame Ear, Tong thought; after the long winter, who wouldn't want to run wild a little? He circled the town and then walked up to the river.

The ice drifts, which not long ago were entertaining teenagers, had melted, while the boys had taken up a new, more exciting game in the alleys, where they formed gangs that bore the names of wild beasts and fought to make their groups' names endure. The fights started harmlessly, with fists and kicks, but soon smaller groups merged into bigger ones, and weapons of all sorts were created by stealing, whetting, grinding, and imagining. The authorities, however, ignored the gangs—parents and teachers and city officials were busy worrying about feeding their families and securing promotions, but this spring they were also preoccupied with the trouble that had intruded on their lives in the form of uninvited, mimeographed leaflets. A line had been crossed. Which side would they choose? they wondered secretly at work, and asked their spouses at home.

The troubles and indecisions of the grown-up world did not trespass on the many worlds occupied by other, less anxious lives. As they did every year, children in elementary school found a new craze. This spring, for the girls, collecting cellophane candy wrappers replaced the plastic beads of last year, and for the boys, gambling with serialized martial arts heroes replaced a similar game with folded paper triangles. Girls in middle school remained aloof to the street fighting, even though some of the rumbles were for their attention. Unaware of the boys' youthful ambition, the girls lavished their passions on their most intimate girlfriends. They sat on the riverbank or in their own yards, their hands locked and their fingers interwoven; they murmured about the future, their voices no more than whispers, for fear they would startle themselves from the dream about a world that would soon open like a mysterious flower.

Tong walked past a pair of girls sitting by the river singing a love song, neither of them noticing his distress. Soon he reached the birch woods, and a young man crouching in front of a shallow cave stood up at his approaching steps. Tong walked closer and saw a gray ball with arrows embedded in it on the ground. "What is it?" he asked.

The man turned to Tong and hissed. "Don't wake up my hedgehog."

Tong recognized the young man, though he did not know his name. "Don't worry," Tong said. "He's hibernating so you won't wake him up by speaking."

"Spring's already here," the man said.

"But it's not warm enough for the hedgehog yet," Tong said. He had read in a children's almanac, retrieved by Old Hua from a garbage can, that hedgehogs would not wake up from hibernation until the daytime temperature rose to 15° C. He told this to the young man and showed him the recordings in his nature journal.

Snakes too would wake up around the same time, Tong said, though turtles would wait longer because it took longer for the river to warm up. The man shrugged and said he had no use for the information. "My home is definitely warmer," he said. He put on his gloves and scooped up the arrowed ball.

"Why do you want to take him home?" The hedgehog looked dead in the young man's arms, though Tong knew better than to worry.

"Because I need a pet. You have a dog named Ear, don't you?"

"Have you seen him today? I'm looking for him," Tong said.

Bashi looked at Tong with a strange smile. He wondered how fast the boy who had killed Ear walked. By now he must be past the city boundary. "He may be running somewhere with his girlfriend now," said Bashi.

"He doesn't have a girlfriend," Tong said.

"How do you know?" Bashi said with a grin that made Tong uneasy. Tong decided not to talk to the man. He turned to walk away but Bashi caught up with him, holding the hedgehog in the cup of his two hands. "I'm teaching you a lesson. Sometimes you think your dog is your best friend but you may be wrong. For instance, all of a sudden he may decide to go home with someone else."

"He won't," Tong said, a little angry.

"How do you know?"

"Of course I know. He's my dog."

Bashi said nothing and whistled. After a while, Tong said, "Why are you following me?"

"You're going back to town, and I am too. So how come it is not you who's following me?"

Tong stopped, and the man did too. Tong turned and walked back toward the river and Bashi turned, walking side by side with the boy.

"Now you're following me," Tong said.

"It just so happened that I changed my mind and decided to go in that direction too," Bashi said, and winked.

Tong flushed with anger. What a shameless grown-up; even a five-year-old would know more of the rules of the world. "I don't want to walk with you," Tong said. "Stop following me."

"I want to walk with you," said Bashi, affecting a child's voice. "There's no law that says I can't walk with you."

"But you don't follow people if they tell you they don't want to play with you," Tong said with exasperation.

"Whose rule is that? You don't own this road, do you? So I can put my feet wherever I want on this road, no? If I like, I can follow you anywhere, as long as I don't go into your house."

Tong was in tears, speechless. He had never met a person like the man in front of him, and he didn't know how to reason with him. Bashi looked at Tong's tears with great interest and then smiled. "Okay, now I don't want to play with you anymore," he said, still in a little boy's voice. He walked away, throwing the hedgehog up like a ball and catching it with gloved hands. A few times he missed and the hedgehog rolled onto the road, which made him laugh.

Ear didn't return by dinnertime. When Tong mentioned this absence to his parents, his father, who slumped in the only armchair and looked at the wall, where there was nothing to see, said dully, "He'll come home when he will."

It was useless to talk with his father about anything before dinner—for him, it was the most important meal and nothing, not even a falling sky, could disturb him while he waited for it. Tong's mother glanced at him with sympathy but said nothing. She put dinner on the table and brought out a bottle of rice liquor. Tong took the bottle from her and poured some of the liquor into a porcelain cup. When his father was drunk and asleep, he would beg his mother for help.

Tong carried the cup with both hands to his father. "Dinner is ready, Baba."

Tong's father accepted the cup and tapped on Tong's head with his knuckles. It hurt but Tong tried not to let it show. "It's better raising a boy than a dog," his father said, his way of showing his approval of Tong. He moved to the table and downed the cup. "Now pour me another one, Son."

Tong did and his father asked him if he wanted to try some. His mother intervened halfheartedly, but his father wouldn't listen. "Try once," he urged Tong. "You're old enough. When I was your age, I smoked and drank with my father every night," he said, and he struck the table with his fist. "My father—your grandfather—wasn't he a real man? I tell you, Son, don't ever do anything less than he did."

Tong's paternal grandfather was, according to his father's drunken tales, a local legend, with a firecracker temper, ready to fight anyone over the slightest injustice. He had died in 1951, in his late forties. The story was that he had had a big fight defending his fellow villagers against a party official, sent down to supervise the process of turning private land into a collective commune. He had beaten the official half to death; the next day he had been arrested and executed on the spot as an enemy of the new Communist nation.

Tong's mother scooped some fried peanuts onto his father's plate. "Don't drink on an empty stomach," she said.

Tong's father ignored her. He poured himself another cup and pointed his chopsticks at Tong. "Listen, your grandfather was a real man. Your father is nothing less. You'd better not disappoint us. Now move here next to me."

Tong hesitated. He did not like his father's breath and his intimate gestures when he was drunk, but his mother moved his chair, with him in it, before he could protest. His father put a hand on Tong's shoulder and said, "Let me tell you this story, and you'll know how a man was made. Have you heard of Liu Bang, the first emperor of the Han dynasty? Before he became an emperor, he had to fight many years with Xiang Yu, his toughest enemy. Once, Xiang Yu caught Liu Bang's grandparents, his mother, and his wife. He brought them to the battlefield and sent a messenger to Liu Bang. *If you don't surrender this very moment, I'll cook them into meat paste and my soldiers will have a feast tonight.* Guess what Liu Bang said? Ah, wasn't he the hero of all heroes! He wrote back to Xiang Yu, *Thank you for letting me know about the banquet. Would you be a good and generous person and send me, your hungry enemy, a bowl of the meat paste?* Think about that, Son. If your heart is hard enough to eat your mother and your wife, nothing can beat you in life."

Tong looked at his mother, on the other side of the table. She gave him a smile, and he tried to smile back. They were on their way, it seemed, to another night during which he and his mother would have to sit and listen to his father tell the same old stories; the dishes and the rice would be reheated a few times, until his father was finally too drunk to carry on with his tales, and eventually Tong and his mother would be permitted to eat.

Tong thought about Ear; his father said that love for a dog was a lowly thing to feel, and his only concern, when it came to Tong, seemed to be to make him into a manly man. Tong wondered if he would disappoint his father. If an enemy were to threaten him with his grandparents' and his mother's lives, he would cry and beg, promising anything in exchange for their lives.

After several more rounds of drinking, Tong's father pushed his chair back and told his mother to get a brick—she kept a pile of bricks in the kitchen for him to demonstrate his kung-fu skills with, and she replenished the stock dutifully when it was running low. When she came back with a red brick, he shook his head and said it would be too easy; he needed a bigger, harder brick tonight. Hear that? he said, stretching his fingers and making cracking sounds with his knuckles. She replied that the red bricks were all they had, and wouldn't it work for him if she stacked two bricks. Tong's father lost his temper, calling her a brainless woman and ordering her to go out and borrow one from their neighbors, who were building an extra shack in their yard for a granduncle who had come to visit and decided not to leave.

When she returned with a heavy construction brick, six times as big as the red brick, Tong's father took it over and put another hand on her neck. "I could wring your neck with two fingers. Do you believe me?" he asked. She giggled and said of course, she had no doubt about it. He snorted with satisfaction and set down the brick in the middle of the yard.

Tong watched his father chanting and dancing a little before he crouched down and, with a bellow, hit the brick with the heel of his hand. Ear would have enjoyed the evening if only he had been home in time—he was always the most excited member of the family when Tong's father put on a drunken show. The brick remained intact, but his father's hand looked red and swollen. Tong hid both hands in his pockets. Only once in a while could Tong's father break a brick in half, by sheer luck perhaps, but he never tired of his brick-hacking trick.

He tried another time with both hands but the brick did not yield to the strike. When he examined his hands, the sides of both of them were bleeding. Unfazed, he told Tong's mother to stop fussing, when she brought a clean, soft rag for him. He tried two more times, and when the brick refused to surrender, he kicked it, which seemed to hurt his toe more than it had his hands. He cursed and hopped on his good foot to the storage cabin, and before Tong's mother could protest, his father hit the brick hard with a hammer. The brick broke but not into two halves; he squatted down to study it and roared with laughter. Tong moved closer with his mother, and they saw three rusty iron rods in the middle of the brick, holding it together. "Where did they steal the construction blocks for their shack?" Tong's father said. He wiped his bleeding hands carelessly on his pants and drank more liquor, content with the fact that he had not lost face. When he was urged once again by Tong's mother to go to bed, he retreated into the bedroom with a last cup, and soon his snores thundered through the closed door.

Tong and his mother sat by the table and she smiled at him. "What a funny man he is," she said quietly, and shook her head with admiration. The dinner was cold now and she stoked the fire to heat it up for Tong, but he was not in the mood for eating. "Mama, do you think something has happened to Ear?" he asked.

He shouldn't worry, Tong's mother said. Before he could reply, he heard a noise. He rushed to the yard and was disappointed to find that it was not Ear scratching on the gate but someone knocking. He opened the gate. In the yellow streetlight Tong saw the unfamiliar face of a middle-aged woman, her head wrapped in a shawl. She asked for his parents in a low voice. Next to her on the ground was a big nylon bag.

"Are you coming because of my dog? Did something happen to Ear?" Tong asked.

"Why, is your dog missing?"

"He's never been out so late," he said.

"I'm sorry to hear that. But don't worry," the woman said.

The grown-ups all said the same thing, without any offer to help. Tong stood aside but before he could invite the woman into the yard, his mother came to the gate and asked the woman what had brought her.

"Comrade, you must have heard of Gu Shan's case by now," said the woman. "I'm here to talk to you about a rally on Gu Shan's behalf."

Tong's mother looked around before apologizing in a low voice that she and her husband were not the type of people who cared for this information.

"Think about the horrible things that happened to a child of another mother," the woman said. "I'm a mother of three. And you're a mother too. How many siblings do you have, boy?"

"Three," Tong said.

His mother pulled him closer to her. "I'm sorry. This household is not interested in politics."

"We can't run away from politics. It'll catch up with us."

"It's not that I'm not sympathetic," Tong's mother said. "But what difference would we make? The dead are dead."

"But if we don't speak up now, there will be a next time, another child maybe. *A thousand grains of sand can make a tower.* We each have to do what we can, don't we?"

Tong watched his mother, who looked away from the woman and apologized again. Once in a while, beggars from out of town would stop in their alley, asking for money and food. Tong's father never allowed these people near their yard, but his mother always looked embarrassed when he shouted at the poor and hungry strangers that he was an honest worker and had no obligation to share his blood-and-sweat money. Sometimes when Tong's father fell into a drunken slumber, his mother would wrap up a few leftover buns and leave them outside the gate. When Tong got up early the next morning, the buns would always be gone. Did the beggars come back to get the buns? he asked his mother when his father was not around, but she only shook her head and smiled, as if she did not understand the question.

"Comrade, please listen to me just for this one time," the woman said. "We're having a memorial service for Gu Shan tomorrow at the city square. Come and meet her mother. Perhaps you'll change your mind then and sign the petition to support the rally."

Tong's mother looked flustered. "I can't go—I—my husband won't be happy with it." She looked around as though to check if he was coming.

"I'm asking for your own heart and conscience," the woman said. "You can't let your husband make every decision for you."

Tong's mother shook her head slowly, as if disappointed at the accusation. The woman unzipped the nylon sack and brought out a white flower. "Even if you don't want to sign the petition, come with this white flower and pay respect to the heroic woman and her mother," she said.

Tong looked at the flower, made of white tissue paper and attached to a long stem, also made of white paper. His mother sighed and did not move. Tong accepted the flower and the woman smiled. "You're a good helper for your mama," the woman said to Tong, and then turned to his mother. "Every family will receive a white flower tonight. It won't pose any danger if you just leave the flower in the basket for us tomorrow. We'll be there before sunrise."

Tong's mother closed the gate quietly behind the woman. She and Tong stood in the darkness and listened to the woman knock on their neighbor's gate. After a moment, Tong nudged his mother and handed her the paper flower. She took it, and then tore the flower off the paper stem and squeezed both together into a small ball. When Tong raised his voice and asked her why, she put a warm, soft palm over his lips. "We can't keep the flower. Baba will find out and he won't be happy."

Tong was about to protest, but she shushed him and said the matter was better left where it was. She led him gently by the arm and he followed her into the front room of the house. His father was still snoring in the bedroom. The dishes that his mother had reheated had grown cold again, but she seemed too tired to care now. She sat him down at the table and took the seat on the other side. "You must be starving now," she said.

"No."

"Don't you want to eat something? There's your favorite potato stew."

"No."

"Don't be angry at me," she said. "You'll understand when you're older."

"Why don't you want to take the flower back tomorrow? The auntie said it wouldn't bring any trouble."

"We can't trust her."

"But why?" Tong asked.

"We don't want to have anything to do with these people," his mother said. "Baba says they're crazy."

"But Baba is wrong and they aren't crazy," Tong said.

Tong's mother looked at him sharply. "What do you know to say so?" she said.

Tong did not speak. He thought about the leaflets he had kept and made into an exercise book. He had read the words on the leaflets; the part that he could grasp sounded reasonable to him— they said that people should have the right to say what they thought; they talked about respecting everyone's rights, however lowly people were in their social positions. Tong himself understood how it felt to be looked down upon all the time as a village boy.

"Don't question your parents," Tong's mother said. "We make decisions that are in our own best interests."

"Mama, is the auntie a bad person?" Tong asked.

"Who? The one with the flowers? I don't know. She may not be a bad person, but she is doing the wrong thing."

"Why?"

"The government wouldn't have killed the wrong person in the first place."

"Was my grandfather a bad person?"

Tong's mother was quiet for a long time and then got up to close the bedroom door. "Maybe I shouldn't tell you this," she said. "But you have to know that the story Baba told was not all true. Your grandpa did beat an official but it was over a widow he wanted to marry after your grandma died. The official also wanted to marry the woman, so they had a fight after an argument in a diner. When the official was beaten, he announced that your grandpa was a counterrevolutionary and executed him. There was nothing grand in the story, and Baba knows it too."

"So was my grandpa wronged?"

Tong's mother shook her head. "The lesson for you is: Never act against government officials. Don't think Baba is only a drunkard. He knows every rule by heart and he doesn't make mistakes. Otherwise, he would not have lived till now, with a counterrevolutionary father."

"But what if the government made a mistake? Our teacher says nobody is always right."

"Let other people be wronged—it has nothing to do with us. Remember Baba's story of the emperor? You have to harden your heart to grow up into a man, do you understand?"

Tong nodded, though he didn't know what to think of her words. She had never talked to him about such things, and she looked unfamiliar, almost intimidating. She watched him a moment longer and then smiled. "Look how serious you are," she said. "You're a little boy and you shouldn't worry yourself with grown-ups' business."

Tong did not reply. His mother urged him to eat again. He shoveled the food into his mouth without tasting it. Then he heard a noise and ran to the gate, but it was only wind passing through the alley. He came back and asked his mother if they should go out and look for Ear.

She sighed and put on her coat. "Another boy that constantly asks for attention," she said tiredly. "Why don't you wash and go to bed now? I'll go out and look for him."

"Can I come with you?" Tong asked.

"No," she said, and her voice, harsher than usual, stopped him from begging again.

Tong's mother walked to a friend's house two blocks away and knocked on the door. She was coming for a chat, she said, not wanting to stay cold in the windy night looking in vain for a missing dog. The friend—a fellow worker—invited her in and they talked over cups of hot tea about the plan for the next day: The friend's family would be having a picnic, it being their ritual to go to the mountain on the day of Ching Ming; Tong's mother said they had no plans, though watching the friend's children pack the food containers with excitement, she wished for Tong's sake that they did.

Elsewhere in the city, white flowers in nylon bags were carried from house to house. People opened their gates, finding themselves facing a doctor from a workers' clinic, a clerk in the optical factory, a retired middle school teacher, a department store accountant, a pharmacist, and a few educated youths who had recently returned from the countryside. Some of the white flowers found their way into trash cans, toy boxes, and other corners where they soon would be forgotten; others, placed more carefully, sat in vigil and waited for the day to break.

That night Tong did not sleep well. He woke up several times and went out into the yard to check Ear's cardboard house, even though he knew Ear couldn't get through the locked gate. Ear must have got himself into some big trouble. Tong cried quietly to himself, and his mother woke up once and told him in a hushed voice that maybe Ear would be back in the morning. Tong sniffled; he knew she did not believe what she was saying. After a while, when he still could not stop crying, she held him close and rocked him before telling him that perhaps Ear would never come home again. Had something happened to him? Tong asked. She did not know, his mother replied, but it did not hurt to prepare for the worst.

THEY HAD NAMED HER PEONY after the kerchief that had come with the bundle, a silk square with a single embroidered peony. The pink of the blossom and the green of the leaves had both faded, the white fabric taking on a yellow hue, and Mrs. Hua, her arms curled around the newborn, had wondered if the baby had come from an old family with status. All the same, a princess's body trapped in the fate of a handmaiden, Old Hua replied, bending down and telling Morning Glory, three and a half then, that heaven had answered her request and sent her a little sister.

The kerchief, Mrs. Hua said to Old Hua now, had they left it with Peony?

They must have, Old Hua replied; there was no reason they would not have. Peony had always known it to be special to her.

Mrs. Hua watched Old Hua work on the pickax, which had a loose head; Bashi had offered to buy them new tools, but Mrs. Hua, worrying that the boy would squander his savings before he knew it, had told him that they would rather use their own pickaxes and shovels, which their old hands had grown used to.

She wondered if Peony's mother had ever found her, Mrs. Hua said, a question she asked often of herself. Old Hua hammered on the pickax and replied that they did not even know if the mother was alive, or whether she ever meant to find Peony. It would be a pity if they had not found each other, Mrs. Hua said, and Old Hua hammered without saying anything.

The girl had taken to dreaming more than her adopted parents and elder sister, more than the younger girls who were added to the family one by one. She was the slowest to sort the rubbish but the first to suggest that a thrown-away wallet, once found in a garbage can, might contain enough money for the family to live happily and comfortably for the rest of their lives, and she was disappointed by the photographs in the wallet, cut so methodically that the fragments were beyond recognition. She wept after each baby found at the roadside, and she made a point to remember the names of the towns where her younger sisters were picked up, not concealing her hope of finding the birth parents, hers and Morning Glory's included.

That had not surprised Mrs. Hua and her husband, as they too had had dreams about Peony's return to her birth parents. The kerchief, an intentional loose end left by a mother in a helpless situation, would perhaps one day be sought out. What was the woman's story? Mrs. Hua wondered, more often than she thought about the mothers of the other girls. Heaven had placed Peony in their care and it would be up to heaven's will to take her back, the Huas believed, but in the end, they had to harden their hearts and let her be taken in, at thirteen and a half, as a child bride for a man ten years her senior. He was an only son, born to parents in their late forties when the hope for a child had almost run out. They would treat Peony as their own daughter, the couple promised, their apparent affection for the girl a relief for the Huas.

Mrs. Hua wondered if Peony's birth mother would have acknowledged and honored the marriage arrangement had she found the girl. Different scenes played out often in her imagination. Sometimes it was the boy and his parents who were greatly dismayed when Peony decided to leave them for a life she had always dreamed of going back to; at other times the mother was hurt when Peony turned her back as a punishment for the abandonment. Mrs. Hua talked about these worries now to her husband, and he stopped his hammering for a beat. Once a mother, always a mother, he said, his voice reproachful, but Mrs. Hua, knowing the same could be said of him as a father, only sighed in agreement. A child losing her parents became an orphan, a woman losing her husband a widow, but there was not a term for the lesser parents that those who had lost their children became. Once parents, they would remain parents for the rest of their lives.

Neither talked for a moment. Old Hua laid the pickax aside and began to work on the dulled edge of a shovel.

When Mrs. Hua broke the silence she said that they should go to the city square the next morning.

Old Hua looked up at her and did not reply.

She felt responsible for Teacher Gu, Mrs. Hua said. It had been on her mind since she had learned of Teacher Gu's illness. They should go there and apologize to Mrs. Gu.

Old Hua said that they were hired for a burial.

They could go early, before they went out to the burial, Mrs. Hua said. Bashi had come earlier in the evening and said that he had a bad cold, and asked the couple to bury his grandmother themselves. Neither Old Hua nor Mrs. Hua had pointed out the lie to the boy's face; he had paid them generously.

Old Hua nodded. So they would go, he said, as she had known that he would.

NINE

Teacher Gu pretended to be asleep while his wife moved quietly in and out of the bedroom on the morning of Ching Ming. He ignored the small noises and tried to focus his memory on another morning, the distant day of his first honeymoon, when his wife had slipped away from the wedding bed and made tea for him. He had willed himself not to hear the small clicking of teacups and saucers, but when he had opened his eyes with feigned surprise at the tea, she had smiled and scolded him lovingly for his playacting. Didn't he know his quivering eyelashes had betrayed him, she said, and he said that he did not, because he had never had to feign sleep for anyone before.

"I'm going out for a few hours," Mrs. Gu said to him, by the bedside. "Here's your breakfast, in the thermos. I'll be back soon."

Teacher Gu did not answer. He willed her to disappear so he could go back to that other morning.

"If you need to use the chamber pot, I've put it here behind the chair."

Teacher Gu thought about the things that he had not known on that newlywed morning, of the intimacies one would never wish to share with anyone but oneself, the vulnerability one was forced into in old age. He thought about secrets too, of sleeping in the same bed with one woman and dreaming about the other, of his wife hiding a

social life from a sick husband half dying in the hospital. Such deceptions must take place under every roof, some more hurtful than
others. His first wife must often have thought about other men during their honeymoon, thoughts without romantic desire but nameless strangers occupying her mind nonetheless; she had arranged the
honeymoon in that specific sea resort so that, with a husband who
served at the National Congress as a cover, she could work as a secret
messenger for the underground Communist Party. These stories,
hidden from him for the duration of their marriage, had been revealed after they signed their divorce papers. He had not doubted
her love then, even after she showed him the divorce application, but
now, thirty years and the death of a daughter later, he wondered if he
had been too naïve to see the truth. Perhaps his first marriage had
been based, from the very beginning, on the merit of his serving the
government that she and her comrades were fighting to overthrow.
He provided cover for her, and brought home government papers
not meant for her to peruse; had she ever considered him an exit
plan, in case her side failed to win?

Teacher Gu struggled out of bed. Mrs. Gu entered the bedroom,
already dressed up to venture into the early April morning, a black
mourning band on her arm. "Do you need something?" she said,
coming over and helping him into his shoes. "I didn't hear what you
said."

"I said nothing," he said. "You were hallucinating."

"Are you all right? Do you need me to find someone to sit with
you while I'm away?"

"What's the good in sitting with a half-dead man?"

"Let's not argue."

"Listen, woman, I'm not arguing with you, or anyone. You have
your business, and I have mine." He pushed her hand away and
limped into the front room. By the door he saw a photo of Shan, enlarged to the size of a poster and framed with black paper and white
silk ribbon. "I see your comrades and you are making her into a pup-

pet," Teacher Gu said. Before his wife answered, he shuffled to the old desk in the kitchen and sat down. He pushed away two glasses and a plate of leftover food.

"She is a martyr," Mrs. Gu said.

"A martyr serves a cause as a puppet serves a show. If you look at history, as no one in this country does anymore, a martyr has always served the purpose of deception on a grand scale, be it a religion or an ideology," Teacher Gu said, surprised by his own eloquent and patient voice. He had been conducting these dialogues in various imagined conversations with his first wife in the past few days. Mrs. Gu said something, but Teacher Gu did not catch her words. Already his mind was floating on to the other woman, who had—or had not, if he still had some remaining luck from a luckless life—intentionally deceived him for three years. He wanted to write a letter to her and request the truth.

Mrs. Gu left with the picture without a farewell. Teacher Gu thought for a moment and remembered he had been looking for his fountain pen. He tried the two drawers by the table, in which he was horrified to find all kinds of odds and ends, as if he had forgotten they had been there for years. After some fumbling, he realized that his wife must have moved his decades-old Parker pen someplace for safekeeping after he had fallen ill. Had she been expecting him to die, so that she would burn the pen with him? Or had she already sold the pen to the secondhand store for a few chickens? This new fear left Teacher Gu in a cold sweat. The pen had been a present from his college professor when Teacher Gu had established the first boys' school in what was then one of the least educated provinces in the nation; the gold tip had worn out and been replaced twice, but the body of the pen—smooth, dark blue, and polished by years of gentle care—retained its aristocratic feel. Even Shan, in her most fervent years as a young revolutionary, denouncing anything Western as capitalist, had spared Teacher Gu the pen by pretending not to know its hiding place, sewn into the middle of a quilt by his wife.

Teacher Gu pushed himself against the table and stood up. There were not many places in the house for safekeeping, and he located the pen in the bedroom in a wooden box, where his wife kept a few of her jewels that had survived the Cultural Revolution as well as a snapshot of all three of them from when Shan had been a toddler. Teacher Gu squinted at the picture, taken by a friend who had come to visit them in the spring of 1954; Shan was staring at the camera while her parents were both watching her. The camera had been a novelty in Muddy River back then, and a group of children and a few adults had gathered and watched the black box hanging from their friend's neck. He snapped shots generously, of Teacher Gu's family as well as of the onlooking children, but this picture was the only one his friend mailed. Teacher Gu wondered what had happened to the other pictures; another letter he needed to write, he thought, before remembering that the friend had taken his own life, in 1957, as an anti-Communist intellectual.

Teacher Gu shuffled back to the front room. He took the pen out of the velvet box, unscrewed the cap carefully, and wiped off the dried ink on the gold tip with a small piece of silk he kept in the box for that purpose.

Greatly respected Comrade Cheng, he started the letter, and then thought the opening ridiculous with its revolutionary ugliness, even though he had addressed her with this formality in his letters, once or twice a year, for the past thirty years. He ripped the page off the notebook and started again. *My once closest friend, colleague, and beloved wife,* he wrote with great effort. "My once closest friend, colleague, and beloved wife," he read it out loud, and decided that it suited his mood.

Remember the umbrella that my father lent my mother at a street corner in Paris that started their lifelong love story? It was in the autumn of 1916, if you still remember. You said what a romance when I first told you the story; I am writing

to let you know that the emblem of this great love no longer
exists. The umbrella did not survive my daughter's death
because her mother, my current wife, thought the daughter
needed an umbrella in heaven. Were there a heaven above, I
wonder if my parents are fighting with my daughter for
possession of the umbrella. The grandparents had not met
the granddaughter in life; in death I hope they do not have
to spend a long time in the company of the girl. My parents,
as you may remember, possessed the elegance and wisdom of
the intellectuals of their generation; my daughter, however,
was more a product of this revolutionary age than of her
grandparents' noble Manchu blood. She died of a poison
that she had herself helped to concoct. Despite art and
philosophy and your beloved mathematics and my faith in
enlightenment, in the end, what marks our era—perhaps we
could take the liberty to believe, for all we know, that this era
may last for the next hundred years?—is the moaning of our
bones crushed beneath the weight of empty words. There is
no beauty in this crushing, and there is, alas, no escape for us
now, or ever.

Teacher Gu stopped writing and read the letter. His handwriting
was a shaky old man's but there was no point in being ashamed at
the loss of his capacity as a calligrapher. He folded the letter in the
special way that young lovers had folded love notes forty years earlier
and put it in an envelope. Only then did he realize he had forgotten
to ask the question. He had wasted time and space in a uselessly
moody letter. He opened his notebook.

Highly respected Comrade Cheng: Please tell me, in all
honesty, if you were assigned to marry me by your party
leaders for your Communist cause. I am getting closer
to death each day and I prefer not to leave this world a
deceived man.

Teacher Gu signed his name carefully and sealed the letter along with the first one without rereading either of them. He put the envelope into his pocket, pulled himself across the room, and stumbled into an old armchair. The writing had exhausted him; he closed his eyes, and returned to the argument he had carried on all night with his first wife, about whether Marxism was a form of spiritual opium, as Marx had once described other religions.

"Greatly respected citizens of Muddy River," the voice from the loudspeaker said, interrupting Teacher Gu's eloquent argument. He recognized the voice as the star announcer, and thought that the woman sounded falsely grave for a holiday of ghosts. "Good morning, all comrades. This is a special broadcast on the current events in Muddy River," the voice said. "As you may not know, there is great historical change happening in our nation's capital, where a stretch of wall, called the democratic wall, has been set up for people to express their ideas on where our country is going. It is a critical moment for our nation, yet news about the democratic wall did not reach us. We've been taught for years that in our Communist state we are the masters of our own country, and of our own fates. But is this ever true? Not long ago, Gu Shan, a daughter of Muddy River, was wrongfully sentenced to death. She was not a criminal; she was a woman who felt immense responsibility for our nation's future, who spoke out against a corrupt system with courage and insight, but what became of this heroine who acted ahead of her time?"

Teacher Gu's hands trembled as he tried to pull himself out of the armchair. The woman continued to talk, but he could no longer hear her. He struggled to open the notebook, his hand shaking so much that he tore several pages before finding an intact one. "I will beg you only for this one thing now," wrote Teacher Gu to his first wife.

May I entrust myself to you when I can no longer trust my wife of thirty years? Only in our culture can a body be dug from its grave and put on display for other people's political

ambitions. Could you please agree to oversee my cremation?
Do not allow traces of me to be left to my current wife, or
anyone, for that matter.

"Comrades with conscience!" the woman continued to speak
over the loudspeaker. "Please come to the city square and speak up
against our corrupt system. Please come to meet and support a
heroic mother who is perpetuating the legend of her daughter."

Stupid women, Teacher Gu said aloud. He put on a coat on top
of his pajamas and got ready to go and post the letters.

THE YARD WAS QUIET in an eerie way when Tong woke up before daybreak. He opened the gate, hoping to see an eager Ear waiting for
him outside, but apart from a few early-rising men loading their bicycles with bamboo boxes of offerings for their outings, the alley was
empty. Tong asked the men about Ear, but none of them had seen
the dog.

Tong left the alley, and at the crossroad of two major streets, he
caught the first sight of people walking toward the city square. They
were silent, men with hats pulled low over their eyebrows, women
with half of their faces wrapped in shawls. Tong stood by the roadside and watched the people pass, sometimes in twos but mostly single file, each keeping a distance from the person ahead of him. Tong
recognized an uncle from his father's work unit and greeted him,
but the man only nodded briefly and then walked faster, as though
eager to get rid of Tong. The shops on the main street would be
closed for the day, and there was nothing but the public event to attract people to the town center. Perhaps Ear, a gregarious dog that
always enjoyed boisterous events, would be found there. Tong waited
for a gap to join the procession.

The eastern sky lit up; another cloudless spring day. The main
street was quiet in spite of the growing number of people coming in
from side streets and alleys. No one talked, and crows and magpies
croaked in the pale light, louder than usual. People nodded when

they saw acquaintances, but most of the time they focused on the stretch of road in front of them. A few men loitered in front of the shop doors that lined both sides of the main street, their faces too covered by hats or high collars.

"Are you still looking for that dog of yours?" someone said, with a tap on Tong's shoulder. He looked up and saw the young man from the previous day, grinning and showing his yellowed teeth.

"How did you know?" Tong said.

"Because he'd be here with you otherwise," Bashi said. "Listen, I'm a detective, so nothing escapes my eyes."

"Have you seen my dog?"

"Do I look like someone who wouldn't tell you if I'd seen him? But I do have a tip for you. You've come to the wrong place. Nobody here and nobody there"—Bashi pointed in the direction of the city square—"cares about your lost dog."

Tong knew that the man was right. How could he ask people about a small dog when they had more important things to think about? He thanked Bashi nonetheless and moved toward the city square, wishing that the man would stop following him.

"I know you're not listening to me," Bashi scolded. He pulled Tong out of the procession. "You can't go there alone."

"Why?"

"How would you get into the city square by yourself? Do you have an admission ticket? They won't let you in without a ticket."

Tong decided that Bashi was lying, and turned to leave, but Bashi grabbed his shoulder. "You don't believe me?" he said, and brought out something from his sleeve. "See, here's the ticket I'm talking about. Do you have one?"

Tong saw a white paper flower, half-hidden inside Bashi's sleeve.

"Look at these people. They all have a white flower in their sleeves or under their coats. If you don't have one, they won't let you in, because they have to make sure you're not spying for their enemies. Did you see those men in front of the shops? Look there. Why aren't they going to the square?" Bashi paused and savored Tong's questioning look. "Let me tell you—they look like secret police to me. How can you prove that you are not working for the police? Of course you're too young for that, you could say, but you're too young to go to a rally also. Unless you're with someone older."

Tong thought about Bashi's words. They did not quite make sense but he found it hard to argue. "Are you going there?" Tong asked.

"See, that's a question a smart boy asks. Yes, and no. I'm going there, for a different reason than these people are, but if you're looking for someone to tag along with, you've found the right person. But here's one thing you have to promise me—you need to listen to me. I don't want you to get lost or trampled by the crowd."

Just then the woman announcer's voice came from the loudspeakers. Both Tong and Bashi stopped to listen. When she finished, Bashi said, "I didn't know that Sweet Pea was behind this. So it must mean the government is behind the rally now. Bad news, huh?"

"What's bad news?"

"Nothing. So, do you want to come with me?"

Tong thought about it and agreed.

"I'm old enough to be your uncle already," Bashi said. "But I'll give you a discount this time, and you can call me Big Brother."

Tong did not reply but walked with Bashi. When they reached the city square, Tong realized that Bashi had been lying—there was no one asking for the white flower as a token for admission, nor was there a confused stampede. The line ran from the center to the southwest corner of the square, and then turned east until it reached the southeast corner, where more people were joining it. Tong stepped behind the last man, but Bashi tugged at him and whispered that there was much more to see elsewhere. Tong hesitated but followed Bashi out of curiosity. A smart and sensible boy, Bashi praised Tong, as they walked to the east side of Chairman Mao's statue, where there was less of a crowd. A few wreaths of white flowers had been placed along the edge of the pedestal; in front of the wreaths was an enlarged photo held up by a makeshift stand of bamboo sticks; the young girl in the picture, a teenager, tipped her head slightly backward, her smile wide, as if the photographer had just made a joke.

Bashi clicked his tongue. "Is that the woman?"

"Who?"

"The counterrevolutionary."

Tong looked at the picture. Hard as he tried, he could not connect the girl, young, confident, and beautiful, to the woman he had seen on the day of the execution, her face an ashen color and her neck wrapped in bloodstained surgical tape.

"Hey, hey, did you lose your soul over a beautiful face?" Bashi said to Tong. "Look there."

Tong breathed hard and stood on tiptoe. Wreaths as tall as a man's height had formed a circle, and the line of people going in and then leaving, through a gap on the other side of the circle, blocked his view.

Bashi looked for a long moment. "Very interesting. Aha, that's her. And he's there too."

Tong did not want to admit that he was too short to see anything. Bashi looked at him and sighed. "Well, I've brought you here so I am responsible for entertaining you, no?" He squatted down and told Tong to hop onto his shoulders. Tong hesitated, but when Bashi told him to stop being a sissy, he climbed up. "Hold on to my head," Bashi said, and stood up. "Ugh. You look like a cabbage but weigh like a stone Buddha," Bashi complained, but Tong did not reply, his attention drawn inside the circle. In the middle a woman was carefully placing a white flower into a huge basket with a diameter of more than two arms. Next to the basket was a table, on which lay a piece of white fabric. A man behind the table pointed to the white fabric and said something to the woman, and she shook her head apologetically and left without looking up at him. Tong recognized the man as a teacher from his school.

"Do you see what I see?" Bashi said, and moved closer to the fence made of wreaths. Tong wavered and held on to Bashi's neck. "Hey, don't choke me."

Tong let his hands free. "That auntie there is the news announcer," he said, a bit too loud.

Kai looked up at a boy's voice but quickly turned back to the woman who was about to leave the circle. "Thank you, comrade," she said. "This is Gu Shan's mother."

"Thank you for your support," Mrs. Gu said.

The woman did not acknowledge Kai or Mrs. Gu when they held out their hands to thank her. She left quickly and thought about her husband and two children, who must be wondering by now why a short stop off at her work unit had taken so long; she had lied and said she needed to readjust a perimeter in the machine she ran in the food-processing factory.

The line moved quietly. One by one people dropped their white flowers in the basket; some of them signed their names on the white cloth, but others, when invited, apologized. Kai greeted everyone in line and spoke to them about the importance of the petition for the nation's well-being. Her voice, soft and clear, sounded reassuring; after all, was she not the official news announcer? Some people, once they had talked to Kai, changed their minds and signed the petition.

"Hey, are you deaf?" Bashi said to Tong. "I'm asking you a question."

"What did you say?"

"How long is the line now? I can't even lift my head because of you."

"Still very long."

"How many people do you see?"

Tong tried to count. "Sixty, maybe eighty. It's hard to count. They're coming and going."

"Have you seen anyone you know?"

"The auntie by the basket," Tong said. "She's the announcer, you know? She just smiled at me."

"Everybody knows that. Who else?"

"A teacher from our school."

"Who else?"

Tong looked at the people waiting and recognized some faces, another teacher from his school who taught an upper grade, an old shop assistant at the pharmacy who liked to give children pickled plums for snacks, the postman who delivered letters to Tong's neighborhood twice a day and who always whistled when he rode by on his green postman's bicycle, Old Hua and his wife, who stood an arm's length apart in line, neither looking up at the people around them. Tong told Bashi what he saw and Bashi told him to keep up the good work. "You could make a good apprentice for me," Bashi said. He greeted everyone passing by as if he knew them all, though few returned his greetings. Some people glanced at Tong but most ignored him and his companion. In their eyes, Tong thought, he was probably only a small child who had come for some inappropriate fun; he was sad that he could not prove himself otherwise. He wondered whether the man he was with had come just for a good time, but it seemed too late to confront him.

Thirty minutes passed, perhaps longer; the basket, already overfilled, was put aside and replaced by a new one. The sun had risen now, casting the shadow of Chairman Mao over the place where Tong and Bashi stood. Bashi moved out of the shadow, still with Tong on his shoulders. After a while, when Tong told him that the line was shorter now, Bashi said that Tong should come down. "Sooner or later you'll break my back," Bashi said, massaging his neck with both hands.

"Are you going to put in your white flower?" Tong asked. His legs had fallen asleep and he had to stamp hard to awake them.

"No," Bashi said. "Why should I?"

"I thought that was why you were here."

"I told you I'm here for a different reason," Bashi said.

Disappointed, Tong limped away.

"You don't want to know where Ear is?"

Tong turned around. "Have you seen him?"

"Not lately," Bashi said. "But remember, I'm a detective, and I can find anything out for you."

Tong shook his head and said, "I'll find him myself."

"Do you want me to lend you my flower?"

Tong thought about the offer and nodded. He wished his mother had not destroyed their flower so he did not have to beg from this man he disliked. Bashi took the flower out from his sleeve and handed it to Tong. "Yours now," he said. "On the condition that you're not to leave me yet."

"Why?"

"Because we're here together, remember?" Bashi said with a wink, and Tong reluctantly agreed. Bashi accompanied him to the end of the line. When it was Tong's turn, he greeted the announcer and told her that he had been sent by his mother. Bashi only smiled, and said nothing.

"Please thank your mother for us all," the woman said. The old woman next to the auntie bowed and thanked Tong as if he were another grown-up. Close up, he recognized her now, the one who had burned the clothes at the crossroad on the day of the execution.

"Mrs. Gu?" Bashi said and shook the old woman's hand. "Lu Bashi here. I hope your daughter's first Ching Ming is great. It's the first for my grandma too. We're burying her today. You know how you have to wait for the spring. Not the best time to die, if you ask me. So have you already buried your daughter?"

Kai patted Bashi on his arm. "Please, we don't have time for your talk."

"But I'm not here to chat," Bashi said, and grasped Kai's hand. "Lu Bashi here. Sister, I really like your program. You know what nickname people have given you? Sweet Pea. Fresh and yummy. Yes, I know, I'm leaving. No problem, I know you are busy. But I am not here to be mischievous. I was asked by his parents to accompany him here," Bashi said, and pointed to Tong. "He's awfully small to come by himself, isn't he?"

Tong bit his lip. He did not want to be seen with this man, but Bashi had given him the white flower and had not said anything when he had lied earlier, about his being sent by his mother. Tong waited painfully while Bashi talked on, asking Kai what she thought of the number of people at the rally, what she planned to do next. She tried to be polite but Tong could tell that she had no interest in talking to Bashi. "I know you're busy, but can I have a word with you in private?" Bashi said. She was busy, Kai said. Bashi clicked his tongue. Too bad, he said; in that case perhaps he would have to talk with Mrs. Gu about her daughter's kidneys.

His voice was low, but Kai looked startled. She glanced at Mrs. Gu and beckoned Bashi to step aside. Tong followed them; neither Kai nor Bashi seemed to notice him.

"What did you hear about the kidneys?" Kai asked.

"It's not a secret," said Bashi. "Or is it?"

Tong watched the announcer frown. "Could you not mention it in front of Mrs. Gu?"

"I'll do whatever you ask me to do," Bashi said, and in a lower voice explained that there was more to the body than the kidneys, and he only wanted her to know that he was working on it. Things were in good hands, Bashi said, and he assured Kai that he would let her know as soon as he solved the case. Tong could see that the news announcer did not understand what Bashi was talking about, and that she was only trying to be patient. A man in a heavy coat approached them; a cotton mask covered most of his face. "Is there anything wrong here?" he asked, his eyes looking alarmed behind his glasses.

Bashi replied that everything was fine. The man looked at Kai, and she shook her head slowly and said nothing. The man, without taking off his glove, shook Bashi's hand and thanked him for coming to support the rally. Bashi answered that it was everybody's cause to fight against evil, and when he saw that the man would not leave him alone with Kai, he signaled for Tong to follow him to the table. "Do you mind if I take a look?" Bashi asked, and leaned toward the white cloth.

The man behind the table, a new teacher at Tong's school—although he did not recognize Tong—replied that it was not for browsing.

"But we're also here to sign, aren't we, little brother?" Bashi said to Tong. "Didn't your parents say you represent them here? By the way," he said to the man, "the boy is a student of yours."

The man turned to Tong. "Do you go to Red Star?"

Tong nodded.

"And didn't you just beg me to let you come and sign the petition?" Bashi said, and turned to the man. "He's a shy boy, especially with a teacher sitting here."

The man looked at Tong and said he might be too young to sign.

"Too young? Nonsense. Gan Luo became the premier of a nation at eleven," Bashi said. "There's no such thing as being too young. Have you heard people say heroes are born out of young souls? Here's a young hero for you. Besides, don't you need as many names as you can get?"

The man hesitated and dipped the brush pen in the ink pot. "Are you sure you understand the petition?" he asked Tong.

"Of course. I just told you he was a young hero," Bashi said, and whispered to Tong. "See how your teacher and your announcer auntie both are behind the petition. They'll be so happy if you sign your name there. Do you know how to write your name?"

Tong was embarrassed and tired of Bashi. He took the brush pen and looked for a place he could put down his name. The teacher was about to say something, and Bashi told him to stop fussing; the boy knew what he was doing, just as a swallow knew where to find his home, Bashi said. Tong breathed carefully and wrote on the white cloth, trying to keep each stroke steady. He had thought of writing down his name, but at the last moment, he changed his mind and wrote down his father's name; after all, he was too young and perhaps his own name wouldn't count.

■ ■ ■

NINI LOCKED THE HOUSE UP once the pedicab her family had hired disappeared around the corner. There was laundry for her to wash, pots and pans to scrub, and the house to sweep and mop, but these, along with the memory of her sisters' muffled giggling when her parents had ordered her to finish the housework before their return, did little to dampen her mood for the day. She had heard her father say to her mother that, on the way up the mountain, the pedicab driver would not be able to pedal and he would have to help the driver push. They should spend as much time as they could up there, Nini's mother had replied, making the most of the fee they paid the driver. It would be a long day before Nini's family returned home, and even if she did not finish everything, what did it matter? The day was a holiday for her too, a special day to be with Bashi. Nini held Little Sixth in her good arm and told her that they were going out to have a good time for themselves. Little Sixth looked back with clear, trusting eyes; when Nini tickled the baby underneath her soft chin and asked her if she was ready for the ride, the baby finally broke out into a big smile and showed her small new teeth.

The sun was up in the sky, blue without a wisp of cloud, a perfect day for Ching Ming. People came out from alleys and moved toward the Cross-river Bridge, women and children on foot, men pushing bicycles loaded with offerings and picnic baskets. Nini walked north, against the flow of people, and she had to stop from time to time to let people pass, some of whom walked right at her without slowing down, as if she didn't exist. Little Sixth sucked her hand and then pointed a wet finger at the people passing by. Kitty, kitty, she babbled, not making much sense.

Halfway to Bashi's house, Nini turned into the alley where the Gus lived. She did not expect them to have holiday treats for her. Even if they begged her to come into their house and spend a few minutes with them, she would reply coolly that she was quite busy and had no time to waste. Or perhaps she would be more generous and exchange a few nice words with them, saying she'd heard that

Teacher Gu had been sick and asking him how he felt now, if he needed any special food from the marketplace that she could bring him the next time. She imagined them speechless in front of her, dumbfounded by her gracefulness and her ease as a grown-up girl. She would smile and say that if they had no important requests, she would come back to visit when she had more time to spare. They would nod and try to find the words to reply, agonized by their secret wish to keep her close to them a moment longer, but she would leave nonetheless, the way a daughter who was married off to a rich husband might bid farewell to her plain parents, her good fortune being the only brightness in their life.

Besides a few sparrows hopping among the chickens, the Gus' alley was quiet. Nini knocked at the gate, first cautiously, and then a little harder. After a long moment she heard some small noises from the yard. For a moment her heartbeat became wild, her legs ready to take her fleeing before she was seen. But what would that make her except a useless child? She persisted, knocking at the gate, loudly this time.

The gate opened. Teacher Gu, leaning on a cane, stared at Nini. "What are you doing here?" he said. "Don't you know that people have important things to do besides waiting to be disturbed?"

Little Sixth pointed at Teacher Gu's cane and giggled for reasons known only to herself. Nini looked at him in dismay. She had imagined Teacher Gu, weakened and saddened by his illness, in need of comfort, and she could not help but feel that the old man in front of her now, like the other old men strolling in the marketplace or sitting by the roadside who enjoyed nothing but being harsh to a world that had, in their minds, mistreated them, was a stranger who had taken up the space of Teacher Gu's body. She breathed hard. "I heard you were sick, Teacher Gu," Nini said, trying her newly discovered confidence. "I'm here to see if you feel better now, and if you need anything."

"Why do you care?" Teacher Gu said. "Don't expect me to entertain anyone who has too much goodwill to dispense." Before Nini could reply, he banged the gate in her face.

Little Sixth, startled, began to cry then hiccup. Nini looked at the gate. She thought of spitting and cursing, the way she dealt with every humiliation in her life, yet she knew that those actions would not bring her the satisfaction they had before. Teacher Gu, whom she had once loved and admired and wanted as a father, had become a lesser person than she.

Bashi seemed anxious when Nini and Little Sixth arrived. A whole table of food, ordered from Three Joy, the most expensive restaurant in town, waited on the table. He offered to take the baby, and when Little Sixth protested with flailing hands, he made funny faces and squeezed his voice to sing a song about a snail, which scared the baby and made her cry. Nini hushed them both and walked straight into the bedroom. Bashi's bed was freshly made, the sheet and blanket and pillowcases all with a matching pattern of a pair of swallows nestling together in a spring willow tree. "The holiday is for dead people," Nini said, not yet recovered from the encounter with Teacher Gu. "You thought it was for you?"

Bashi smiled mysteriously. "Don't give me that stupid smile of yours," Nini said. She brought the baby to the other bed, stripped after the old woman's death. Nini took a rope out of her pocket. The bed was much smaller than their brick bed at home, so she had to double and then double the rope again before binding it around the baby's waist and tying it to a pole on the inner side of the bed. Bashi seemed concerned, but Nini reassured him: Little Sixth was used to the rope; it would be a miracle if she were able to strangle herself or loosen the knot and fall headfirst to the ground.

Bashi watched Little Sixth explore her new territory. "What a nice baby," he said. He knelt at the bedside so that he was at eye level with her. He made squeaky noises and funny faces, which Little Sixth did not appreciate, and when she cried again, he stood up with resignation. "What if she gets bored?" he asked.

"Why would she get bored?" Nini said. "She lives this way every day."

Less than convinced, Bashi went to the kitchen and fetched a whole bag of crackers. At each corner of the bed, he put a stack of crackers. He rummaged in the closet and found a pair of old silk shoes that had belonged to his grandmother, who had had bound feet, so the shoes were no bigger than a child's palm. More intrigued by the shoes than the snack, Little Sixth grabbed them and chewed on the embroidered flowers.

Nini looked on as Bashi busied himself making Little Sixth comfortable. What a strangely good man he was sometimes, she thought, wasting his time on a baby. She went out to the living room and sank into a huge cushioned chair. Bashi's solicitousness made her feel important; she could easily be the mistress of this household, making him her servant.

After a few minutes, Bashi came out and said, "I've got a present for you."

Nini turned to study him. When he was not behaving oddly, he looked almost handsome.

"Do you want to guess?"

"How would I know? Who knows which screw has come loose in your brain?" she said.

He laughed. "You're right," he said. "It'd take you a million years to guess." He went out to the storage room and, a moment later, came back with a cardboard box. The box was not a big one, but the way Bashi carried it, carefully balanced between his two hands, made Nini think of something expensive or heavy, or both. She wondered if it was a present she could hide from her parents and sisters.

Bashi put the box on the table and opened it; then he stepped aside, gave her a great bow, and invited her to step forward, as if he were a master magician. She squatted by the box and looked inside. She found neither expensive food nor jewelry; instead, the box was filled with ripped newspaper, and in the middle was a little gray ball with quills. She moved it with a finger and it rolled to one side, revealing nothing but more newspaper under its small body.

"So," Bashi said. "What do you think?"

"What is it?"

"A hedgehog."

Bashi watched Nini's face closely, which made her impatient. "What kind of present is that? You think I'm a skunk that needs a hedgehog for lunch?" she said.

Bashi guffawed as if he had heard the funniest joke in the world, and despite her wish to remain stern and angry, Nini laughed too. She lifted the hedgehog by its quills and put it on the table. It remained motionless, hiding its small face and soft stomach away from the world. "It's dead," Nini said.

"Silly girl," Bashi said. "It looks dead because I put it out in the storage cabin last night." He picked up a dustpan and scooped the hedgehog into it. "Let me show you the trick," he said, and carried the hedgehog to the kitchen. The fire in the stove was roaring and the kitchen was hotter than the rest of the house. Bashi took off his sweater and rolled up his shirtsleeves. "Now look," he said, and placed the dustpan on the floor, close to the stove. After a while, the hedgehog started to move, slowly at first, and then it grew longer and flatter, its face showing up underneath its uncurled body. Nini looked at its pale pink nose and small beady eyes—the hedgehog looked confused, its nose twitching helplessly.

"Is he hungry?" Nini asked.

"Wait and see," Bashi said. He put a shallow plate of water on the floor nearby, and soon the hedgehog crawled toward the water. To Nini's amazement, when it found the water, it gulped it all down without taking a breath.

"How did you know he was thirsty?" Nini asked.

"Because I tried this trick before you came," Bashi said. "You freeze a hedgehog and then unfreeze him and he thinks he's just out of his hibernation and he's thirsty."

"Stupid animal," Nini said.

Bashi smiled and said he had another trick to show her. He took a jar of salt out of the cupboard and asked for her hand, and Nini stuck out her good hand in a fist. He grabbed her fingers and uncurled them, and she felt a small tickling sensation coming not from her hand but from somewhere in her body that she had not known existed before. He poured a tiny mound of salt onto her palm. "Hold still," he said, and bent down to lick from her palm. She withdrew her hand before his tongue could touch it and the salt spilled all over the counter. "What are you doing?" she said.

Bashi sighed. "I'm teaching you how to do the trick," he said. "You need to hold still or else the hedgehog will be scared."

Nini looked at Bashi with suspicion, but he seemed preoccupied with his demonstration. He poured salt onto his own palm and told Nini not to make any noise. He knelt by the hedgehog and held his hand out to the hesitant animal, his palm flat and still. After a moment, the hedgehog moved closer and licked Bashi's palm, his tongue too small for Nini to see, but Bashi winked and grinned as if he were being tickled. Soon the small pile of salt in his palm disappeared. The hedgehog moved away, slow and satisfied. Nini looked at Bashi questioningly. He smiled and signaled her to wait, and a minute later, the hedgehog started to cough vehemently. Nini was startled and glanced around, even though she knew nobody had come into the house—the noise the hedgehog made was low and eerily human, as if from an old man dying of consumption. Nini stared at the hedgehog; there was no mistake that the animal was coughing. Bashi looked at Nini and started to laugh. The hedgehog coughed a minute longer and curled back into a painful ball. Nini poked it a couple of times and when she was sure it would not cough for her again, she stood up. "Where did you learn this mischief?"

Bashi smiled. "It doesn't matter. What's funny is that the hedgehog never learns to stay away from the salt."

"Why is that?"

Bashi thought about the question. "Maybe they like to be tricked."

"Stupid animal," Nini said. She lifted the balled hedgehog and put it back into the box. "What else can it do besides cough?"

"Nothing much."

"What are you going to do with it?"

"It's up to you," Bashi said. "It's a present for you."

Nini shook her head. She could not think of anything to do with the hedgehog, and it made her feel empty, all of a sudden, after the good laugh with Bashi. "What do I need a hedgehog for?" she said.

"You can have it as a pet."

"Why don't you keep it?" she said, and went into the bedroom to check on Little Sixth. The baby had discovered the crackers. Nini watched Little Sixth nibbling one. Today was a day that she had been waiting for, but now she was agitated for reasons she did not understand.

Bashi followed her into the bedroom and offered more crackers to the baby. Nini snatched them away before Little Sixth got ahold of them and the baby started to cry. "Are you going to fill her to death?" Nini snapped.

Bashi scratched his scalp. He seemed perplexed by Nini's sudden change of mood. After a moment, he offered cautiously, "I've got another idea."

"Your ideas are boring," Nini said.

"Maybe not this one," Bashi said. "We can eat the hedgehog. I've heard hedgehog is one of the best tonics."

"We're not eighty years old and don't need ginseng and hedgehogs to keep us alive," Nini said. "Who wants to eat that ugly thing with all the quills?"

Bashi smiled and told Nini to come over with him so he could show her one more trick he had heard about. She was not interested, but anything was better than staying in the bedroom with Little Sixth, who, after crying halfheartedly for a minute, began to suck her fist. Nini knew that soon Little Sixth would doze off. She went out to look for Bashi and found him in the yard. He was digging the freshly thawed dirt with a shovel, and when he got a pile of it, he poured some water over it and patiently kneaded the mud, as if he were an experienced baker.

"Are you cooking a mud pie with the hedgehog?" Nini said.

"Close," Bashi said. He went into the room and brought the box out. The hedgehog was still a frightened small ball. Bashi lifted it out of the box and put it in the mud dough. "Do you know how beggars cook the chickens they steal?" Bashi said. "They wrap the chicken up in mud and put the whole thing into hot ashes. When the roasting is done, you break the mud shell and eat the tender meat. The same with hedgehog, I heard." Bashi rubbed mud onto the hedgehog until it was totally enclosed. He rolled the ball in the mud a few more times and worked to make it perfectly round.

The fire in the stove hissed. Bashi tried in vain to blow on the fire to put it out; Nini laughed at him and slammed the damper shut. Soon the fire went out, smoldering quietly. Bashi poked the mud ball into the amber ashes. Together they stood and watched the mud ball in the belly of the stove, the outside drying into a crust. After a moment, Nini sighed and said, "What do we do now?"

Bashi turned around with his two muddy hands sticking out like claws. "We can play eagle-catching-the-chick," he said, and bared his yellow teeth. "Here I come."

Nini limped away with a happy scream, and Bashi followed her, always two steps behind, making a funny screeching noise with his grinding teeth. They circled the living room and then Nini ran into the bedroom. She threw herself onto Bashi's bed and panted. "I don't like this game," she said, with her face buried in the pillow.

Bashi did not reply. Nini rolled over and was surprised to see him standing by the bedside, gazing at her with a strange half smile. "Don't stand there like dead wood," she said. "Think of something better to do."

"Do you want to marry me?" Bashi said.

For a moment, Nini thought he was joking. "No," she said. "I don't want to marry you."

"Why not?" Bashi said. He looked hurt and disappointed. "You should consider it before you decide. I have money. I have this place all to myself. I'm your friend. I make you laugh. I'll be good to you— I'm always good to women, you know?"

Nini looked at Bashi. His eyes, fixing on her face with a seriousness that she had never seen in him before, made her nervous. She wondered whether her face looked especially crooked. She turned and hid the bad half from his gaze.

"Think about it," Bashi said. "Not many men would want to marry you."

Nini did not need him to remind her of that. Anyone who had eyes could see that she would never get a marriage offer. She had blindly hoped that Bashi would not notice her deformed face, but of course, like everyone else, he could not get it out of his mind. "Why do you want to marry me then?" she said. "Aren't you one of them?"

Bashi sat down by Nini and ran a finger through her hair. She did not move away even when she saw that he had mud on his hand. "Of course I'm different," Bashi said. "Why else do you think I'm your friend?"

Nini turned to look at Bashi, and he nodded at her sincerely. She wondered if she should believe him. Perhaps he was what he said, a man different from everyone else in the world; perhaps he was not. But what harm was there even if he was lying? He was her only friend, and even if he did see her as a monster, he seemed not to be bothered by it. She had no other choice; he was not a bad one, in any case. "Will you marry me if I agree to marry you?" Nini said.

"Of course. What do I need other women for if you agree to marry me?"

Not many women would want to marry him, Nini thought. She wondered if she herself was his only choice, but no matter how strange a man he was, she was on the bottom rung when it came to marriage and he was somewhere higher up. "What do we do if we agree to marry each other? When do I get to move out of my parents' home?" she said.

Bashi circled Nini's eyes with his muddy finger and then sat back to look at the effect. "Look in the mirror and see what a silly girl you are," he said. "If people heard you say this, they would all laugh at you."

Nini felt the tightening of her skin around her eyes. "Why would they want to laugh at me?" she asked.

"No girl should express such eagerness to marry a man, even if you can't wait for another minute."

"I can't wait for another minute to move out of my parents' house. I hate everyone there," Nini said. As if to dispute her, the baby babbled on the other side of the curtain. Nini got up from the bed and peeked at Little Sixth. She was crawling to reach half a cracker she had missed earlier. She sucked her lips with satisfaction after she ate the cracker and then began to play with the rope. She was a good baby; as long as she was not hungry, she could entertain herself for a long time. Nini let go of the curtain and sat down next to Bashi. "Do you think I can bring Little Sixth with me if I marry you?" she said.

"Two at a time? I must be a man hit by good fortune right on the forehead," Bashi said.

If she were not there to watch out for Little Sixth, who knew what might become of her, especially if her mother gave birth to a baby brother soon. If her parents did not like the idea, Nini thought, she would find a way to sneak the baby out of the house. But why wouldn't they be happy to get rid of two daughters without any trouble? The longer Nini thought about this, the more she was convinced that Little Sixth belonged to her more than to her parents. She could find a good husband for the baby when the time came. She turned to Bashi and patted his face to stop his grinning. "I'm serious," she said. "When can I leave my parents?"

"Wait a minute," Bashi said. "How old are you?"

"Twelve. Twelve and a half."

"Honestly, I would like to get married now," he said. "But there's a problem. You might be a little young yet to marry me."

"Why?"

"Because there are people who might not be happy about it."

"Who? What does it have to do with them?"

Bashi wagged a finger at Nini and hushed her. He knocked his forehead with his fist and Nini watched him. There was an unusual aroma in the room, and Nini twitched her nose hard to identify the smell. "The hedgehog," she said finally. "It's ready."

Bashi put a hand on Nini's mouth. "Don't distract me," he said, and let his palm touch Nini's lips. The mud on his hands had already dried up. Nini thought about the hedgehog, roasted in the ashes. With Bashi there were always things unexpected that made her happy. Nini began to think that perhaps it was a very good idea to marry him.

"I know," Bashi said after a moment. "Have you heard of child brides?"

"No."

"Ask Mrs. Hua and she'll tell you about it. Sometimes people send their young daughters to live with their future husbands and their families, and when the girls are old enough, they get married. Maybe you can become my child bride."

"Will those people you talked about be unhappy with this?"

"Why should they be, if you're my child bride? We can even ask Mr. and Mrs. Hua for help if your parents don't agree with the idea. You can live with the Huas, because they're good friends of mine. They won't mind having you around. I can pay them for your expenses. Will you be happier that way?"

Nini thought about the arrangement. Would her parents let her, a free maid, go so easily? But what could they do if she insisted on leaving for her own husband? People in the marketplace always said that a daughter who was ready to marry had a heart like the water splashed out of a basin—no matter how hard the parents tried, they would never get the water back. Of course her parents would understand this. Perhaps they would even celebrate her success in finding a husband; perhaps they would be generous enough to give her a tiny dowry. "Let's find the Huas and talk to them," Nini said.

"What an impatient girl," Bashi said. "They're burying my grandma at this moment. We'll see them later. We have something more important to do."

"The hedgehog?"

Bashi smiled. "More important than that. Have you heard of the bride check?"

"No."

"It used to be that the matchmaker checked the bride's body and made sure she was in fine shape for a wife," Bashi said. "In the case of a *love marriage,* like ours, the husband does the checking himself."

Nini thought about her crooked face, her chicken-claw hand, and her crippled foot. Was there a possibility that he could still reject her, even if he promised to take her in as a child bride?

"Don't look so nervous," Bashi said, and moved closer. He pulled Nini to her feet and let her stand in front of him. Then he put his hands on her shoulders and worked his thumbs underneath Nini's old sweater. "Just like this," he said, and rubbed her collarbone with his thumbs. "Does it hurt?"

Nini looked at his face, serious with a studying expression. She held her breath and shook her head. He moved his hands downward and cupped her rib cage in his two big palms. Tickled, she wiggled with laughter. He shushed her and said, "The sweater is a problem. Do you want to take it off?"

Nini looked at Bashi suspiciously and he smiled. "You don't have to," he said, and squeezed his hands beneath her sweater and under-shirt and enclosed her washboard body again, his hands hot on her cool skin. She shuddered. He moved his fingers up and down, as if he was counting her ribs. "A bit on the skinny side," he said. "But it's an easier problem to solve than having a fat hen."

Nini looked up at Bashi's face, close to her own. It wasn't right for a stranger to touch a girl this way, Nini knew, but Bashi was no longer a stranger after their talk of marriage. His hands on her skin made her feel good. She wasn't nervous now, yet her body still shivered as if it had its own will. When his hands wiggled downward she did not protest. He let his hands stay around her waist for a moment and said with a hoarse voice, "I need to check you down there too."

"Do you think the hedgehog will be overdone when we finish?"

Nini asked. The aroma of slightly burned meat from the kitchen was getting stronger and she was surprised that Bashi did not notice it.

Bashi did not reply. He picked Nini up and laid her on his bed. She felt his hands working on her belt, a long and threadbare piece of cloth she had ripped from an old sheet. Let her do it, she said, and pushed him slightly aside, feeling embarrassed in front of him for the first time. She untied the knot and he helped her take her pants and underpants down to the crook of her knees. She looked up at Bashi but he seemed to be shaking more than she was. Was he cold? she asked curiously. He did not answer, and covered her exposed body with a blanket. He needed a flashlight to go under there so she did not catch a cold, he said in a hushed voice, and he left the bedroom.

Nini waited. The hedgehog would be badly burned when they were finished, she thought. She wondered what Bashi would do to her—the *bedroom business,* as the men and women in the marketplace talked about? Whatever it was, Nini believed that it was a good thing, because those shameless women always pretended to be uninterested but their flushed faces and giggles told a different story.

Nini wondered why it was taking Bashi so long to find a flashlight. Little Sixth started to cry on the other side of the curtain. "I'm here," Nini said in her gentlest voice, and when the baby did not calm down, Nini started to sing Little Sixth's favorite lullaby, a song Nini had made up herself and sang to the baby when she was in a good mood. Little Sixth stopped crying and babbled to herself; Nini continued singing, lost in the wordless song of her own creation.

When Bashi finally returned, he seemed less flustered.

"Where were you?" Nini asked. "It took you so long."

"Ah, I just suddenly needed to go to the outhouse," Bashi said. He shone the flashlight on her face. "The best one a detective could have," he said, and crawled underneath the blanket, his legs dangling by the bedside. Nini felt him gently move her legs apart. She was about to ask him what he was doing under there, when a finger tentatively touched her between her legs. She badly felt a need to pee but she held it in and waited. The finger moved around a little, so gentle she almost did not feel it. After a long moment, Bashi emerged from beneath the blanket. "You're great," he said.

"Are you done?"

"For now, yes."

Nini was disappointed. She had once heard her mother and father panting at night for a long time, and only later did she realize that they had been engaged in their *bedroom business.* "Why didn't it take you long?" she said.

"What didn't take me long?"

Nini got up from the bed and got dressed. "I thought husband and wife did more than just looking," she said.

Bashi looked at Nini for a long moment before he stepped closer and held her in his arms. "I didn't want to frighten you," he said.

"What would frighten me?" Nini said. "We're husband and wife now, aren't we?"

Bashi smiled. "Yes, you're perfect for a wife, and of course we will be one day soon."

"Why not now?"

Bashi seemed baffled and unable to answer her question. "People need a wedding ceremony to become husband and wife," he said finally.

Nini shrugged. She did not care about a ceremony. He had checked her body and he had said everything was fine. That was all she cared about now that she had finally found herself a place to go. She was eager to make it happen. After a moment, she said, "How's your hedgehog now?"

Bashi was startled, as though he had only just now remembered the roasted animal. He ran to the kitchen, and when Nini followed him there, she was not surprised to see that when Bashi knocked open the dried mud ball, the hedgehog was a ball of charcoal, no longer edible.

Part III

*K*ai walked alone to the city square, a tired sadness taking hold. In the falling dusk the street was gray and empty. By now most people had returned home after their outing in the mountain, Ching Ming ending, like all holidays, a bit too soon.

An official at the courthouse had been assigned duty and was waiting for them when they had delivered, at midday, a copy of the petition with the transcribed signatures, requesting an investigation of Gu Shan's trial and the restoration of her posthumous reputation; the official, an acquaintance of Kai's, had pretended not to recognize her and, without further comment, had signed the official paperwork for receipt of the petition.

The enlarged picture of Gu Shan remained untouched on the pedestal of Chairman Mao's monument, the black mourning ribbons around the frame loose in the evening wind. The paper flowers gathered earlier in the day had been made into three wreaths, and in the dim light they bloomed like huge pale chrysanthemums. Underneath the wreaths was the white cloth that bore more than three hundred signatures, the four corners weighed down by rocks. Wildflowers and new twigs of pine trees, brought back from the mountain by people Kai had or had not met in the rally earlier, had been left in bouquets on the cloth. Kai studied the improvised memorial to Gu Shan; no order had come from the government for a cleanup, which seemed another confirmation of their achievement.

Earlier that afternoon Kai had stopped by Jialin's shack. His friends had all been there, basking in the day's success. A woman introduced by Jialin as Dr. Fan thanked Kai for her beautiful speech; a middle-aged man nodded in agreement. The town's librarian turned out to be a friendly person despite her quietness, and she poured tea for Kai from a thermos she had brought to the shack. There were four men and four women other than Jialin and Kai; Mrs. Gu, who had gone home to take care of her husband, was the only one missing from the celebration. The group talked about their rally, and wondered how soon they would hear from the city government. They needed to be patient, Jialin reminded them, but his eyes betrayed irrepressible excitement. The British and American radio stations all predicted a drastic change in the central government, he said, and so did the broadcast from Hong Kong. Kai confirmed the news and revealed that Gu Shan's execution was being investigated in the provincial capital. Exhilarated, a woman embraced Kai and thanked her for being one of them. Perhaps she was among the ones who had suspected Kai earlier, Kai thought, but they received her as their friend and comrade now, and that was all that mattered.

Jialin turned on his shortwave radio and found a station that was playing a waltz, a chorus of accordions. The music filled the shack with a festive mood, and an engineer in his late fifties stepped into the middle of the shack and invited someone to dance. Three of the four women, an accountant, the schoolteacher, and Dr. Fan, protested in laughter. What was wrong with having a good dance? the engineer said, as if feeling offended. Kai thought of volunteering but before she stepped up, Jialin shook his head slightly at her. Kai turned and saw the librarian walk up to the middle of the shack, putting her hands in the hands of the blushing engineer. The man winked at Jialin and led the dance in the shack's limited space. Kai watched the librarian's face turn to a deep crimson, like a young girl in love for the first time.

Kai had not been able to talk to Jialin alone that afternoon. She wondered if he felt as grateful as she did for the distractions the rally had brought. Would they have made different decisions had there been a future they could look forward to? He tried to conceal his exhaustion as the afternoon progressed. If his illness saddened his friends as much as it did her, she could not tell.

A woman, her belly slightly protruding from under an old jacket, approached the square now. Kai nodded, but the woman, reading the signatures on the white cloth, took no notice. It was not too late to sign, Kai said, wondering if the woman, like so many others, had not been able to escape her husband's supervision for the rally in the morning. The woman turned to look at Kai, hatred in her eyes. "I wish a horrible death to every one of you," she said, not hiding the venom in her words.

Kai watched the woman spit at the memorial before waddling away. It takes all sorts to make a world, dragons and phoenixes along with snakes and rats, she remembered her father saying, but how easily one could forget, after an afternoon with Jialin and his friends, that the world was still the same place of cold-heartedness and animosity, and that the small fire of friendship could do only so much to keep one warm and hopeful. She thought about her in-laws, who must be enraged by now. Her own mother, whom Kai had avoided thinking about in the past few hours, must have locked herself in her flat, bracing for her in-laws' rage. Kai dared not even think of Han.

The flat was dark when Kai entered. Out of habit she called Ming-Ming's name, and the nanny quietly came out of the nursery, also unlit. Kai turned on the light and the nanny blinked, her eyes swollen with fresh tears. Where was Ming-Ming? Kai asked; the girl did not answer but looked in the direction of the bathroom with trepidation. A moment later, the door opened and out came Kai's mother, her face puffy and wet. Kai signaled for the nanny to leave them alone, and when the girl closed the door to the nursery, Kai's mother said, "Where have you been?"

"Where's Ming-Ming?"

"Your parents-in-law took him home with them. They left word to let the nanny go tomorrow morning."

"Who did they leave the order with?"

Kai's mother looked at her for a long moment, her lips trembling. "Who did they leave the order with? Your own mother. Your mother had to stand here and beg your in-laws for forgiveness because you were out of your mind. Tell me, Kai, why did you do this to me? I'm an old widow and don't I deserve a moment of peace?"

Kai watched her mother crying. She realized that she had never, since her father's death, looked into her mother's eyes. With her tear-streaked face she looked more than ever like a stranger. "I'm just happy that your father's long gone so he didn't have to be humiliated as I was, being called all sort of names in my own daughter's home, in front of my grandchild and his nanny," Kai's mother said between sobs.

"What else did they say?"

"What's the point of repeating their words to you? What's been said had better be buried with me."

Even though Kai's mother had always been dominating at home, she was known to be easily intimidated by her superiors. One could not be expected to be repressed all the time, Kai's father had once said, in explanation to Kai of her mother's behavior; she needed to vent her anger, he had said, and it struck Kai now that her father had served as a receptacle for her mother's bitterness; that must have been what killed him. "Stand up for yourself," said Kai now. "Ignore my in-laws."

"How easy for you to say that. They left word that you and I would not be allowed to see Ming-Ming anymore. Tell me, how do you ignore that?"

Kai looked away from her mother. Under the newly finished television stand she saw something blue. She bent and picked it up. It was Ming-Ming's favorite rattle, in the shape of a whale. She wondered if the nanny knew he had lost it, or if he had put it there as one of his games of hide-and-seek. One time before she had found a small rubber ball in her boot, and for three days after that, she had found different toys there, and she had known then that it must be a purposeful action on his part. She wondered if he would soon settle for a grandparent's shoe for the game.

"Why did you do it? What is it that you want that you haven't got?"

This question had never been put to Kai before. She shook her head. It was not what she wanted that mattered, she said.

"What do we do now?" Kai's mother said. "Do we know how much trouble we're in?"

Kai was struck by her mother's including herself in her daughter's fate. She thought of comforting her mother, but she would not listen. "You've always been such a good child," her mother wailed. "You've always followed your parents' and your teachers' instructions and never made a mistake."

Again Kai told her mother not to worry, knowing her words were too vague to do any good. Such a trustworthy child, Kai's mother repeated as if in disbelief; people had always told her it was her fortune to have a daughter who would not step on the wrong side of the line and who had helped her siblings prosper.

Kai left her mother and walked to the nursery. When she pushed the door open, the nanny, who had been eavesdropping behind the door, stepped back, panic and shame on her face. Kai pretended that she had not noticed; she asked the girl if she was willing to take some extra money and leave for home the next morning.

The girl stared at Kai as if she did not understand Kai's question. Kai sighed and explained that it was best for the girl to go back to her own parents, at least for now. "Are you worrying that your parents will be angry at you? I can write them a letter and tell them that you did nothing wrong here," Kai said.

"My parents—they don't read."

"Can you explain to them? Tell them that we'll send someone to get you back as soon as we settle things here," said Kai. She wondered how much the girl understood the situation, and if this lie would be enough to offer her and her parents some comfort and hope.

"Who will take care of Ming-Ming?" the girl asked.

"He's with his grandparents for now."

"But someone has to take care of him," the girl said. "Do they know what Ming-Ming wants when he cries?"

"He'll be all right."

"But they have never taken care of him. They don't know him," said the girl. "They were pushing him to drink milk when he'd just wet his diaper."

Tap water was being run in the bathroom behind the half-closed door, but Kai could still hear her mother crying. "Ming-Ming will be just fine," Kai said. "You don't have to worry about him."

The girl looked down at her hands without replying. She must have hurt the girl's feelings somehow, Kai thought, but she was too tired to think about what she had said wrong. She counted out money equal to an extra month's pay and handed the bills to the girl.

The girl did not take the money. She unbuttoned the top of her blouse and brought out a small jade pendant. "Could you give this to Ming-Ming?" she said. "I don't have anything else to leave for him."

"Is it something special?" Kai said. "Don't give it away to a small child so easily."

The girl gripped the pendant and insisted that Ming-Ming would not sleep without touching it.

"He'll do without it," Kai said. She put the money into the pocket of the girl's blouse, and thanked her and then apologized for the disruption. The girl begged again to leave the pendant with the baby so that he could have something by which to remember her.

Kai accepted it; the girl bowed to Kai, then wiped her tears. Ming-Ming was the first baby the girl had taken care of other than her siblings; Kai wondered if there would be other babies in the coming years, and if farewells would become easier once they were a regular part of the girl's life.

"And please tell his grandparents that Ming-Ming likes to have someone touch the back of his ears before he goes to sleep," the girl said.

Kai looked down at the pendant, a carved jade piece in the shape of a fish. It was an inexpensive one, the carving rough and amateur, the kind that a peasant's family could afford for their daughter. Han's parents would not allow such a thing near Ming-Ming, but Kai thanked the girl and said that she would buy a silver chain for the pendant so Ming-Ming could wear it around his wrist. She was welcome to come back and visit them, Kai said, and promised that once things settled down, the girl would be rehired. Her lie was delivered and received without much faith on either side; after a moment, Kai had little left to say but to wish the girl good luck in her own life.

HAN RETURNED TO MUDDY RIVER on the night of Ching Ming, after he had phoned the mayor with news of the victory they had been waiting for. In Beijing, the situation in the central government had taken a drastic turn after a late-night meeting, with the democratic wall now defined as an anti-Communist movement; the man to whom they had provided the new kidneys was on his way to cleanse the provincial government of the supporters and sympathizers of the democratic wall, and rumors were that he would either become the leader of the province or be promoted and move to the central government in Beijing. Yet the mayor had sounded halfhearted in his praise of Han's work, and it was only when his own parents got on the phone that Han understood the reason for the mayor's lukewarm response. Did he know what his wife had been up to? Han's mother yelled at him over the telephone, and then without waiting for an answer, she ordered Han to come home straight away.

On the trip home, Han practiced his defense, saying that he had been away and he had no idea what Kai had been doing in the past weeks. In his imagined conversation, he begged his parents and the mayor to help Kai out, and by the time he reached the door of his flat, he believed in his fantasy. Despite the request of his parents for him to report to them first, Han went straight home. It was in the middle of the night when, discovering his own wife absent from their bed, he woke the nanny up. Mrs. Wu—Kai's mother—had come that night and had asked Kai to go back to her flat, the nanny said, frightened by Han's grip on her arm; his parents had brought the baby home with them. Han looked at the nanny hard, as if she were lying to him, and when he saw that the trembling girl in her night-clothes was about to cry, he told her that she had better have a good sleep, as he would get Ming-Ming back first thing in the morning. The girl mumbled and said that she was to leave for home in the morning, as his parents had fired her. What nonsense, Han told her; he and Kai would both come home with Ming-Ming the next morning.

Han thought of knocking on his mother-in-law's door, but in the end he went to his parents' flat instead. His parents, both smoking in the living room, showed no sign of having slept. "That wife of yours," Han's father said at the sight of Han. "She has spoiled our victory."

Han looked at his parents' expressionless faces. Despite the defense he had rehearsed, he began by saying that he was the one to blame, as he had not detected early enough what Kai had been doing. Now that all this had happened, could they think of a way to protect her before it was too late?

"Protect her? We need to think about protecting ourselves," Han's mother said. "The only thing we can do now is to draw the line with her and pray."

"But she's my wife," Han said.

"She won't be after tomorrow," Han's mother said. She motioned for Han's father to continue the conversation. He laid out the plan, obviously devised by Han's mother: Before daybreak, Han was to prepare a divorce application, and he would turn it in in the morning.

"Start with the divorce application," his father said. "Say that you and she disagree on the most fundamental problems of ideology—now use your brain to elaborate on this—and say that the knowledge of your wife's role in the antigovernment scheme was shocking—explain 'shocking' to mean that you had no previous information about it until being told by someone, not us, of course, but someone irrelevant, someone unimportant, that she was a leader at the rally—and that when you learned of this, it was too late to correct her wrongdoing. Also, write a sincere self-criticism. I mean flesh-and-bone sincere, blood-and-marrow sincere. Dig and dig into the real depths and open yourself to show you regret your lack of political alertness. Ask for punishment—now this is tricky—ask to be punished in a way that means really it was not your mistake except getting married to the wrong person—and then ask for an opportunity to make amends. You know what that means? Say you want to put your life in the hands of the party so you can demonstrate that your life is a worthy one."

"What will happen to Kai?"

"What will happen to her is not our concern anymore," Han's mother said. "Didn't you hear what your father said? Now is the time for you to act. If you miss this chance we'll all be dragged down by her foolishness."

Could they at least reconsider their strategy? he begged his parents again; did they want their grandson to become a motherless orphan? Halfway into his argument Han began to cry.

Wordlessly, Han's mother brought him a towel. He buried his face in its wet warmth and wept. His parents watched him, patiently waiting for him to gather himself, and when he finally did, his mother reminded him to think about his parents' careers and his own political future; her voice was unusually gentle and sympathetic, and Han could not help but think, for a brief moment, that he would have to give up his wife to earn tenderness from his own mother. There was Ming-Ming's future to take into consideration, she said, and asked him if he wanted his son to lose all privileges because of his mother's stupidity. Kai was not the only woman in the world, Han's mother said, and once this crisis passed, they would look for a better wife for him, more beautiful and obedient, kind as a stepmother. This talk went on for a while, and when Han cried again and said he could not let this happen to Kai, his father sighed and told his mother not to waste her words anymore. From a desk drawer he produced a draft of the divorce application they had written for him. Just sign the paper, his mother said to him, her voice still gentle and unfamiliar.

Han signed his name, his spirit crushed and his heart filled with a pain and sadness that he had not known could exist in life. His mother poured a cup of tea and left it by his side, and then retreated with his father to their bedroom to sleep before daybreak. Han sank into his parents' sofa; a new television set, on its beautifully crafted stand, watched him like a dark, unblinking eye. Han had imagined years of happiness with three children, the youngest one a daughter as beautiful as Kai and spoiled by her big brothers. If he closed his eyes he could see them in ten years, a loving family sitting at the dinner table on a New Year's Eve, the steam from the fish and chicken and pork making their mouths wet with appetite; when the firecrackers began to pop outside their window, announcing the approach of midnight, he would walk his wife and children, all bundled up in brand-new down coats, to the city square, where his sons would launch their fireworks with boyish bravado and his daughter would scream with joy, her upturned face cupped in her mother's hands.

WHAT ON EARTH did she want? Han asked Kai later, in her mother's flat. His parents had forbidden him to see his wife, but he had threatened to withdraw his divorce application, and in the end, they had agreed that he could talk to her once. When Kai's mother had opened the door for him at dawn, he saw that she too had had a sleepless night, her eyes red and puffy.

"Please save her," Kai's mother had said before she showed him to

Kai's room. "Kai is a headstrong person. If something ever happens to her, you'll be the only one she can rely on."

Han dared not meet the old woman's eyes.

"You have to help her," she said. "Tell your parents that I will crawl to their door and beg for their mercy if that is what they want me to do."

Han tried to comfort Kai's mother, but half a sentence later he choked on his own tears. The old woman handed him a handkerchief, and then turned away to wipe her eyes. They had been close ever since Han had come to her six years earlier, asking her to teach him to cook Kai's favorite dishes; together they had kept this secret from Han's parents.

Kai was in her sister's bedroom, where an extra bed had always been kept for Kai, even though she had already married Han when he arranged for the family to move into the new flat. When Kai and her mother had returned earlier that evening, they had found a note left by Lin, Kai's little sister. She was to spend a few days at her best friend's home, Lin wrote, and in the note she called Kai the last person she wanted to see now. Lin, at twenty-one, had just begun to enjoy being courted by the most suitable young men in town. Earlier in her life, she had taken up, from her mother, the shame of living in the alley, and made it a source of her own unhappiness. She was sixteen when Kai married Han, and at the time, Kai could see that the move made Lin blossom with confidence and joy.

Kai did not seem surprised when Han came in. She asked if he had seen Ming-Ming in his parents' house.

"Ming-Ming is well," Han said. He moved the only chair in the room next to where Kai was sitting, an arm's length between them. "He has grown a lot since I last saw him."

"That's a child's job," Kai said. "Growing. Isn't it?"

"He's a good baby," Han said, and before he knew it, tears fell onto his lap and darkened his gray trousers.

When Han told her about the crackdown in Beijing, the news came more as a disappointment than a shock; Kai wondered if Jialin had heard similar reports on his transistor radio. She wished they were with each other tonight. She smiled when Han asked her what it was she had wanted that they didn't have. She had done what her conscience demanded, Kai said.

"What about Ming-Ming?" Han asked. "Has he ever been on your conscience?"

Not all women were meant to be good mothers, Kai said, and she apologized for the first time that day.

When Han sobbed, it was as though he were a small child again. He was, before anything else, his mother's son; despite her lack of feminine gentleness, his mother had always considered him the center of her life and had never failed to let him know that all she had achieved in her career had been done for him. Han had not known that a mother could discard her son so easily; such cruelty, beyond his understanding, crushed his universe. He thought of begging Kai, for the sake of his son and himself, but even before he opened his mouth he could see through his tears that, before she stood up and left, she was looking at him with pity and disgust. He cried, for his son and for himself, until his head dropped in exhaustion. In a half dream he remembered a spring day not long ago when he had become the first person in Muddy River to own a camera imported from Germany. He had been dating Kai for two months then, and he remembered looking through the viewfinder at her before he clicked the shutter.

A while later, Kai's mother entered with a look of panic and despair, and Han quickly wiped the corner of his mouth, his head aching dully. The police had just come and taken Kai away, she told Han. Please, could he help Kai, because he was the only one, now, who could save her.

RUMORS AND SPECULATION, born out of insufficient information and vivid imaginations, took hold in Muddy River on the morning after Ching Ming. People woke up to the seven o'clock news, read not by Kai but by a male colleague of hers. Two retired engineers, who took morning walks together, contemplated what could have happened. It might come down to a political earthquake now, they said to each other. Those who won the game would become kings, they said, citing the old saying, but neither ventured a guess about who would be the winners. The men had both escaped unscathed the various revolutions in their lifetimes. They had known each other for three years now, since meeting in the hospital morgue, two new widowers; in the twilight of their lives they found one another irreplaceable. They had discussed the situation on their daily walks in the past two weeks, each trusting the other as the only one with whom such sensitive matters could be voiced. Neither of them had any expectations, nor did they take a stand—at their age they considered the only role left for them to be theater spectators, and they took their seats and coolly watched from a distance. For every poor soul who was dragged down by this, the two wise men contemplated, there would be another one up for a promotion. A balance of the social energy, one said, and the other nodded and added that, indeed, to climb up in this country, you'd have to use someone else as a stepping stone. Neither bothered to take up his own past, as both understood that to be safe and sound in their age, they had had their share of bodies underneath their feet to keep them afloat, and those stories were no longer relevant, their shame and guilt absolved by old age.

Elsewhere, a woman commented to her husband at the breakfast table that the female announcer was in trouble. One could not tell merely from a changed schedule of her broadcast shifts, the husband argued, but the wife insisted that she herself had been the farsighted one; if not for her, he would have let himself be summoned by the woman's speech to the city square like a fool. The husband ate his dinner in silence, but this gesture was not enough to placate his wife, who, along with several of her close friends, despised the woman reading the news in her beautiful voice to their husbands, making them deaf to their wives' domestic nagging. "I tell you," she said now, her voice drowning out the announcer's report on the record-high revenue of the city of Muddy River for the first quarter. "I tell you, that woman is a nightmare for any man."

In the emergency room of the city hospital, where no one was dying or being rushed in to die, a boy lay in the recovery room and his mother dozed by the bedside. The boy had taken part in a gang fight the night before and had his scalp cracked open by a brick. The doctor who had given him twenty-five stitches was off duty now, and her colleagues, two women who had both been at the rally the day before, stood by the window of the recovery room without talking. If it came to a crackdown, the one who had signed the petition thought to herself, she would divorce her husband so his promotion to head of hematology would not be affected; the other woman, more positive due to her optimistic nature in general as well as her decision not to sign the petition, believed that nothing serious would happen, because the law never punished the masses for going astray. No discussion occurred between the two colleagues, yet when they parted for their morning duties, one comforted the other with a pat on the shoulder, and all was understood.

Jialin leaned on his pillow. When his mother entered the shack with a late breakfast he did not move. She had forgotten the kettle of boiled water for the heater, but he did not ask. The night before, his three brothers had come home with blood on their hands and shirts. They had, in a gang fight, smashed a boy's head and, for the first time in their lives, understood the taste of fear. All night they couldn't sleep, taking turns looking out the gate for possible enemies coming with bats and bricks, or worse, policemen with handcuffs. Jialin's youngest brother, who had never talked much to him, came into the shack before daybreak, asking Jialin to take care of their parents if it reached a point where the three of them had to flee for a few years.

Jialin had thought the boy's dramatic behavior laughable but had not said so. Before the boy had entered, Jialin, with his transistor radio tuned to the Hong Kong station, had heard the news that in Beijing the secret police had started to carry out arrests.

"I heard people talk about yesterday's event in the marketplace," Jialin's mother said, and put the food on the makeshift table made of an old tree stump.

"What did they say?"

"They said the government wouldn't let anyone get off so easily."

Jialin did not move. "What else did they say?"

"They said the woman announcer is married to an important figure so there's no need for her to worry," Jialin's mother said, and then glanced at him. "You were with them, weren't you?"

Jialin had always told his family that his friends came to read books with him, but he knew that his mother could easily have guessed the connection. "Other things? What else did people say?"

"They said she must be using the rally to become famous," Jialin's mother said. "But I don't understand. She's already famous. Why did she need to become more famous?"

"Don't listen to rumors," said Jialin. "People think they know more than they do."

"So were you one of them?"

"Yes."

Jialin's mother did not speak, and after a while, he looked at her and saw her quietly wiping her eyes.

"Mama, don't worry," he said. "Nothing has happened, and people are just indulging their imaginations."

"There must not be a heaven above us," Jialin's mother said, dabbing at her eyes with the corner of her blouse. "Or else, why were you given a brain only to get sick, while your brothers are healthy and strong but empty-headed?"

"They'll learn their lesson."

"How about you? I can't afford to lose you," Jialin's mother said, and tears dampened the front of her blouse.

Jialin smiled. It was no secret that he would die soon. What mattered to him was how he left this world. His mother wanted him to die in her arms; she wanted him to belong to her, and her only.

"Do you think there'll be trouble? People say different things and I don't know whom I should believe."

"Listen to nothing and believe no one," Jialin said.

"What will happen to you?"

Jialin shook his head. Perhaps it was only a matter of days, or hours, before someone would come into his shack and break his mother's heart, but he did not want to share this knowledge with her. "Think about it, Mama, I wasn't meant to live forever."

Jialin's mother turned her head away.

"There's nothing to be sad about," Jialin said. "Thirty years from now—no, let's hope it's not that long. Ten years, or five years, from now, they will come to your door and say to you that your son Jialin was a hero, a pioneer, a man of foresight and courage."

"I would rather you were as unambitious as your brothers."

"They'll live their lives in their ignorance, but not I. Why do I read books if not to live up to principles that are worth striving for?"

"I would rather you had never touched a book in your life. I wish I had never stolen a book for you."

"That's a stupid way of thinking, Mama," Jialin said, shocked by his own vehemence. After a bout of coughing, he said in a gentle voice, "What else can I leave for you, Mama? I can't give you grandchildren."

Jialin's mother left the shack without answering; on the way out she bumped into the door frame. He listened to her broken sobs disappear into the depths of the house and had to force his heart to remain hard, untouched by his mother's tears.

THE TEACHER'S HEART was restless on the Monday after Ching Ming. She gave the class an assignment of copying the textbook, and sat for a while at her desk, then went to the hallway to talk to another teacher. The children, still excited, could not keep quiet. Boys exchanged tales of ghosts and wild animals they had spotted on the mountain; girls showed off souvenirs offered by nature— bookmarks made by pressing new leaves and wildflowers between the pages of a book, feathers of bright colors, bracelets made from linked dry berries. Only when the classroom became boisterous did the teacher come in and bang on the wooden blackboard with a ruler. They were to copy every lesson in the textbook three times instead of one, the teacher announced, and they would not be allowed to go home for lunch before finishing the work.

The children, terrified by the prospect of being kept behind for the midday break, stopped wiggling on their benches and started to write, their pencils scratching on the paper like a thousand munching silkworms. Tong counted the few blank pages in his exercise book—he did not have enough pages for the assignment, but even if he had the space to copy all the words in the world, his heart was not in it today. Ear had not come home for another night, and Tong's hopes were dimming.

Dogs got stolen and eaten all the time, his father had said the night before, and there was no reason to cry over it; the world would become a crowded place if dogs, or, for that matter, little children, did not disappear. Tong's mother had held his hand while his father ran on with his drunken philosophy about stolen children and butchered dogs. However, when Tong's father fell into a stupor, she herself repeated the same message. Once the mating season started, she said, they could find him a new puppy; she suggested that he name the new puppy Ear, too, if that would make him feel better.

The idea of replacement puzzled and disappointed Tong, but it seemed natural for the grown-ups to think that way. Even Old Hua had said the same thing, as if there were endless duplicates or substitutes for anything, a jacket, a dog, or a boy.

Tong's eyes stung. It would be a shame to cry in class, and he sniffled and tried to hold back his tears. After a while, his chest hurt. He had cried the night before, quietly, for a long time, and then had felt embarrassed by his tears; he had wondered what the people back in his grandparents' village would think of him if they knew he was softhearted. Perhaps losing Ear, like taming Kwen's black dog and uncovering nature's secrets from the weather forecast, was another test for him to prove himself, but even this thought could not relieve the weight on his chest.

At the break, Tong rushed to the hallway and squatted in a corner. It did not make him feel any better when the long-held-back tears fell onto the cement floor. When an upper-grade teacher discovered Tong and asked him what was wrong, he could not say a word, his body shaking with the effort not to wail. It must be some sort of stomachache, the teacher wondered aloud; she asked Tong if he could walk home all by himself, or if he needed a ride to the hospital. He nodded and then shook his head, confusing the teacher, so she decided to find the school janitor to send the boy to a clinic. It took her a while to locate the janitor, who was dozing behind a pile of firewood in the school basement. He seemed upset when he was shaken awake, and when he followed the teacher to the hallway, the sick boy had disappeared, leaving behind a small puddle of tears on the floor. The janitor grumbled and wiped the tears with the soles of his shoes, eliminating the only proof that the teacher had not told a lie to disturb his morning nap.

Tong wandered around town. There was no use combing through the streets and alleys yet again, as he understood his parents' and Old Hua's conclusion that if Ear had not come home by now, he had very possibly landed on someone's dinner table. Still, walking under the clear morning sky, away from the classroom with its low ceiling and small, soot-covered windows, he felt a tiny hope rise again. He went from block to block, trying not to make eye contact with the grown-ups, who, like his teacher, seemed in no mood to catch him playing truant. Housewives and workers leaving the night shift talked in twos and threes in the street; a few shop-owners came from behind their high counters and stood in front of the doors, exchanging talk and looking at every passerby for possible business.

"Why are you not in school now?" yelled an old man as Tong entered an alley. The man was wearing a heavy sheepskin coat and a cotton-lined hat, even though spring was in full bloom. He propped himself up with one hand on a wooden cane, and the other hand, holding an envelope, was on a wooden fence for extra support. "I'm asking you. It's ten o'clock on Monday morning and what are you doing here in the alley?"

Tong inched back. If he started to run, he could easily leave the growling man behind, but growing up in the countryside, where old people were respected as kings, he did not have it in his nature to ignore questions put to him by an old man.

"Which school do you go to?"

"Red Star," Tong replied, the truth slipping out before he could think of a lie.

"Then what is the reason for you to be in my alley and not in school?"

"I don't know," replied Tong.

"Is that the answer you give to your teacher? Listen, I'm a schoolteacher. Two weeks ago I had boys like you in my class, and I know all your tricks. Now, one more time, what makes you think you can play truant today?"

"Our teacher said we had to copy the whole textbook before lunch," Tong said in a low voice. "I don't have enough pages left in my exercise book."

"What kind of teaching is that!" the old man grunted. "You may as well stay away from such a useless place."

Tong wondered if he should leave the old man who claimed to be a schoolteacher but talked like a grumpy old illiterate. "You want to run away from me now?" the old man said. "You think I'm talking nonsense? Let me tell you: You could learn all the characters in the dictionary, and write the most spectacular articles in the world. You could be more learned than Confucius—do you know who Confucius was? Well, how could one expect you to learn anything from school these days? In any case, you could be as knowledgeable as a scholar, but still you could be more ignorant than an illiterate peasant or a beggar. Do you understand?"

Tong shook his head.

"What I'm saying is this"—the old man hit his cane on the

ground—"you don't get real intelligence and wisdom from text-books. As far as I can tell, you may as well run away from your stupid teacher who stuffs your brain with nothing but lard."

Tong smiled in spite of himself.

"Now, if you want to be a good and useful human being, help me get this letter to the mailbox."

Tong accepted the letter from the old man and was surprised by its weight. He glanced at the envelope, which bore several stamps. "No peeking!" the old man shouted, and then changed his mind and asked Tong to hand the letter back.

"I can help you, Grandpa. There's a mailbox there."

"I know it perfectly well. Call me Teacher Gu. I'm no one's grandpa."

Tong returned the letter to Teacher Gu, who patted it and then put it in his coat pocket. Tong held the old man's free arm with both hands. "I'll help you to walk," he said.

"Thank you, but no, I can walk perfectly well," Teacher Gu said, and he pushed Tong aside and let his cane lead him forward.

Tong followed Teacher Gu, for fear the old man's cane would catch in the gutter. Teacher Gu, however, stumbled forward without paying attention to Tong, as if all of a sudden the boy had ceased to exist for him. When they approached the mailbox, Teacher Gu studied the collection schedule, in small print, on the side. "What time does it say?" he said after a long moment of frowning.

Tong read to Teacher Gu, who looked at his watch. "Twenty past ten," he mumbled aloud. "Let's wait then."

Tong thought it strange that someone wanted to wait for the postman. Wasn't that the reason that a mailbox was installed in the first place, so that people could just drop their letters in and not have to wait?

"Why are you standing here?" Teacher Gu said after a while. "Were you sent by someone to spy on me?"

He thought he had been asked to wait, Tong explained, but Teacher Gu acted as if he had forgotten his own words. He checked the street and then tapped a finger on his watch for Tong to see. "Whoever is responsible for this mailbox is late," he said. "Don't ever believe in what's written down."

NEVER BEFORE had the midday break seemed so long. Teacher Gu drummed on the table with his fingers and waited for his wife to finish her lunch and go back to her bank teller's window. Near the end of the previous week, his school had sent a request for his early retirement, due to health reasons, and seeing that he was qualified for three-quarters of his pension, Teacher Gu had signed the paper without a moment's hesitation, or consultation with his wife. There were plenty of educated youths returning from the countryside; he might as well leave his position, no longer fulfilling to him anyway, to a young man for whom the dream of a family would make the long hours among noisy, pestering children endurable.

"You don't have to sit here and wait for me," Mrs. Gu said. "Or do you need more rice?"

"I'm fine as I am."

Mrs. Gu finished her lunch. When she cleaned up the table and washed the dishes, she poured a cup of tea and left it by his drumming hand. "Do you want to take a nap?" she asked.

"Don't you need to go to work now?"

"Yes."

"Then go. I can take care of myself perfectly well."

Mrs. Gu, to his disappointment, took a seat at the table. "Do you think we need to hire a girl from the mountain to help with the housework?"

"Are we rich people?"

"Or perhaps Nini? I've been thinking—you need a companion. You may need help too," said Mrs. Gu. "Nini would be a good person in many ways."

"I thought you hated her."

Mrs. Gu looked away from his stare. "I know I've been unfair to her," she said.

"She'd better learn to live with that then," said Teacher Gu. "You won't be the last person to treat her unfairly."

"But we could make it up to her," said Mrs. Gu. "And her family too. I saw in the street that her mother was expecting again. They will need some extra money."

Teacher Gu thought about how his wife had been brainwashed by her young comrades. Her desire to do good and right things disgusted him. "Don't we have enough spying eyes?" he said. "No, I would rather be left alone."

"What if something happens to me?" Mrs. Gu looked at him and then shook her head. "I'll go to work now."

"Yes. It's good not to ask questions we don't have to answer now," Teacher Gu said to his wife's back, and when she closed the door behind her, he retrieved his fountain pen from the drawer and found the page in the notebook that contained another halfway-composed letter to his first wife. He reread it, but hard as he tried, he could not resume the thought that had been interrupted when his wife came home for lunch. He ripped the page off and put it in an envelope that already contained three similarly unfinished letters. Let her decide how she wanted to sort these out. On a new page he began writing:

Recently, I have been going over the Buddhist scriptures. No, they are not in front of my eyes—the scriptures my grandfather left me, as you may imagine, did not survive the revolutionary fire, started by none other than my own daughter. The scriptures I have been reading, however, are written in my mind. I am sure that this is of little interest to you with your Communist atheism, but do imagine with me, for one moment, the Buddha sitting under the holy tree and speaking once and again to his disciples. He who was said to be the wisest among the wise, he who was said to have vast and endless love for the world—who was he but an old man with blind hope, talking tirelessly to a world that would never understand him? We become prisoners of our own beliefs, with no one free to escape such a fate, and this, my dearest friend, is the only democracy offered by the world.

Teacher Gu stopped writing when he heard someone walk into the yard through the unlocked gate. He looked out the window and saw his neighbors, the young revolutionary lunatic and her husband, coming to his door. The wife raised her voice and asked if there was anyone home. The door to the house was unlocked too, and for a moment, Teacher Gu wondered if he should move across the room quietly and bolt the door from the inside. But the distance to the door seemed a long, exhausting journey. He held his breath and closed his eyes, wishing that if he remained still long enough, they would vanish.

The couple waited for an answer and then the woman tried the door, which she pushed open with a creak. "Oh, you're at home," the woman said with feigned surprise. "We heard some strange noise and thought we would come to check."

Teacher Gu replied coldly that things were perfectly fine. Discreetly he moved a newspaper to cover his unfinished letter.

"Are you sure? I heard you had a stroke. We'll help you check," the woman said, and signaled for her husband to come into the room from where he stood by the door, his two hands rubbing each other, as if he was embarrassed. "Is your wife home?" the woman asked.

"Why should I answer you?"

"I was just wondering. It's not a good thing for a wife to leave her husband home."

"She's at work."

"I know, but I'm talking in general. When you were in the hospital, I saw her leaving home after dark at least twice," the woman said, and turned to her husband. "Why don't you check and see what that noise is? Maybe it's a litter of rats."

The man stepped up unwillingly and looked around, avoiding Teacher Gu's eyes. The woman, however, did not conceal her interest as she walked around the room and checked all the corners. When she took the lid off a cooking pot and looked in, Teacher Gu lost his patience. He hit the floor with his cane. "You think we're too old to take care of a rat in our cooking pot and need you snakes for that?"

"Why, it's not good manners to talk to your neighbors this way," the woman said, throwing the lid back on the pot. "We're here to help you before things get out of hand."

"I don't need your help," Teacher Gu said. He supported himself with one hand on the table and stood up, pointing to the door with the cane. "Now leave my house this very instant. You don't happen to have a search warrant, do you?"

The woman ignored his words and moved closer to the table. She lifted the newspaper, uncovered the half letter, and smiled. Before she had a chance to read a word, Teacher Gu hit the tabletop with his cane, an earsplitting crack. The cup of untouched tea jumped off the table and spilled onto the woman's pants; the saucer, falling onto the cement floor, did not break.

The husband pulled his wife back before she could react; her face remained pale when he assured Teacher Gu that they did not mean him any harm. The husband's voice, a polite and beautiful baritone, surprised Teacher Gu. The man was a worker of some sort, as he wore a pair of greasy overalls and a threadbare shirt. Teacher Gu realized that he had never heard the man speak before. If he closed his eyes, he could imagine a more educated mind for that voice.

The wife, her face regaining color, stepped from behind the man. "What do you think you are doing? This is a civilized society."

The woman's voice was shrill. Teacher Gu could not help but feel sorry for the husband, whose beautiful voice—were it to have a life of its own—would probably be disappointed beyond words by the mismatch of the other voice, blade-thin and ugly.

"Don't think you can scare me with that Red Guard style of your daughter's," the wife said. "Let me tell you, truth is not to be enforced by violence in our country."

Teacher Gu pointed his cane at the woman's face, his whole body shaking. "Do not come and shit in my house," he said slowly, trying to enunciate every word.

"What vulgarity for a schoolteacher," the woman said. "The earlier you are fired, the better for the next generation."

The husband pulled her back and moved between her and the shaking cane, apologizing for the misunderstanding. She pushed her husband aside and said there was no need to succumb to the rudeness of the old man. "Now I dare you to hit me. Hit me now, you counterrevolutionary fox! Hit me so we can put you under the guillotine of justice."

Teacher Gu watched the woman, frothing with a hatred that he did not understand; she was his daughter's age, without much education perhaps, without a brain for sure. He let the cane fall to the floor and said to the husband, "Young man, I beg you—this request is between two men—and I beg you sincerely. Why don't you tell your wife that such behavior will only make her an ugly, unwanted woman in the end?"

The woman sneered. "What a rotten thought. Why should I be taught anything by my husband?" she said. "Women are the major pillars for our Communist mansion."

Teacher Gu sat down and wrote in big strokes on a piece of paper, his handwriting crooked, with no beautiful calligraphy to speak of. *SHUT UP. GO AWAY.* He showed the paper to the couple. He had decided not to waste one more word on the woman.

"Who are you to order us around? Let me tell you, you and that wife of yours are like the crickets after the first frost. There's not much time left for you to hop."

The man dragged his wife away, and when she resisted, he said in a low voice that she might as well shut up now. She raised her voice and questioned him. The man half dragged and half carried her out of the house. Through the open door, Teacher Gu heard her shouting and cursing at her husband's cowardice even in front of an old, useless man. Teacher Gu gathered all his energy to move across the room and close the door. When he returned to the table, his hands were shaking too hard to write. The visitors, even though farcically obvious in their intention to uncover some firsthand secrets, spelled danger; but while waiting for the noose to tighten around his neck, what could a man do except close his eyes and believe that the possibility of escaping one's fate lay not in the hands of others but in one's own will?

UNDER THE SHELTER of a dark evening sky on the day after Ching Ming, ten houses were entered and searched. Arrests were made, and none of the suspects resisted. By nightfall the first victory against the anti-Communist disruption was reported in a classified telegraph to the provincial capital.

A high-ranking party official, flown in from the provincial capital to take charge, was met by the mayor and his staff. Han and his parents, once considered the most trustworthy assistants to the mayor, were excluded from the meeting. Special security teams, formed to ensure an impartial investigation and cleansing of Muddy River, and made up of police and workers from a city a hundred miles away, were transported into the city in ten covered army trucks. During the ride, a young man who had recently inherited his father's position in the police department, worked loose a knot in the tarp cover and peeked outside. The silver stars in the sky and the dark mountain, even from afar, made him shiver like a young dog. He had just turned twenty, and had never left his hometown. He imagined the stories he would tell, upon his return, to the young clerk at the front desk; she would call him a braggart, insisting she did not believe a single word, but her blushing smile would tell a different story, understood only by the two of them.

The people of Muddy River, despite speculation and uncertainty, trusted in the old saying that the law did not punish the masses for their wrongdoing. This belief allowed them to busy themselves with their nightly drinking, arguing, lovemaking—their grand dreams and petty desires all coming alive once again on a night like this, when wild peach and plum trees blossomed along the riverbank, their fragrance carried by the spring breeze through open windows and into people's houses.

A carpenter and his apprentice walked on the Cross-river Bridge in the direction of the mountain, the young man pushing a wheelbarrow with his tools and watching the red tip of a cigarette dangling from his master's mouth. The carpenter had bought the cigarettes with their last money, as he had sworn before coming to the city that he wanted to have a taste of cigarettes. There had been other promises, made to the carpenter's wife and the apprentice's parents, before they had left the mountain, but their hope of making a small fortune was defeated by the officials who hired them to make, among other things, three television stands without paying more than the minimum compensation. City dwellers, the carpenter said between puffs, were a bunch who'd had their hearts eaten out by wild dogs; he warned his apprentice not to make the same mistake again, but the young man, who had been puzzled by the television sets he had seen in the officials' homes, imagined himself sitting in one of the armchairs he had helped to make and enjoying the beautiful women who appeared on the television screen at the push of a button.

A blind beggar sat in front of the Huas' shack and ran a small piece of rosin along the length of the bow for his two-string fiddle. He had been on his way from one town to the other when he met Old Hua and his wife, who had invited him to stay at their place for the night and had treated him to a good meal. The beggar had not met the couple before, though it did not surprise him, after a round of drinking, that they began to tell stories about their lives on the road. People recognized their own kind, despite all possible disguises, and in the end, the three of them drank, laughed, and cried together. The couple asked the beggar to stop drifting and settle down with them, and it seemed natural for him to agree. But now that the magic of the rice liquor had waned, the blind man knew that he would leave first thing the next morning. He had never stayed with anyone in his life, and it was too late to change his fate. He tested the bow on the string, and the fiddle sighed and moaned.

The door opened, and the blind man stopped his bow and listened. The husband was snoring from inside the shack, and the wife closed the door as quietly as she had opened it and took a seat near the beggar.

"I'm waking you up," the blind man said.

"Go on and play," Mrs. Hua said.

The blind man had planned to sneak away without waking the couple up, but now with the wife sitting next to him, he owed her an explanation. "It was nice of you to invite me to stay," he said. "I don't mean to be a man who changes his mind often, but I think I may have to decline your kindness."

"You have to be back on the road. I don't blame you."

"Once destined to be homeless, one finds it difficult to settle down."

"I know. I wish we could go back on the road too," Mrs. Hua said. "Now go on and play."

The blind man nodded, knowing that the couple would not take his departure as an offense. Slowly he drew the bow across the string and played an ancient song called "Leave-taking" for his day-old friendship.

ELEVEN

*B*ashi was in love, and it perplexed him. The desire to be with Nini for every minute of his life seemed not to come from between his legs but from elsewhere in his body, for which he had no experience or explanation. He thought hard and the only similar experience had been when he was three, not too long after his mother had left him with his grandmother: Winter that year had been particularly harsh in Muddy River, and every morning they would wake up to frozen towels on the washstand, even though his grandmother had not spared one penny on coal. Every day they slipped into bed together straight after dinner, and often in the middle of the night Bashi would wake up with icy cold feet. He would whimper, and his grandmother, still dreaming, would grab his little feet and hold them against her bosom, not one layer of nightclothes in between. The soft warmth made Bashi shiver with inexplicable fear and excitement, and he would lie awake, wiggling one toe and then another, imagining the toes in their adventure until he fell asleep.

Bashi longed to be with Nini the way he had once yearned for his grandmother's bosom. Sometimes he worried that something was wrong with his male root, but it never failed to rise dutifully when he was thinking about Nini. The problem occurred when she was next to him, a tangible body, warm and soft. He could not desire her the way he wanted to. The prenuptial bridal check he had made, on a whim, haunted him; that glimpse into a secret pathway she had opened to him, with trust and ease and even playfulness, shamed him. Her thin hair, cut short carelessly by her mother, looked like a bird's nest. Her pointed chin, her bony arms, and her forever-chapped lips made him want to take her in his arms and rock her and croon to her. But even this desire made him nervous in front of her. What would she think of him, a man with more than one screw loose in his brain?

Nini, however, seemed unaware of his struggle. The morning after Ching Ming, she had come into the house as naturally as day-light. She had moved around as if she had grown up there. Bashi waited for her to bring up the topic of marriage again; he believed everything he had told her when he had conducted his bridal check, but he knew that marriage to a twelve-year-old was easier said than done. Nini, on the other hand, did not press him, as he had dreaded she might. She talked more, even a bit chatty; she jokingly criticized his messy bedroom, and before he had a chance to defend himself, she took it upon herself to put everything in order for him. She did not blink when she discovered his foul-smelling socks and under-wear beneath the bed. He protested when she gathered the laundry to wash, but she refused to listen. If a man knew how to take care of himself, she said, what would he need a woman for?

Nini seemed not to understand her value, Bashi thought. She did not put on any of the airs that other women did when be-ing courted—or perhaps she was just a golden-hearted girl. Over-whelmed by his good fortune, Bashi was eager to find a friend with whom he could share his love story, but there was no such person in his life. Through his mind ran all the people he knew—the Huas nat-urally came up first, as the more Bashi thought about it, the more he believed the Huas to be the only ones willing to offer the assistance that he and Nini needed. But suppose they were old-fashioned and didn't approve of a marriage arranged by the two young people themselves?

Bashi found Mrs. Hua in the street in the morning; the arrests, made the night before, had caused little ripple in the everyday life of Muddy River. "Was your marriage to Old Hua arranged by your parents or his parents?" Bashi asked.

The old woman did not stop sweeping. She was aware of being addressed, yet ever since her dream about the death of her youngest daughter, Bunny, she had found it hard to concentrate on a conversation. The blind fiddler, coming and then leaving with his heartbreaking tunes, had made her nostalgic for her days and nights on the road. She talked to her husband about giving up their home and going back to the vagrant life. They could visit their daughters, the married ones and the ones who'd been taken away from them, before they took their final exit from the world; he said nothing at the beginning, and when she asked again, he said that he imagined these visits would not do the daughters, or themselves, any good.

"Mrs. Hua?" Bashi touched her broomstick and she gazed at him. More than any other day he looked like someone she had known from a long time ago. She closed her eyes but could not locate the person in her memory.

"Did you have a matchmaker to talk to your parents and Old Hua's parents?"

This boy, who was serious and persistent at asking irrelevant questions, baffled her—who was the person returning to her in his body?

"Mrs. Hua?"

"I met him as a beggar," she said.

"You mean, nobody went between your parents and his parents as a matchmaker?"

"No matchmaker would visit a couple of dead parents in their graves. My husband—he had been an orphan since before he could remember."

Bashi was elated by Mrs. Hua's answer. He himself was an orphan, and Nini was nearly one. Of course they needed no blessings from their parents, alive or dead. "What do you think of Nini?"

Mrs. Hua looked at Bashi with an intensity that frightened him.

He wondered if he had made a mistake bringing up the topic. Would the old woman become suspicious and turn him over to the police?

It was the boy flutist, Mrs. Hua thought. The boy who had once come and begged to become their son. Mrs. Hua looked up at the sky and counted. What year was that? The year that she and her husband had first thought of their deaths and the girls' lives without them—1959 it was, when the famine had just begun, a hard blow for everyone but hardest for beggars. They had four daughters then, Morning Glory at thirteen, Peony at ten, Lotus at eight, and Hibiscus, seven. The flutist was not older than twelve himself, an orphan who went from village to village, as they themselves did, and begged with his flute.

"Do you play flute?" Mrs. Hua asked Bashi.

"Who is Flute? I don't know him. Does he know me?"

The boy twenty years earlier had talked in this glib way too, but the music he had played could make a stone weep, such was the sadness that his flute had carried; he could make a dead man laugh in his coffin too, when he was in the mood. The boy had made much older girls fall in love with him; even some married women, when their husbands were at the fair or in the field, stood in front of their doors and teased him with jokes usually meant only for married men and women, behind closed doors. Despite all the attention he got, the boy came and begged Mrs. Hua and her husband to adopt him; he would call them Baba and Mama and would support them with his flute, he promised, but her husband refused. With his flute and his sweet words, he would put all their daughters through hell, Old Hua said to Mrs. Hua afterward; she agreed but not without regret, and now the boy had come back to her in another incarnation, flute-less, yet she recognized him.

"What do you think of Nini, Mrs. Hua?"

"Why do you ask, Son?"

"What do you think of my marrying her?" said Bashi. "Mrs. Hua, don't look at me like I have two heads. You're scaring me."

"Why do you want to marry Nini?"

"She'll be so much better off with me than with her own parents," said Bashi. "And I'd be the happiest man in the world if I could spend my days with her."

Mrs. Hua looked hard at Bashi. For a year after the flutist boy had left them, Lotus had been in a cheerless mood, unusual for an eight-year-old. Among the sisters, she had been the closest to the boy; she had learned to sing to his accompaniment, and he had joked that they would make the best beggar couple, with his flute and her voice. Mrs. Hua had wondered then whether they had made a mistake by refusing the boy, but Old Hua, upon hearing her doubt, shook his head. Lotus was the plainest of the four girls, and the boy, with a face too smart for his own good, would one day shatter her heart. Besides, Old Hua said, did they want their daughter to repeat their own fate, married to another beggar, without a roof over her head?

"I'm serious," Bashi said. Mrs. Hua's silence made him nervous and eager to prove himself. "I'll treat her well."

"I've seen you grow up these years, Bashi," Mrs. Hua said. "I've known you enough not to suspect you as a bad person, but anyone else who hears you say this will think you crazy."

"Why?"

"She's still a child."

"But she'll grow up," Bashi said. "I can wait."

Indeed, why couldn't the boy have the right to think of marrying Nini? What if they had let the young flute player be part of the family—they might have more now to their names, a daughter and a son-in-law to see them off to the next world, music that added color to their dull lives, grandchildren to love.

"Who would marry her and treat her well if not for me? I love her," Bashi said, and he stood up straighter as he made the bold claim. "She's never happy in her own house. Can you be my match-maker? Can you talk to her family on our behalf? They can't get a better offer."

"She's too young," Mrs. Hua said.

"You married your daughters young to other families, didn't

you?" Bashi said. "I can wait for her to grow up. I can pay for Nini to live with you. I just need to have their word that Nini will be mine."

Mrs. Hua looked at Bashi. The wheel of life, with its ruthless revolving, could be merciful at times. The boy had come back to her, giving her a second chance, but what was the right thing, for any mother, any woman, to decide? "Let me talk to my husband," she said. "Can you come to our place in the afternoon? We'll have an answer for you then."

IT TOOK TONG a long walk to gather his courage for school. He imagined his teacher asking for an explanation about the previous day. He would never get the red scarf now that he was a dishonest boy, pretending to be sick and skipping school. The teacher had once said that a small crack in the bottom of a ship would wreck it in the open sea, and Tong imagined himself a deteriorated soul heading toward a sinful life, and the thought made his eyes fill with tears. He would admit his wrongdoing first thing this morning, before the crack widened and made him into a young criminal.

The teacher, however, was in no mood to question Tong. Classes had been canceled from the first through the sixth grades. The principal had announced an emergency meeting for all teachers and staff, and the students were herded into the auditorium, watched by nobody. Soon the unsupervised auditorium exploded with noise. Boys from the upper grades ran wild along the aisles, and the younger boys, even though they dared not leave their seats, hurled paper planes at one another. Girls shrieked when they were bumped or hit by the boys, and some brought out colorful plastic strings to weave key rings in the shape of goldfish or parrots. No question was asked about why they were kept there, or how long it would go on; as far as the children could see, this day of happiness would last forever.

Tong sat among a few quieter classmates, boys and girls who could sit still in their seats for hours when required by their teachers. There was a war coming, the girl sitting next to Tong whispered to him. What war? Tong asked, and the girl did not answer, saying only that she had overheard her father say so to her mother. She was the kind of girl who blushed at every word she said, and Tong looked at her crimson face, finding it hard to believe her.

Half an hour later, the principal led the teachers into the auditorium. He blew his whistle with all his might, hurting everyone's eardrums. The students quickly returned to their seats, and the auditorium soon became quiet. The principal stood at the podium and, as usual, cleared his throat several times into the microphone, which cracked and magnified the sound, before beginning his speech.

"An outbreak of a counterrevolutionary epidemic has caught Muddy River unprepared," he said. "I want you all to understand that the situation is urgent, and if we don't watch out for ourselves, we may be the next ones infected by this virulent disease."

Some children shifted in their seats, a few coughing and others rubbing their noses.

"It is time that we cleanse our hearts and our souls with the harshest disinfectant," the principal said, banging on the podium to emphasize each of his words, the children's hearts pounding along with his fist.

"You've all been born under the red flag of revolution and grown up in the honeypot the party has provided," the principal continued. "Sometimes this privilege may be the exact reason that one forgets to appreciate one's happiness in this country. Now answer me, children, who has given you this happy life?"

It took a moment of hesitation before some upper-grade students answered, "The Communist Party."

"I can't hear you," the principal said. "Say your answer louder if you have confidence in it."

A few teachers stood up and signaled to the auditorium, and more voices joined the chorus. It took several rounds for the principal to be satisfied with the roaring answer. *"Long live the greatest, the most glorious, and the ever-correct Chinese Communist Party,"* he said again with a thump-thump of his fist. "Do you all understand these words? What does this mean? It means our party has never been wrong and will never be wrong; it means that anything we do will not escape the scrutiny of the party. I know you've all been taught to respect your parents, but what are they compared to the party, our foremost parents? You are the party's children before you are the children of your parents. Everybody is equally loved by the party, but when someone makes a mistake, just as when a child makes a mistake, the party will not let a single wrongdoer slip by. No one will be spared; no crime will be tolerated."

Tong's eyes were swollen and hot. How could he, a child loved by the party, skip class only because of a missing pet? How could he have forgotten that he was destined to become a hero? Softheartedness would make him useless, as his father had said; he was meant to be a special boy, and never again would he allow himself to forget it. He shouted the slogans with the other students—he could not hear his own voice, but he was sure his voice would reach the party, asking for forgiveness.

After the meeting, the students lined up and went back to their homerooms. The upper grades were required to write down in detail what they and each member of their families had done on the day of Ching Ming. The smaller children were given the time to think and recollect, their teachers patrolling the aisles so those boys and girls who tended to daydream in class would be constantly reminded to focus.

His dog had disappeared the evening before so he had been looking for his dog on the day of Ching Ming, Tong told the teachers in the separate classroom, when it was his turn to confess. The two interrogators, sitting behind the desk with notebooks open, were both strangers—they had been called in from another school, as the school district had instructed that schools swap staffs so the children's answers wouldn't be influenced in any way by their own teachers. The younger one of the two, a woman in her thirties, took notes and then said, "What's your dog's name?"

"Ear."

The two teachers exchanged looks and the other one, a man in his fifties, asked, "What kind of name is that?"

Tong wiggled on the chair, made for an adult, his feet not reaching the floor. The chair had been placed in the middle of the room, facing the desk and the two chairs behind it. Tong tried to fix his eyes on his shoes, but having their own will, his eyes soon wandered to the four legs underneath the desk across the room. The man's trousers, greenish gray, had two patches of a similar color covering both knees; the woman's black leather shoes had shiny metal clips in the shape of butterflies. Tong did not know how long he would be questioned—even though the principal and teachers had said nothing of the signed petition, he knew that it was one of the things he had to hide.

"Who could prove that you were looking for your dog?" the male teacher asked.

"My mama and my baba," Tong said.

"Were they with you when you looked for the dog?"

Tong shook his head.

"Then how could they know what you were doing?" the male teacher said. "What were they doing when you were looking for the dog?"

"I don't know," Tong said. "I went out early. They always get up late on Sundays."

"Do you know what they do on Sunday mornings?" the male teacher said in a particular tone, and the female teacher looked down at her notebook, trying to hide a knowing smile.

Tong shook his head again, his back cold with sweat.

"What did they do after they got up?" the male teacher asked.

"Nothing," Tong said.

"Nothing? How could two adults do nothing?"

"My mama did some laundry," Tong said, hesitantly.

"That's something. And then?"

"My baba fixed the stove," Tong said. It was not exactly a lie—the damper of their stove had been broken and his mother had asked his father many times before he had fixed it the week before. It was something that a father would do on a Sunday.

"What else?"

"My mama cooked the breakfast and the supper."

"But not lunch? Did she or your father go out to buy lunch?"

"We eat only two meals on Sundays," said Tong. "They did not go out. They took a long nap in the afternoon."

"Again?" the male teacher said with exaggerated disbelief.

Tong bit his lips and did not speak. His mother always said sleeping was the best way to save energy so they would not have to spend extra money for a lunch on Sunday, but how could he explain this to the teachers?

"Did your parents leave home at any time in the morning?" the male teacher asked. "Say, between seven and twelve o'clock?"

Tong shook his head. He had a vague feeling that they did not believe him, and sooner or later they would reveal his lie to the school and his parents. What would they do with him then? He would never get the red scarf around his neck by June.

"Are you sure?"

"I went home for breakfast and then they said it was a waste to look for Ear so I stayed home with them."

"Did you find your dog?" the female teacher asked while she screwed the cap back onto her fountain pen and glanced at the roster, ready for the next student.

Tong tried hard to hold back his tears, but the effort gave way to the fear that he would be punished not only for lying but also for signing his father's name on the white cloth. The two teachers watched him for a moment. "Don't cry over a missing dog," the woman said. "Ask your parents to get another one for you."

Tong howled without answering. The male teacher waved to dismiss him and the female teacher led him out of the classroom by his hand. For a moment he wanted to confess everything to the female teacher, whose soft and warm palm calmed him a little, but before he could open his mouth, she signaled to his teacher to take him back and called out the name of the next student.

Tong waited in his seat, not talking to the other children. Nobody asked him why he was crying; already two girls and a boy before him had come back sniffling or sobbing, and no one had shown any surprise or concern.

It was past lunchtime when the principal, talking through the PA system, announced that it was time for an hour break for lunch. They were not to discuss anything with their classmates or their parents, the principal said. Anyone who broke the rule would find himself in grave trouble.

Tong walked slowly. That morning he had noticed the sudden appearance of many black caterpillars nicknamed "poplar stingers," and now, only half a day later, hundreds more had appeared on the sidewalk and the alley walls. Many had been crushed by careless feet and bicycle wheels, their tiny bodies and innards drying in the sun.

When Tong entered the room his parents both looked at him and then returned to their conversation. "Who knows?" his father said. "Maybe the government means it only to be a setup to scare people a little and nothing serious will come of it in the end."

Tong sat down at the table, a bowl of noodle soup in front of him. His mother told him to hurry up, as both of them needed to return to work within half an hour. "The way this is carried out gives me palpitations."

"A woman's heart palpitates at anything," Tong's father scoffed. "A crushed sparrow could make your heart jump out of your mouth. Let me tell you: The law does not punish the masses. You don't even need to go far—just think how many people were beaten by the Red Guards in 1966. Now that their behavior is considered bad and illegal, do you see any former Red Guard being punished? No."

Tong ate slowly, each mouthful hurting him while he swallowed. When his mother urged him to eat faster, he said, "Baba, why doesn't the law punish the masses?"

"So you finally have a question about something other than that dog of yours," Tong's father said. From afar came drawn-out sirens. Tong's mother stopped her chopsticks and listened. "Sounds like a fire engine," she said to his father.

His father went out into the yard and looked. In a minute, he came back and said, "You can see the smoke."

"Where is the fire?"

"East side."

On any other day he would ask to be excused and rush to the fire, but Tong only sat and nibbled on a noodle that seemed endless. His mother felt his forehead with her palm. "Are you sick?"

"Lovesick for a dog," Tong's father said.

Tong did not answer. He forced himself to finish his lunch so his father would not comment on his eating habits. Perhaps nothing bad would happen, after all, as his father said. This hope cheered him as he walked to school. But what if his father was wrong? Grown-ups made mistakes, as they had said nothing would happen to Ear. Plunged back into despair by the thought, Tong felt cold in the spring breeze; his legs stumbled, as if he were walking in cotton clouds.

Two different teachers, from yet another school, were assigned to Tong's class, and one by one the students went in to answer the same questions for a second time. The two teachers were less intimidating this time, and Tong was able to look up at their eyes. They seemed to find nothing unusual in the sleeping patterns of Tong's parents. "Are you sure?" one of the teachers asked every time Tong answered a question; her voice was gentle enough that Tong did not find it hard to lie. By the end of the questioning, Tong felt relieved. The teachers were nice to him—they wouldn't have been if he had already been found out. Indeed, he had done nothing serious except look for Ear; the more Tong thought about it, the less real the signature he had left on the white cloth became, and soon he stopped worrying about the petition.

. . .

NINI HAD NEVER KNOWN that a secret could have a life of its own. That she had a place to go someday consumed all the space in her chest in no time; expanding still, it made her small breasts ache. Her limbs, even the good hand and leg, seemed to get farther away from her, the joints becoming loose and out of control. Nini studied herself in an oval-shaped, palm-sized mirror that her second sister had hidden underneath her pillow; even though the mirror was only big enough for part of her face at one time, the person in the mirror was no longer the ugly self she remembered, her lips fuller, her cheeks rounder now, always flushed.

It was not the first time her mind had been occupied. Before Bashi there had been Teacher Gu and Mrs. Gu, but some longings seemed to be more demanding than others, and Nini felt her body was too small to contain her secret now. She had to bite the inside of her mouth to avoid blurting the news to a stranger on the street or, even worse, to her own family. In the end, when it seemed that she was going to explode, Nini picked up the baby and told Little Fourth and Little Fifth that she was taking the baby to the marketplace. The two girls begged to tag along, but Nini said she had other things to tend to, and they would not be of any help. To appease the girls, Nini gave them each a candy she had brought home from Bashi's house. She promised more snacks if they remained well behaved in the house. Couldn't they play in the yard? Little Fourth asked, and she promised that they would not step into the alley. Nini hesitated. The two girls were growing into a pair of twins, and once they had each other, their world was complete. It was usually fine to let them play in the yard, but Nini decided that this time it would not hurt for her to exercise more authority so that each favor would be returned with gratitude and obedience. She told the girls that she would have to lock them in the house. They looked unhappy, yet neither complained. They stood side by side, each sucking on the candy and watching Nini close the door and padlock it from the outside.

"I've found you a brother-in-law," Nini whispered to Little Sixth in the street, her lips touching the baby's ear.

The baby pointed to a police car with lights flashing on a side street and said, "Light-light."

"I'll find you a good husband too, and people will be so jealous that their eyes will turn green," Nini said to Little Sixth, imagining the helpless infuriation of her parents and the two older girls. If Little Fourth and Little Fifth behaved, she would consider helping them too. She pulled gently until the baby had to look at her instead of the police car. "Listen. Do you want a better life? If you do, you have to stick with me. Don't ever love anybody else in the family. Nobody will make you happy except me, your big sister."

"Sis," Little Sixth said, and put her wet mouth on Nini's cheek.

"Your brother-in-law," Nini said, and blushed at her audacious name for Bashi. "Your big brother, he knows how to make a stone laugh."

The baby babbled, practicing saying "brother," a new word for her.

"He's rich and he'll give you a dowry when it's your turn to get married. Don't ever expect that from anybody else."

When they entered Bashi's house through the unlocked door, for a moment nobody replied to Nini's greetings. The bedroom door was closed. Nini knocked on the door. "I know you're inside. Don't try to play a trick on me," she said.

There was no reply from the room. Nini put her ear on the door and heard a rustling of clothes. "Bashi?" she said.

A second, he replied, his voice filled with panic. Nini pushed the door open. Bashi rushed to her, a hand buttoning his fly. "I didn't know you were coming," he said, panting a little.

She studied his flushed face. "Who's here?"

"Nobody," Bashi said. "Only me."

Nini shoved Little Sixth into Bashi's arms and went in to check. She found Bashi's reaction suspicious, and instinctively she knew it was another woman he was hiding from her. She picked up Bashi's unmade quilt from his bed but there was no one hiding underneath.

She peeked under the bed. On the other side of the curtain, his grandmother's bed was empty. So was the closet.

"What are you looking for?" Bashi said with a smile, the baby sitting astride his shoulders and pulling his hair.

"Are you hiding someone from me?" Nini asked, when she could not find a trace of another woman in the bedroom.

"Of course not," Bashi said.

"Why else were you sleeping in the middle of the morning?"

"I wasn't really sleeping. I came back from a walk and thought I would take a rest in bed," Bashi said. "In fact, I was dreaming about you when you came in."

"What idiot would believe you?"

"Believe me," Bashi said. "I have no one to think about but you."

Nini thought of laughing at him but he gazed at her with a desperate look in his eyes. "I'll believe you," she said.

"I talked to Mrs. Hua."

Nini felt her heart pause for a beat. "What did she say?"

"She did not say no," Bashi said.

"But did she agree?"

"She said she needed to talk to Old Hua, but I think they will agree. I can't see why not. Mrs. Hua looked like she was ready to kiss me when I said I wanted to marry you."

"Nonsense. Why would she want to kiss you? She's an old woman."

"Then do you want to kiss me, young woman?"

Nini punched Bashi on his arm. He jumped aside, which made the baby shriek with happiness. Nini opened both arms, trying to catch Bashi, and he hopped around, all three of them laughing.

Nini was the first to calm down. She was tired now, she said, sitting on Bashi's bed. Little Sixth pulled Bashi's hair, demanding more rides. He marched around in the bedroom, singing a song about soldiers going to the front in Korea, the baby patting his head and Nini humming along. When he finished the song, he lowered the baby and put her next to Nini. Then he took the baby's kerchief and folded it into a small mouse and played tricks with his fingers so that the mouse jumped onto Little Sixth as if it had a life of its own. The baby screamed with joy; Nini was startled and then laughed.

"What a lucky man I am to have a pair of flower girls here," Bashi said.

Nini stopped laughing. "What did you say?"

"I said with one trick I made both of you laugh."

"No, you said something else," Nini said. "What did you mean?"

Bashi scratched his head. "What did I mean? I don't know."

"You're lying," Nini said, and before she knew it, tears came to her eyes. She sounded like the bad-tempered women she saw in the marketplace; she sounded like her own mother, and she was ashamed.

Little Sixth chewed on the tail of the kerchief mouse and watched them with interest. Bashi looked at Nini with concern. "Do you have a stomachache?"

"What ideas do you have about the baby?" Nini said. "I tell you— she's not yours. She'll have the best man in the world."

"A man even better than I?"

"A hundred times better," Nini said, though already she was starting to smile. "Don't ever set your heart on Little Sixth."

"For heaven's sake, she's only a baby!"

"She won't always stay a baby. She'll become a big girl and by then I know you won't like me, because she'll be prettier and younger. Tell me, is that your scheme, to marry me so you will one day get Little Sixth?"

"I swear I've never schemed anything."

"And when the baby is an older girl—"

"I'm her big brother so of course I'll watch out for her. Pick for her a man a hundred times better than I."

"Brother-brother," Little Sixth said, the kerchief still between her teeth.

She did not believe him, Nini said, trying to keep her face straight.

"I'm serious. If not, all the mice of the world will come and nibble me to death, or I will be stung by a scorpion on my tongue and never talk again, or some fish bone will stick in my throat and I will never be able to swallow another grain of rice," Bashi said. "I swear I only have you in my heart."

Nini looked at Bashi and saw no trace of humor in his eyes. "Don't swear so harshly," she said in a soft voice. "I believe you."

"No, you don't. If only you knew," Bashi said, and took a deep breath. "Nini, I love you."

It was the first time he had said love, and they both blushed. "I know. I love you too," Nini said in a whisper, her arms and legs all in the wrong place, her body a cumbersome burden.

"What? I can't hear you. Say it louder," Bashi said, with a hand on his ear. "What did you just say?"

Nini smiled. "I said nothing."

"Ah, how sad. I'm in love with someone in vain."

"That's not true," Nini said, louder than she'd intended. Bashi looked at her and shook his head as if in disbelief, and she panicked. Did he misunderstand her? "If I were not telling the truth, the god of lightning would split me in half."

"Then the goddess of thunder would boom me to death," Bashi said.

"No, I would die a death a hundred times more painful than you."

"My death would be a thousand times more painful than yours."

"I would become your slave in the next life," Nini said.

"I would become a fly that keeps buzzing around you in the next life until you swat me to death."

Neither spoke, as if they were each entranced by their desire to demonstrate their willingness to suffer for the other. In the quietness they listened to the baby babbling. Nini wondered what they would become now that they knew how much they desired each other. When Bashi touched her face, it was only natural for his lips to touch hers, and then they let the rest of their bodies drag them down to the bed, onto the floor, without a sound, and they held tight to each other until their bones hurt.

Bashi picked her up and put her on his grandmother's bed. Little Sixth watched and then, when the curtain was drawn, she lost interest. She crawled on Bashi's bed, from one end to the other, exploring the new territory, enjoying the freedom without the rope that bound her to the bed. Soon she rolled off the bed, but the pillow she had been dragging along cushioned her. She cried halfheartedly and then crawled to the other bed, past the curtain that threatened to tangle her, around a pair of big shoes and then another pair, bigger, and finally she reached the place she had set her mind to, under the bed where her big sister and big brother were panting in their inexperienced joy and agony. She picked up half a stick of ginseng from under the bed and chewed it. It was sweet at first but then it tasted awful. She took the stick out and threw it as hard as she could, and it landed in one of the big shoes.

"Bashi," whispered Nini.

Inches away, Bashi gazed at Nini, and then buried his head into the curve of her neck. "Let's wait until we get married," he whispered back. "I want you to know that I'm a responsible man."

Nini looked at her undone clothes and smiled shyly. He buttoned her shirt and together they listened to the baby talking to herself.

"I'm going to find Mrs. Hua and Old Hua right after you go home," Bashi said.

"Tell them we want to get married tomorrow," Nini said. "My parents won't care."

"How lucky I am," Bashi said.

"I am the lucky one."

They lay in each other's arms. From time to time one or the other would break the silence and talk of plans for themselves and the baby, their future life. After a long time Bashi looked at the clock and looked again. "It's near noon now," he said.

Nini looked at the clock and then listened. It was quiet for the time of the day, when normally schoolchildren and grown-ups would be going home for their lunch break. She sat up and said it was time for her to go; she moved slowly, as if her body were filled with lazy dreams too heavy for her to carry. She might as well let her parents and her sisters wait.

"Are you coming in the afternoon?" Bashi asked. "I'll have talked to Old Hua and Mrs. Hua by then."

"I'll come after lunch," said Nini. She turned her back to him and straightened her clothes. Before she left she put a small bag of fried peanuts in her coat pocket. For Little Fourth and Little Fifth, she said, and Bashi added some toffees.

When Nini left Bashi's yard, two old women stared at her and then exchanged looks. It was the first time she had left his door in broad daylight—she used to be careful, sneaking in and out of Bashi's house in the semidarkness of the early morning—but let the women suffer in their nosiness and jealousy. She was his, and he was hers, and Old Hua and Mrs. Hua were going to marry them very soon. She had nothing to fear now.

The street was eerily empty. The marketplace was locked, and in the main street, most of the shop doors were shut. When Nini walked past an elementary school, the school gate opened and out ran children of all ages. School was letting the children go home late, she thought, and quickened her steps. She wondered if she could get home before her parents and sisters came back. They might not even discover her absence.

A few blocks away from her house Nini saw the smoke rising. People with buckets and basins ran past her. When she entered her alley, a neighbor saw her and cried out in relief, "Nini, thank heaven you're not in the house."

Nini looked at their house, engulfed by fire. The smoke was black and thick against the blue sky, and the orange tongues of fire, nimble and mischievous, licked the roof. The neighbor shouted for her to stay at a safe distance; her parents were on their way, and so were the fire engines, he said.

A few schoolchildren ran past Nini. They cried warnings at anyone passing by, more out of excitement than alarm, and soon they were ordered by the grown-ups to leave the alley. Nini looked at the neighbor who was running toward the house and who had, she hoped, forgotten her by now. She held the baby tight and slipped into a nearby alley, against the running crowds, wishing she could turn herself into a wisp of air.

TWICE BASHI HAD WALKED PAST Nini's alley, but none of the neighbors who answered his knocking would provide him with any clue when he inquired about the whereabouts of Nini's family. The brick walls remained standing, but the roof had collapsed. The front room of the house, with its blackened holes where the two windows and a door had been, reminded Bashi of a skull, and he spat and scolded himself for the unlucky connection. An old woman who was probing the ruins with a pair of tongs, upon hearing his steps, looked up with alarm. Thinking that she was a neighbor, Bashi tried to start a conversation, asking her if she knew the family stricken by the disaster, but she seemed to be caught in panic and hurried away with a straw bag of knickknacks. It took Bashi a moment to realize what the woman had been doing, and he shouted at her to return what did not belong to her, but she was soon out of sight.

Bashi decided to go to the city hospital to find any news. Someone there must have information if the two sisters, as Nini believed, had been caught in the fire. He had found Nini curled up in a ball in front of his locked door earlier that afternoon when he had returned from his visit to the Huas. Wake up, girl, he had said, saying he had brought great news, but when she opened her eyes he was struck by how, in less than an hour, she had become a stranger—Nini always had everything on display in her small face, hunger and anger and curiosity and determination, but now the blankness in her face frightened him. Little Sixth, hearing him, crawled out of the storage cabin and smiled.

Did he still want to marry her, a bad-luck girl who had murdered her sisters and left her family homeless? Nini asked. It took Bashi a few minutes to understand the question. He tried to think of something to lighten Nini's mood, but his brain seemed frozen by her unblinking eyes. The Huas had agreed to take her in if her parents agreed to the marriage proposal, Bashi said, the news delivered with less confidence and joy than he had imagined. They could have been in heaven, Nini said; they could have been so happy. They could still be happy, Bashi said, but Nini shook her head, saying she was being punished for her happiness. Heaven was the stingy one, taking back more often than giving—Bashi remembered his grandmother's favorite saying and told it now to Nini. Heaven was the mean one, Nini said, and Bashi replied that, in that case, he would go to hell with her. For a while after that they watched Little Sixth crawl in the yard, their hands clasped together. They were two children for whom the world had not had any use in the first place, and in each other's company they had grown, within half a day, into a man and a woman who would have no more use for that world.

On the way to the hospital, Bashi saw unfamiliar faces loitering in twos and threes in the street. If not for the fire he would have been talking to these strangers, trying to strike up conversations, but now Bashi watched them with detachment. The world could have been collapsing but it would not have made any difference to Nini or to him.

The receptionist at the emergency room was unfriendly as always, and when Bashi could not pry any useful information from her, he thought of the two strangers in front of the hospital. "A busy day, brothers," Bashi said when he approached them.

The two men looked Bashi up and down and did not reply. He offered them a pack of cigarettes. The younger one, not much older than Bashi, held out a hand and then, taking a quick glance at his companion, shook his head and said they had their own cigarettes.

"How disappointing. No offense, but I think it's unacceptable to refuse a cigarette offered to you. At least here in our town."

The older man nodded apologetically and brought out two cigarettes, one for himself and one for his companion. The younger man struck a match and lit the older man's cigarette first. When he offered Bashi the match, already burning to the end, Bashi shook his head. "So, where are you from?" he said.

"Why do you ask?" the older man demanded.

"Just curious. I happen to know a lot of people in town, and you don't look like one I've seen."

"Yes? What do you do?" the older man said.

Bashi shrugged. "Have you heard anything about this fire?" he said.

"There was a fire?"

"A house was burned down."

"Bad luck," the younger man said.

"So you haven't heard or seen anything? I thought maybe you would know, the way you have to stand here all day."

"Who told you we stand here all day?" the younger one said. The older man coughed and pulled his companion's sleeve.

Bashi looked at the two and smiled. "Don't think I'm an idiot," he said. "You're here because of the rally, no?"

"Who told you this?" the two men said, coming closer, one on each side of Bashi.

"I'm not a blind man, nor deaf," Bashi said. "I can even help you if you help me."

The older man put a hand on Bashi's shoulder. "Tell us what you know, Little Brother."

"Hey, you're hurting me," Bashi said. "What do you want to know?"

"All that you know," the older man said.

"As I said, you need to promise to help me first."

"You don't want to bargain on such things."

"Oh yes? Do you want to know what that person did?" Bashi pointed to a middle-aged man, who exited the hospital and crossed the street.

The older man gave the younger man a look, and the younger

man nodded and went across the street, running a few steps to catch up with the middle-aged man.

"If you can go into the ER and ask them if there was anyone hurt in the fire, I'll tell you what he did," Bashi said, when the older man pressed again.

"Tell me first."

"Then you won't help me."

"I will."

Bashi studied the man and then said, "I'll take your word. That man—I don't know his name but I know he works in the hospital—he signed a petition for the counterrevolutionary woman. Now you need to go in there and help me."

The older man did not move. "Just that?"

"Why? This isn't important enough information for you?"

"Use your brain, Little Brother. If he signed the petition, why do we need you to tell us?"

"Then what do you want to hear?"

"Did you see anyone, say, who went to the rally without leaving a signature?"

That was what they were after, Bashi thought, and nodded with a smile, pointing to the entrance of the emergency room. The older man looked at Bashi and then flipped his finished cigarette into the gutter. "I'll do this for you and you better have something good for me in return."

A few minutes later, the man came back and said nobody had died in the fire, but two little girls, badly burned, had been transferred that afternoon to the provincial capital. Bashi thought about the small bodies engulfed by the fire and shuddered.

The man studied Bashi. "The girls didn't die—I'm not sure if that's good news or bad news, but I've found it out for you. Now your turn."

"What do you want to know?"

"I've said, all that you know."

"This old woman—the mother of the counterrevolutionary, if you know whom I'm talking about—is a master behind the scene."

The man snorted, unimpressed. "What else?" he said. "Tell us something we don't know."

"I saw so many people I can hardly remember all their names."

"At least you remember some?"

"Let's see," Bashi thought, and listed the names, some he had seen at the rally, a few others who had, at one time or another, offended him. The man seemed uninterested in checking the validity of his report, so Bashi went on more boldly, giving as many names as he remembered from the rally and then throwing in a bunch of people he considered his enemies. The man wrote down the names in his notebook and then asked for Bashi's personal information.

Bashi gave the man his name and address. "Anytime you need help," he said.

"Wait a minute," the old man said. "Why did you go to the rally?"

"Just to see what was going on," Bashi said, and bid farewell to the men.

THE JOY OF YOUTH shortened a day into a blink; the loneliness of old age stretched a moment into an endless nightmare. Teacher Gu watched his slanting shadow, cast onto the wall of the alley by the evening sun. The envelope in his hand was heavy, but for an instant he could not remember what he had been writing to his first wife. How long did it take for his letters to reach her desk, be opened, read, reread, and answered? He counted and calculated the time it should take for her letter to arrive, but the number of days eluded him.

His wife had been taken away the night before by two policemen, and now he remembered he had mentioned the arrest in a matter-of-fact way in the latest letter. The police had come and pushed open the door after one knock, and she came out of the bedroom and let them cuff her wrists without saying anything. Teacher Gu was sitting at the table, his fountain pen in his palm even though he wasn't writing a letter. Neither the policemen nor his wife said anything to him, and for a moment he felt that he had become transparent, according to his own will. He wrote a long letter to his first wife, the spell of his liberation turning him into the poet that he had long ago ceased to be.

His wife did not return for breakfast or lunch, and by now, when homebound people were starting to fill the streets and alleys with their long overlapping shadows, Teacher Gu knew that she would not come home for dinner, or, as far as he knew, for the rest of his life. They all disappeared in this manner, not giving him any chance to participate, or even to protest: his first wife, late from work one day and the next thing he knew she had left a letter proposing divorce, written in her beautiful penmanship, next to a pot of tea that he had brewed for her and that later turned cold, untouched; Shan had been reading a book in her bed when the police came for her, close to bedtime because that was when all the arrests were customarily carried out, and there had been scuffles, resistance on Shan's side, questioning the legality of the arrest, but in the end Shan had been dragged away, leaving the dog-eared book by her pillow; his wife, the night before, had said nothing to question the police when they informed her of the arrest, nor had she resisted. She had said some words of apology to her husband's back, but what was the point of it, her heart no longer with him in the house they had shared for thirty years, but floating to a farther place, ready to occupy an altar? They all took their exits so easily, as if he were a dream, neither a good nor a bad one but an indifferent one filled with uninteresting details, and they would wake up one day and continue their lives, oblivious to his absence. Would they have a moment of hesitation and think about him, when they saw his face between two tree branches, or heard him in an old dog's coughing? Was his wife, wherever she was now, thinking about him, this aged invalid who had nothing better to do than wait and weep in the alley? Teacher Gu tried to steady himself with his cane but his hand shook so hard that, for a moment, he thought this was the end he had been looking forward to, when his body would exert its own will and throw him into the gutter before his mind could stop it.

"Are you all right?" It was the neighbor with the beautiful voice, whose name Teacher Gu had never bothered to find out and whose wife had been so keen on spying on them. He braked his bicycle next to Teacher Gu and supported him with a hand.

Teacher Gu, in a moment of confusion, tried to wriggle his arm free and run away. The man's grip, however, tightened like an iron clamp. He got off the bicycle, and with one hand still on Teacher Gu's arm, he said, "Do you need to go to the hospital?"

"I'm going to the mailbox," Teacher Gu said, when he regained his dignity.

"I can do it for you," the man said.

Teacher Gu shook his head. He wanted to hear the thud of the letter dropping into the metal box. How many days had it been since he had sent out the first letter? He counted again, not knowing that the letter, bearing his name and address, would be, as were the other thick letters he had sent out, intercepted and read by a stranger first. The man who read the letters, an older man serving his last year in a clerical position at the police department, agonized over the almost-illegible passages, which reminded him of his dying parents and his own imminent retirement. He could circle the lines that spelled some unfriendly message to the government and make a big fuss, but in the end, finding no reason to cause undue pain to a fellow-man in the final, joyless years of old age, he stamped the letters as harmless and let them continue on through the post. He even wondered, at night, when he could not fall asleep, about the woman who would be reading the letters and writing back. He wished it was his duty to read the letters sent back to the Gu address, but that job belonged to another colleague, a woman in her late thirties who always sucked hard candy when she read, and the small distracting noise the candy made, clicking against her teeth, annoyed the old man. He could not bring himself to ask her about letters from a certain woman to Teacher Gu, but he was curious, almost as eager as Teacher

Gu, for the woman to write back. Neither knew that the letters were sitting unopened in a study, along with other mail, the woman in question dying of cancer and loneliness, in a hospital for high-ranking officials in Beijing.

"I'll help you to the mailbox," the man said now to Teacher Gu.

Teacher Gu did not speak. He freed himself from the man and walked on, but after a few steps, when the man offered again, he did not protest. He had not eaten anything since the night before, and when the man came back and found him barely supporting himself by the wall, he picked Teacher Gu up easily and placed him on the back rack of his bicycle. "I'm taking you to the hospital, all right?" he said in a raised voice, one hand gripping the handlebars of the bicycle and the other stabilizing Teacher Gu.

Teacher Gu protested so vehemently that he almost caused both of them and the bicycle to fall over. Another neighbor came to help, and together they rolled the bicycle slowly to Gu's gate. The man leaned the bicycle against the wall and helped Teacher Gu to get down from the rack, but before they could enter the yard, the man's wife appeared as if from nowhere. "What's going on here?" she said, clicking her tongue. "Aren't you the one who hates us proletariats?"

Teacher Gu stopped, and it took him a moment to realize she was addressing him, her eyes enlarging in front of his face, as she stood ridiculously close. "Where's that wife of yours?" she said. "Do you now believe in the power of the people?"

The other neighbor slipped away, and the man said to his wife, "Go home now. Don't make a scene."

"Why shouldn't I?" the woman said. "I want to see these people rot in front of my eyes."

Teacher Gu coughed and the woman shielded her face with her hand. "Go ahead. Come on in," Teacher Gu said weakly. "It won't take too long."

The woman opened her mouth but the husband said again in a pleading voice, "Go home now. I'll be back in a minute."

"Who are you to order me around?" the wife said.

Teacher Gu, past the bout of dizziness now, carefully pried the man's fingers off his own arm. "Thank you, young man," he said. "This is my home and you can leave me here."

The man hesitated and his wife laughed. "Come on," she said. "He's not your father and you don't have to follow him around like a pious son."

The man left with his wife without a word, as she continued to ask why he was being courteous to an old counterrevolutionary. Teacher Gu watched them disappear through their own door. After a while, he entered the quiet house, dim and cold. For a moment he wished for a garrulous wife like the neighbor's. He wished she would flood the house with her witless words so he did not have to find meaning to fill in the emptiness himself. He stood and wished for things unwisely before pulling himself together. From a kettle he poured lukewarm water into a teacup and then added spoonfuls of powdered sugar to the water. He would need the energy to take care of all the necessary things first, the empty stomach and the full bladder and later the filled chamber pot. There would be other things to tend to afterward, plans to locate his wife, the procedures to go through to see her, all the things he had once done for his daughter and now would have to do again, less hopefully than ten years earlier, for his wife. Teacher Gu sipped the sugar water, chokingly sweet.

A single knock on the door announced once again an uninvited visitor. Teacher Gu turned and saw his neighbor, still in his worker's outfit, dark grease on the front of his overalls. "Teacher Gu," he said. "I hope you don't mind my wife's rudeness."

Teacher Gu shook his head. He invited the man to sit down at the table with a wordless gesture. The man brought out a few paper bags from his pocket. He ripped them open and let their contents—fried tofu, pickled pig's feet, boiled peanuts, seaweed salad scattered with white sesame seeds—spread onto the flattened paper. "I thought you might want to talk to someone," the man said, and handed a small flat bottle of sorghum liquor to Teacher Gu.

Teacher Gu looked at the palm-sized flat bottle in his hand, green thick glass wrapped in a coarse paper with red stars. "My apologies for having nothing to offer you in return," said Teacher Gu when he handed a pair of chopsticks to the neighbor.

The man produced another bottle of liquor for himself. "Teacher Gu, I've come to apologize for my wife," he said. "As you said, man to man."

Teacher Gu shook his head. As an adult, he had never sat at a table with someone of his neighbor's status, a worker, a less educated member of the all-powerful proletarian class. His only similar memory was from when he had visited a servant's home as a small boy—her husband was a carpenter who had lost the four fingers of his right hand in an accident, and Teacher Gu remembered staring at the stumps when the man poured tea for him. The smell from the man's body was different from the men he had known, masters of literature and teachers of the highest reputation. "What do you do, young man?" Teacher Gu asked.

"I work in the cement factory," the man said. "You know the cement factory?"

Teacher Gu nodded and watched the man put two peanuts at a time in his mouth and chew them in a noisy way. "What's your name? Please forgive me for being an old and ignorant invalid."

"My name is Gousheng," the man said, and then, as if apologizing, he explained that his parents were illiterate, and that they had given him the name, a dog's leftovers, to make sure he would not be desired by devils.

"Nothing to be ashamed of," Teacher Gu said. "How many siblings do you have?"

"Six, but all the rest are sisters," Gousheng said. "I was my parents' only good luck."

A son was not what Teacher Gu had consciously hoped for, but now he wondered whether he was wrong. It would make a difference if he had a son, drinking with him, talking man-to-man talk. "Still, better luck than many other families," Teacher Gu said.

Gousheng took a long drink from the bottle. "Yes, but I wouldn't have felt so much pressure if I'd had a brother."

"You and—your wife—don't have children?"

Gousheng shook his head. "Not a trace of a baby anywhere," he said.

"And you are"—Teacher Gu struggled for the right words—"active in trying to make a baby?"

"As often as I can," Gousheng said. "My wife—Teacher Gu, please don't mind her rudeness—she is a soft woman inside. She feels bad about not being able to have a child. She thinks the whole world laughs at her."

Teacher Gu thought about the wife, her words that issued like razor blades. He could not imagine her as a soft woman, but it pleased him, for a moment, that she was in well-deserved despair, though the joy of Teacher Gu's revenge soon vanished. They were all sufferers in their despicable pain, every one of them, and what right did he have to laugh at the woman whose husband was pouring his heart out to him, a man in sincere confession to a fellowman?

"I worry that her temper is making it harder for us to have a baby. But how can I tell her? She's the kind of person who wants everything, all the success and glory."

Teacher Gu picked up the bottle and studied it. Gousheng pushed the food toward him. "Eat and drink," he said. "Teacher Gu, I'm a man who doesn't know many words in books, and you are the most knowledgeable person I've met. Please, you tell me, Teacher Gu—is there something we could do better? I worry that my wife is mean to too many people and we're being punished because of her behavior."

Teacher Gu drank carefully from the bottle and braced himself for the coarse liquid. "Scientifically speaking," he said, and then cringed at his words, which would probably alienate the man who was saving him from a lonely night. "Have you been to the doctor's?" he asked.

"My wife doesn't want to go—we've been married for three years. It's enough that she can't get pregnant—if we go to the doctor, the whole world will know our trouble."

Teacher Gu thought of explaining that she might not be the one fully responsible for the situation, but then why would he want to release her from her shame and humility? He drank and popped the peanuts into his mouth the way Gousheng did. "There's no other way. Just try again. But you have to know that some hens never lay eggs," Teacher Gu said, disgusted and then exhilarated by his own crass metaphor.

Gousheng thought about it. After a few gulps he nodded. "I would be doomed, then," he said. "My parents didn't agree with our marriage when they saw her picture. They worried that she looked too manly for a wife."

"And you liked her?"

"She was already a branch leader of the Youth League, and I was only a common worker. How could I reject such a match? A blind man could see how lucky I was, especially since she was the one who initiated the matchmaking."

"Why did she choose you, then?" Teacher Gu said. "But, of course, you are a handsome man," he offered unconvincingly.

Gousheng shook his head. "She said she wanted someone trustworthy, someone from the proletarian class, someone who earned a living with his own hands. But why on earth did she choose me? There are many men who would have fit her standard! Sometimes I wish she had not chosen me—to think I could have had a more obedient wife instead of being the obedient one!"

Teacher Gu looked at the young man, in drunken tears. "Women are unpredictable," agreed Teacher Gu. "Men certainly want to understand their logic, but let me tell you, they act with little sense. Why don't you divorce her? Let her suffer. Don't suffer with her. They are all the same—they don't know how to make men's lives easier!"

Gousheng seemed to be shocked by Teacher Gu's sudden vehemence, but Teacher Gu drank and talked on with new energy. "Take my wife, for example—look at where she's gotten herself!"

Gousheng drank quietly and then said, "Teacher Gu, your wife . . ."

"Don't feel you have to defend her in any way. I know what she did."

"She's probably an accomplice at most," Gousheng said. "She's older and they probably won't be too harsh on her."

Teacher Gu ignored Gousheng's effort to comfort him. He drank now with a speed that matched Gousheng's. "Let me tell you, the worst thing that ever happened in this new China—not that I'm against the new China in any way, but to think of all these women who get to do what they want without men's consent. They think they know so much about the world but they act out of anything but a brain! Your wife, forgive me if I offend you—she is the same creature I have seen in my own wife. And my daughter too—you may not know her but she was just like your wife, full of ideas and judgments but no idea how to be a respectful human being. They think they are revolutionary, progressive, they think they are doing a great favor to the world by becoming masters of their own lives, but what is revolution except a systematic way for one species to eat another alive? Let me tell you—history is, unlike what they say on the loudspeakers, not driven by revolutionary force but by people's desire to climb up onto someone else's neck and shit and pee as he or she wants. Enough bad things are done by men already, but if you add women to the equation, one might as well wish not to bring a baby into this world. What do you see in this world that is worthwhile for a baby to be born into? Tell me, give me one good reason."

Teacher Gu felt his heart spill out onto the table like the rolling peanuts that his fingers were now too clumsy to catch. He had never felt such passion about the world. Why should he remain respectful and humble when he had to suffer, not only from the men he hated but also from the women he loved? Why did he have to love them from the beginning, when the Buddha had made it clear that every beautiful woman was only a bag of white bones in disguise? How could he be deceived by them, wives and lovers and daughter—who were they but creatures sent to destroy him, to make him live in pain, and die in pain?

"Teacher Gu, don't get too loud," Gousheng said in a whisper. "You're being imprudent."

The young man, who sat at his table but whose name had already eluded Teacher Gu, tried to take the bottle away. Teacher Gu pushed his hand, ready to fight the young man and the world standing behind him. This was his home and he could do what he wanted to, Teacher Gu said aloud. He could feel the world take a timid peek from behind the young man's tall and heavily built body. If it looked again, Teacher Gu decided to smash its head with the thick green bottle, but when he looked down at his hand, he did not know where the bottle was.

HALFWAY THROUGH THE CHANTING of a revolutionary song, Tong's father trailed off and soon started to snore. "Not many people can remain cheerful after drinking," Tong's mother said in admiration, as if to explain her indulgence of her husband's drinking. She knelt down next to him to loosen his shoelaces and take off his shoes. "He has the best virtue of a drunkard."

Tong sat on the edge of the chair and looked down at his own dangling legs. He was waiting for his father to pass out into happy oblivion. Nobody had mentioned anything about the signature on the petition; still, Tong could not convince himself, and he decided to talk with his mother for reassurance.

She peeled the socks off his father's feet. "Get some warm water," she said, not looking up. And when Tong did not move, she told him to hurry up before his father caught a cold. Tong dragged himself to where the water kettle sat high on the counter, a pair of cranes strolling on its pink plastic cover. He looked at the cranes, one stretching its neck to the sky and the other lowering its head for something he did not see. When his mother urged him again, he climbed onto a chair and held the water kettle to his chest like a baby. When he jumped down, the loud thump made his mother frown. Tong pulled a basin from underneath the washstand with his foot. The bottom of the basin scratched the cement floor, the noise of which seemed to make him feel livelier than he had felt the whole day. He nudged the basin, first with one foot and then the other, as if the basin were a ball he was trying hard not to lose on the playing field. One, two, one, two, he counted, and almost bumped into his mother.

She went for the basin first and checked the enamel bottom carefully before she said in a disapproving tone, "Tong, you're old enough to know what you shouldn't do."

He felt the sting of tears but it would be wrong to cry. He hugged the water kettle and waited for harsher words from his mother, but she grabbed it from him. Tong watched her test the water temperature with the back of her hand first and then splash water onto his father's big feet. He moved a little in the chair and snored on.

Tong asked her why she did everything for his father.

"What a question!" Tong's mother said. She looked up and when she saw Tong's serious face, she smiled and rubbed his hair. "When you become a man, you'll have a good wife and a good son who will serve you on their knees too."

Tong did not answer. He carried the water out to the yard and poured it into a corner by the fence. When he came back to the room, his mother was half dragging and half supporting his father to the bedroom; Tong's father complained and flailed his arms but when she tucked him in, he fell into a drunken sleep. She watched him for a moment and turned to Tong. "Did you finish your homework?"

"There's no homework today," Tong said.

"How come?"

Tong glanced at his mother but she seemed not to notice it. "There were emergency meetings all day at school," he said.

"Oh yes, now I remember," she said. "The thing about the rally."

"What happened on Ching Ming?" Tong asked, not knowing if she could tell he was hiding a secret from her.

"It's too complicated to explain to you. It's all grown-ups' business."

"Our principal said horrible things happened."

"Not as bad as you think," Tong's mother said. "Some people think one way and some think the other way. People are always like this. They seldom agree on anything."

"Which side is right?"

"The side where your teachers and principal stand. Always follow what's been taught and you won't make a mistake."

Tong thought about a few teachers he had seen the day before at the rally, the teacher who had sat behind the petition, and a couple of others standing in silence in the line, with their white flowers. "Don't think too much about these meaningless things," Tong's mother said. "If you stay in line you'll never be in the wrong place. And if you do nothing wrong, you will never fear anything, even when the ghosts come to knock on your door at midnight."

Tong thought of asking more questions, but before he could speak, someone pounded on their gate. His mother laughed. "The moment you talk about someone, here he is tapping on your door. Who would come at this late hour?"

Tong followed her to the yard and all of a sudden, his throat was gripped by fear. There was nowhere to hide in the yard except in the tipped-over cardboard box that had once served as a home for Ear. When his mother opened the gate to two bright beams of flashlights, Tong climbed into the box, holding his breath.

Tong's mother asked the visitors what they wanted, and someone answered in a low voice. Could there be a mistake? Tong's mother said, and Tong recognized fear in her voice. There must be a misunderstanding, she argued in a pleading tone, but the visitors seemed not to hear her, and one of them must have pushed her, because she stepped back with a small cry of surprise. Tong looked out and tried

to recognize his mother's cotton shoes among the four leather boots
of the visitors. Two men were walking toward the house now, his
mother trailing behind; her husband was sick and he was in bed
now, she lied, but the visitors ignored her entreaties. They went into
the room and soon Tong heard his father, being awakened, question
the intruders. They spoke in low and undisturbed voices, and hard
as Tong tried, he could not hear what they were saying. "Let me be
clear with you," Tong's father said. "I didn't leave this house one step
that morning."

The visitors replied in indiscernible voices.

"There must be a mistake," Tong's mother insisted. "I swear we're
both law-abiding citizens."

Tong climbed out of the box and crawled closer to the house.
Through the open door, he heard one of the visitors speak in a calm
voice: "We're not going to argue with you now. Our job is to get you
to the station. You can talk all you want at the station, but here's the
arrest order that you've seen. If you're not going to move, don't
think we can't use force to get you out of here."

"But, sir, can you wait till tomorrow morning? Why do you need
him tonight, when you can let him sleep at home?" Tong's mother
said. "We promise first thing in the morning we'll come in and clar-
ify the misunderstanding."

The visitors didn't reply, and Tong imagined the way they were
looking at his father without acknowledging her voice. Tong had
seen many men behave this way, ignoring women and, for that matter, all children, as if they didn't exist. He wished his mother could
understand this and leave things for his father to deal with. "A
woman's insight," his father sneered. "As short as an ant's legs.
Haven't you heard of the saying that *if the ghosts want to invite you for a
talk, you can't stay longer than a minute*?"

"There you go," one man said, with a short chuckle.

"But what did he do, really?" Tong's mother mumbled.

"Black words on white paper," another man said. "You can't
argue with the police order."

"Don't fuss, woman," Tong's father said. "It seems that I have to condescend to a journey tonight. Why are we still standing and wasting our lives, brothers?"

"Here you go. A smart man you are," one of the visitors said, and then clanked something metal.

"Do you need to do that?" Tong's father asked. "It's not like I'm causing a riot."

"Sorry." The handcuffs clicked. "Can't exempt you from that."

"Can he bring some snacks?" Tong's mother asked. "It might be a long night."

The visitors did not say anything. "What silly talk about snacks," Tong's father said. "Cook a good breakfast and I'll be back tomorrow morning, when the misunderstanding is cleared up."

"Some hot tea before you go? Is the coat warm enough? Do you want me to get the sheepskin out for you?"

"A good wife you've got for yourself," one man said.

"You know how it goes with women," Tong's father said. "The more you treat them like crap, the more they want to crawl to you on their knees. Now stop fussing like an old duck. Sleep tight and I'll be back soon."

Tong retreated to the box and watched his father, still tipsy, leave with the two men in black uniforms. His father's hands were cuffed behind him but that did not stop him from talking intimately with the visitors, as if they were his long-lost brothers. His father's ease and confidence frightened Tong. He imagined his father's shock when he was shown his own name signed on the white cloth. Would his mind be lucid enough for him to point out that the handwriting was not his? But would the police then come with another pair of handcuffs for him? Tong wondered, and the thought frightened him. They would never give him the red scarf of a Young Pioneer.

When the two men left with his father and slammed the gate in his mother's face, she stood in a trance and then called Tong's name, and when he did not answer, she raised her voice and called to him again.

He did not reply, holding his breath, his blood pumping in his ears in heavy thumps. He watched her listen for a minute and then go into the house, still calling his name. If he tiptoed to the gate, he might have enough time to run before she caught him; if he jumped onto a passing night train, he might be able to get back to his grand- parents' village by the next day. Back at the village, nobody would blame him for anything; they knew him to be a boy destined to make a big and important name for himself.

Tong's mother came out to the yard, still calling his name in a low voice, but he could hear her panic now. He crawled out from the box and stood up. "Mama," he said. "I'm here."

IF SHE KEPT STILL ENOUGH in the chair, Nini thought, the ghost of Bashi's grandmother, if the old woman's ghost existed at all, would perhaps think Nini was part of the furniture in the room. Nini looked at the posters, Chairman Mao shaking hands with General Zhu, a fat boy holding up a cheerful golden carp, and a pair of red magpies chirping to each other as messengers of good luck, all of them dusty from coal ashes now, hanging dimly on the wall. The old woman would not like it if Nini did not keep her house neat and clean, Nini thought, slowly pulling one leg and then the other onto the chair and crossing them. In the bedroom Little Sixth stirred and cried a little, but after a while she fell asleep again. They were a fam- ily now, Bashi and Nini and the baby.

The fish soup was steaming hot on the table, the two bowls of rice looking invitingly delicious; the fried tofu and steamed sausages and pickled bean sprouts all beckoned to her rumbling stomach. This was her first supper with Bashi, and she had gone to great lengths to make it a special meal. She picked up one chopstick and dipped it into the soup and then sucked it. The taste made her hun- grier, yet she dared not steal a bite, for fear that it would bring bad luck to the life she would share with Bashi from now on.

It had been a while since Bashi left, and she wondered how long it would take for him to return with news about her sisters. Could he have bumped into her parents or other suspecting adults? Would they ask him where she was? Nini wiggled her toes, which were falling asleep, and looked up at the ceiling. There were no eyes watching her, and she picked up the chopsticks and caught a slice of ginger from the fish soup. That led to another ginger slice and then a small bite of the fish, from under its belly. The tender flesh cheered her up—why should she care about a future she had no control over? If indeed there was heavenly justice, she would be heading to hell— she had destroyed the lives of Little Fourth and Little Fifth, and she'd better enjoy her own while she still could. Nini took another bite, and then another. When she had finished a whole fish, she wrapped up the bones in an old newspaper and threw them into the flames in the stove. The remaining fish looked lonesome, and she wondered if it was one more sign of misfortune for her, as married couples should do everything in twos.

A strange smell came from the stove, reminding Nini of her father's sheepskin hat that had been shoveled into the belly of the stove under their bed at home; it was Little Fourth and Little Fifth who had dreamed up this mischief, for reasons that Nini didn't understand, but it was Nini who had received a good beating on their behalf, her back swollen for a week afterward.

Nini poked the burning fish bones with the iron tongs but the nauseating odor became stronger. She went into the bedroom and rummaged through the closet and chest of drawers, and found nothing but an old bottle of floral water that must have belonged to Bashi's grandmother, the green liquid already sticky. She opened the lid and poured a small amount in her palm, and was horrified by the pungent fragrance condensed by years of sitting in the bottle. It made her sneeze.

Nini put her hand under running water for a long time and then sniffed her palm. It was less noticeable. She was relieved when she found half an orange left next to Bashi's pillow. She peeled one slice and sucked it while putting the rest of the orange into the fire. The fire engulfed the half orange and soon the room was filled with a more pleasant smell.

Someone knocked on the gate. She turned off the light in the room and slipped out of the house and into the storage cabin. The pounding of something metal on the thin wooden gate frightened Nini. Soon these people would come in, devils sent by her parents to destroy her hope of a happy life, and Bashi was not here to protect her; soon they would drag her away from this house and put her back into the jail run by her parents.

"Hello, what are you doing to my gate?"

Out of gratitude Nini almost wept when she heard Bashi's voice.

"Are you Lu Bashi?"

"I don't know any other Lu Bashi in my life."

"Then come with us."

"Where to?"

"You'll know when you get there."

"That sounds exciting," Bashi said. "But I can't go with you just now. I have more important business to deal with."

"Be disappointed, then," the man said. "Nothing is more important tonight than coming with us."

Something metal was shaken outside.

"Are the handcuffs real? I remember I had a toy pair when I was this small," Bashi said.

"Try them on."

"Sorry, but I would rather be the one to cuff others," said Bashi. "What are you here for?"

"You know better than we do."

"I truly can't think of anything I've done wrong."

"Well, you can keep thinking about it when we get to the station."

Nini thought about opening the gate and dragging Bashi in before the men registered her existence. She could bolt the gate from the inside, and by the time the men broke it down she and Bashi would be gone from the yard, the house, and this world of horrors.

"But I'm busy tonight. Can I come tomorrow morning?"

A man grunted. "Look here. Do you know what this is? Can you read?"

"Arrest order. Now what is that for?"

"Well, let's go. I've never seen a person who talks as much as you."

"Please, brothers, give me a hint. Is it because of a girl? Do you know if this has anything to do with a girl?"

"A girl!" the men said, laughing. "Did you get lost in your own wet dreams to think that we would come to get you because of a girl?"

"So it's not girl-related," Bashi said.

Her parents, after all, did not care about her enough to go through the trouble to find her, Nini thought. Perhaps they would celebrate their good fortune in her loss.

The men again urged Bashi to go with them.

"Wait a second. Comrades, you are very gracious. Do you want to give me a minute to get a few things settled in my house?"

"You look enough like a man but fuss like a girl," one man said, shaking the handcuffs again. "We have other houses to visit. We don't have the whole night to entertain you."

"Please, just one minute. I have to tell my grandmother that I will not spend the night at home. You know how it goes with old women—they worry all the time even when there's nothing much going on."

"Now don't fool us. Here it says you're the only resident in this house, isn't that correct?"

"True for the household register, but think of the ghost of my grandma—she raised me and she wouldn't leave me here all by myself so I talk to her every day and let her know where I am. If you take me away without informing her, what if she followed me to the station? What if she made a mistake and followed you two home instead and disturbed your children's sleep? Don't say you're from out of town and you don't worry about such things. Ghosts travel faster than you and me."

Nini shivered in the darkness. She looked up at the ham hanging just above her head. What if the ghost was watching her? But what kind of a ghost was she if she didn't come to rescue her own grandson? Nini said a low prayer to the old woman and asked her to understand who her real enemies were.

"Are you bluffing? You know this is a new society where superstition has no place."

"Well, if you don't trust me, take me away now. The thing is, you never know. Ghosts don't read newspapers and they don't listen to government broadcasts."

"That's all right," the voice that belonged to the older of the two men said. "Let's give him a minute. It's not like he can run away from us."

"No, I won't run away from you," said Bashi. "You have my word—I'll only be a minute."

"What do you mean by that? We're coming in with you."

"But my grandma hasn't invited you."

"We'll be good houseguests."

The gate opened and the three men came into the yard. Nini, squatting behind a jar in the storage cabin, remembered Little Sixth fast asleep in the bedroom, and her heart began to pound. "Do you smell that?" she heard Bashi say, after the door was open.

"What's the smell?"

"My grandmother's floral water," Bashi said. "How long has it been since I smelled it? The last time she used it I was still a child going into the street without my pants."

The two men coughed uneasily and one of them said, "Now hurry up."

"You're not coming in with me? Perhaps my grandma knew you were coming and prepared some food for you."

"Let's go now," one man ordered suddenly with a sharp voice. "I'm tired of your superstitious nonsense."

"Are you scared, comrade?" Bashi said, but his laughing was interrupted when one of the men yanked him back and made him stumble down the steps. He cried out loudly, but the two men grabbed him and dragged him out the door. "Nana," called out Bashi. "Did you hear the gentlemen? I need to be away for a night. No need to worry, Nana. I'll be back in a blink and you be good and stay here. Don't ever think of being naughty and following the gentlemen here, all right? I don't want you to get lost."

Someone cursed and then Bashi screamed in pain. Nini squatted in the darkness and cried. She heard the neighbors' gates open with creaks and then close. After a while, she came out of the storage cabin. A crescent moon was halfway up the sky, reddish gold. The gate to the alley was open just a crack. Nini walked quietly to the gate and looked out. The neighbors had returned home, every gate closed in the alley. She pushed Bashi's gate, inch by inch, until it shut soundlessly. There was no ghost in the world, she thought; the old woman was buried, cold in the dirt, and she would not come to rescue Bashi or be offended by Nini. They were at the mercy of strangers, as always.

THE WATER DRIBBLED in a slow, hesitant rhythm, as the raindrops had done many years earlier in his grandparents' garden, dripping from the tips of the banana leaves to a small puddle beneath. Any moment now his nanny would come, and he would have to shut his eyes, but she was always able to tell that he'd been crying. Look at your pillowcase, his nanny would say, and stroke his wet eyelashes with a finger, the light from the red lantern in her other hand warm on his face, but they were never able to expel his gloom, just as he was never able to find an explanation for his tears. Young Master has been crying again, he heard her say to his grandparents after she walked out of the bedroom, and his grandmother would explain, once again without losing her patience, that children cried so that all the sadness they had to carry from their last lives would leave with the tears.

A perfect cycle it was, Teacher Gu thought, one's life starting with the pain carried from the previous life, growing up to shed the burden only to accumulate fresh pain for the next life. Slowly the world came back to him, and with great effort he turned on the bedside light. He was in his shirt and underwear. His jacket and pants— soiled by his vomit, he supposed—had been washed and now hung on the clothesline, dripping into a small puddle on the cement floor. Gousheng had left a pot of tea by his bedside, still warm to the touch. How long had he been unconscious? Teacher Gu opened his mouth but no sound came from his scratchy throat. So this was what he was reduced to, an old man hung over, from nothing other than his own illusion of staying alive. Staying alive had been his faith since his divorce, and for this he had given up dignity, hope, anger, and his loved ones; but where did this faith lead him except back to this cycle that no one could escape?

Dearest love, my mind is as clear as a mirror wiped spotless under the silver light of a full moon, Teacher Gu wrote, and put it with other notes to his first wife in a large envelope. For the last time he spelled out her name and address, and then screwed the cap carefully back on his Parker and inserted it, with his letters, in the envelope.

Underneath the bed was the old wooden chest where his wife had kept their precious possessions, and it cost Teacher Gu a great effort to drag it out. There was a Western-style suit in the chest. The suit had belonged to her grandfather, Teacher Gu told Shan the night before she and her comrades planned to come and cleanse him of his bourgeois possessions; the umbrella next to the suit, a souvenir of his parents' love story. He would appreciate it if she could spare the few things he had kept from his parents. At the time, Shan sneered at his pleading, but the next day she decided to overlook the suit and the umbrella while she threw the other stuff into the fire, including her mother's silk blouses and Teacher Gu's college graduation robe.

Teacher Gu buttoned the suit and tidied his hair; it was one's responsibility to leave the world as a clean person.

The distance to the mailbox was longer than he'd thought, and twice he had to stop and catch his breath. The letter weighed no

more than his own heart, and no sound came back when he dropped
it into the metal box.

A dog barked; a feral cat whined and another answered in a
shriller voice; a child cried in a nearby house and a mother sang a lullaby; the world was a beautiful place under the spring sky, with the
new moon surrounded by silver stars and a gentle breeze combing
its unseen fingers through the long branches of the willow trees.
Teacher Gu listened. His heart was a bottomless well; each small
sound, a sigh and a whisper and the flapping of the most tender
wings, was welcomed with deep-felt serenity.

"Where are you going?" two men said, stopping Teacher Gu as he
was leaving the alley.

"The Muddy River," Teacher Gu replied.

The men looked at each other and told Teacher Gu he was not allowed to go there. Why? Teacher Gu questioned, but the men only
shrugged and said nobody was allowed to move around town after
eight o'clock. They pointed to where he'd come from and ordered
him to go back home. Elsewhere similar requests were made, the cur-
few enforced by workers from another town.

Beware, Teacher Gu said, full of sympathy for these people who
lived in blind faith and who would die, one day, without a single
light shining into their souls. Butchers one day and the next day you
will be the meat on the cutting board, he said to the men; your
knives that slit open others' throats will one day slit your own.

The two men, infuriated, pushed Teacher Gu and threatened to
place him under arrest. Their mouths opened and closed with useless words and empty warnings. You stupid human beings, Teacher
Gu said; with the resolution to meet the water that would carry him
away, he struck at them with his cane and ordered them to let him
pass. It did not take long for the men to pin the old man to the
ground. Cold as water, the thought of relief passed through him like
a whisper as he moved his head slightly so his cheek would hurt less
from the smashed glasses.

Unknown to Teacher Gu's fading consciousness were the screams and howls of tortured flesh, muffled by unfeeling walls as well as unfeeling hearts. Tong's father, beaten into a stupor, for a moment was lost in one of his drunken dreams in which, behind his warm eyelids, his mother stirred a single egg, but the beat-beat of the bamboo chopsticks on the china bowl was then disturbed by the heavy thumping of boots on his head. Not far away, in another room, a man, father of two daughters who had once been among the girls dreamed of by Bashi, cried on the cold cement floor after having pressed a bloody fingerprint onto the confession thrust at him. Cautious man as he was, he had never been near any leaflet, but in Bashi's made-up and unsubstantiated account the man had turned up at the rally with a white flower.

In a different room Bashi cried too, rolling on the floor and grasping his crotch with both hands. Please big brothers please uncles please grandpapas please please, he begged; he was smaller than their smallest toenail he was smaller than his own fart please he would confess to everything anything they wanted him to; yes he was a counterrevolutionary yes he had been to the rally but please big brothers please uncles and grandpapas he remembered all of the people he had seen; he would give their names he would point out their faces in pictures please please don't kick don't beat because he was so low he would soil their shoes and their hands; please he had everything and anything to tell please he could tell them about the man who said bad words about Communism and the woman who spat at Chairman Mao's statue and yes yes he could tell them all about this man who raped and mutilated female corpses and who would do the same thing to their wives and their sisters if they did not catch him in time.

TWELVE

*M*any years later, parents in Muddy River would point Tong out to their children, some saying he was the sole culprit for his father's deafened ears, broken skull, and forever-paralyzed body; others, out of fairness, would add that, despite Tong's stupidity, he was a good son who had never allowed bedsores to grow on his father's body, or let his mother suffer under the reign of a daughter-in-law. He went to work as a clerk at the administration building by day and read by night. He read till after midnight, and when his mother fell asleep, he took out a thick notebook from a locked drawer and scribbled in it, though he never went back to read what he'd written, and there was no one else in his world who demanded to read the words.

Regardless of how dismal his life would turn out to be, when Tong entered the principal's office the morning after his father's arrest, he saw nothing but the blossom of his belief, more splendid than all the flowers, purer than pure gold. He listed the names of the people he had met at the rally, uncles and aunties from his parents' work units, teachers and neighbors, Old Hua and Mrs. Hua. He described unfamiliar faces and vowed to point out every one of them if given the opportunity. He would put his life into the punishing hands of the party and the people, and his father, please, could the principal let the officials know that his father was nothing more than a drunkard?

What a heaven-sent boy, the principal thought, studying Tong, with his odd accent and villager's looks. The boy was a slate for him to color, the principal thought, and whether it was red or black it all relied on his own genius.

The principal picked up the telephone and waited for the sweet-voiced woman at the switchboard to get him an education official at the city council. The boy sat in the middle of the office, looking at his shoes, and the principal had to signal twice for the boy to raise his head for him to get a better look. They were crickets bound by the same string now, the principal thought, his hands shaking yet his heart filled with the thrill of a gambler: The boy could be the youngest counterrevolutionary in this political storm and he, the failing educator, could lose the career he had diligently built up; or, if he could convince his superior that the boy could be turned into a young hero who would stand up to denounce all the criminals, including his own father, they, the architects of a boy hero, would win a bright star for their résumés.

He was ready to die for his cause, Jialin said to his mother when she was granted a visit the day before the trial, and it was time for her to feel happy for him instead of grieving. Some lives were lighter than a feather, and other deaths weighed more than Mount Tai. Jialin's mother pressed a handkerchief to her eyes and replied that a son's life, no matter how trivial it was to the world, was irreplaceable, and how could he expect her to celebrate her own son's misfortune?

Eight hundred and eighty-five people, those who had gone to the rally with the white flowers and those who had been accused of doing so by their neighbors and enemies, were investigated and later expelled from their work units. Among them was a doctor at the emergency room of the city hospital. Why was fate so blind? the doctor's daughter wrote in her journal, her mother's misfortune growing in her fourteen-year-old girl's mind into a poisonous tumor. A young receptionist, her wedding scheduled to take place in two weeks, on May Day, received a letter from her fiancé apologizing for the frailty of love and wishing her good luck in finding a new job and a new husband. A teacher in the middle school said farewell to his students in class; two best friends who had both had a crush on the teacher started to cry; their tears led to many visits to the principal's office and in the end they were turned against each other, both competing to reveal the other one's dirty thoughts over a man their fathers' age.

Mrs. Hua and Old Hua were released from the makeshift detention center, a training camp for the local militia, a few hours after their arrest. Later Mrs. Hua learned that her boss, the old bachelor Shaokang, had been the one to help them out. They would forever remain grateful to him, Mrs. Hua said when she saw him again, and he replied in a stern voice that he did not have a job for her anymore. But how had he done it? she asked, still in disbelief of her luck; he must have some powerful connection in the government; was it a brother, or a relative, or a friend? Shaokang looked up at Mrs. Gu. Let it be forgotten, he said in a near-pleading tone, and she realized for the first time that there were well-guarded secrets in his bachelor's life that he had risked for their sake.

Nini ate, slept, and cried for four days in Bashi's house before she was discovered by the police. They had not come for her but to seek nonexistent evidence for a nonexistent crime, as Bashi was alleged by Kwen to have been an accomplice in his criminal actions against the body of the executed female counterrevolutionary. Both men's places were searched. Two glass jars of formaldehyde, in which a woman's severed breasts and private parts were on display, were uncovered by the police in Kwen's shack after they shot his growling guard dog in its forehead; in the other house they found a girl, along with her baby sister, intimidated into self-imprisonment by the criminal. The girl kept talking about a marriage arrangement that nobody believed to have existed and later, when she was escorted away from the house, she screamed and kicked her captors. A medical examination proved her to be mentally normal and still a virgin, and it mystified the police that she kept talking about her marriage to Bashi, her kidnapper. When questioned about why they had not reported the two missing daughters, her father said nothing but that he had forgotten the girls when he had to tend to two daughters who had been burned in a house fire as well as a wife who had miscarried. How could parents forget a daughter? a young policewoman asked her colleagues, and they replied that worse things had happened to other children, and she'd better toughen herself up for her line of work.

The tales, of the body parts from the executed woman, and the incarcerated girl discarded by her own parents who had begun to have feelings for her kidnapper, traveled from mouth to mouth, ear to ear; for the time being, they were the only topics safe to discuss in Muddy River, and people invented details, their imaginations drowning their fears of a life they did not understand.

Under the policy of giving the harshest punishment to all antigovernment organizations and individuals, three hundred and eleven people who had signed the petition were tried as counterrevolutionaries, their sentences ranging from three years for the followers to lifelong imprisonment for the leaders. Upon reviewing the cases, the provincial officials pointed out that a warning to the masses would not be effective without a death sentence. *Kill a chicken to frighten all the mischievous monkeys into obedience,* one top official urged in writing, and several others chimed in with their consent.

SHE HAD NOT EXPECTED the quietness. The sounds that had once made up the natural course of her day—Ming-Ming's crying in the middle of the night, Han's joking, her mother's complaining, the patriotic music she played for the town, her own voice, reading the news to the same uninterested ears—did not leave her; rather, they blocked out the everyday noises for Kai: water dripping, the crying and whispering of women in nearby cells, the unlocking of the window where meals were delivered, her own footsteps measuring the cube of her cell.

It was not a surprise that, after the first day of her confinement in the best guesthouse in Muddy River, Kai had been transferred, wrists cuffed, to her present cell. She did not know what to expect in the hours and days to come, yet in a strange way she was looking forward to it, as someone floating above unknown territory looks forward to landing on solid ground.

And now the phantom limbs of the once-familiar sounds pulled her down, and in the quietest nights she thought about Ming-Ming, for whom she would be slowly reduced, by his father and his grandparents, into a nonexistence. Of all the people she missed—her mother and her siblings, Jialin, and even Han—Ming-Ming was the one who would not have any memory of her once this page was turned. Had Autumn Jade wished, in her fearless waiting for death, that there could be a parallel world in which she could continue mothering her children?

Kai began to sing to take her mind off the pain. She sang the songs that had long ago been stored away with her youthful dreams. Her voice sounded different than what she remembered from years ago, but the open stage had not taken a grip on her then as the cold walls did now.

She sang the songs that Gu Shan must have been singing in her long years of imprisonment. *The flowers of May bloom on the prairie, and the red petals fall and cover the martyrs' blood.* She had never felt this close to the people in her songs—the man and the woman who wedded themselves minutes before their execution, a jailed daughter asking her mother to bury her with her tombstone facing east so she would see the sunrise, a mother's lullaby to her child who had been tortured to death by the secret police in front of her eyes. They had been alive once before legend had claimed them, and they lived in her singing now, sharing their secrets with her and holding her hands, waiting with her.

Many years later, in his memoir, one of the imprisoned activists would write about listening to her singing. He had been released and depurged, and she had, by then, long ago been claimed by legends.

· · ·

THE MAY DAY CELEBRATION was marked by the public denunciation of Wu Kai and her accomplices in the antigovernment uprising. On the morning of the denunciation, Tong got up early and washed his face, wiping the backs of his ears with extra care. His mother had sewn a pair of blue pants and a white shirt for him the previous two nights, and after he dressed, she ran a hand across his clothes to get rid of the tiniest wrinkle. Tong was going to be one of the speakers at the denunciation meeting, along with Han and a few other model citizens of Muddy River who would be granted the title of Guardian Hero of Communist China. A special ceremony was to take place, before the denunciation meeting, for Tong to become a Communist Young Pioneer. He looked at his shirt, which would soon be decorated with the red scarf; when he looked up, his mother was gazing at him with awe and a sadness he did not understand. Be a very good boy, she said, and told him that she and his father were both very proud of him; Tong glanced at his father in bed—he had not recovered enough to recognize Tong's face—and said that he would win all the prizes and make them the happiest and proudest parents in the world.

Two women officers unlocked the cell door and came in, neither meeting Kai's eyes. A package from your mother, one officer said, and handed a bundle of clothes to Kai. Since her arrest, Kai had refused to see her mother, who had come several times to visit. What a hard-hearted woman she was, the judge had said to her at the first trial, which had been carried out in secrecy with only a few officials from the courthouse present; she had betrayed not only the party that had nurtured her but also her own mother, her husband, and her son. Kai remained quiet and aloof, and she was not surprised by the retrial, carried out in a similar manner. What was there to fear about death? she asked when the sentence was read to her; she imagined the same message being read to Jialin, knowing he was as ready as she was.

Kai unrolled the bundle, new clothes and shoes her mother must have wrapped up for her. It was her mother's misfortune to have a daughter like her, Kai thought, and she forced herself to focus on the small task of changing her clothes. She was not a daughter, or a wife or mother; she was herself, and she would remain herself for the rest of the day.

At half past nine she was escorted to a covered police van, her arms heavily bound behind her and already growing numb. The officers, two men and two women, were silent; the leader of the four, about ten years older than the rest of them, was almost courteous when he told her that she was not to make any counterrevolutionary speeches at the denunciation ceremony.

Why didn't they cut her vocal cords to ensure her obedience, as they had done to Gu Shan? Kai asked, almost out of curiosity. The three younger officers seemed unaware of what she was talking about, their faces remaining blank. Kai fixed her eyes on the older officer as the van pulled off; his eyes dropped from her stare but after a while he replied that all prisoners deserved civilized treatment, and if any extra procedure was to be carried out it would be done out of humanitarian consideration.

When they reached the East Wind Stadium, Kai could tell, from the slogan shouting and from her own past experience, that the ceremony must have reached its climax. When she walked onto the stage, she realized that her comrades had been escorted there before she had, and that the slogans must have been meant for them. Their arms were all bound, each with two officers standing behind them. Kai did not have a chance to meet their eyes when she was pushed to the middle. When the audience finally calmed down, a female voice announced the crime of the counterrevolutionaries.

Kai listened to the new announcer, her voice as perfect as her own had once been. A young boy with a slight rustic accent came onto the stage and read his script aloud, followed by a few others, every one of them having assisted in one heroic way or another to cleanse

Muddy River of its most dangerous enemies. Han was the last to speak, of his struggle and then awakening at finding his ex-wife to be a leader of the uprising against his mother country.

It was only when the sentences were read that Kai was surprised for the first time that day. Hers was the last to be announced, the only death sentence among the ten. She was too young to die, Mrs. Gu shouted, breaking down before she was dragged off the stage. Only then did Kai realize that her sentence had been kept secret from her companions, for the greatest shock effect, perhaps, or just for mere protocol. Despite the two officers who tried hard to push her head down, she managed to look up at Jialin, who had turned to her, his eyes behind his glasses filled with a strange look of longing. Before either of them could speak, Jialin was pushed off the stage. Kai was the last one to be taken offstage, and for a moment, she remembered an essay her father had drafted for her when she was in the fifth grade. *A man with a revolutionary dream is never a lonely soul*— she remembered the title, and when she closed her eyes, she could almost see the essay, posted as the top winner of the provincial contest, her father's perfect words in her less than perfect handwriting.

OLD HUA AND MRS. HUA left Muddy River the evening before the May Day celebration. There was little left for them to cling to in the town, or anywhere else in the world, their hearts rekindled by the hope of going back to the freedom of a begging life. Leaving with them was Nini, who had been disowned by her parents and who had pleaded with the beggar couple to take her along. It did not matter that she no longer remembered her daughters' faces, Mrs. Hua thought; Nini would be their last daughter. They did not know that Nini had taken out all the cash from Bashi's trunk and hidden it in her socks; the stacks of bills rubbed the soles of her feet now, hardened into calluses from many days of blistering, but nobody found her limping suspicious.

She would take care of the couple, when they were too old to work, with the money in her socks, Nini thought. There was no reason for her to linger in Muddy River, though she knew she would be back in seventeen years, after Bashi served his sentence for molesting and kidnapping a young child. She had tried to visit him once, but the guards said only families and relatives were allowed. There was no point in making them understand she was his child bride; there was no point in explaining anything to anyone, the Huas included. The only thing to do was to count the days and years to come.

For raping and mutilating a dead woman's body, Kwen was sentenced to seven years. The morning of May Day, when the music and slogan shouting came from the loudspeakers outside the high walls of the prison, Kwen signaled for Bashi, who had been curled up in his narrow cot, to listen. They had both been beaten repeatedly by their cell mates, on account of their being newcomers as well as their women-related crimes. They were considered lower than the lowest creatures. The beatings seemed not to bother Kwen, and it would not take long before he became the one who organized such beatings, but at this moment, when Kai was driven in the police van to Hunchback Island, both Kwen and Bashi were slow in moving around because of their fresh wounds. Hear that? Kwen said to Bashi; another life on the way to the otherworld. Bashi did not reply, looking up at the old man with fear and disgust. Remember the other day, when we became friends over the woman's body? Kwen patted Bashi's shoulder and told him not to look so frightened. Heaven's door is narrow and allows only one hero at a time, but those going down to hell, Kwen said, always travel in pairs, hand in hand.

Acknowledgments

I am very grateful to: Elizabeth McCracken and Edward Carey, who gave sunshine and water and plenty of love to the novel when it was only a seed; Richard Abate, Chen Reis, Katherine Bell, Jebediah Reed, Barbara Bryan, Timothy O'Sullivan, John Hopper, and Ben George, for reading and rereading the manuscript; the Lannan Foundation and the Whiting Foundation for their generous support; Andrew Wylie, Sarah Chalfant, and Scott Meyers, for their hard work; Mitzi Angel and Kate Medina, for their insights.

And also to:

Brigid Hughes and Aviya Kushner, for their friendship, which makes my small world big;

James Alan McPherson and Amy Leach, for their beautiful minds;

Vincent and James, for keeping their mother from living solely in words; and Dapeng, for making the maps and the curtains, for keeping the memories, and for love.

Mr. William Trevor, for stories and hope.

ABOUT THE AUTHOR

YIYUN LI is a recipient of the Frank O'Connor International Short Story Award, the Hemingway Foundation/ PEN Award, the *Guardian* First Book Award, and a Whiting Writers' Award. She was also selected by *Granta* as one of the best young American novelists under thirty-five. She lives in Oakland, California, with her husband and their two sons.